Books by Julie Midnight

<u>Monstrous Hearts</u>
Wolf's Wife
Wolf's Bane
Wolf's Kin

Wolf's Kin

Monstrous Hearts
Book Three

Julie Midnight

ISBN: 978-1-7367836-2-7

Any references to historical events, real people, or real places are used fictitiously. Names, characters, and places are products of the author's imagination.

Front cover image by Julie Midnight
Book design by Daniel Young

Printed by Kindle Direct Publishing in the United States

First Printing Edition 2021

Hellcat Press LLC
www.hellcatpressllc.com

Table of Contents

PROLOGUE
The Black Wolves   1

CHAPTER ONE
Into a Fairy Tale   7

CHAPTER TWO
Sensing Danger   29

CHAPTER THREE
Hidden Graves   55

CHAPTER FOUR
Lost in the Woods   71

CHAPTER FIVE
A Painful Wait   89

CHAPTER SIX
The Ritual   107

CHAPTER SEVEN
The Shell of Suburbia   137

CHAPTER EIGHT
The Hunt Begins   167

CHAPTER NINE
The Party   181

CHAPTER TEN
A Challenger   203

CHAPTER ELEVEN
Grandma's House   229

CHAPTER TWELVE
Recovery   243

CHAPTER THIRTEEN
The Coven   271

CHAPTER FOURTEEN
The Hole   291

CHAPTER FIFTEEN
The Hermit   303

CHAPTER SIXTEEN
A Future Seen in the Past   315

CHAPTER SEVENTEEN
Tricked   341

CHAPTER EIGHTEEN
The King   353

CHAPTER NINETEEN
Gruesome Discovery   365

CHAPTER TWENTY
No More Words   371

CHAPTER TWENTY-ONE
Endless Slaughter   377

CHAPTER TWENTY-TWO
From the Ashes   387

CHAPTER TWENTY-THREE
The First One Known   399

CHAPTER TWENTY-FOUR
A Painful Answer   409

CHAPTER TWENTY-FIVE
A Final Fight   423

EPILOGUE
Forever   435

The Black Wolves

All who live in the shadows of the mundane world know about the black wolves. Most who whisper about these creatures are damned themselves: squatting in stone ruins once tourists leave with the sun, sucking fat from the bones of any who wander too far into the gloom of the woods, sliding off the silk of suits or dresses so that spilled blood will run down bare skin.

They know how to hide their endless appetites in the light of day and hunt with their true faces at night, how to shrink from revealing fire and thrive in the dark. And yet even these fiends of glut and malice regard the black wolves as something strange, something unknown. Something to be feared.

What are they?

It's a question hissed over ritual knives being cleaned, through hair writhing with lice, in the quiet of crumbling churchyards. *Not human nor monster. Not spirit, not witch. What, then?*

The answers are always the same. *Vargr. Men who came back from the grave as wolves. Hunters you'll never wish to meet. They slip past all boundaries as easily as they slip between fur and skin. Do you understand yet, my pretty? They can't be killed or caged. They have no loyalty, not even to each other, and whatever they want, they catch. Even we must fear crossing their paths.*

Anything more is embellishment, exaggeration. None know how many vargr there truly are. Few enough that it's rare to meet one. Few enough that most are recognized as more than eyes flashing in the dark. Names change with the centuries, but the black wolves hold true to their appetites no matter what carcass of civilization they slink from, still hungry as their reputations fill the shadows...

The most feared of these doesn't let himself be seen. Not now. Something precious found him, and every night he slips into her bed, marveling at how she bares her body to him with such trust. He tests her throat with his teeth and yet she only smiles, offering her heart. The warmth of her skin and the sweet smell of her hair always draw a word from him, this wolf who has spent decades at a time in silence. Even now, his voice sounds rough from disuse, more of a growl as he speaks against the pulse in her neck.

"Alice."

She shivers at the sound of her name, but it's not fear that floods her scent while he kisses along her collar bones, savoring her taste. In the moonlight, her eyes are as mesmerizing as the first time he saw her, a girl who looked lost as she peered through a window in the darkest hours of night.

"Four days," she says. "We haven't been apart for that long since..."

He remembers but simply nips at her shoulder. For him, the past is the past. When she continues shivering, his mouth turns gentle. "Nervous?"

Her voice sounds shy. "I'll miss you."

He's taken antlers to the gut and gunshots to the face, yet hearing this hits him harder. His kiss is rough, insistent, telling her everything he'll never put into words, and her body soon relaxes against his.

The moon drifts through the sky for some time before she speaks again, now drowsy. "I don't mind going on a family trip, and I love spending time in the wilderness. I don't think I could ever fear a forest. Not now."

It makes him think of how beautiful she looks as a wolf, running lightly among the trees while moonlight brightens her fur into silver. When he brushes strands of hair from her eyes, she sighs, and he knows the reason for her worry is about to come out.

"But I *am* scared. For the past week, I've had dreams about my mother, and all of them are about her leaving me alone in the woods."

"Tell me." He doesn't miss how she shifts closer, or how her fingers clutch at him as if she expects to be pulled away and lost to the darkness.

"It starts off the same way as my memories, but this time I somehow follow her even while staying behind in the car. I can see her face. She looks frightened, like she wants to go back but can't. I always thought she wanted to leave, but what if she didn't? What if she was somehow... forced?"

He's seen a lot, this wolf, and while she's the one with witch blood, he knows her kind far better. Witches like sniffing each other out. They like using each other even more. "It's possible."

At the hitch in her breath, he cups her chin, coaxing her to look at him. "You won't end up like her. I'd find you and get you back out."

"I know you would. But what if I'm too far gone to want to leave?"

"It's not hard to throw you over a shoulder."

Her laugh is small yet real, and he runs a thumb over her mouth before adding, "Hunting a witch is no harder than hunting a rabbit. If it comes to that, I'll show you how."

She nods, some of the worry fading from her scent, and her heart returns to a steady beat while she settles against him for sleep. Yet even after her breathing slows, he remains awake, stroking her back and feeling his teeth sharpen whenever he thinks about losing her.

And as the moon hangs heavy in the nearing dawn, the final glimmer of its light pierces the heart of a forest and the figures hunched there in a circle. As they sharpen knives for a new ritual, their whispers blend into the hissing of blood dripping into their fire.

She'll be here soon.

Very soon, yes. We're ready for her.

CHAPTER ONE

Into a Fairy Tale

The mountains loomed dark and sullen against the bright blue sky, their jagged shapes nothing more than shadow from peak to gulch. The thin roads cutting through them stood out like veins, pumping cars into pockets of civilization. One in particular glittered from the amount of traffic on it, a sluggish line of roofs burdened with kayaks, bicycles, and other luggage —tourists escaping to the wilderness for the weekend.

Alice studied the distant highway as their own truck barreled down a back trail Colton had found, her gaze drifting to the narrow tunnel of the mountain pass. It looked like a mouth there among the split stone and scrubby pines, as if the earth itself swallowed the road and every car on it. She found herself biting her lower lip, pain taking the edge from her anxiety.

Then Colton's hand stroked along her leg, calm and reassuring. "What's wrong?"

His deep voice always sounded rough as a growl. Indifferent, too. Its curtness was that of a beast far preferring the certainty of teeth to the frailty of words. A hunter used to living in silence. Yet when he looked at her, his eyes revealed everything he refused to say, everything that she meant to him.

It steadied her breath. It drew out her smile. She didn't think she'd ever get used to him, this wolf hiding as a man. So many months they had lived together, so many times they had explored each other body and soul, and yet baring her heart to him still left her feeling raw and open and overwhelmingly free.

She sighed, already feeling lighter. "I was thinking about my mother and wishing I knew why she left. Why she picked that day, why she took me along in the car... and where she ended up. I realize they're all questions that will never have answers, and that *why* doesn't matter, not really. But sometimes I still want to know."

Old worries, old pain, and voicing them suddenly left her impatient to strip them from her thoughts. She shook her head and asked the first question that came to mind. "How did you find this trail? There's no one else on it."

"I know the area and all the nearby towns." Despite the constant twists and turns in the road, his hand remained on her thigh. "Not the hotel you're staying in, though."

"It's very new. Denise heard about it from a friend. She said it's deep in the woods because it's supposed to feel old-world. Like you're stepping into a fairy tale."

Colton gave a short growl that was his version of a scoff. "People in fairy tales end up dead. Or wishing they were."

A laugh bubbled out. "I think they're using the romantic versions for their inspiration. Magic, enchantment, and wonder instead of torment, loss, and murder. From what Denise said, the hotel even looks like a castle."

"We'll find out soon enough." Then they turned onto a paved road. The open view of the mountains disappeared as pine trees loomed all around. The ground leveled out before he added, "Under a mile to go."

Her heart beat a little faster. Four days and three nights without him. Tonight without *anyone.* She dreaded it but put on a pleasant smile while looking over at him, determined to see this trip through. The afternoon sunlight warmed the green in his eyes and picked out stubble already shadowing his face. She couldn't help reaching out to brush his jaw. "You'll probably have a full beard by the time I come back."

Something changed in his expression, there and gone as swiftly as a breath, but she still saw and understood it. He didn't like the idea of leaving her. More than that, he would miss her; their little house back home would echo without her presence. He probably wouldn't even step inside it until she was back, instead living as a wolf in the surrounding forest.

Then his hand caught hers, and he said, "You sure about this? You've been quiet since hearing you'll be alone until tomorrow."

She nodded, firm about the decision despite a fresh wave of fear. "I'm sure. It'll be fine."

He gave her an intent look but took the final turn. The first glimpses of white buildings and neat shrubs appeared between the trees.

After a few hundred yards, the road straightened out and revealed a massive stone archway carved with the words WONDERWOOD RESORT AND SPA. When they passed through it, the pines on either side melted away, exposing the grounds of the resort. Alice could only blink at the buildings nestled among cultivated hedges and pristine lawns. The place was *massive*.

The driveway circled a marble water fountain surrounded by rose bushes, each bloom striped red and white like peppermint candy. Beyond it waited the hotel itself, a towering giant with turrets and chimneys. It looked bizarre, even out of place among ancient pine and weathered rock, as if it were something that had been lost to time and rediscovered as an artifact. A sword recovered from an eroding mountain. Gold unearthed from centuries of soil. A wedding dress preserved long after its owner had withered away to bone.

Inside, the lobby was just as impressive, with overstuffed furniture upholstered in red and gold and a lit fireplace guarded by crouching marble lions. Dark wooden beams spanned the pale ceiling like massive ribs, and Alice somehow felt both lost in a chasm and utterly trapped as she and Colton approached the receptionist at the front desk.

The girl was probably her age, blonde hair in an immaculate bun and smile as crisp as her navy uniform. "Welcome to Wonderwood Resort and Spa. My name is Gwen. How may I help you?"

"I'm Alice Corrigan. There should be a reservation for me."

After a few seconds of muted tapping, Gwen said, "Oh, yes. We have you down as a guest with Denise Corrigan and Fleur Corrigan for three nights in our Gold Villa."

"That's right, but they won't make it in until tomorrow." Alice kept her expression confident despite the small tremor that ran through her.

"We understand. It won't be a problem in any way. However..." Gwen's gaze flickered over to Colton, who eyed the stuffed boar's head mounted on the nearest wall. "If you were planning on a fourth guest, then I'm sorry. I'm afraid we require 24 hours' notice for adding anyone to the original reservation."

"I'm here to settle her in," said Colton, scanning the rest of the room. His flat tone dared her to argue against him being there at all.

Gwen didn't try. "I understand. This will only take a few more minutes."

Then she offered Alice a document holder stamped with the resort's insignia. The sleek leather looked burnished in the warm lamplight. "This is your party's personalized itinerary. It'll help you keep track of the experiences and activities you've signed up for."

As Alice peeked inside and tried not to wince at Denise's choices, the other girl took an antique key from the hook board behind her. It gleamed like gold as she handed it over. "And this is your room key. Wonderwood policy is to have our guests experience bygone elegance and luxury. Other than modern plumbing and electrical lighting, we avoid technology when old-fashioned simplicity will do."

"No phones?" said Colton, finally looking at her. There was a sudden alertness in his eyes.

"None outside the lobby. But since the villa is separate from the rest of the hotel, there are call buttons in both bedrooms. Please be assured, our service is always prompt, discreet, and ready to attend to a guest's slightest need." Then Gwen tried a bright smile. It wilted beneath his full stare. "This policy *was* mentioned very clearly during the reservation process, sir."

Alice ran fingers along his arm to get his attention. "She's right. It's one of the reasons why Denise picked this place. That and because guests can't bring their phones along."

"You're correct, ma'am. Personal phones, tablets, and other devices must be left at home." Gwen pitched her voice to sound slightly apologetic but firm. "The proprietress of Wonderwood firmly believes it's an essential step to enjoy the peace and beauty of our surroundings inside and out."

Colton's expression suggested exactly what he thought of that, but he remained silent as Alice matched Gwen's smile with one of her own. "I understand. How do I find the villa?"

Gwen offered to have a staff member escort them to the private trail, but Alice declined, already tired of the smothering politeness. Within a few minutes, she and Colton were on a path that curled around the immense bulk of the hotel to lead deeper into the woods. It wasn't long before they reached the villa, itself a miniature of the hotel, yet the closeness of the trees made it feel as isolated as if they were in the heart of the forest.

"It's very quiet," said Alice, glancing at Colton as she unlocked the door.

He only nodded, the tightness in his jaw revealing he didn't like any of this.

When they stepped inside, Alice understood why her stepmother had been so excited. The interior was even more luxurious than the lobby, with the walls painted in rich shades of red and brown. There was a crystal chandelier in the salon, replicas of ancient Greek sculptures in the library, and fireplaces in both bedrooms. All the furniture had claw feet and intricate floral upholstery, and all the floors had antique Persian rugs. There wasn't an inch of space undecorated, with tasseled drapes, oil paintings, bronze figurines, and vases of flowers all creating a sense of being surrounded by unbearable elegance.

It felt hard to even breathe, and Alice soon found herself sitting on the huge poster bed in the nearest bedroom, staring all around. "They weren't joking about the luxury. I can't believe Denise called this a vacation cabin."

Colton eyed the bed as if he didn't want to touch it, instead circling around the room once more. The tension in his shoulders was obvious even beneath his jacket.

"What is it?" said Alice, her voice falling soft.

He looked at her. There was a feral gleam in his eyes. "No phone, no car... no way out. I don't like it."

Whatever she said in response would direct the next few days. If she wanted to go home, he'd take her without a second thought, without one word of complaint over driving eight hours total for nothing. If she insisted she felt safe, that this all felt like stepping into a dream and she'd be fine, he wouldn't grind her down until he got the answer he wanted. Sometimes it still stunned her, how this nightmare creature who tore throats without hesitation and knew tenderness only through his teeth was also the first figure in her life to let her have her own thoughts. She could show him the most vulnerable parts of her heart without going away bleeding.

Tomorrow, she would have to put on a smiling mask for her stepmother, but right now she could still bare herself—and she wanted to. "I don't like it either. And I won't like being on my own until they get here. But Denise asked me to be part of this, and asked me to still come here today when she found out they'd be late. I want to do this for her."

Now Colton sat beside her, the brush of his hand coaxing her body to relax against his. As she melted into his touch, she found herself saying, "She thought it would be a perfect place to have a girls' getaway. And with the way she and Fleur have been fighting lately... I think she's desperate to try anything that might give them bonding time."

"And you?" His voice rumbled against her cheek.

"Denise never treated me like I was just a stepdaughter. She really did everything she could to make me feel loved. When she first talked about this trip, I could hear how worried she was about Fleur, and how much she wanted me to come along to smooth things over. That's why I agreed, because I knew she needed help. And that's why I'll stay."

There was a soft growl from him that sounded more like a sigh. Then he caught her chin, tilting it up, yet she was the one who leaned in for the kiss. The heat of his mouth felt real in a way that nothing around her could compare, transforming the heaviness behind her ribs into a sweet ache. Her fingers grabbed at the thick hair at the back of his head to pull him closer, losing herself in the dangerous press of teeth, in the way his hand held her firmly, almost desperately, as if nothing could make him let go. Even once he broke off to let her breathe, her nails dug into his shoulders in a silent demand for more.

"I don't want to say it," she said, the words hardly more than a whisper. "I don't want to have to tell you goodbye."

"I know."

The rasp in his voice had turned almost soothing, but she still shuddered, memories swirling. "I know it's silly by this point. I know this is nothing like what happened with my mother. And once Denise and Fleur are here, I'll be fine. But the idea of sleeping here by myself... *being* here by myself...

when Denise called this morning with the news they'd be late, I felt sick. I still do."

"Alice." The sound of her name drew her gaze back to his face as he murmured, "You really think I'd leave you alone and frightened?"

She released a shaky breath. "I thought I hid it pretty well."

"You did, but I know you." He traced the curve of her cheek before adding, "I'll get the truck out of here. Make it look like I left. Won't be hard to hide from the staff."

Relief cracked through her voice. "You might as well have fun exploring the area. I'll be busy throughout the evening. Denise signed up for dinner at the resort's restaurant and then a spa treatment afterward. But tonight..."

For the first time, a hint of teasing entered his eyes. "Tonight, I'll be here."

Then he kissed her again, this time slow and rough, each flick of his tongue tantalizing her with what to expect.

The sun hung low in the sky when she left the villa to go to dinner. She took the trail without fear, aware of a shadow moving among the trees. Colton tilted his head until his eyes flashed at her, his version of a wink while he was a wolf, and disappeared into the gloom the same moment she stepped onto the main path. Then she put a smile on her face and pretended to be a normal girl.

Other guests were also drifting toward the restaurant, an ornate building reminiscent of a Mediterranean mansion. The inside was lit with chandeliers, their antique brass arms glowing against the gold and cream walls. The patrons sparkled as much as their table settings, and Alice was glad she'd changed into heels and a nice dress. The hostess sat her at a booth, handed her a menu personalized with her name, and then left her alone to choose what she wanted.

It was all very rich, delicate, and exquisitely presented. Field greens with a champagne vinaigrette, pomegranate seeds glittering among the glazed leaves like rubies. A slender cut of lamb drizzled with sauce dark as blood. Panna cotta the color of lavender, paired with honeyed figs split open and seared. There was nothing she could find fault with, and yet it all felt uncomfortable in its very indulgence. Like the heaviness of diamond earrings, or the pressure of a gold ring meant for another's finger. It was a relief to leave.

Back at the main grounds of the hotel, the stone firepit for the outdoor lounge was being lit, shooting sparks into a darkening sky. Several guests already sat around it, sipping wine while a man played classical guitar. Staff drifted here and there, somehow both obvious and invisible in their starched uniforms while they offered elegant parfaits.

As Alice lingered, reluctant to fulfill her appointment at the spa, she grew aware of a figure watching her from a cluster of hemlock trees. Her skin prickled even before she looked over, knowing gut-deep that it wasn't Colton.

It was a man, one who seemed about her age. He wasn't dressed in a formal uniform, instead wearing the sturdy boots, jeans, and all-weather jacket of someone used to working outdoors. When their gazes met, he smiled and approached, the light from the fire revealing more of his features. He was blandly handsome, not enough to intimidate but enough to charm.

When he spoke, his voice sounded easy-going. "Hi, I'm Steve. You must be one of the new guests that arrived today."

Alice nodded, keeping her smile small and cool. Whatever he wanted, she wasn't interested in giving it. "It's a beautiful place."

"Oh, yeah. Pretty as a picture." Gravel crunched beneath his feet as he stepped closer. "But you don't look too interested in sitting around and listening to folk music. In fact, you look pretty bored."

She eyed him, wondering what his playfulness hid. "Do you work here?"

"Yep, I'm one of the handymen. I know every inch of this resort and can show you around anytime you want. The most popular areas, the less popular areas... even the areas that nobody knows about." Then he flashed a grin that probably tempted some guests to seek out more than his knowledge.

Alice bit back a laugh at the idea of him trying to seduce her. "It's nice of you to offer, but I know where I want to go." Then she nodded at the spa facility in the distance, its lit windows muted by burgundy drapes. "Thanks anyway."

As she turned and left, her skin tingled unpleasantly, and halfway down the path she glanced back to see if he still stood there. He did but spoke with a couple, appearing as interested in them as he had with her. Maybe she'd misunderstood things.

Then the door to the spa loomed before her. The cherubs carved into its wood had maniacal grins. She could already smell the eucalyptus and rose oils inside, and mentally resigned herself to whatever service Denise had signed her up for.

It turned out to be something called a *purifying mud experience*, and Alice soon found herself at the mercy of Olga, a woman whose teeth were as white as her esthetician's jacket. For the next two and a half hours, she was scrubbed head to toe with a dry brush to stimulate and polish her skin, ushered to a mud bath where she was buried up to her neck in the thick glop, and given a hydromassage to relax her muscles.

Her final treatment was thirty minutes of being covered in a special mud paste harvested from a Scottish peat bog and then wrapped in layers of plastic and flannel sheets to encourage her body to absorb it. Olga offered a lavender spritz and a scalp massage to help pass the time, leaving Alice to stare at the dainty cocktail in front of her while clinical fingers rubbed at her head. It was hard not to feel like a sausage about to burst from its casing.

Soon, the sensation of muddied plastic sticking to her sweating skin brought certain memories to the surface, ones that she hated: those sharp, painful flashes of crawling around in the hot car while waiting for her mother to come back. Strange how she couldn't remember her mother's face on that day but could visualize with perfect clarity the way light winked off the rearview mirror as the sun set for that first night. Hot and trapped and thirsty from screaming so much. Sweat running down her back even as the crickets began singing.

Why could she remember that so well and not what she ached for: a hint of her mother's reason for leaving?

The cocktail glass was empty by the time Olga gave her a shower cap to protect her hair while washing off the mud, and Alice wasn't sure whether she felt like screaming or laughing during the finishing treatment—a layer of peat mud lotion applied to her skin to give it "velvety softness."

Finally, she was allowed to leave, staggering into the darkness of true night without hesitation. Even with those heavy memories, she didn't fear the woods. She easily walked among the trees while thinking about the orange shirt of the hiker who'd pulled her out of the car, and the plastic taste of the water he'd given her. The confusion and fear in his face when he realized a small girl had been left at the edge of a state park long enough that her crying was nothing more than hoarse breaths. Everyone in the little group who'd found her had looked around in terror, suddenly aware of how implacable the wilderness was, and how horrors could disappear in its silence without a single footstep to mark them.

And yet that terror had never touched her, for it wasn't the forest swallowing her mother whole that frightened Alice, but that she never once looked back while walking away... and the fact that Alice still wasn't sure what aspects of her mother survived through her, passed through their witch blood in the way that eye color might appear through generations of a family. Yes, the wilderness had taken her mother, but what had it also left behind?

The key felt heavy in her hand while she unlocked the villa's front door and stepped inside, already glancing around for Colton. His name died on her lips as she realized the salon looked... different. A note on the table revealed why.

Little elves and fairies came while you were away and set things back in their proper place.

Everything had been touched in some way. Her clothes folded and put away in drawers, her suitcase zipped up and taken off the bed, her toothbrush back in her toiletry bag. Even the laces on her sneakers had been tied, and she shook her head while setting the key on one of the bedside tables.

Then teeth nipped at the back of her neck, familiar, teasing, and she laughed as Colton's hands slid under her dress, tracing her hips. "Were you here when they came in?"

"No, but I watched them. They didn't take anything."

"That's not what bothers me. It's the idea of them touching everything." She shuddered and then relaxed again as he kissed the skin on her back bared by the dress. "I'm really glad you're here with me."

The words made him growl while he teased the strap of her bra with his teeth. "Went that bad, hm?"

"Yes. I'd love a drink, but right now I couldn't handle someone from the resort trying to impress me with the wine list."

"Here." He let go of her long enough to pull out a bottle of whiskey from his jacket. "This place didn't look like it'd have anything strong."

"Where did you...?"

"It's a tourist area. There's always a liquor store around." He found a glass and poured a shot in it while Alice sank back on the bed. "So. What happened?"

She told him while sipping at her drink, enjoying the sweet burn that came with every mouthful, and still had a little left as she finished with, "It just felt really weird. She was *so* cheerful, and the figurines around the room looked like they were all staring at me. By the time she brought out the plastic, I thought I'd been picked for a secret snuff film."

"Snuff film?" Colton had taken a few hits straight from the bottle but was unaffected as always, standing at the foot of the bed to ease off her high heels. They were dropped to the floor without care, but his hands turned gentle while they ran over her feet and ankles, leaving her body flushed with a new kind of warmth.

She managed to murmur, "It's where a real murder is filmed for depraved people who want to watch something like that."

He raised his eyebrows. "They don't do it live anymore?"

When she only blinked at him, he gave her one of his rare smiles before leaning in to lick the traces of whiskey from her mouth. "I'll tell you about ancient Rome sometime."

"Why not now?" she whispered as he settled against her, pressing their hips together. The rough denim of his jeans pushed up the thin silk of her dress.

In the dim light of the room, his eyes looked dark and intent. "Because I'd rather fuck you."

The crude words left her gasping against his mouth, already trying to pull off her dress. Her skin felt clammy from the spa treatment, even alien, and she wanted his teeth and sweat and semen on her instead. She wanted *him*.

He teased her, letting her tug off his jacket and unbutton his shirt before he pulled back, rising to his feet and reaching for the whiskey as if to pour her more. She only teased back, sitting up to tug at his jeans with one hand while her other ran up along the hard muscles of his stomach. Surprise flashed in his eyes—the hunter startled by such willingness—but they turned hot as her mouth followed her fingers. She licked at the dusting of hair there, smiling against his skin just to feel him jerk.

Then his hand caught her hair and pulled it free of that intricate bun, rough and demanding. She gasped against the fly of his jeans, and when his cock twitched in response, licked along it. He gave her that short growl that was the closest he ever came to a groan, fingers tightening.

His cock was already half-hard when she pulled it free, and she kissed up its length just to feel him shudder before taking it all in her mouth. The smooth burn of whiskey lingering in her throat deepened into something sweeter in her chest, something heavier. So many nights spent afraid even while in a relationship, so many hours crawling by as her heart beat like a panicked rabbit's at the thought of being alone because she wasn't worth another's time or attention.

So many things she had done to stay close to someone, to take on the sharpest love, to open her arms to the cruelest behavior in return for never being left behind, and now here she was in the company of a beast, panting and writhing and free. How could she fear the forest when a piece of it had found her, howling until she had learned how to let her own voice rise with his?

Alice had no answers for what she felt, only knew that the taste of his sweat and the roughness of his growls made her feel as alive as when his teeth were locked onto her neck. She worshipped him with every slide of her tongue, with every planted kiss, with every gasp against his straining cock. And when his fingers snarled in her hair and his breathing changed, she grew frantic, sucking until salt and musk exploded in her mouth.

Still insatiable, she kissed up his stomach again, shifting until her breasts brushed against his still-hard cock. When he growled in response, she started rubbing against him, wanting to feel his semen against her skin. The sensation sent pulses of heat straight to her cunt.

"I love you," she said against the throbbing vein at his hip that led to his cock, her voice hardly more than a whisper.

At that, he caught her by the chin and pulled her up, crushing his mouth against hers. His tongue was hot, devouring, and she was panting for breath when he finally broke off, their lips still touching.

"Words," he said, but his voice was gentle, and the look in his eyes made her forget the twisting desperation she'd felt throughout the day. Made her feel safe and whole.

Later, she settled against him, almost believing they were back home, back in their own woods. His fingers ran through her freed hair, the slow rhythm coaxing her mind toward sleep.

"Will the pain ever go away?" she whispered, knowing he couldn't give her an answer. That no one could.

His next kiss was tender, that dangerous mouth aware of how many times she had been hurt. "However things turn out, I'll be there with you."

It gave her enough peace to fall asleep, cheek pressed against his heartbeat. Most of the resort slept with her.

Most... but not all.

In a small room beneath the hotel, a woman sat at a desk littered with papers. She called herself Portia Valcott and was the proprietress of Wonderwood and its facilities. In truth, this was merely her latest disguise, but she was trying to be dutiful this time around, and so on this night, at this late hour, she was paying bills. It wasn't cheap to run a resort, and they quickly piled up if she didn't keep on top of things.

She sensed someone approach the door long before the knock came, yet decided to act irritated, as if she'd been disturbed out of her concentration. "What is it, Stephen?"

He entered the room with his face already set in a scowl. "She didn't like me."

Portia sighed. "Why did you even speak to her? Didn't you check the guest notes? The full party for the villa hasn't even arrived yet. It won't until tomorrow, which means our plans will be delayed by a day."

She watched his scowl deepen. "I couldn't help it. She's the one I want."

"You'll get her." Her gaze returned to the pile of bills, but the unusual silence from him drew her attention once more. "What else?"

"Gwen said there was a guy hanging around her when she checked in. Said he had bad vibes."

"Gwen is a sweet little girl who truly believes she's working for a normal resort. I wouldn't trust her perception of anyone if she thinks I'm just a businesswoman." Then she raised an eyebrow at him. "Or that you're just a handyman. You were sizing her up for your *appetites* as well."

"I changed my mind once I saw this other girl. Listen, whether this guy is human or something more, I want her. You promised me I could have my first pick this time."

"And I always keep my promises." Then Portia sighed. "Dear boy, stop worrying. In two more nights, we'll have our ritual... and you'll have yours."

CHAPTER TWO

Sensing Danger

Branches reached for Alice as she followed the stream. It was a trickle of water, hardly enough to cover the smooth pebbles of its bed, yet it remained a sure path through looming pines and drifting fog. A silver arrow pointing a way out of the suffocating forest.

She dreamed. She knew she dreamed because the sky looked black as pitch even while the whippy branches on either side gleamed like knives. Her feet took step after step, steady and numb as her gaze remained fixed on a spark of light hidden deep within the trees.

Something cried in the distance, a high-pitched shriek that could have been human or animal. The voice cut off just as Alice reached a point where the stream dwindled to a muddy path. A chill ran along her spine while she listened for any other noise.

All was silent. Still. Only the hint of wood smoke warned she would meet someone if she took this new trail.

There was no way to go back; she knew that bone-deep. And whatever waited beside that pinprick of a fire felt heavy with malice, poisoning the forest with its very presence, thickening the air into a raw, throbbing heartbeat.

Yet Alice stepped onto the path without shivering, and when thorns caught at her hair, she didn't flinch. Her lips curled back to reveal her fangs, and her hands snapped the branches trying to scratch and sting. She was nothing to be toyed with.

The trees opened into a clearing as quickly as a gasp, and Alice stumbled to a stop, bloody and hot-eyed and shaking. A bonfire burned in the very center, the logs at its heart long and curved like bones. As it crackled, a sound that seemed very much like laughter, the cages around it grew clear.

They were built from branches and mud, squat and filthy and marked with fingernail scratches. The lingering smells of blood and terror choked Alice with each breath even as the flames brightened, revealing the cages weren't empty. Hunched things convulsed with each breath, ruined as roadkill but somehow still alive. Firelight flickered on exposed bone and missing muscle, on mouths opened in silent screams because their voices were gone, taken along with everything else.

Alice flinched back, her own voice catching in her throat. Then a figure rose from behind the bonfire, the uncertain flames hiding its face. All she could see was long, ragged hair and skin streaked with blood.

The things in the cages grew frenzied, filling the clearing with wet, ripping sounds while their ravaged flesh tore under the strain of struggling, but it was the weight of the figure's gaze that broke through Alice's shock. When several shadows slipped over to flank it, hardening into silhouettes that all beckoned, she snarled and dropped into a crouch, limbs shaking with the first spasms of her shift.

Agony wracked every inch of her, bone and sinew twisting in protest of their raw rebirth, but within a heartbeat she lurched upright again, already steady on the long, lean limbs of a predator, already frothing at the air with jaws that could shatter bone. The dim figures watched with cocked heads, their bodies flickering with the fire even as hers found its fearsome form.

Wolf-Alice shook away the last of the tremors, fur bristling as she growled at them. *Come closer if you dare*, she said with a snap of her teeth. *Just try turning me into your prey*.

A rush of laughter in response. Then the fire roared, flames swelling out to catch her. She ducked away unharmed, but when the smoke and sparks cleared from her sight, everything had vanished. The cages, the figures... even the fire itself. Only a smoldering pit of ash and some bloodstains remained.

Wary, cautious, she circled around the clearing, sniffing over the ground for any clue as to where they had fled. Magic always smelled horrible to her, sharp as fear and acrid as smoke. Thick enough to overwhelm everything else. Even so, she caught traces of sweat, hair, and skin. The forest had hidden the figures but couldn't strip away their scents—all female, all entwined with magic. All of them ravenous.

A nearby branch suddenly jabbed at her with a life of its own. So did another. She stepped back with a growl as the trees leaned closer, bark creaking while they choked off the clearing. They weren't going to let her leave. As they continued to tighten like a knot, the first thorns raking against her fur, she realized they weren't even going to let her *live*. She snapped at the closest branches, ignoring the sting of scratches, but soon found herself crouching low as they closed in.

Then the trees behind her shivered. She turned toward them with defiant jaws, ready for a fresh attack, but the branches only shrank back, bark rubbing against itself with a sound like frantic whispers. A dark shape lunged out from their midst, eyes as bright as the moon, teeth ready to tear, and Wolf-Alice's growl rose into a yelp at the sight of the black wolf. He pressed close, responding to her frantic nuzzle with a few tender licks at the scratches on her nose, but his slanted ears warned of further danger even as the trees withered around them.

They fled together, the black wolf leading her through a forest as stark as charcoal until the sky deepened and the land opened wide. As soon as the moon appeared, large and luminous and just rising over the horizon, the black wolf urged her toward it, his presence grounding her as the unflinching light filled her senses and then her very being.

It was a smell that came back to her first—the rich, bitter heat of coffee. Her eyes opened, and then she realized she was awake, curled up in bed while Colton leaned over her. His gaze was intent, furious, and she knew without a word passed between them that the dream had been something more. Something real. "Where was I?"

His words came out as a growl. "The shadow world."

Her skin prickled. She hadn't been there since... well, since Magdalene had lured her to it. She still didn't truly understand what that strange land was, or where it existed. Only that she could be called there in her dreams and would bear the marks of her visit once she woke up. "Did you see them? Did you hear their laughter?"

"No. Just saw you there by the firepit." Then he stopped her hand as she unthinkingly tried to rub at the areas of her face that still stung.

"How bad is it?" she asked, now remembering how the branches had slashed at her.

"It's already healing." Despite the curt words, his thumb gently stroked over her palm.

She nodded and pushed herself upright, wincing from the hot tenderness in her bones that always came after she ran as a wolf. As Colton caught her waist, steadying her, she realized he was fully dressed and that a styrofoam cup of coffee waited on the bedside table. So did a takeout box.

Even as lingering shivers wracked her body, she looked up at him with a faint smile. "You brought me breakfast."

"Figured the food would be as fucking weird as everything else."

"Quail egg with wild mushroom mousse. I checked the menu plan yesterday." Then she dropped her head against his shoulder, realizing she needed to explain what had happened in her dream. It didn't take long, and she soon finished with, "There's something happening here, isn't there? Something nasty."

The brightening sunlight only intensified the feral look on his face. "We're on someone's hunting ground."

"I wonder if the handyman is involved," she murmured. "The figures in my dream all seemed female, but... he gave me the creeps."

"Handyman?"

"He came up to me while I was walking the grounds after dinner and offered to show me around. The way he said it felt very practiced and smooth, and I got the feeling he'd been watching me for awhile. He seemed like one of those types used to getting laid on the job." Then she grew aware of how Colton's shoulders had bunched beneath her fingers. "You're really tense."

"He either wants to fuck you or kill you. You think I'd take that well?" Despite his flat tone, the green in his eyes seethed bright and vicious. At that moment, they didn't look human at all.

She stroked the side of his jaw without fear. "I thought it was laughable. He didn't seem dangerous at the time... and no one could seduce me away from you."

"Willingly." His pupils had narrowed to pinpoints.

The implication left her quiet, all words crushed beneath the weight of vague fears hardening into true danger. She was being hunted again. Whatever those figures were, they wished to catch her. Use her.

Did she still seem so vulnerable in the eyes of others? So tempting a morsel, so sweet a sacrifice? It galled her that anyone might believe she was something to steal away and feed on.

She found herself looking up at Colton. A savage edge slipped into her voice. "We're the hunters. I'm no one's prey."

He tilted his head at her, eyes still hot, still feral, yet a new light entered them. "Then you want to stay."

"Whatever this is, I won't leave my family to face it alone. And I..."

When she faltered, embarrassed to reveal what had scratched and howled against her ribcage from the moment those figures had jeered at her, he raised his eyebrows. "Don't be ashamed. Not with me. We've seen each other good and bad."

"I know. But I'm feeling different than I would have before. I'm not relieved we found out in time. Instead, I'm mad that it's happening at all." She hesitated again, falling quiet until his fingers traced the curve of her jaw. The touch drew her closer, drew out words that felt dangerous to reveal to anyone, even him, because they mapped out a part of her that had changed. A part she didn't quite understand. Exposing herself still felt stunningly vulnerable, an offer of trust that might lead to a new scar.

But it wasn't just anyone who listened to her now. It was a beast who had shown her the delight of teeth, who had brought blood and moonlight into her bed. Her next words came out as a snarl. "I don't want to hide. I want to hunt."

At that, Colton nearly smiled. "Then we will."

Could it be that simple? The possibility left her breathless. "Even if it means I've become less sweet? More savage?"

"Alice." The growl didn't leave his voice, but the undertone to it changed as he leaned in close. "I like your teeth as much as the rest of you."

His mouth felt hot against hers as she began shaking again, this time in excitement, yet just as she felt the first hint of his tongue, a knock came at the front door. Then the sound of a key scraping in its lock. "Ms. Corrigan? We're here with breakfast."

She muffled a groan. "Thank you. Could you leave it in the library?"

"Of course, ma'am." There was nothing but politeness in the voice, and yet even after the villa fell quiet again, she remained tense, her exhilaration soured by the intrusion until Colton's hands squeezed her hips.

"They're gone," he said, nipping at the curve of her ear.

"For now, but it must already be seven o'clock if breakfast is here. Which means Denise and Fleur will arrive in a few hours. That's not enough time to find these bastards, is it? I'll have to put on a pleasant smile and pretend everything's all right."

"It's probably better to watch over your family during the day. Humans are oblivious."

She nodded, clinging to him as her heart churned. She wanted to bite, not to smile. She wanted to rip and claw and scream. Her tension was mirrored in him; she could feel it in the way his muscles tightened whenever her body shifted against his, in how he never once looked away from her. The air between them felt electric.

"Colton?" She turned her face into his neck, breathing in the hints of blood, musk, and tree sap that were always there against the clean warmth of his skin. "I really want to fuck. But I..."

"Want it rough."

She laughed. "You know. You always know."

His response was a growl, a deep one promising the delicious burn of teeth. He was still too on edge to smile, but the charge in the air took on new intensity while his fingers tangled in her hair. She reached for the fly of his jeans, hot excitement sparking in her chest. He let her pull his hardening cock free before jerking her head back hard enough to make her gasp against his mouth.

His kiss was slow but unrelenting, tasting every inch of her, keeping her to his rhythm as her nails dug into his hips. Then he pulled her head back even further, until her neck arched, until the vulnerable length of her throat was fully exposed. She panted against his first bite, her voice rising as he then sucked against her skin to take away the sting.

It was his strength that always undid her—teeth scraping against her pulse, mouth intent and patient even as she threw away all control. His erection pushed against her stomach, giving away his hunger, but he continued to taste at her skin as if savoring it. As she stroked the length of his cock, she marveled at its thickness and strength as much as his total control. Even when she rubbed a thumb over its head, he merely growled against her, keeping to his measured pace.

Then his mouth found the heavy flesh of her breast, sucking hard enough to draw a yelp out of her. When he found her nipple, he bit instead, teasing with his teeth, with the hot press of his tongue, with the rasp of his stubble. She clutched at his hair as he drew her further into the delicious torment, stoking her gasps into moans until she dimly wondered whether they'd be overheard.

As if sensing her thoughts, he moved enough to kiss her once more, muffling her voice. The wet heat from his mouth lingered on her nipples, leaving them flushed and aching as he pinned her down and teased, rubbing his cock against her hips. She arched in response, eager to feel him push inside her.

Instead, he straightened up again, humor glinting in his eyes. "No. I'll decide when."

"How are you so patient?" she groaned, letting her head fall back against the bed. She was always the frantic one, feverish for the bliss within reach, her need as sharp and forceful as a flash of lightning.

His only answer was to push her legs open until she felt the seam of her cunt part. The rush of air against her swollen folds had her panting even before the velvet heat of his tongue found them. That dangerous mouth was just as unrelenting as before, magnified by the hard rasp of his chin. He found her clit, teasing until she was beyond desperate, fingernails tearing at the sheets as she begged him with each moan. A pinch from his teeth and she thrashed into a white-hot climax, only his weight and strength keeping her still as he moved from teasing to sucking, stoking her into wave after wave of release. Only once she was too limp to do anything but shiver did his attention soften into gentle licks, cleaning her up.

When his cock finally pushed in, sheer exhaustion kept her from climaxing on the spot. He stretched over her, their mouths nearly brushing as she managed to say, "You always outlast me."

He seemed amused at that, licking her parted lips as she continued to pant. "I'll draw this one out."

And he did, moving slow, hard, and deep, each thrust feeling like it would split her in two even as he bit at her breasts and sucked the sweat from her neck. He was sweating, too, his body slick against hers while the bed shuddered to their rhythm.

Then his teeth found his favorite spot on her throat, where her pulse beat hard and fast, where she arched just from the hint of his tongue. He bit down while pushing in hard enough to make her howl, her fingers digging into the hard muscles of his back as he snarled through his release.

Her body held onto a warm afterglow even after the windows brightened with true daylight and noise could be heard outside. Colton seemed just as unconcerned, letting her curl against him as their sweat dried.

"What will you do while I'm busy with my family?" she said, unwilling to get up and get dressed.

The answer rumbled against her forehead. "Search the surrounding forest for anything trying to hide. Check in on you."

"Kill the handyman?"

"I'm tempted."

"He might be innocent."

"Is that what your gut says?"

"No. But the figures in my dreams felt very different. I couldn't see any of them clearly, but they felt... inhuman." Then she licked her lips, feeling some of her nervousness return. "Do you think they were witches? And that maybe there's a reason why I've been dreaming about my mother the entire week before coming here?"

His nose nuzzled hers. "Don't know. But we'll find out."

Alice sighed, stroking his hair a final time before rolling for the edge of the bed. "We'll be busy until late tonight. I'll meet you outside the villa."

Despite her reluctance, she couldn't help smiling at him as he also got up, moving with a hunter's silent grace. A final kiss and then he stepped away to shift form.

In the clear light of day, it was like a flickering shadow, a gasp of breath. The wolf that had been a man shook his black fur into place before circling to her, the set of his ears relaxed, even reassuring. Alice ran fingers through his fur, burying her face against his shoulder in a brief hug before he slipped out through the opened window. She watched him disappear into the gloom of the forest, the love bites on her skin still hot and delicious.

She had a pleasant expression in place when her stepmother and sister arrived at the villa. Denise's smile, always bright, now turned brilliant while she hugged Alice with one arm and steadied her suitcase with the other. "I'm so sorry we didn't make it in until today. Were you all right last night? I booked the villa because I didn't want us to feel cramped and all the cabins in this area are tiny, but having a space as big as this to yourself must have been overwhelming."

"I was fine." Alice pulled back enough to give her a smile even as concern trickled through her.

Her stepmother always looked like the embodiment of understated luxury in her tailored clothes, subtle makeup, and simple jewelry, yet strain now showed through that well-kept appearance. She looked tired, determined instead of carefree, and her voice sounded artificially cheerful while she turned back toward the doorway. "What do you think, Fleur? Isn't it breathtaking? I feel like a princess in a fairy tale."

Alice's thirteen-year-old sister stepped inside with only a backpack slung over her shoulder, looking around in obvious disgust. "It's weird here."

Alice blinked in surprise. She hadn't seen Fleur since last fall, and the girl's appearance had drastically changed. She and Denise still looked stamped from the same mold, both willowy in build and heart-shaped in the face, but Fleur had seemingly rejected everything her mother embraced. Her hair fell past her shoulders limp and unstyled, and she made no attempt to mask the angry clusters of acne on her face with makeup. A baggy sweatshirt and beat-up jeans and sneakers completed her appearance, and the metal braces on her teeth flashed with each word as she added, "This whole place is weird. Why couldn't we bring our phones?"

Denise's smile shifted into something desperate. "Because we're here to get away from the frantic pace of our daily lives. This trip is all about enjoying ourselves and making new memories."

Alice tried not to wince, remembering how similar comments had always felt so contrived during her own awkward teenage years. Everything from an adult's mouth had only increased her sense of feeling alone and uncomfortable, and she remembered not wanting advice or lectures but instead to be left the hell alone.

The thought kept her quiet as Fleur shrugged. "Whatever. Which room is mine?"

"The one with twin beds. You'll be sharing it with your sister."

Alice offered her a brief smile, all too aware that she knew some strangers better than this girl, separated by their age gap and Alice's own wish for distance during the time she had lived with her parents.

When Fleur only nodded and walked toward the bedroom, Denise called after her. "Sweetheart, we'll unpack later. Let's take a nice walk and explore the resort."

"No." The door slamming shut killed any chance of an argument.

Denise's shoulders slumped. "Once there's a closed door between her and me, she might as well be dead to the world."

"Maybe she just needs some space to herself after the long drive up here."

"Space is all she has. She never does anything anymore. I just don't—" Then Denise cut herself off with a shake of her head. "Let's take that walk. I'll explain everything."

It was a crisp day, the sunlight bright and colorless as it winked between the pines surrounding the trail. The sense of privacy seemed to unleash her stepmother's worries, and Alice found herself nodding along while Denise elaborated on what had gone wrong in an uninterrupted flow of words.

"I'm so sorry about getting here late. We had to go to a teacher's meeting that Fleur tried to hide from us. She failed her English Literature class after not turning in an essay that was 40% of the grade. She refuses to explain why. I know she loves to read, and at the beginning of the school year she was so excited to get in. It was her top pick."

"Will she have to retake the class?" said Alice, trying not to sound distracted as the trail opened into a view of the resort and the various staff members bustling around in their stiff uniforms. Who was the hidden predator? Which of them had cackled behind filthy hair while blood dried on their skin?

"The teacher said if she turns in the essay next week and shows she really worked hard, then she'll pass. But I'm not worried about a silly grade—your father looked ready to swallow his tongue at hearing she might be held back a year over it, but to my mind it's much worse that she failed on purpose. She had a partner with this assignment, and it was her best friend, Hayley! Fleur won't talk to her anymore. She won't speak to *any* of her old friends. I just don't understand it."

Alice made a sympathetic noise, glancing over the bulk of the hotel as they passed by. The vast windows of the lobby revealed the receptionist inside, her face tight and unhappy while she spoke to a woman who stood with her back to Alice's curious gaze.

Alice glimpsed greying hair in an elegant French bun and a flash of gold jewelry before Denise caught her arm, voice falling urgent. "Alice. Please. Talk to your sister. Not about the failed class. I mean... about anything. All she wants to do is stay in her room and play video games. She won't talk to me or to your father, and we wasted three therapy sessions with her sitting in silence the entire time. We just want to know she's all right. She's so different now, as if something happened."

Life, thought Alice. It left her skeptical about her own chances at breaking a shell that didn't want to crack, but the near panic on her stepmother's face left her nodding in agreement. "I'll try."

"Thank you. You're an angel." Denise let out a final sigh, as if expelling the last bits of stress, and then glanced at her watch. "Oh. We have to hurry back and get her. It's already time for our spa appointment. Did you go to the one I scheduled for last night? The 'Serene Bedtime' treatment?"

"I did. It was definitely a new experience."

"Oh, good. This one is even more luxurious. It takes three full hours, which will give us lots of time to catch up."

Alice managed a smile, hoping she didn't look as horrified as she felt.

Olga was still there, and her pleasant expression didn't waver an inch while she explained all the steps in reaching full-body rejuvenation, even when Fleur interrupted to say, "I'm not taking my clothes off."

"Sweetheart, it's not quite like that," said Denise, as the esthetician nodded along. "We'll be in towels the entire time."

"Fresh linen scented with lavender for utter relaxation," added Olga.

"I am *not* taking my clothes off."

Alice glanced at their various expressions and then took a closer look at the pamphlet explaining the spa package they were about to experience, a germ of an idea forming.

"Well... how about a swimsuit underneath the towel?" said Denise, looking at the esthetician.

Fleur's voice flared into a shriek. "Why are you making me do this? Because of some stupid body-positive article you read?"

"Fleur, please." Denise's tone finally lost its brightness. "You're too old to make a scene."

Before Fleur could do more than scoff, Alice looked up and said, "What if she skips the herbal bath and body buff? Everything else seems to be for our feet or faces."

There was a brief silence. Fleur looked torn between rage and relief. Denise just looked uncertain. When all gazes jumped to Olga for a final verdict, the esthetician's smile turned serene. "Of course. We'll set something up so that she can sit nearby and enjoy the calming atmosphere."

Fleur muttered an *okay*. Denise mouthed a *thank you* at Alice, who nodded and quietly hoped the next three hours would go better.

They did, with Denise's chatter filling the gaps in conversation left by Alice's natural reserve and Fleur's stubborn silence. As Olga's explanations of the health benefits of seaweed washed over Alice, she idly wondered whether the esthetician was involved with that strange ritual from her dream.

Some part of her marveled at herself for being so willing to hunt down those shadowy figures, to face their threats with teeth rather than run for safety. In truth, she liked the idea of seeking out their true identities, of seeing their shocked realization that she wasn't helpless prey right before she bit into the first throat. She'd always known she was a little depraved. She hadn't known she was bloodthirsty.

The thought drew a smile out of her while she and Denise went through the massage treatment. Fleur sat in a corner of the small room, ignoring the marble cherub behind her left shoulder while staring out the window, fingers twitching as if she longed for her phone.

The sound of the front door opening reached them all, as did a female voice gently calling Olga's name. Despite the friendly tone, a shiver ran through Alice, and she immediately looked up when its owner brushed the curtains aside to enter the room. It was the same woman she had glimpsed in the lobby. "There you are, my dear. How are the new guests enjoying their spa day?"

The esthetician murmured something appropriate while working over Denise's back, preventing her from looking up to say hello. Fleur ignored her entirely. But Alice... Alice fought to breathe while something vicious writhed in her chest, snarling even as the woman smiled at them all with a warmth that filled her next words. "I'm Portia Valcott, the proprietress here. I just wanted to welcome you to Wonderwood and make sure you've settled in comfortably."

"Oh, yes!" Denise exclaimed, able to look up when Olga moved to her legs. "It's wonderful here."

Alice just stared, knowing bone-deep that this had been one of the figures at the ritual. If she had been asked for reasons, she couldn't have given any. All she knew was that the mere sight of the other woman took her back to the bloodstained cages and frantic fire.

When their eyes met, Portia kept her smile. In fact, it even broadened. "I'm so glad to hear it. I do hope you enjoy dinner tonight, especially... Fleur, isn't it? As a special welcome, I've had the chef at the restaurant prepare a full multi-course meal to accommodate your dietary needs as a vegan."

Fleur blinked and then turned beet red.

Denise gasped. "I can't believe it. That is so kind of you."

The proprietress held up a hand. "Please. We just wish to make our guests feel fully welcome and looked after. If there's anything else, let me know."

Alice forced herself to smile as the other woman said her goodbyes, but the final, all-too-knowing glance from Portia left her fingers curling into claws. Olga *tsked* as she started to work on Alice's back. "You're very tense."

Denise didn't even notice, still bubbly over the gesture. "Can you believe that? They really do treat you like royalty here. I've never felt so pampered in my life."

Not pampered—fattened, thought Alice, but before she could think of a more neutral response, Fleur spoke up from her corner.

"I can't believe you told them I was vegan."

"To be honest, I don't remember doing that, but the receptionist asked so many questions when I made the reservation." Then Denise glanced at Alice, perhaps realizing how long her silence had stretched on. When Alice just chewed on her knuckles, the ghost of laughter lingering in her mind, her stepmother added, "Anyway, I'm sure it will be much more delicious than my sad attempts at cooking. I can't wait to see."

Hours later, as they walked back from the restaurant amid the silence of the trees, Fleur said, "It wasn't delicious. It was weird."

"Just because something is different doesn't make it weird, sweetheart. It's good to have new experiences." Despite her optimistic words, Denise looked tired, and Alice wasn't surprised when she told them she was going to bed as soon as they stepped inside the villa.

"It's the food," said Fleur, once she and Alice were alone in the bedroom they shared. "I can't believe she ate it. Half of what was on our plates looked like cat puke."

Alice couldn't disagree. As she unpacked her suitcase, noting the maids had once again opened it up to fold her clothes, she said, "I'm guessing you didn't like yours."

Fleur climbed onto her bed and hugged her knees to her chest, looking as tired as her mother. "No. I'm not really a vegan. Mom just read that it can help clear up acne. I'd rather keep the bad skin if it means getting real pizza back."

"Maybe tomorrow you and I can go into town and get some."

Fleur's eyes almost lit up. Then her expression resumed its usual wariness. "Did Mom suggest that? Us having *bonding time* so I can have more *positive influences* in my life?"

Alice pulled out some pajamas before looking over. "No. I just don't like the food here either."

Fleur seemed unconvinced, fingers picking at the ratty sleeves of her sweatshirt. "But she *has* told you that I turned into a loser who fails her classes and is about to fall behind by a year, right?"

"She used nicer words." Then Alice sat on her own bed to face her sister, seeing no reason to lie. "Look, I know how Dad is when it comes to grades, so I'm happy to help you with the essay. It's for English Lit, right? What's the topic?"

"*Hamlet.*"

Alice kept her expression confident despite the fact that trying to understand Shakespeare had always been her most hated homework. "I won't write the paper for you, but if you want, I'll help you pick apart and analyze the play."

Before her sister could answer, someone knocked on the front door. Alice glanced at the nearest clock and then at Fleur, who looked as startled as she felt.

"Stay here," she told her sister, trying to sound calm even as the back of her neck prickled.

She stepped into Denise's bedroom long enough to hear the shower running, and decided not to interrupt her stepmother. The knock came again just as she reached the front door. Fleur appeared in the corner of her eye as she called through the thick wood. "Who's there?"

"Is this Alice Corrigan?"

She already recognized the voice, and let an edge slip into her own. "I asked who's there."

"It's Steve. We talked yesterday, remember?"

"Is there a problem?"

"I just found out there's a leak in the plumbing that wasn't fixed before your party arrived. Thought I'd get to it tonight before it gets any worse. Or before Ms. Valcott fires me for incompetence."

The words sounded innocent enough, even disarming, but she didn't trust them for a second. A glance back at Fleur's frightened face only reinforced her decision. "We're about to go to bed, so please come back in the morning. We'll avoid using any water until then."

If he was disappointed, he was good enough to hide it. "Sure. I'll be back at around nine tomorrow. Have a good night."

The clear crunch of footsteps moving away over gravel drifted through the door, but Alice remained leaning against it, muscles tensed and ready to brace the wood in case he suddenly returned and tried kicking it in.

"You didn't believe him."

The sound of Fleur's voice startled her into glancing over her shoulder. Her sister looked pale, shaken.

"No. What place would fix a pipe this late at night?"

"Are you going to say anything?"

"To Denise? I don't see the point."

"I meant to your boyfriend."

For a moment, Alice could only blink at her. Then she relaxed and laughed. "Sure, if he didn't already see it for himself."

Fleur frowned a little. "Does that mean he's hanging out by our window like a perv?"

"No." Then Alice returned to the bedroom, surprised by how serene she felt. Amazing, how bare honesty felt lighter on the tongue than a practiced lie.

"Aren't you going to swear me to secrecy? Beg me not to tell?" Something in her sister's expression told her that the words were bitter with experience, heavy with anticipation.

"Say whatever you want, Fleur. I stopped hiding a while ago."

The response left her sister quiet. Alice let the silence stretch on while Denise poked her head in to wish them both goodnight, and then while Fleur took her own shower and crawled into bed.

Afterward, she simply settled on the window seat and stared out into the night, alert and still. Excited at the chance to go out and meet Colton. It was a strange echo of those liminal days spent at the cabin with Magdalene, and those secret nights spent in the forest with him. How differently she now felt, as though she could no longer fit her own outline in those memories.

When the villa slipped into true silence, Alice carefully cracked open the window. Again, the dizzying sense of the past swept through her as she peered out, searching for any sign of another person. The glass frosted against her breath, just like the first time she had seen him. A mere shadow at the edge of the forest. A flash of eyes shaping the darkness. Yet tonight it was exhilaration that left her shivering, not desperation, and tonight she would go out to meet him.

The window was as well-polished as the rest of the villa, opening without so much as a squeak. Alice dropped to the ground just as quietly, enjoying the chilly bite to the air. She'd barely taken a step when Colton was there beside her, the heat of his mouth against her ear. "I saw the fucker knock to be let in. Anything else happen?"

The words came out of her in a rush. "I met one of the figures from my dream. I can't prove it, but I swear it's her. She's the owner of this resort. Portia Valcott. What about you? Did you find anyone who might be one of them?"

The glitter in his eyes was strange, both grim and amused. "Better than that. I found bodies."

CHAPTER THREE

Hidden Graves

Bodies. Alice felt a chill as the word sank deep into her mind. "Where are they?"

"In graves in the forest. I left without looking them over. Wanted to check on you." Colton scanned their surroundings as he spoke, alert to the distant lights glimmering between the trees—the only hints of the hotel and the rest of the resort from where they stood. Then he looked back at her, eyes gleaming with a vicious energy that always filled him on hunts. "Ready to find out what's happening?"

An answering thrill rose within her, but she had enough presence of mind to turn back toward the villa. Denise and Fleur were surely asleep by now, oblivious to the strange things stirring outside their windows. "Is it safe to leave them?"

The roughness in his voice turned sly. "I made a distraction at the hotel. One they'll be working on all night."

He didn't give her curiosity time to crystallize into a fresh round of questions, instead shifting form and laughing a wolf-laugh at her indignant huff. He lingered close while she stripped down and changed over, still amused as she shook her fur into place. She kept quiet, well-aware of the need to remain unnoticed, but rubbed against him in a wish to know more. *Show me everything.*

Their path wound through shadows bordering the pathways around the resort until the dim shape of the hotel hardened into harsh lamplight and sharp voices. The smell of wet earth filled the air, bright and mineral-rich, as water erupted from the back garden. Froth caught the tallest branches from a nearby pine; the patios were already flooded. Staff still in their uniforms slipped and slid while trying to erect a barricade, their words swallowed by the roaring. Now it was Wolf-Alice who laughed—a plumbing leak, indeed.

Into the forest, then, away from the tar and smoke and fences of the civilized world. The land grew rough and uneven between the trees, with branches tangling over streams and ferns clustered around jutting rock, but they ran without care, fast and sure beneath the moon. For Wolf-Alice, running by the black wolf's side was sheer joy after a day of hiding her hunger behind a sweet smile, and a hot ache filled her full while the rhythm of his panting matched hers.

The first hints of rot sobered her. Their pace slowed when the black wolf took them around a slab of granite worn with age, their paws sinking into the gritty soil. To human eyes, the stretch of earth there might have seemed as untouched as the rest of the forest, nothing more than ground cover growing over rock and root. But Wolf-Alice let her nose guide her to where the smell of death strengthened into something definite, into hints of hair and rotting cloth and porous bone. Beside her, the black wolf began to dig, and she soon joined in.

Trees loomed in silence as they clawed away the soil, unearthing teeth along with pebbles. The reek of decay intensified. When they were finished, Wolf-Alice whined low in her throat as the moonlight shone on bones that had been hidden for years, now uncovered like grisly jewels, like shameful secrets.

The curve of a femur. The empty cavern of a skull. The jumble of ribs. All of them were dirt-stained, picked clean by grubs and beetles. Clothing had disintegrated into scraps bleached of color. These were old remains, long forgotten.

Still more used to hands and their dexterity, she changed form, waiting for the shaking to pass before reaching for a jawbone. Her touch held care, reverence, but some part of her winced over examining these sad bones, tossed together as casually as bits of trash.

Then her fingers ran over a deep mark on its surface. A few shallower ones were present, too, all of them thin and straight as if made by a blade. "Were they hacked to death?"

At that, Colton changed over as well, eyes still gleaming in the dark. "No. The cuts would be deeper. More destructive. These are made from removing the flesh."

"They were fed on." It wasn't the cold night air that brought goose bumps to her skin.

"And now whoever did it is hungry again." He turned enough to guide her gaze toward a patch of earth hidden between the massive roots of a pine. Someone had dug a large pit there, the upturned soil fresh and damp.

Alice understood the implications but still had to say the words, still had to unearth the horror behind such a simple sight. "They're ready to bury more people. But... what are they waiting for? Why dig a grave before you even have the bodies?"

"The feeding isn't done here. This is just the garbage pit. It's an entire fucking cycle. Graves scattered everywhere, each one older than the last."

"And each one with multiple bodies." She closed her eyes then, trying not to think of the vivid images from her dream even as her fingers curled into claws. "So, they *are* witches."

A brief growl from him was the only confirmation she needed. "Is there anything else we can find out about them?"

"No. There's nothing left to do until they make a move. Expose themselves."

She frowned while pushing the dirt back over the bones. It seemed kinder to keep the pitiful remains in their grave rather than leave them exposed to scavengers. An image flashed before her eyes of Fleur's face disappearing beneath soil, of Denise's body dropped against others. It made her stomach twist. "What if their next move is killing people?"

Colton's voice remained steady. "Then we fight over fresh bodies."

She jerked to her feet, shock spiking through her. "But..."

When the rest of her words faded into silence, he moved closer. That hunter's tension hadn't left his face, but something in his eyes turned almost tender as he said, "The safest thing for your family is leaving this place, but they won't believe the truth and won't listen to a lie. Next safest thing is killing the staff since we don't know who's in on this besides the owner and that handyman fucker. But a slaughter brings the wrong attention. We'd have to hide afterwards. All that's left to us is waiting until we can pick them off."

She couldn't disagree with what he'd said. It was practical if harsh, a coldly realistic look at things. Even so, she found herself circling away to stare at the moon, serene and heavy in the sky while she shivered with frustration, worry, and a little embarrassment over how inexperienced she must have seemed to a seasoned hunter like him.

Then he caught her from behind, arms wrapping around her waist, coaxing her into relaxing again. Dirt rasped against her skin even as his voice rasped against her ear. "You were laughing when we left. Excited to hunt. What makes it different now that we're a step further?"

Each word hurt, drawn up from somewhere deep inside. "It's the fact that I can't do anything yet. The last time I waited, you were shot and burned alive."

The tension in his body changed. Then the heat of his mouth pressed against her neck, as tender as a kiss against a bruise. "Alice. Don't put that on yourself. I came out of it fine, and in the end we were the ones shaking blood from our fur."

She nodded, but he must have sensed how unconvinced she was, because his next breath was a sigh. "You know I hate words. But for you, I'll say this. Things will get messy. A hunt always does when it means more than eating. You think I didn't want to tear you away from that fucking woman? Especially when you said you'd stay with her?"

She shuddered while turning enough to face him. "I was too scared to leave with you."

"I know. And I knew killing her then wouldn't have helped your fear. I had to wait." His hand stroked along the line of her back, the tension in it suggesting just how hard *that* had been, before he added, "But I did, because what happens on a hunt doesn't matter. It's what you gain from it. Or what you protect."

Then he caught her chin, urging her to look at him. "Don't bite at yourself over this. You've lived with people who expected you to follow cues like a dog. Hunting's nothing like that. It's always a struggle."

Her fingers dug into his back as she nodded, silent until she was sure her voice wouldn't tremble. "I just want to keep them safe."

"We will. We'll look out for them until there's more to do. It's not as empty as it sounds."

The sick pit in her stomach eased slowly but surely, and within a few breaths, she managed a faint smile. "Thank you. I know that took a lot. You haven't talked that much in months."

He shrugged. "If you need to hear it, I'll say it." He brushed a few strands of hair from her face before adding, "Ready to go?"

They traveled back swiftly, the stars above fading in the growing greyness of dawn. The moon remained a faint ghost, and only it and a few startled deer were the witnesses to their arrival at the villa.

After they shifted back to human form, Alice smiled at him, wishing there was time for a long goodbye. Not wanting to wake Denise or Fleur, she only teased—running fingers along his jaw in that one way that always made his eyes dilate—before turning toward the window. It was cracked open just as she'd left it, and she clutched her clothes to herself while crawling inside, trying not to wake Fleur.

Then the light flicked on, revealing Denise waiting there in a fluffy pink robe. "Alice! Why are you sneaking out at night like a..."

Alice froze as her stepmother's voice faded, realizing how it must have looked, her coming in naked, disheveled, and still panting.

When she said nothing, Denise started to stutter. "You—you didn't... you're not cheating on..."

Colton leaned in through the window, already in his jeans. "No."

Denise's expression changed yet again. "Oh, I can't believe this. You couldn't go four days without seeing her?"

"No."

With a huff, her stepmother walked over to the window, forcing him to duck back outside. "I'll talk with you later." Then she slammed the window shut and pulled the curtains, already looking at Alice. "At least I don't have to ask what you were doing all night."

"Mm." Alice had already pulled on a robe and now picked pine needles from her hair. She glanced over at Fleur's bed and found her sister holding a pillow over her head, clearly uncaring of anything except going back to sleep. Deciding there was no use in playing coy, Alice looked back at her stepmother and said, "Why are you up so early? It's not even dawn."

"Food poisoning." Fleur's words drifted out from the pillow, the glee in them obvious despite being muffled by fabric.

"The food was delicious and perfect," said Denise, rubbing at one temple. "It's a stomach bug. It was going around back home, and I'm sure I caught it. Simple bad luck."

Then the door to the room opened, and Colton walked in fully dressed. Alice circled over to him even as her stepmother sighed. "I'm too exhausted to fight about this, so I won't. To answer your question, Alice, I came in here to look at our itinerary for today. I don't think I could do anything as demanding as horseback riding, but—"

"Horseback riding?" Fleur pulled the pillow away and sat up. "But Dad said no more lessons until my grades went back up."

"I know what he said, but I wanted to surprise you," said Denise, smiling faintly. "That's what the 'Spend a Day in Nature' package is—riding to various outlook points."

With both of them distracted, Alice took the chance to glance at Colton, wondering if she was the only one who saw the ominous potential in a group of people riding in remote areas. The sudden glitter in his eyes was answer enough.

Alice tried to keep her voice neutral as she asked, "Is it really all day?"

"Close enough. It's six hours total, which is more demanding than anything I could do today, but the rest of our planned activities will be fine. I was thinking that if none of us wanted to go, then—"

"No!" The syllable exploded from Fleur as she tossed the pillow aside. "I want to do it. Please, Mom."

At the look on her stepmother's face, Alice knew the chance to err on the side of caution and cancel the riding trip had just been snuffed out. Denise and Fleur both turned to her then, and for a moment, the resemblance between mother and daughter was uncanny as Denise said, "Alice, how about you?"

It had been years since she had been on a horse, but the idea of Fleur riding into a trap alone made her want to snarl. "I'll go, too."

"Then it's all settled." Despite the dark circles beneath her eyes, Denise's expression had regained some of its usual glow. When her gaze fell on Colton, though, her smile faltered. "Except for the fact that you're here. Normally, I think it's very sweet that you adore each other—don't take this to mean you can start neglecting her—but this was supposed to be a trip just for the girls."

Alice took in a breath, ready to argue, but Colton's amused glance calmed her while Denise added, "I'm guessing you planned to hang around until we went home tomorrow."

"Sure. Shouldn't be a problem."

"Of course it is. You're not a registered guest. As soon as a staff member sees you, you'll be asked to leave." Then her expression brightened. "I know. While they're riding, we can go into the historic parts of Mariposa and look at the preserved buildings and gift shops."

If there had been anything less than a threat of death hanging over her stepmother, Alice knew those words alone would have pulled an inflexible "no" out of him. As it was, he didn't even hide the reluctance in his voice. "Shopping?"

"Yes. Oh, don't worry. I won't overdo it. You can never be too sick to shop." Then Denise glanced at the nearest clock. "We should all start getting ready. Breakfast will be here in under an hour."

The rest of them stared after her as she left the room, fingers already working at her hair. Then Fleur jumped out of bed and grabbed her toiletries bag, expression still ecstatic. When her sister disappeared into the bathroom, Alice brushed Colton's arm in a silent signal before moving for the privacy of the library.

As soon as there were walls of books to muffle her words, she said, "There's no way I was going to let Fleur go alone. A group of people led deep into the wilderness sounds like a trap to me."

"Hm. Horses are neurotic. Easy to have an accident while riding. Or to make it look like there was one." Then he cocked his head at her. "You feel up to this? Watching over her alone?"

She nodded. "What about you and the shopping trip?"

"Shopping's fucking annoying, not dangerous."

It wasn't fear she felt. It wasn't even nerves. Instead, as she pressed her tongue against her teeth, testing their feel, a diamond-hard determination settled within her ribs. "I know. But Denise needs protection, too. And there's no way you could be around horses. They scream as soon as they smell you."

He grimaced but couldn't disagree. When he remained quiet, she ran a hand along his jaw, feeling the tension there. "I'll never be afraid of the woods, no matter what's in them."

There was a strange look in his eyes as he studied her, and suddenly nothing about him seemed human. "I know. Knew it from the first time I saw you."

Such simple words, and yet her heart throbbed at hearing them. As their noses brushed, she whispered, "Look, if something does happen..."

"I'll find you even if it means razing the entire forest." His voice seethed, hot as a kiss, savage as a bite.

The sound of Denise calling her name broke through, drew her back. Without the warmth of his presence, her skin suddenly felt chilled, but she still smiled. "I don't think it'll come to that."

The intensity in his gaze didn't leave, even when Denise called for her again, and she couldn't resist running a hand through his hair a final time before pulling away. "I'll see you soon."

The morning light appeared watery and weak as Alice and Fleur joined eight other guests going on the ride. Alice was given an Appaloosa mare called Pepperjack, who remained docile as the line started moving. Fleur was a few horses ahead, her grey gelding easy to spot even once the brush thickened around the trail.

Alice didn't pay much attention to the guide, instead scanning her surroundings whenever she wasn't watching Fleur. The plodding gait of the horse was strange but lulling, a rolling movement that threatened to seep her caution along with the growing heat of the sun.

They went uphill, the earth firm whenever the trail dwindled to flattened grass between tall trees. Some of the clearings they passed reminded Alice of the one from her dream, and a shiver ran through her as they stopped at an old mining site to listen to the guide talk about the local history. One or two of the horses snorted uneasily at being so close to the rusted equipment, but all fell back in place when they continued along the tour.

Fleur was the happiest Alice had ever seen her, her smile big enough to split her face as she cooed to her horse. She also helped the rider behind her remember how to hold his reins, and when they paused for a break, took a photo for a couple. It was as if being around the horse melted her anger, frustration, and pain—or at least let her forget about it.

The sunlight strengthened into something that glared from the sky, and Alice heard murmurs of relief as open land closed into thick forest. This time, the shadows from the trees seemed darker than before, and colder, too. After a few minutes, Pepperjack began shaking her head uneasily, the reins jingling with each twitch as Alice tried soothing her with pats to the neck. One of the horses ahead snorted, its tail swishing.

Movement flickered off to the right, too obscured to make out what it was. The horses were no longer walking, instead milling and stamping as the guide shouted back instructions for keeping them from being spooked by deer or birds. Fleur's gelding whinnied and jerked his head, the whites of his eyes visible, but she managed to coax him still even as another horse startled, nearly dislodging its rider.

Then something brushed the edge of Alice's senses, a laugh so faint that she thought she misheard it over Pepperjack's nervous stamping. Another laugh, this one strong enough to send chills down her spine, and then twigs snapped in the distance, sharp as gunshots.

The horses bolted.

Alice was off the trail within a heartbeat, the world shuddering as Pepperjack carried her into the thick brush. Hoofbeats, shrieks, yelling. Horses thrashing through trees in all directions, some with their riders and some without. Despite the chaos, Alice somehow caught sight of Fleur's grey and pointed Pepperjack after them.

Pepperjack resisted, tossing her head until the rough leather of the reins ripped against Alice's hands. Gritting her teeth against the pain, Alice dug her heels in until the horse ran in the right direction.

Trees flashed past. Noise faded to her pounding heart and her cracked voice as she called out to her sister. Then branches slashed across her face, blinding her. Just as Fleur and her horse both screamed somewhere ahead, Pepperjack stumbled. Alice felt a sickening weightlessness, and then the ground slammed into her. Shock shot through her limbs as the taste of blood filled her mouth, as the sound of hoofbeats faded. The forest fell silent.

Eventually, she was able to push herself up, raking hair from her face with a shaking hand. The cracked bark of mammoth pines surrounded her, as idyllic as the grass and ferns growing over their roots. Then her eyes cleared enough to look further, to find her sister's body among some ivy.

"Fleur!" Alice stumbled up on shaking legs, reaching her sister just as she groaned and rolled over. "Wait. Take it easy. Does anything hurt?"

"I don't think so." Fleur's expression remained dazed as Alice helped her upright. "Where are the others?"

"We got separated." Then Alice glanced around, taking in the indifferent silence of the forest. Deciding it would be better to save her breath rather than call out and risk unwanted attention, she added, "Want to try standing up?"

Fleur nodded, accepting Alice's offered hand in silence. Her face paled as she looked around at the pines, all of them the same in appearance. "Oh, God. The trees didn't look like this near the trail. And why don't we hear anyone?"

Alice just studied the pockets of gloom, searching for any hint of figures watching them.

Fleur grabbed her arm, hysteria rising in her voice. "Are we lost? Are we going to die out here?"

"No." Alice kept the word firm and reassuring. "We'll find our way back. The trail runs north and south, and we're on the west side of it. All we have to do is walk east until we reach it."

"Are you sure?" Fleur held onto her arm, breaths closer to frightened gasps.

"Positive. Colton and I hike without a compass all the time."

One heartbeat, two, and then Fleur reluctantly said, "Okay. Maybe it's better to move around anyway. It was a big group and all the horses bolted. There has to be someone else out here."

Alice merely nodded, biting back her honest response as they started walking, the forest around them still eerily silent. *That's just what worries me.*

CHAPTER FOUR

Lost in the Woods

"Do you think they're all right?" asked Fleur. It was the first time she'd spoken since they had started searching for the trail.

Alice scanned their surroundings, alert to the position of the sun. "The other riders? Hopefully."

"No, not them. I meant the horses." Fleur's tone implied there was something wrong with anyone who thought about humans before animals. "A lot of them bolted. What if one broke a leg or got their reins caught on a branch? What if something attacks them? Aren't there bears here?"

Compared to the malevolent hunger that seethed somewhere in the far-reaching gloom, a bear would be the safest thing to meet. Yet Alice knew such an answer couldn't be spoken out loud, not to her sister anyway, and struggled for something more reassuring. "The horses know the area better than any of us. I'm sure the ones without riders are already back at their stable."

"Yeah, I guess." Still frowning, Fleur swatted at a nearby branch.

They were now in the middle of dense brush that reached up to their waists, leaves and twigs catching their clothes with every movement. Trees towered all around, slender giants that reduced the sun to indistinct glitters of light. Rocks and roots pushed up from the damp earth, turning each step into a test of balance. There were no birds, no insects. No hints of noise.

Alice kept a hand stretched toward Fleur in case her sister stumbled, her own feet sure while she searched for any hint of movement, for any sign that they were being stalked as prey. Her head throbbed from the fall and so did most of her body, leaving her disinclined to speak at all, especially when every word could distract her and alert others.

Yet Fleur veered in the opposite direction, flinging her voice into the silence with the same vicious intent as throwing rocks at windows. "You look worried. We're lost, aren't we?"

"No, I'm sure of where we're going."

"I'm not."

Alice kept her voice calm, refusing to be needled. "Do you want to try something else?"

"No. I think we're going to die out here no matter what. Be found months from now as skeletons."

Alice checked the sun again. The day had already passed noon. People were likely looking for them and anyone else who hadn't returned. For the second time in her life, she'd be listed as missing and searched for.

It was a cutting realization, sharpening her determination not to be the only survivor found. Her next words to Fleur came out raw and unthinking. "We're both getting out of this alive. I won't let anything happen to you, all right? It's going to be fine."

Fleur studied her face, her own still tight with fear. "I don't think so. I've been hearing that a lot—that I'll be fine, or that I'm just going through a phase, or that I better toughen up because life only gets harder as an adult. And it's total bullshit. It's what people use when they don't know what else to say."

Even as Alice remained quiet, some part of her understood the cynicism. How many times had she found herself wanting to scream and scratch at glib phrases when her own life had been a ragged mess? A trite handful of words, well-meaning or not, had felt like a bandage offered to a heart bleeding out. Unaware to the point of being infuriating.

In the fresh silence that followed, Fleur started shredding a leaf. "That was your cue to change my mind with an inspirational quote. Did you know that's how Mom grounds me now that I never leave my room? I have to find a positive message and make a scrapbook page out of it. She changes the wifi password if I don't. So, whatever you're thinking of, it's probably something I've written in glitter."

"Fleur, I'm not going to say anything to make you feel better." The words had the desired effect, shocking her sister into looking up. Then Alice offered a smile, one small but not unkind, and added, "I don't know what your problems are, so

I won't pretend I know the solution, or that you'd want my advice in the first place. But... I'll listen to whatever you want to say. Anything at all. Because I remember how much it hurt when talking felt like dropping words into a void. How nothing I said would make someone understand or even just pay attention."

Fleur looked uncertain, wary, as if the offer was a trap. "What if I want to talk about you? Ask you questions?"

"Sure. Go ahead." Alice was as surprised by her sister's sudden curiosity as she was over her own lack of concern.

A heartbeat of silence passed before Fleur took the plunge. "Mom and Dad never talk about it, but I still heard that you dropped out of college and moved away to live with your girlfriend. That Dad almost disinherited you because of it."

Alice nodded, keeping her expression casual.

"So, it's true? You were going to throw away all that money to be with her?"

Admitting to it was uncomfortable, scraping at areas that would still bleed with enough pressure put to them. "Yes. I loved her."

The answer drained all suspicion from her sister's face and replaced it with embarrassment, as if she'd abruptly realized how intrusive the questions were.

"It's all right," said Alice, and meant it. "I opened myself up to this. Ask whatever you want."

"Well... I also heard things turned bad in the end. Really bad. Like, there were articles that came out. How she cheated on you, and that she was linked to a creepy sex ring along with some photographer. Did you know about that? Is that why you left?"

"I left because she finally took too much from me." For a moment, the memory of that precious pelt blackening in the fire overwhelmed Alice. Even now, in her new life and sure of her own teeth and fur, the pain felt fresh. She supposed it would always hurt, the final blow that had broken the last of her trust. A wound running so deep that healing from it had reshaped her very being.

"I'm sorry." The words sounded small and hesitant, as if Fleur half-expected them to be slapped away.

Yet Alice just smiled. "It's all right. I survived it and moved on. Found someone better."

"Colton. Mom and Dad talk about him a lot. Dad hates him, you know."

Now she laughed. "I did know that, yes."

"But he also admits you're happy with him. We all see it." Then Fleur paused again, and Alice looked over, sensing that the conversation was finally winding toward the tender, beating heart behind Fleur's interest. When her sister spoke again, she sounded strangely vulnerable. "How did you know he'd be different from..."

"Magdalene."

"Yeah." Fleur's eyes burned with the question, desperation suddenly etched into her expression. "When you meet someone, how do you know they won't end up hurting you?"

Something sharp as pain and heavy as grief sliced through Alice, and she suddenly had the urge to pull her into a hug, this girl who had asked a question with only razors for answers. To hold her tight against the world and all its agonies. Instead, she sat on a nearby log, inviting Fleur over with a pat against the moss-covered bark. When they were side by side, she said, "You don't. Not until they do hurt you."

Fleur shook her head, her mouth trembling. "There must be some way. I mean, why would you jump into another relationship if you weren't sure... some of those articles had interviews from ex-girlfriends who said she made them take nudes and everything. There had to be something that showed you he was different. That your heart wouldn't be ripped to shreds by someone who promised to always be there, someone you *trusted*..."

Then Fleur hunched over as if the rest hurt too much to say. Alice hugged her close, murmuring soothing nothings while her sister's voice dissolved into tears. Her crying went on for some time, the gut-deep sobs of emotions shoved down and left to fester. Alice kept rocking her, not minding how her shoulder grew soaked or how the sun sank lower in the sky.

She made no attempt to coax meaning from the choked words, but eventually Fleur's voice thinned into something coherent. "We were supposed to be best friends forever. We always said that. We always *meant* it. But this year, Hayley and the others started sneaking out to high school parties and kept wanting me to go along. I finally did, and it was so stupid. Pot smells like a skunk. Beer tastes like you're licking one. But the worst was…"

Then Fleur shivered so violently that Alice had to squeeze her close to keep her from sliding off the log. When it passed, her sister said, "There was this one jerk there, a friend of the guy who snuck us into the party. He wanted me to do… things. When I wouldn't, he started shouting. Calling me stuff. Hayley found out what was happening and got pissed off, too. At first, I thought she was mad for me, but she wasn't. She was mad *at* me.

"She took his side over mine. Told me to stop being a baby and that this had been a big favor. And then I started crying like I really was a baby. We've been friends since preschool. She's known him for three months. But she still took his side because he can get her into parties, and has a car, and buys her anything she wants. So, I… I told her that I'd never suck dick for such a stupid reason, and that I never wanted to go to a party again. And after that, she stopped talking to me. Everyone did. Now they don't even remember I exist unless it's to laugh at me for being a *little girl who still likes horsies*."

Anger burned behind Alice's ribs, but she kept her voice gentle. "Is that why you didn't do the essay?"

"Yeah. The teacher assigned us as partners. I couldn't believe it when Hayley expected me to do her part, too. Like it was all still the same. Like I wouldn't mind that she'd been laughing at me for months. But you want to know what's really stupid? She's already moved on from the guy. Now she's dating his jerk friend. I don't think she likes them any more than I did. I think she likes what they can do for her. And now when I look around, that's all I see. Everybody is just using each other. So, fuck it. Why should I spend time with people if they're fake? At least animals are honest. Either they like you or they don't."

Alice just rubbed at her back, letting the silence seep in like an anesthetic. Fleur's breathing slowed, steadied. Then she sat back and wiped her eyes with the sleeve of her sweatshirt. "You're not going to tell Mom, are you?"

"No. Not even if she asks."

"Thanks." Despite her swollen eyes and reddened nose, Fleur looked a little happier. Then she glanced around at the trees as the first tendrils of fog thickened the air. "God. It's been hours since we left. She's probably having a heart attack right now."

"Probably," agreed Alice, rising from the log. "But I think we're close to the trail now. I recognize that clump of—"

"Shh!" Fleur jumped to her feet, staring past Alice's shoulder. "Did you hear that?"

Alice turned to look with her. "No. What was it?"

"People shouting." After a few tense moments, Fleur broke into a smile. "They're calling our names."

Alice still heard nothing, still saw nothing. A chill ran down her spine, and she grabbed at Fleur just as her sister stepped away. "Wait. *Wait*."

"Why? They're looking for us."

"Fleur, I don't hear anything."

"I do, and it sounds like they're just past those trees."

Even as Alice shook her head, Fleur turned frantic. "They're getting fainter. They must be moving away from us. Hey!"

With that last word, she lunged forward, ripping herself free from Alice's grip.

"No!" Alice ran after her as the trees stirred with a sudden wind, their branches reaching out. Thick fog rushed in. "Fleur, stop. Stop!"

Her sister only called out to whatever she heard, pushing through the brush with blind abandon. Within a breath, she was nothing more than a silhouette. Alice followed her voice, raking at the mist with furious fingers. Then Fleur's shape ducked around a massive pine, and the fog thickened until Alice could barely see. She shook off its chill as if she were in her fur, slipping around the same tree her sister had passed a moment before.

Then the mist cleared. Alice stumbled to a stop, panting at the meadow stretched out before her. Fleur was nowhere in sight.

"Fleur!" She took a hesitant step into the clearing, blinking against strains of sunlight that managed to penetrate the lingering fog. An echo of her sister's voice hung in the air. Her heart pounded as if it were about to explode.

A twig snapped somewhere behind her. Alice spun around, her sister's name on the tip of her tongue. It faded unsaid at the sight of a figure leaning against one of the trees bordering the meadow, his arms folded. She didn't need a good look to recognize him—Steve, still wearing the affable smile he'd used on her while pretending to be a harmless handyman.

Her lips parted in a silent snarl even before he spoke. "She's gone. We're all alone."

He still sounded easy-going, but the look in his eyes had turned eager, calculating.

"Where's my sister?" Alice's fingers curled into fists.

He hardly seemed to hear her, instead studying her from head to toe. His tongue licked at the corner of his mouth before he said, "I see a lot of beautiful girls at my job, but you seemed like something special. You looked like someone who wouldn't scream right away. I like that. I like hearing someone break."

"Where is she, you bastard?" repeated Alice, the words bubbling in her chest as a growl.

"Not with me, so there's no reason to yell." Then he reached toward the back pocket of his jeans.

She didn't wait to see what he had, instead leaping for him with a snarl that shouldn't have come from a human mouth. He was bigger than her, almost Colton's size, but she was furious and he was surprised. Her lunge drove them both to the ground. Then her fingers found his neck, digging in with the sharpness of claws. As his eyes widened, she leaned in and bared her fangs. "You picked the wrong prey."

Metal winked from the corner of her eye. A knife slashed at her face. She dodged it unharmed, fast from hunting bucks and their deadly antlers. Then she grabbed onto his arm, not caring what his free hand might do to her, and bit down with all her strength. The meat of his flesh gave. The bones in his wrist cracked. His ragged yell as the knife dropped to the ground was the sweetest sound she'd ever heard. She bit again in a frenzy, the taste of iron filling her mouth.

Fingers dug against her scalp, grabbing a fistful of hair to jerk her head away.

"Fucking bitch," he gritted out, eyes deranged.

She just spat blood into his face, using his flinch to grab the knife from its bed of leaves. When she pushed the blade against one of the big arteries throbbing in his neck, he froze, back pressed against the tree.

"Where is she?" Despite her shaking voice, the blade remained steady.

"Shit," he panted, twitching as the knife pressed in. "You really think I'll tell you? Forget it. You can't do anything worse than them."

"Them?"

For a moment, he almost looked like a normal man again, his smile bright and real. "You have no idea what you're dealing with."

"Witches."

Surprise flickered in his expression. "You know what they are but can't find them yourself?"

Gut-deep, she knew it would be a mistake to admit to anything close to a weakness. She moved the tip of the knife to the soft point between his chin and neck, angling it so that he could feel how one jerk of her hand would drive the blade all the way up to his brain. "It's quicker to ask you. But if you don't want to talk..."

At the first hint of pressure, he groaned. "All right. All right, ease up. I'll tell you what I know."

Even as she nodded, he drew in a deep breath. "They're planning to—"

Then he broke off into a cough, face reddening. "They want... *fuck*."

Something in his eyes changed. His features rippled strangely. Alice readied the knife, muscles tensed for a trick as his mouth fell open. Black fluid gushed out, thick as tar, slick as oil, and she flinched back, stumbling to her feet while his body convulsed.

He managed one ragged scream before his voice dwindled to a gurgle. She could hear his teeth rattling in their sockets. Then his skin peeled away from his face, dry as paper.

Alice bit down on her hand to keep from gagging when flesh sloughed off and revealed bone. Eyes bulged and then withered to nothing. There was a final rasp that might have been a plea, and then she found herself staring at a skeleton collapsed in on itself, submerged in a pool of dark slime. The jaws were slack in a final scream, but otherwise the bones looked bleached and old, without one hint of flesh left behind.

"I knew you were going to be trouble," said a voice close behind.

Alice turned, hand tightening around the knife at the sight of Portia Valcott. Her pearl earrings and crisp business attire looked at odds with the blood speckled on her face.

When Alice said nothing, the other woman raised her eyebrows. "Stephen had been our poppet for years. It's hard to replace such experience."

Confusion must have bled into her expression, because Portia then laughed, a contemptuous huff of breath. "You're completely untaught, aren't you? A poppet is a witch's servant, darling. The moment it betrays its mistress... well."

Alice raised her chin. "I'm not interested in a conversation. Where's my sister?"

"No, really, I was convinced for some time that you were merely human. Then I wasn't sure if you were being sly about things. But you're simply a weak witch raised away from her own, stumbling onto our plans out of sheer ignorance. A minor inconvenience."

As soon as Alice drew in a fresh breath, Portia added, "Your sister is out of reach. By tomorrow morning, she'll be dead. There's nothing you can do about either of those things."

"Do you think that's enough to make me give up?"

"I won't risk it either way." Then Portia reached for her.

Alice lashed out with the knife, throwing all her strength into it, but the blade passed through the other woman as if she were nothing more than shadow.

Portia smiled.

Then hands grabbed Alice from behind, one twisting her wrist until she lost her grip on the knife. She snarled while being dragged to the ground, fighting against the two women holding her down. They were just like the figures from her dream, hair filthy and matted, skin smeared with blood. In the uncertain light of the forest, she couldn't make out much of their faces, only their unblinking eyes and thin smiles.

The sight of her fangs sent the one on her left shrinking back. "Her teeth changed. She's trying something."

Portia remained out of sight, but her voice sounded close by as she sighed. "Then you ought to finish subduing her."

"Here," said the witch on Alice's right.

There was only a heartbeat to glimpse something thin and sharp in her hand before she jabbed at Alice's neck. The object punctured her skin like a splinter, and Alice shrieked against the searing agony, trying to bite and kick. Fingernails scratched at her from all sides while she tried shifting into her fur. Her body didn't respond, instead growing heavy and numb. Her growling died away.

"Why don't we just kill her?" muttered the woman on her left as they fought to pull her hands together and tie them. She resisted them sluggishly.

"Because she's still one of us." Then Portia leaned over until Alice could glare at her. "The less you fight, the easier this will be."

Alice just bit at the nearest hand, feeling blood run down her neck.

The woman she had snapped at caught her jaw and squeezed it hard. "Maybe we should knock all your teeth out with a rock. Would you prefer that?"

"Hurry, girls," said Portia, tone silken as she walked away.

The woman on Alice's left jerked, as if cringing against the mild rebuke. Then she twitched again, this time as the sharp crack of bone shuddered the surrounding air. Alice twisted and saw bristling fur and ferocious jaws. The black wolf's teeth were locked into the witch's neck.

A jerk of his head ripped away flesh, splattering blood on the leaves around them. His eyes glowed as the woman slumped, ruined throat gaping. Her hands spasmed until he bit at those as well.

Alice raked clumsy fingers through the leaves, trying to find the knife as the second witch stumbled to her feet with a shriek. The smile had left her face. When the black wolf bit at the gushing neck a final time, shearing vertebrae until the head rolled away from the rest of the body, the other woman fled without a backwards glance.

The black wolf circled away from the remains and approached Portia, too intent to even shake the blood from his fur. Alice tried to warn him about the knife sliding through the witch, but the sickening numbness had spread up her throat, leaving her tongue limp and unresponsive. It was all she could do to pull herself upright as Portia faced him.

"It'll be much better for you to simply leave. I can forgive losing Bettina. She never would have amounted to much in the end. Girls often don't. But thinking yourself a match to the golden antlers of our—"

The black wolf lunged. His weight slammed into Portia, bringing her down in the span of a breath. Alice caught a glimpse of the woman's stunned expression before teeth snapped shut on her entire face. The grisly crunch disappeared beneath her scream. Blood mixed with froth dripping from the black wolf's jaws as he tore off flesh and bone fragments.

A fresh wave of dizziness came over Alice then, and she had to close her eyes. Instinctively, her fingers clawed where that thing remained lodged beneath her skin, trying to scratch it free. Then a callused hand caught hers, and she opened her eyes again to find Colton's bloodstained face inches from her own.

"Easy. I'll get it out." His gaze remained intent on her wound as he carefully arched her neck, growling softly when she whimpered in pain. "This'll hurt less than when it went in."

She managed a nod, going limp in his arms as those dangerous teeth pressed against her skin. A sharp pinch made her jerk, a strangled noise working its way from her throat, but then he was sucking it out, the pressure of his mouth replacing numbness with heat. He cradled the back of her head while spitting the thing out, and then the softness of his tongue returned, licking the blood away, soothing the burning.

She clung to him, trying to force out words. "They took her. They're going to kill her."

At that, he stopped long enough to look at her. He never showed much expression on his face, her nightmare creature, and now was no different. Yet the green in his eyes looked as hot as molten metal, and his pupils were mere pinpoints. Many times, she had seen him violent with both hunger and anger, his gaze flattened to the ruthlessness of an unthinking predator.

This was something else. He was truly enraged, and the intensity took her breath away. It was like facing a fire and realizing nothing would stop it until it chose to burn out. And yet she touched his jaw without fear, fingers leaving trails in the blood there.

He moved enough to lick them clean, his tongue still gentle, but his voice held a growl brutal with the promise of spilled blood. "No. They're not going to kill her. We're going to kill them."

CHAPTER FIVE

A Painful Wait

"Is there anything else you remember?" The deputy's voice was kind yet firm. "Even the smallest detail can help us find your sister and the others."

Alice shook her head, trying to remain calm while something scratched and screamed deep inside her, trapped behind her ribs like a second heart. Her head throbbed as she clutched at the styrofoam cup of coffee that had been given to her, and she could hear crying in the distance—family members of the missing riders.

If the deputy noticed them, she didn't show any sign of it. Despite her neat bun and crisp uniform, she already looked worn out and grim, rubbing at her temples as she said, "All right. Here's my card. Please call the number on it if you think of anything else. We'll let you know as soon as we learn anything."

Alice tried to smile. "Can I go?"

"Not yet." The deputy rose from her seat and reached for her hat. "I believe one of the search and rescue leaders had a few questions."

Alice nodded but didn't watch the other woman leave, instead dropping her gaze to hide any hint of her impatience. Once the door closed, she pushed away from the table, pacing as if still in her fur.

She was in one of the staff-only areas of the hotel, the room hastily set up for one-on-one interviews away from the chaos of different organizations working together in a rush. The air smelled like burned coffee and stale cigarettes, and the lone window revealed nothing more than the staff parking lot, the glass panes vibrating from helicopters passing overhead.

Staff had apparently ignored the no-tech rule, for a small radio sat on a stack of cardboard boxes. After a few more heartbeats of walking around aimlessly, hating the ticking of the clock, Alice turned it on and found it set to the local news station.

"This morning, twelve people and their guide went missing while on a horseback riding tour that included trails into the Sierra National Forest. When the group failed to return on time, authorities were immediately notified. Several search parties have already been sent into the forest, but only one missing rider has been found. Officials haven't yet released her name, but we are told that she is being interviewed by the sheriff's department and other organizations in the hope that she can provide information on what exactly happened."

At that, Alice had to turn it off again, stomach churning for new reasons. She wasn't looking forward to another round of queries from the media, or how her name would be quickly recognized. Alice Corrigan, lost in a forest once before. Alice Corrigan, who had lost a girlfriend to a wild animal attack in the woods. Hers was a history of mysterious vanishings and grisly deaths, and this was simply one more notch to her name —permanent as a scar, marking out how her future always circled back to her past.

The room felt even smaller as she resumed pacing, fighting with the growing sense of being trapped by walls seen and unseen. Then a flash of neon caught her eye, and she looked out the window to see several people in hiking gear milling in the parking lot. One man had a bloodhound, his free hand offering a piece of clothing to help the dog lock in on the scent. The hound's drooping ears and wrinkled face turned its expression into something mournful as it sniffed at the fabric.

When Alice realized it was one of Fleur's sweatshirts, the last of her patience finally snapped, and suddenly it was too much to wait for another interview, too much to hide behind the mask of a confused girl who didn't know why she had been the only one lucky enough to return from the woods and their silence.

Compared to the claustrophobic size of the room, the hallway stretched like a gullet, packed full of people talking to each other or into their phones. Alice pushed through as quickly as possible, badges winking at her until she felt dizzy.

The noise thickened the very air, a frantic hum that hurt the ears, and she could smell fear in the sweat and breath of those around her. There were only a few more hours until dark, until those missing people had to survive night and the creatures that stalked through it. Alice's nose burned by the time she finally broke free, and she panted as if she'd been running.

The tea room waited before her, its ornately carved doors stretching all the way to the ceiling. Voices drifted through that sturdy oak, subdued, wavering. Watery with tears. All relatives of the missing riders had been invited in there while waiting for news or to be interviewed.

A fit of guilt burst through Alice. She'd asked Colton to wait with Denise, had assured him that she was fine and her stepmother was the one who would need to cling to someone. That was true, but it was equally true that she wasn't sure she could face lying to Denise about what had happened, even though the truth was too bizarre to be believed.

After a deep breath, she opened the door as quietly as possible, trying to avoid attention. It was a massive room, with countless tables set up for high tea. Gold cherubs stared at her from every corner as she stepped inside, searching among the rose bouquets and plush chairs for her stepmother.

Denise was just as Alice had last seen her—crying into a napkin while a porcelain cup of tea and a sugar-crusted scone waited untouched. But instead of Colton sitting with her, it was Alice's father, still in his suit from work. He cradled his wife in his arms, tightening his grip when her face turned into his shoulder. His expression left Alice's vision blurred with tears. They escaped in hot tracks down her cheeks as she stumbled back out into the hall, quickly closing the door behind her. There in the dim light, with the brocade pattern of the wallpaper rising all around like a strange forest, memories flooded her full...

The stiff folds of the blanket were itchy, but whenever she tried to throw it off, the paramedic and police officer waiting nearby told her to be a good girl and keep it on. She didn't like the way they looked at her, or the way those other people looked at her mother's car. And she didn't like how they kept asking where her mother was, as if the answer would change. As if she really knew.

It was hot, and the policemen going through her mother's car seemed irritated by the sweat soaking their uniforms. The sun glared from far above, bleaching scrubby weeds into the color of straw. As Alice sat there, twitching every time a police radio squawked to life with voices, the oak trees past the yellow caution tape swayed in a sudden breeze, their gnarled branches heaving as if they were something alive, something that breathed. The gloom between their thick trunks looked like a sweet relief from the heat and noise, and she twitched again, now wanting to jump out from the back of the ambulance and run into it.

Then a car engine rumbled close, and everyone except Alice turned toward it. She only looked over when she heard a voice call her name, a familiar voice that she always connected with the smell of ink from a fountain pen, with stories read to her at night, with a big hand holding her own. Her father's voice.

He had never looked so scared, and that scared *her*. She remained quiet even when he swept her into a hug, the wrinkled collar of his suit pressing against her face as he held her tightly. Then he pulled back enough to look at her, and his voice cracked as he asked, "Where is she, Alice? What happened to your mother?"

Alice only shook her head, tongue feeling thick and useless.

The lines in his forehead deepened. "Try to remember."

"Sir..." said the officer.

But her father's tone only hardened, rising above Alice's hitch of breath as she began crying, too scared to do anything else. "You have to remember something, anything. Where is she?"

Where is she?

Hands caught her wrists as she clutched at her face. Then there was a rasp of a voice against her ear—not her father's but instead one that chased the childhood terrors away, that was darker than the worst nightmares, that terrified the other monsters. "Easy. You're all right."

And then she realized she was back in the hallway of the hotel, all years of life since that soul-cracking day now settling in and throbbing like a dislocated bone snapped back into place. She wasn't a child anymore, and Colton was there with her.

When she finally let her hands drop, his thumbs stroked the inner skin of her wrists, right where her pulse beat hard and fast. Then they moved to her face. His eyes were bright green and absolutely feral, but his touch remained feather-light while he wiped the tears from her cheeks.

"Your father," he said. It wasn't a question.

She nodded. "We didn't talk. He didn't even see me. I just... I feel helpless and I hate it. Fleur might be dead by now, and all I can do is lie to his face about it."

Colton shook his head. "She's not dead. And we're close to catching them. I wouldn't say these things unless I was sure."

When a shiver ran through her, he added, "I found something while you were being interviewed. Thought you might want to look at it."

"I do. I want to do anything that will help us find her."

He took her down a stairway away from the buzz of conversations and the vibration of helicopters, the purple carpet beneath their feet shifting into tile floor and then concrete. The final stair led to a plain door painted a dull red. The brass plate read STORAGE ROOM 5. As soon as they stepped inside, Alice gasped. Stacks of cardboard boxes had been thrown away from the back wall, and there was a gaping hole in it higher than her and three times as wide. "What..."

He kicked the larger pieces of rubble out of her way. "I noticed the floors of this place didn't line up like they should. It's a good sign of hidden rooms or passageways."

"You did this? It looks like a truck rammed through the wall," she said, staring at the ragged mouth of the hole. Beyond it, stone steps sank into darkness.

"It took two minutes with a sledgehammer. The bitch didn't even pay for wood paneling. It's sheetrock and plaster." Then he handed her a flashlight. "I've already been down there. It's safe."

As they descended, the air turned damp and cool, and she thought she heard the scrabbling of a rat. Their steps sounded hollow on the stairs, but once they reached the end, the ground turned powdery and firm. A quick scan with her flashlight revealed it was nothing more than packed dirt, as if they were in a root cellar. The room was equally modest, unfurnished and with a single overhead lamp for lighting. Wooden shelves marched from floor to ceiling on each wall, burdened by glass jars of every shape and size. Everything looked aged and forgotten, but not suspiciously so. Some of the things in her grandmother's cabin had looked far older.

Then Alice started, implications snapping into place. "Denise told me the hotel is hardly a year old. Portia must have built it over this room on purpose."

Colton's eyes held a strange gleam. "It's her larder."

Simple words, but they filled Alice with gnawing dread even before her flashlight revealed the contents of the nearest jar. Eyeballs stared at her, irises dulled by the yellow fluid surrounding them. Alice swallowed hard, and then swallowed again as she recognized mustard seeds and pepper flakes caught in the optic nerves. "She pickles people."

"Means she stays in this area. And with how old the dust smells, she's been here for years."

"What about that... that thing they shoved into my neck? Was that human?"

"No. Tasted like a buck's antler."

She aimed her flashlight away from the rest of the jars, not wanting to see what else waited in them. A horrible thought had occurred to her, and she turned to look at him. "They take what they want and dump the remains in graves. We found cut marks on those bones, but that can't tell us whether they were *dead* when they were butchered. Is that why you're so sure Fleur and the others are alive? Are they being—"

"No." The steadiness of his voice calmed her. "I'll explain everything after we're through the trapdoor. You're miserable in here."

She hadn't even noticed the wooden ladder in the corner, or the faint outline of light in the ceiling above it. Colton went up first and then leaned back through to steady the ladder for her. This new room looked like a normal office, its centerpiece an antique desk covered with stacks of paper. As Colton shut the trapdoor, Alice glanced through a few of them and found bills, handwritten notes, and room registration cards.

One piece of paper was a simple list of names that included hers, Fleur's, and Denise's. Her stepmother's had a line drawn through it. Her own had the brief note *for Stephen* written beside it.

She bit back a snarl. "There are twelve names if you don't count mine or Denise's. That's how many riders they kidnapped if you include the trail guide. Twelve people."

"Twelve points on a royal stag." When Alice glanced up at him, he grimaced. "I know that didn't make sense. It's easy to recognize patterns. Harder to explain them."

She managed a ghost of a smile. "And you hate explaining things."

The deadly calculation in his eyes faded as he glanced over, but he continued to prowl around the room, feet silent yet sure. "The witch that built this hotel is part of a coven. The riders were kidnapped for a ritual they'll perform tonight."

Portia's mocking voice echoed through her mind. *You're completely untaught, aren't you?*

She ignored a wave of shame while admitting, "I don't know what that means outside of mythology books."

"Alice." His curt tone softened as he stopped before her. "Don't be embarrassed. Not with me." His thumb traced along her cheek before he added, "A coven is a group of witches bound together. It gives them more power than they'd have on their own. The oldest of them is the hag mother or elder crone. Whatever she decides to call herself. The words change, but the role is always the same. She's the leader of their rituals."

"But not of the coven?" said Alice, reading between the lines.

"No. That'd be their hag king. A warlock stronger than any of them. Warlocks are lazy fuckers who tie themselves to covens because it's easier to share their power in return for being treated like a god and looked after like a baby."

"Are there a lot of covens? How would we find out which one is Portia's?"

Nothing changed in his expression, but she had the sense that he picked his next words with care. "I already know it. She slipped by mentioning 'golden antlers.' Has to be the Golden Stag coven. It's been based in Europe for a few centuries, but that warlock lets his witches live away from him."

"And that's what you meant about the royal stag having twelve points on its antlers. They're sacrificing those kidnapped riders in his name." Then she studied him, aware of how violence had seethed beneath his every word since the first mention of the hag king. "What made you so angry about them trying to take me as well?"

When he gave her a look that all but said, *You know the answer to that*, she added, "No, I mean... I haven't seen you that furious since Magdalene. What were they going to do?"

His answer was very flat. "A coven will always feed on humans. Sometimes they want more from a witch."

Before she insisted on a better explanation, footsteps sounded from somewhere outside the room. They both fell still, listening until whoever it was walked past.

The silence lasted for a heartbeat or two before she turned back to him and whispered, "We should probably get out of here."

He nodded, but his tension remained while they slipped out and found their way to the staff parking lot. After the stuffiness of the rooms, the mist-tinged air felt crisp and alive, and she breathed in deeply while studying the edge of the forest. For all that the hotel loomed behind them, civilized life suddenly seemed very far away. The anger shoved down, restrained, and ignored now flared into that first thrill of bloodlust, and she looked over at Colton with an intensity that matched his. "You said we're close to catching them."

In the late afternoon sunlight, his eyes looked more yellow than green as he reached inside his jacket. "Found the backup map from the search and rescue teams. It shows all the areas they're searching."

She looked at it with him, taking in the various markings and notes. "It seems like they're spread out from the trail pretty well."

"Except for here." He traced an area where the color changes marked a rise in elevation. "It's higher terrain. Lots of rocks and steep angles. There's also a river you have to cross to get there."

"So, basically, no one who's scared and injured from falling off a horse would ever end up there. Which makes it a perfect place for Portia to hide them. But she wasn't expecting us."

He now studied her, not the map, and the intensity of his attention made her laugh. "What?"

Something flickered in his eyes, wild as a howl, tender as a tongue. "I like seeing you excited."

Coming from anyone else, such a statement would have sounded grudging, even half-hearted. But Alice recognized the reluctance that roughened his voice, the voice of this beast who hated using words in place of his teeth, and found herself smiling as shyly as if she'd just been offered a bouquet.

The sound of her name broke the moment, and she looked over to find her father crossing the hotel grounds. Her heart bucked as she realized he'd already seen them.

"You want to do this?" murmured Colton.

"I have to." Then she sucked in a breath, searching for words with a mind that had tightened into a knot of guilt both fresh and remembered.

When they were close enough to speak without shouting, her father repeated her name, looking a decade older than when she'd seen him the week before. He rubbed at the new grey in his hair while saying, "They told me you were being interviewed."

"I just finished."

He nodded, looking merely tired until he pulled her into a hug. It was then that she felt how fierce and desperate his grip was, as if he tried to make sure she was really there in his arms. His shoulder was still wet from Denise's tears.

When they separated again, he glanced at Colton without the usual dismissal in his eyes. "I'd like to talk in private. Just the two of us."

Her stomach tightened. "All right. Where?"

"In the car. There are reporters everywhere, and some of them are starting to sneak inside the hotel." Then he headed for the guest parking lot, trusting her to follow.

She lingered long enough to give Colton a brief smile. "I'll be fine."

When he shrugged, she knew that he would remain close by. "It's going to be a while before you let me wander out of sight, isn't it?"

His kiss was answer enough, brief but devouring, and she could still feel the pressure of his teeth as she started off after her father.

Once they settled in the car, neither of them spoke for several minutes. Helicopters whirred in the distance, small as birds. News crews packed up their bulky equipment. The frenzy was fading with the sun, and for the same reason: it would soon be night.

Sensations from Alice's memories seemed to dim her sight like a veil, figures from the past superimposed on the present. When her father spoke, it took her a moment to recognize where she was, and that his words were real breath and air instead of painful remembrance.

"The news stations reported all afternoon that only one missing rider was found. Nobody yet knows that it's you. As soon as that detail breaks, our family will be back under the microscope." Her father sounded very calm and mechanical, as if he read from a how-to manual.

Even so, a fresh wave of guilt rolled over her. "I'm sorry."

He shook his head, looking straight ahead. "I didn't say that to draw an apology out of you, Alice. It's just very difficult to think about how this might end. Denise can't grasp that yet, but you and I both understand it bone-deep. That's why I... I need to say this."

When she nodded, his hands flexed against the steering wheel. Then his eyes closed, as if the next words would be a physical struggle, things torn out with the same sheer will that had borne him through those early, unbearable months of losing his first wife.

When he looked up again, his gaze had grown distant. "I once saw something I've never been able to understand or explain. I didn't tell anyone about it and for years afterward tried to forget. It happened a few weeks after I married your mother. One day, I came home early from work to surprise her. She wasn't in the house, but as soon as I saw that the patio door had been left open, I knew she was out in the garden.

"I don't know if you can remember much about that place, but the backyard extended all the way to the national park. Whoever lived there before us had built it into a formal garden. Hedges that blocked the neighbors, flowering vines trained to cover archways... your mother used to say it felt like stepping into another world. She loved it."

Then her father paused, closing his eyes again. When Alice saw the pain on his face, she reached out to squeeze his arm, but her fingers faltered as he resumed speaking. "Anyway, I went into the garden to look for her. She was singing to herself. Dancing. Unaware that I stood there. She looked happy, but something felt off. Wrong. It took me a moment to realize what it was—she was floating a few inches above the ground. And just as I decided that I was seeing things, she floated higher. A foot in the air, then two. Then three. Laughing and spinning slowly in a circle, like when we went ballroom dancing. All the branches from the nearest trees and bushes reached toward her like they were alive. I'd never seen her that happy."

Her father finally looked over, embarrassment, exhaustion, and relief fighting each other in his eyes. "I thought I hallucinated it. There was no other rational explanation. There still isn't. Over the years, I came to realize that I simply can't... understand what happened that day. That there were things about your mother I'll never be able to comprehend. I've accepted it. What's always scared me, Alice, is recognizing that whatever your mother had, you have some of it as well."

Alice didn't know what to say. She didn't know what she *could* say. When her mouth started trembling, she bit her lip hard enough to make it stop, hard enough to feel a flare of pain.

Her father didn't seem to expect an answer but continued to watch her with that distant expression. She half-wondered whether part of him looked at her face and saw her mother's instead. "I don't know what happened in the forest today. I'm not sure you do either. But there was never a moment where you worried about getting lost, was there? Just like your mother. She disappeared because she wanted to. There was a lot I never knew about her, but I'm sure about that."

"I wanted to come back." Alice's voice shook, but she meant every word she forced out. "And I did."

"I know. I used to be terrified you wouldn't." Then her father rubbed at his face. "Fleur doesn't have any of that. She needs help. Please. Find her, Alice. Find your sister and bring her home."

"I will." Then Alice licked her lips, tasting the salt of tears and the iron of blood. "I promise."

CHAPTER SIX

The Ritual

Blood gushes between stiff fingers as the witch clutches the ruins of her face. Bright and thin, splattering the ground until the soil is soaked through. Filling her throat until her breath is reduced to a gurgle. The black wolf wasn't kind, and the witch's remaining acolyte can barely look at her, instead tearing up fabric for makeshift bandages.

Curses are spat out with broken teeth. Hands tremble while wrapping strips around missing features. Only the figure beside them remains calm, studying the grotesque sight with a puzzled air. She's hardly more than a girl, this one, dark hair spilling over a gown as delicate as froth and eyes bright despite the dourness of dusk. In the final rays of light, the slab of rock she perches upon appears unremarkable, squat and misshapen in its bed of ferns. Only the many red stains give hint to its true purpose.

Oh yes, this is damned ground, and only damned creatures gather here, hidden in the shadows of an abandoned quarry long reclaimed by the wilderness. The reek of fear always hangs heavy in the air, and now these witches add to it, disbelief souring their sweat. Their most precious ritual will happen tonight, and each rasping breath proves they're no longer the most dangerous creatures in the forest. Something else has arrived. Something else now hunts.

"Stop flinching, Babette." Only Portia's eyes remained visible, flat and furious as they peered out from a mask of white fabric rapidly turning red. "He didn't so much as bite you."

"But he saw me," said Babette, tying off the final strip. Her gaze darted all around, as if she expected teeth to flash out from the nearest shadows. "He looked right at me while tearing off Bettina's head, as good as promising I'd be next. And how could he do this to you? The bleeding hasn't stopped at all."

"Hush," hissed Portia, the word clotting in her throat.

Too late. The girl on the altar turned toward them, still stroking the rough granite and its gruesome stains. "Yes, what was he, Mother? How could he hurt you?"

Portia's tone immediately sweetened. "Don't trouble yourself, my pet. There are more important things to think about, especially for you. Nothing must stop this ritual. We've worked too hard for it."

The girl's expression cleared. Her mouth curved into a dreamy smile. "*I've* worked too hard. After all, he's coming for me."

"Of course, my darling." Portia waited until her daughter looked away. Then her voice lowered to a livid hiss meant for

Babette's ears only. "I don't know what that creature is. All I'm sure about is that the girl he's guarding was part of Vanna's offering."

"Sabotage?" breathed Babette. "Would she be that bold?"

"Possibly. We'll learn more once she arrives." Then Portia gingerly pressed at her face, testing where blood had already seeped through. "It's such a pity, not having time to fix this. I wanted to look my best in front of the others while they're being forced to honor us. But it doesn't matter. After tonight, his favor will lift us far above them."

"Including me?" asked Babette. "Surely, being Celeste's dear friend will give me a glimpse of his power."

"We're not friends," said the girl, watching the rising moon. "Being friends means you like each other."

"As your loyal acolyte then." Babette stared at Portia in fresh desperation. She was just a girl herself, pinched in the face and thin in the body, hair and eyes equally colorless. It was as if every inch of her that could be spared had long since disappeared, given over to Portia in the effort to move from acolyte to coven member. When silence stretched on, she trembled like a beaten dog, leaned forward like an eager vulture. A ragged little ghost that had lost everything except her hunger.

A note of humor joined the gurgle in the older witch's voice. "Dear Babette. Always looking out for yourself. No, don't be embarrassed. It's why you're here and Bettina isn't.

But you must avoid being so obvious. Some people dislike feeling used."

Just then, a ragged shout drifted up from below, hardly more than an echo among the dark swathes of forest.

Portia dismissed her acolyte with a twitch of her hand. "They're beginning to wake up. Control any that make too much noise, but leave the rest alone. The less they're touched, the better."

As Babette slipped away, steps silent on the steep trail down, Portia returned to where her daughter waited on the altar, her gaze as distant as the horizon. As she began arranging Celeste's hair in perfect waves over her shoulders and down her back, the girl murmured, "They'll have to love me after this, won't they? Even while seething with jealousy over not being chosen themselves."

Portia traced the curve of her cheek. "Some might. Others will hate you as much as they dare. The important thing is that after tonight, all will worship you and what you can do for them."

"It's such a laugh to think about. Becoming their queen." Celeste's smile looked delicate, but the remote light in her eyes had hardened. "Especially the ones who thought I couldn't catch his attention just because they failed to."

Then she really did laugh, a sound as swift and sharp as a bird's cry. It echoed in the darkness, sinking down to the circle of cages waiting far below. They were crude, heavy things, nothing more than branches lashed together and hammered into the ground. Their weathered appearance revealed a pedigree of past horrors: gashes left by frantic fingernails, bloodstains as black as the clusters of mushrooms growing here and there on the rotting bark.

And inside them, roused by smoke and starlight and unseen danger, people began to stir...

Fleur's head hurt. Sweat or blood trickled down the side of her face, but she didn't touch it to find out which. Even dazed and half-aware, she felt how filth crusted her hands from digging at the ground in animal panic. She had tried shaking at the cage, too, but the attempt had only lodged splinters into her palms.

Now she stayed very still there in the darkness, trying to think of what to do. There were torches stuck in the ground, casting light on the other cages but not on the people stuck inside them. Even so, she didn't have to guess who they were— there had been shouting earlier. Hoarse calls for help that had sounded as confused as she'd felt. A few people had calmed down and tried puzzling things together, but she'd kept quiet, too scared to do more than listen and realize they were all from the riding group.

Then someone had emerged from the darkness, coming from the direction of a nearby ledge. A woman as naked and dirt-streaked as if she'd clawed herself out of the earth, a woman whose hair fell into her face while she squatted before the nearest cage and reached for the voice that rose within.

The torchlight had been too weak to reveal what happened next, but Fleur had heard a shriek that ended suddenly, and had seen the woman rise back to her feet with bloodied hands. A few others had kept yelling, unable to believe what was happening until she visited them, too.

Now the forest was silent and the woman was gone, but Fleur couldn't stop shivering, her gaze always circling up to the ledge and the torches glittering there like fireflies. A few times, she pressed her face against the cage, trying to find Alice in any of the others. She gave up just as quickly, unable to make out more than vague shapes that rocked back and forth, or shook at the branches penning them in, or that didn't move at all.

The moon hung high when footsteps crunched through the ferns. Fleur slumped to the ground, staying as still as possible even as her breath quickened. At the sound of voices, she opened her eyes just enough to see.

Two women approached, both at odds with their surroundings. One wore a sharp business suit. The other, the type of breezy, pastel-colored dress that Fleur always associated with her mother. Red-stained bandages covered the first one's face, and Fleur swallowed hard, about to throw up.

Then the second woman spoke, near enough to be clearly heard. "How awful for you, Portia. And here I thought I'd practically gift-wrapped them. Denise is as threatening as a puppy. I didn't expect her family to be any different."

As they circled the cages, the torchlight flickered enough to reveal the second woman's face. Fleur clapped a hand over her mouth to stop her gasp. It was Vanna, one of Mom's college friends.

A muffled noise came from the bandaged woman. It sounded wet and strained, and when they drew closer, Fleur saw thick trails clotting on her neck and staining the collar of her crisp jacket. Then the name "Portia" clicked in her head, and she realized it was the resort's owner standing in front of her. *Bleeding* in front of her. Her fingers were now clamped so hard over her mouth that her cheeks hurt.

Portia continued to check the cages, her voice thinning enough to form words. "How could you not see that the girl was different? Or that she had such a strange creature with her?"

"I knew nothing about her. She drifted away from her family years ago and only recently returned."

"And you expect me to believe that?"

Vanna's tone remained silken. "Why not? You didn't recognize her either. And why are we checking the cages? I thought you had acolytes to watch them."

"One was killed by that fiend. The other is now scared silly. I want to be sure they're all here before I grow too absorbed with the final preparations."

They both stopped before Fleur's cage. Every hair on the back of her neck rose as she remained slumped and still, trying not to whimper beneath the weight of their attention. A heartbeat of silence passed.

Then Vanna sighed. "Well? There she is."

When Portia remained silent, the other woman's voice changed, rising until she hissed like a snake. "I'm so sick of your shit, Portia. Even with a missing face, it's obvious what you're thinking. You could never be as blind as the rest of us, right? You're so much savvier. Farsighted. And now... so much more in his favor. It must have been a trick of mine, because you would never be stupid enough to underestimate a silly little girl. Nothing is ever your fault. Tell me, if tonight's ritual fails—"

"It won't," snarled Portia. The violence of the words left fresh blood soaking the bandages.

"But if it does, who's to blame? Me? Our king? Perhaps your precious daughter. It has to be someone else. It's always someone else."

Portia's hand cracked across the other woman's face. Her nails left scratches behind.

Vanna only laughed. "You *are* worried."

"This means everything to me." Then Portia tore the bandaging off, revealing what waited beneath. As shock replaced the viciousness in Vanna's eyes, she added, "I've waited years for another chance, and I'll see it through all the way. No matter what."

"Do you believe that makes you special? I felt the same way when it was my turn. And while I'll hardly wish the best for you and your daughter, the fact is that we're all too cowardly to move against each other. Especially if Celeste succeeds tonight."

When Portia said nothing, Vanna's smile returned, and she added, "Even if you don't believe me, what harm was done? The older girl wasn't part of my offering, so you didn't exactly lose her. The tour guide works well in place of Denise. And I'm sure your face will turn out fine. Anyway, it's about time you took a new one. You were beginning to look tired."

"That's not the point," snarled Portia. "The other girl and her creature are still loose. If they ruin the ritual out of revenge..."

"While we're all there? I doubt it." Then Vanna turned away from the cages, heading for the trail that led up to the ledge. Her final words were offered over her shoulder. "Try speaking with the hag mother about this black wolf. She knows something about him."

"Bitch," rasped Portia, but quietly, as if to herself. A final glance around, and then she walked away as well. The smell of blood lingered.

Fleur once more found herself alone, shivering against the leaves. Silence fell. The torches flickered and smoked. She felt numb, curling in on herself as the air grew colder. The only way she could measure time was by her heartbeat.

Shapes bounded out from the darkness. Two pairs of eyes glowed at her. She flinched to the other side of the cage and stuffed the ragged sleeve of her sweatshirt in her mouth to keep from screaming. The moonlight picked out sharp muzzles and thick fur, rangy limbs and white teeth. Wolves.

The larger one was black as the shadows, almost invisible while prowling around the cages, but the second wolf was lighter, easier to see when it moved close to sniff at her.

She squeezed her eyes shut, leaning as far away as possible, and muffled another shriek when something brushed her shoulder.

"Fleur," whispered a voice, soft but urgent. "Fleur, it's all right. It's me, Alice."

Fleur stared at the hand shaking her arm, and then at her sister's face. "But—the wolves. There were wolves just here. And then Mom's friend before that, talking with the hotel owner about you. And... and why are you naked? Is any of this even *real*?"

She fell silent when Alice's hands caught hers. "I know. I know it's all strange, but right now you have to stay quiet and patient while we get you out. We don't want them to hear us."

At that, Fleur looked over her sister's shoulder, finding the distant ledge. A big fire had appeared at the very tip, illuminating several figures.

A flicker of movement pulled her attention back to the cage's door. The black wolf crouched there, teeth snapping at the twine knotting the door shut. The cage jerked from the force. Fleur's breath dwindled to a squeak.

"He's on our side," murmured Alice. "You can trust him."

"Are you kidding?" managed Fleur, as wood chips flew from his second bite.

"No. I'll explain everything later."

Then the door buckled, swinging open with a creak. The black wolf melted into the darkness while Alice motioned at her to hurry.

"You've got to be shitting me," she muttered, crawling out even as her mind struggled to accept a wolf and her naked sister appearing out of nowhere. After hours of being hunched in the cage, her body trembled, trying to remember how to work. She stumbled several times while Alice helped her toward the nearest cluster of trees. Then those massive trunks were looming all around, hiding the ledge and its voracious fire.

Just as she opened her mouth to demand an explanation, a flashlight beam caught her in the face. She flinched back, aware of Alice's grip tightening on her arm. Her stunned eyes made out a figure with long, matted hair and skinny limbs. Then she gasped, realizing it was the same woman who had gone around the cages to silence anyone shouting for help.

The light remained fixed on her face as the woman said, "Nice try. Now get back in your cages, or I'll cut the tendons in your legs and drag you there."

Beside her, but still in the shadows, Alice growled. It was a deep, inhuman sound, and the woman's expression changed into sheer terror. Before she could angle the flashlight toward Alice, a man slipped out from the shadows behind her and caught her head, giving it a vicious twist. A sharp *crack* and the woman crumpled to the ground, unmoving.

Fleur whimpered, too stunned to even run.

Alice tried to turn her away from the sight. "It's okay. It's Colton, and he's not going to hurt you."

"He just killed someone with his bare hands," said Fleur, her voice very flat. "And he's also not wearing any clothes. What the fuck is happening?"

He ignored the question, instead glancing at her sister. "Not much time left. Want to get any of the others?"

Alice hesitated, but when she spoke, her voice sounded firm. "No. I want Fleur away from here and safe before anything else."

Fleur watched him nod and pull the body away into the thickest part of the shadows, his movements casual and efficient as if he'd done this a thousand times before. When her sister tried to urge her away again, she shook her head, some part of her insisting that she stay and watch and understand. Then a black wolf loped back out into the moonlight, eyes flashing at her sister before he circled around them, obviously impatient.

"No. No way," said Fleur. Her gaze jumped to Alice, pieces clicking together in her mind. "There were *two* wolves. Then you suddenly appeared. Does that mean you're the—the other wolf?"

"It's a lot to take in, I know." Then Alice glanced behind them at the glimmer of light that could still be seen between the trees. "Trust us a little longer. We'll get you safely home."

"But..." The rest of Fleur's words faded as her sister suddenly hunched over, hair falling into her face while convulsions wracked her body. Skin and muscle and bone writhed in a way that should have been impossible, twisting and reknitting itself as her sister gave a soft gasp, obviously in pain. At that, the black wolf returned to her, pressing close.

When he moved away again, it was a grey wolf that rose from where her sister had been, a grey wolf who looked at her and then trotted further into the trees. A soft whine urged her to follow before it was too late.

Fleur did, feeling dizzy. Heartbeats passed. Her feet slid in the soft soil, crunched against dead leaves. The moon flickered in and out of sight, hardly enough to light their uneven descent into thicker forest. The black wolf was completely invisible; she couldn't even hear him, much less see him there in the dark. But her sister remained close by, letting her grab onto the thick fur between her shoulder blades whenever she stumbled.

Then—a distant scream, ragged and echoing. Fleur stopped short. When it came again, wet heat ran down her cheeks. Her pulse hammered in her throat so hard that it hurt.

A cold nose pushed at her hand, coaxing her on. Instead, she sank back against the nearest tree, not caring how the damp leaf litter clung to her jeans and sweatshirt. The whole world seemed to spin. "I can't do this."

There were a few moments of silence before Alice approached her, human once more. Her long hair and the surrounding shadows obscured all except her face, which held the same composure she'd had when they'd first been lost. For a single breath, Fleur could almost believe this night hadn't happened at all, that they hadn't been separated and the only things to fear were exposure and thirst. It was a comforting thought, a flashlight to cling to in the darkness, but it evaporated as soon as her sister spoke.

"We're almost there. It's just two miles to a ranger's station."

Fleur shivered and hugged her knees, aware of how her fingers were growing numb from the chill. As she stared at the sky, she said, "What if they're part of this shit?"

"They aren't."

"But how can you know?"

Alice moved close enough to settle beside her, also looking up at the stars. "Do you remember what I said earlier today? That I wouldn't lie just to make you feel better?"

Fleur nodded, scrubbing at her cheeks with her sleeve.

Her sister's hand squeezed hers. "You'll be safe at the station. I promise."

The forest had fallen quiet again. The black wolf reappeared, his eyes glowing while he paused beside Alice. Fleur watched her sister rest her head against his fur without a hint of hesitation, moonlight tracing them both. She looked so at ease, so natural, that Fleur could only stare, overcome by this glimpse of a world that had always existed just out of sight, a world impossible to explain or rationalize.

"They'll think I'm crazy. *I* think I'm crazy." Then she surprised herself with a laugh. "But then, how many people really want the truth?"

Her sister smiled a little, but her expression remained serious. "A lot less than you'd guess. Ready to walk some more?"

"All right." Fleur stood after the second try, feeling her legs wobble, and let Alice steer her in the right direction. She couldn't say how fast or how slow they traveled. Any sense of time had drifted away, and all she knew was the distant sound of running water, the sharpness of rock protruding from damp earth, and her sister's soft steps beside her own.

There were no other screams, but fear still itched at her, driving her forward even when every tree looked the same. She started to feel weightless, as if she floated over the ferns and roots. She stopped wincing against the cold, stopped seeing the stars. All that mattered was putting one foot in front of the other.

Then light glittered. Her heart jumped, caught by the idea of them somehow getting lost and circling back to those cages waiting beneath torches.

"That's it," said Alice, pushing a branch aside to reveal a long, double-story building with all its windows lit. A few cars were still parked there.

Fleur only swallowed, suddenly terrified now that the safety of electricity, blankets, and civilization waited feet away, just out of reach. She stumbled closer, clawing past the final trees until her sneakers reached the first pool of light from the parking lot. Then she stopped, looking back at her sister, who remained in the shadows.

"Aren't you coming with me?"

Some part of her knew the answer even before Alice responded. "We're going back."

"No!" Fleur found herself grabbing at her sister, desperate to keep her close. "They'll kill you. They're total freaks."

Alice only shook her head.

Fleur felt herself crumple. When her sister caught her into a hug, she clung back fiercely, trying to convince her not to go back, not to disappear forever.

As if sensing her thoughts, Alice murmured, "You'll see us in the morning. I promise."

"What am I supposed to tell Mom and Dad? They won't believe any of this."

"Sometimes, it's easier to say only what they *need* to know." Then Alice pulled away, stepping further into the shadows with a final smile.

"Shit." Fleur ran hands through her hair, trying not to cry again. But as she stepped out into the full light, shaking so hard her teeth chattered, the black wolf was suddenly there beside her, ears alert while he matched her pace. Making sure she was safe all the way to the door.

When she glanced back at her sister, she could just make out Alice's silhouette there among the trees, the light catching her tangled hair and little else. She looked unreal, inhuman, and Fleur's skin prickled from a sense of having stepped past some invisible barrier between the brightly lit mundane world and its secret, unknown shadow.

Then she was at the door, the black wolf slipping away while she knocked on the worn wood. Her hands didn't stop for a response, instead pounding harder and harder until all her weight was thrown into her fists. At the sound of footsteps on the other side, she shrieked. When the door opened, she nearly fell inside against the rangers standing there, staggering until hands caught her.

"I got lost earlier today," she muttered, trying to focus on their startled faces. "I'm part of the horseback riding group."

"My God," said one, as they carefully ushered her in. "Is there anyone else with you?"

Anguish filled her voice for more than one reason. "No."

She told them her name and let the rest of their questions flow over her, ignoring everything except the station's cat, a fluffy calico that curled in her lap and purred, not minding how her tears dampened its fur.

Back among the trees, Alice watched what was visible through the windows. "She's safe," she murmured, but a chill ran down her spine over how close it had been.

Beside her, Colton changed form, his gaze on her instead of the station. When his mouth pressed against the curve of her neck, she leaned into the heat of his body, trying to ignore a second shiver.

He must have felt it, because his voice then rumbled against her throat. "Sure you want to go back? You're tired from changing form so much."

She sighed, closing her eyes. The first hint of a helicopter could be heard. Fleur would soon be flown out. If she wanted, she and Colton could just return to the resort and rest. Her bones throbbed and ached, urging her to give in.

She resisted, some part of her snarling for more. "I couldn't live with myself if I just let the rest die. If I didn't at least try. Besides..."

Then she looked up at him, feeling her teeth bite into her lips. "Portia has a lot to answer for. She's felt your anger, but she hasn't felt mine."

Four witches stood in a circle around the altar, stripped to their skin despite the wild sparks from the nearby fire. The moon was at its highest, and the air had taken on a strange tension, all nearby shadows stretched and thin. Anticipation lit their eyes while they watched Portia attempt to calm her daughter.

Celeste's shrieks split the night as Babette hunched by her feet, knowing better than to speak or even look up. She still seemed in disbelief that the black wolf had left her to recover, unresisting whenever Celeste slapped and scratched at her in between bouts of sobbing.

"It's ruined! He won't come with only eleven sacrifices."
The girl was hardly more than a heap of fabric in her mother's
arms.

"Everything will be fine, my darling. Vanna will pay for
this." Those last words gained a particular edge as Portia glared
over at the other witch.

Vanna scoffed, remaining unconcerned. "Why is it my fault?
It was your acolyte who lost her. And it was *you* who lost the
other two."

There was a low hiss from Portia, but one of the other
witches shook her head and said, "Enough bullshit. She's
here."

All stared as the hag mother emerged from shadows.
Despite her title, she didn't look old, skin soft and flushed as a
girl's and face fresh and unlined. She moved with a stiff grace,
smiling a little while the rest dipped their heads in a show of
respect. The glitter to her eyes suggested she was well-aware of
their hidden hatred and that it amused her, but her expression
grew serious at the sight of Celeste. "No tears, darling. You
should be saving every part of yourself for our king."

As the girl frantically waved at her face, trying to keep the
rest at bay, the hag mother turned to Portia. "Tell me what
happened."

The torches flickered while she listened. When she'd heard
enough, she cut Portia off with a sharp motion of her hand, the
same one that held the ritual knife. Then she glanced at Vanna,
who looked sullen. "Find a replacement. There must be twelve

sacrifices, and we owe our king more respect than to immediately give up."

Vanna knew better than to argue, and at first her mouth only tightened. Just as quickly, it relaxed into a smile. She walked over to Portia's acolyte—hunched by Celeste to blot the tears from her face—and grabbed her by the hair. "Here."

"What?" Babette scratched at her, panicking when her grip only tightened. "Portia, tell her to let me go."

The other witch said nothing, still holding her daughter.

Babette's eyes widened. "You can't do this. You can't! Let me find someone else. Just let me go and I'll find a new sacrifice. Please!"

The hag mother raised her eyebrows at Portia, another smile playing on her face. "Will you accept this gesture of Vanna's? To refuse this replacement would mean an effective end to this ritual."

"Portia," managed the acolyte, fingernails ripping at the hand that held her. "Please. Not to me. I've done so much for you without ever complaining. Ever!"

Portia finally looked at her. Her eyes were the only recognizable feature in her ruined face. "And believe me, I'm always impressed. You're very obedient, Babette, and now there's only one more thing to do."

"No!" The acolyte writhed as the hag mother handed the knife to Vanna and then screamed as the fingers snarled in her hair wrenched her head back, exposing her throat. The blade's edge gleamed as Vanna raised it high, licking her lips. Then it sliced down, flashing with moonlight. Babette's ragged scream cut off into gurgling.

As Vanna continued cutting at the neck, Celeste managed a tremulous smile at her mother. "Will it be all right?"

Portia smoothed her hair. "As long as you remember what to do. It's begun, my dear, and now it all rests on you."

The girl nodded. "I won't fail like you did. I swear it."

As she resettled herself on the altar, once more composed, Vanna tossed the head into the bonfire. The smell of burning flesh seemed to both excite and terrify the other witches, and they all stared at the blackening features, watching one of their own burn beyond the point of return.

Vanna began taking cuts from the body, as experienced with the knife as a butcher. The others watched, leaning closer when the slick, heavy guts were pulled free. Already bloodied up to her elbows, Vanna cut out the heart and offered it to the hag mother, who took it gently, as if it were something more precious than gold. Then she bit into it viciously. Her smile turned ghastly as she chewed.

Vanna's own grin disappeared entirely when she took the heart over to Portia.

"You're such a cunt," hissed Portia, brandishing her own knife. The tip quivered, as if she ached to stab it into Vanna instead.

"As if you even liked her," said Vanna, squeezing the heart until fresh blood ran down her arm. Then she handed it over.

Portia was also experienced, quickly tearing off her mouthful and then slicing off a second piece for her daughter. She fed it to Celeste in tiny morsels, taking care not to smear that perfect, waiting mouth. The girl already seemed to be in a trance, face glowing with each fresh taste.

Witch by witch, the heart was passed around until all had fed. The sad remnants were given back to Vanna, who threw it into the fire next to the head. Then the hag mother spoke again, her eyes bright in the firelight. "Bring your second offering, Vanna."

Soon, screaming reached them. All the witches waiting for her to return from the cages now shifted impatiently, eyeing the mutilated body that they couldn't touch and sucking blood from their fingers.

The second sacrifice was hardly dragged within reach of the torches before they were all on her, tearing at her with fingernails and teeth as she kicked and shrieked. When Vanna hit one of the other witches in the face with the hilt of her knife, she spat in response. "Hurry the fuck up."

Vanna smiled again, but something had gone sour in her face while she cut up through the stomach. Only the hag mother, Portia, and Celeste ate from the second heart; the rest still tore at the body, squabbling over choice parts like scavengers.

After Vanna threw the second heart into the fire, she wiped at the blood smeared on her face, fingers digging at the soft flesh of her throat in a pulse-like rhythm. She stopped only to squeeze her nipples instead. When she looked at Celeste there on the altar, delicately accepting another bite from her mother, she pinched them harder, teeth bared in what could have been a snarl as much as a grin.

She offered the knife to the witch beside her even before the hag mother spoke from her place at the altar. "Your offerings now, Cleo."

The bodies piled up, blood softening the ground into mud. Celeste continued to eat whatever was given to her, expression serene while those around her grew more frantic with each sacrifice. Blood smeared over every inch of their bodies as they fought and fed. The air thickened with the smells of smoke and burning flesh, with split intestines and sweat.

By the time the final body was thrown onto the others, most of the witches already had one hand working furiously between their legs, crawling back to their places around the altar.

Vanna seemed the angriest, leaning back against a tree while her fingers raked across the planes of her body. Scratches were left on her chest and stomach, some of them bloody. She pulled at her hair, pinched at her thighs while the palm of her hand crushed the seam of her cunt, her panting hoarse and low as she glared at the altar and the girl upon it. Her hot gaze never left Celeste or how the dark tips of her breasts pressed against her pristine gown. Froth bubbled from her lips during her first climax.

The hag mother had moved within full reach of the torchlight, exposing every inch of her body as she worked herself into a frenzy. The smile never left her face, but it did grow pained, sweat leaving her hair damp against her neck, leaving trails through the blood on her skin. Her hips worked in hard, sharp jerks, the only hints of something far more raw and ragged living beneath her composure.

Others hunched in the damp ground, backs curved until it seemed their vertebrae would burst out through their skin while they shivered and shook. One rubbed her entire body against the ground, throwing her head up whenever a rock or root pushed against her clit. Her fingers left deep furrows in the earth. Another bit her lip until it bled and spat at those nearest to her, her voice rising as laughs or sobs while her fingers pushed in deeper.

Yet it was Portia who was the most changed; all hints of the refined proprietress had disappeared. She hunched there as ugly and obscene as the rest of her coven, fresh blood oozing from her face from the effort. Her eyes remained unblinking on her daughter, who stayed still and silent, watching the sky instead of the writhing bodies circling her. The firelight cast her in gold, the moon in ivory. She looked perfect, too perfect to be real, and something like pain filled Portia's gaze even though her fingers never faltered.

One scream rose, and then another. The stench of spilled blood and ripped apart bodies was joined by something muskier, something seething. Then there was a sixth cry, the last cry. The hag mother's cry. The pile of bodies shifted, and each witch turned toward it, exhausted and sticky and enthralled.

It moved again from somewhere within, as if a great force gathered beneath the lifeless meat and bone. Celeste stiffened, shivering lightly as she stared with the others. Her fingers fluttered beside her thighs, as if she desperately wished to join in with the rest, but instead she stayed still, stayed obedient, and watched.

Antlers pushed up from the slack flesh. A stag's antlers, giant and with tines as sharp as teeth. Soft gasps rippled among the witches when a dark-haired head followed. Strong hands appeared, and then arms that bulged with muscle. A final heave sent bodies rolling away as the figure rose to its full height, shaking its head to cast lingering scraps of flesh from those terrible antlers. The hag king had answered their call.

Silence fell. He stood there, blood running down his chest and stomach as he breathed. He was tall and broad-shouldered, face hidden in shadow, but there was something else unnerving about him, a sense of the untouchable. When he approached the altar, the firelight flickered over his powerful frame, revealing his thick, erect cock.

The witches all sank to their hands and knees in supplication, watching with gleaming eyes as Celeste stared at him in rapture. The smells of blood, rotting earth, and musk reached her even before he stopped in front of her—huge, towering, the tilt of his head suggesting he stared down at her.

He was filthy, unwashed even beneath the blood, and his hair hung past his shoulders in snarled tangles, the color impossible to tell from the erratic light and mud. Yet the girl knew the part she had to play, and immediately stroked along the hard muscles of his torso, her lips already parting.

Her fingers found the thick nest of hair surrounding his cock, jerking when she realized lice writhed there. More could be seen in his hair as well, and Celeste swallowed hard, realizing any hesitation would ruin her chance. Then she forced a smile and ran her hand along the length of his shaft, rising to her feet to press her flat belly against its head.

One of the other witches hissed when he let her cling to his shoulders, her legs wrapping around his waist. Another swore when his hand slid between her thighs and squeezed. Yet Celeste's smile looked identical to her mother's as she shifted, trying to brush against his cock as his hands caught her by the hips. One thrust, and he would be in her. One thrust, and she'd be the most powerful witch in her coven.

Then the hag king threw her aside, the movement casual, almost careless. She landed on the ground in a disheveled heap, shrieking even as that head with those magnificent, imposing antlers shook side to side slowly, deliberately.

"No!" Celeste's voice cracked on the word as she crawled toward him.

He was already gone, fading as quickly as a shadow, as silently as a gasp, and she was left panting and rubbing furiously at her mouth with the back of her hand.

The hag king had refused her.

For one agonizing moment, there was only the crackling of flames. Then Vanna laughed, a high, clear sound that shattered the air as much as Portia's expression. Another witch joined in, and then a third. Soon, it was only her mother who turned away in silence, hunched over as if she'd been stabbed in the stomach. The others all jeered, breasts heaving, hands clasped over mouths.

"Stop it. Stop it!" Tears ran down the girl's flushed face.

The laughter only continued, drifting down from the ledge and into the trees beyond. It reached the two wolves racing past the empty cages, intent on the scent of blood. Up the trail they went, fast and quiet, until they could watch the witches from the shadows and remain unnoticed. Only the black wolf's presence kept Wolf-Alice from whining in shock at what she could see.

The witches were disappearing one by one, their derision hanging in the air. The fire burned sullenly. Once they were alone, Portia picked up her knife and looked at it, still ignoring her daughter.

"Mother." Celeste sounded bewildered while pulling the folds of her gown closer to her. The delicate fabric was now smeared with blood and filth from the hag king's touch. "I don't understand. I did everything right."

"He found you worthless." Portia finally looked at her.

"But it's not my fault." The girl drew in a shuddering breath. "You saw me, Mother. You saw what I did."

"Yes. You ruined my last chance." Then Portia grabbed her daughter and pulled her head back to expose her neck. The knife shivered in her hand as it slashed down.

The act spurred Wolf-Alice into lunging out in the open, an unthinking reaction to the girl's panic. Yet Portia already held one of the torches to her daughter's face, hand steady even when the gurgling rose into a broken scream.

Wolf-Alice slammed into the witch, ignoring the sparks singing her fur. She bit at whatever she could reach. Hands, arms, hair. Fury left her frothing, clumsy, but then the black wolf joined her. Within a heartbeat, he caught Portia by the throat and began suffocating her in one steady, unrelenting bite. Only when the witch stopped kicking did Wolf-Alice returned to the altar, changing form to face the body there.

It was a terrible sight, and Alice felt herself tremble as she looked around, taking in the carnage, the smell of arousal and excitement, the fire burning down. Her gaze returned to the burned girl and remained there while Colton changed into his skin and dragged Portia's body over to the flames.

When he circled back to her, she finally spoke, voice unsteady. "She called her 'Mother.' I heard it. She was begging her mother."

He nodded. "Looks like a failed ritual."

"And she killed her own daughter over that?" Then she looked up at him, unable to say why tears filled her eyes. "This is what witches are like?"

"Most of them."

The response drove her away from the altar, back to the shelter of the trees. He followed and pulled her into a hug, understanding why it hurt so much.

She tucked her head under his chin, closing her eyes so that even the glimmer of flames disappeared. "Is there anything we can do?"

He knew she meant the bodies. "Bury them, maybe. No way to explain what really happened without Fleur getting pulled into it."

"No, I don't want that. But their families... well, they'll never stop looking. Or wondering."

He remained silent for a moment, hand stroking along the lines of her back while she listened to his heartbeat. "Best we could do is scatter belongings around the forest. Wallets, rings. Things that might be found later."

She nodded, hating how hollow she felt. "Would you mind doing that?"

"Not for you."

Later, they returned to the outskirts of the resort, finding where they'd hidden their clothes in a tree. Despite the early hour—it wasn't even true dawn—Alice could see activity. People seemed agitated, even excited, crossing the lawn in their hurry to get to and from the hotel.

One man paced the line of trees marking the entrance into the forest, and Alice started when she recognized him. Her father. She quickly finished dressing and then, with a final glance at Colton, slipped out from the shadows.

"Alice." He grabbed her into a hug, his next breath coming out as a huge sigh. "A ranger station called in to say Fleur found them. She's been in the hospital for about an hour. I told your stepmother I would stay behind and wake you up with the news when it grew closer to morning."

She pulled back enough to look at him. "But you're not waiting by my room."

"No. No, I'm not." His expression remained as controlled as his voice, but something in his eyes softened. "Thank you for finding her."

She nodded. Then her chin trembled. "I still don't know what happened to Mom. I really don't."

"It's all right." He hugged her tighter, rocking her as if she were four years old again. "Sometimes, the ones left behind can never know what happened."

CHAPTER SEVEN

The Shell of Suburbia

Alice studied the front of her parents' house while she and Colton pulled into the driveway. It had been a week since they had all returned from the resort, a week since she had seen them. She didn't know what to expect.

The path through the yard looked freshly swept and the surrounding hedges neatly clipped. Bird feeders coaxed in finches with their full trays of seed. Flower beds blazed with color, the lush scent from the roses following them up the porch steps. With its neat brickwork and white trim, the house fit with its neighbors like perfectly aligned teeth. Only a note taped to the front door indicated recent troubles.

TO THE MEDIA: WE HAVE ALREADY MADE A STATEMENT. FOR FURTHER INQUIRIES, PLEASE CONTACT JOHN GARNER & ASSOCIATES AT THE NUMBER BELOW.

Alice read it and murmured, "It's the same one Dad told me to use. And now I remember why the name sounded familiar

—it's the firm he hired after a documentary about my mother's disappearance came out and implied he murdered her. He must expect the frenzy to linger."

"Probably will," said Colton, tone already sinking into a particular indifference that was his form of civility during get-togethers. Considering how his usual response to anything social was to disappear if he grew bored and maul egos if he grew irritated, Alice felt flattered that he tried this much with her family.

She watched while he knocked on the door, movements easy and calm. "It really doesn't bother you, does it? Being part of so much scrutiny when you're used to living away from humans."

Even before he shook his head, she knew the answer and marveled at it. A childhood in suburbia had shaped her ideas of danger like a back brace correcting a crooked spine, and she always felt stunned by the concept of simply not caring what others might say. And yet it came so naturally to him, this monster from the woods. What reputation was there to ruin? What weakness could be exposed? The power of whispers shriveled against jaws that crushed throats.

It made her smile despite the numbness behind her ribs and the headache pounding her skull. It made her remember how to tease him. "Does *anything* bother you?"

"Sure." In the late afternoon sunlight, his eyes looked more yellow than green, bright and wry and direct. "When you stop sleeping, eating, and talking."

At that, Alice realized he'd waited all week for her to admit the obvious: that something kept her awake at night and left her sick in the day. That she wouldn't speak about Fleur's kidnapping or the glimpses they'd caught of the coven. That she withdrew into a shell of silence unless answering a question.

It hadn't been a conscious decision, not at first, but the more her heart had hurt, the less she'd wished to examine it.

"I'm fine," she said, and then knocked on the door herself. "Just a little tired."

That drew out his full stare, the one that left people shrinking back. She rarely experienced this side of his intensity but understood what it meant. *Don't bullshit me.*

A pang went through her—not fear, nothing he did could ever scare her. It felt more like anguish. "I'm not trying to shut you out. It's just that…"

Then the door opened, revealing Denise with her brilliant smile. "You're here!"

Alice felt a smile of her own snap in place, the tension between her and Colton thickening even as she focused on her stepmother. There were streaks of flour on Denise's face, and splatters of chunky, green sauce covered her peach-colored apron, but she otherwise looked as fresh and well-kept as ever. "I'm so sorry nobody answered right away. Fleur and I were up to our elbows in sauce, and whenever your father is in his office, he can't hear anything outside it. Come in, come in!"

She pulled Alice into an awkward hug to avoid staining her clothes and then ushered her inside, leaving Colton to follow behind. "Fleur might need a few minutes. Some of the ingredients for dinner had to be made in advance, and things got a little messy, especially when we tried making pesto in the food processor. She's just gone into the shower to wash it out of her hair."

"What are you making?" said Colton, a trace of resignation in his voice. He never trusted Denise's idea of a meal.

"Pizza," said Denise, and beamed again. "It's Fleur's favorite."

Alice hardly listened, too struck by all the changes made in the rooms. A large oil painting had replaced the TV. The modem setup in the corner of the kitchen had been unplugged and hidden behind a vase of flowers. The original curtains, all pastel hues and transparent fabrics, were now wooden blinds that could be pulled shut. It was a house transformed into armor.

As Denise set steaming cups of coffee for them on the granite countertop separating the living room from the kitchen, Alice asked, "How bad have things been?"

Her stepmother's hesitation proved answer enough. "I wouldn't call it bad. Compared to what those other poor families are going through, we've got nothing to complain about at all. I just thought some time away from the TV and internet would be good for us."

Then her phone rang. She declined the call without looking at the screen, and her smile remained fixed while she stirred at a pot bubbling on the stove. The air smelled vaguely of basil and desperation. "It's so sweet of you to help Fleur with her essay. Everything is set up in the dining room. There's usually more light in the sunroom, but now with the new blinds... it's nothing to worry about though. We bought a ceiling fan with a light to replace the one that's in there, and your father will try installing it when he has a few hours free."

Alice nodded, fidgeting with her cup while trying to remember when her father last attempted anything involving wiring. No one in her family had much self-sufficiency outside the narrow confines of an office meeting or a cocktail party.

"I've done those," said Colton, already halfway through his coffee despite its scalding temperature. "Tell me where it is, and I'll have it up in an hour."

Denise looked torn between elation and doubt. "Are you sure? I don't want you getting electrocuted on our behalf."

"It won't be a problem." Then he drained his cup to the dregs, obviously ready to get started.

Before Alice could catch his eye, her stepmother said, "Well, it would be a huge help. Tom will certainly appreciate it. I think the box is in the garage."

Alice felt sick at the idea of the friction between them continuing any longer. A whole evening of this stiffness? Of his quiet seething and her feeling like she was starting to rot from the inside? No, she couldn't bear it, and as soon as he was out of sight, she straightened up from the counter, working hard to keep her tone casual. "I'll say hi to Dad while Fleur's getting ready."

"Of course, sweetheart," said Denise, measuring cashews into a blender. Intent on her work, she didn't notice how Alice followed after Colton instead, slipping through the doorway that opened into the second half of the house and then down to the garage.

She caught up to him on the stairway, her voice no longer steady. "Wait."

He stopped and looked, already halfway down. There were no windows and no lights, and in the dimness he appeared even more feral than usual, what little light there was now picking out the sharpness in his jaw, the strength of his outline. When he started back up to her, she shook her head and took the last few steps herself until she could touch him, until he was more than one shadow among many.

In the dark, it was easier to let the words out, and they left her in a rush even as the narrow stairway pressed them close. "I'm sorry. Sometimes, I still put on a mask because it feels like the safest way to get through something. But I don't like hiding from you, even when I end up doing it."

"Alice." Despite the roughness to his voice, his touch was gentle as he traced her cheek, urging her closer. "Fuck apologies. You've been miserable. I just want to know why."

"I'm not sure. I can't stop thinking about my mother, or what those witches did. That night cut me in ways I don't understand, and I'm scared that talking about it will only open the wounds further."

There was a soft growl from him. The heat of his hand matched his mouth as their lips brushed. "Not if they're licked clean."

Even as she closed her eyes, the numbness of her heart burning away with every beat of his, a noise came from somewhere upstairs. Nothing more than a creak of floorboards, but still enough to break the illusion of privacy. She sighed, limp against the lingering tension in his body. "I'll talk about everything when we're back home. I promise."

His kiss was brief but devouring, the slide of his tongue a promise of his own. Her lips tingled as she returned upstairs.

Fleur hadn't yet appeared. Alice found herself drifting in the direction of her father's office, aware that it was only polite to say hi. Fresh nerves stiffened her spine as she drew near, and she wondered whether she'd ever be able to talk to him without feeling like each word had to be as carefully chosen as a chess move.

Then she sighed and forced her chin up. She wasn't four years old anymore, and she had faced things much more terrifying than her father's opinions on what she was doing with her life.

The door waited ajar. She knocked on it out of courtesy and pushed it all the way open. The familiar smells of computer paper and leather furniture reached her just as she saw him.

He sat behind the large desk set near the back of the room, rubbing at his forehead while he spoke into the phone. When their eyes met, he motioned at her to come in and wait.

She did so, gaze drifting along the walls. It had been years since she'd stepped inside his office, but it looked as stern and sterile as ever, a relic back to her childhood. The only difference she could find was a number of picture frames added to the plaques and awards scattered throughout the room.

Most held photos of Denise or Fleur, spanning years and marking occasions. Fleur grinning in a dirty soccer uniform. Denise planting flowers. The two of them together on the beach, wearing matching hats against the sun. There was even a picture of Denise glowing despite the circles beneath her eyes, a newborn Fleur in her arms.

Then Alice started, seeing one of herself. It was from her high school graduation, taken right after the ceremony had ended. She remembered how hot it had been, leaving everyone except her stepmother short-tempered and sullen. Her father had barely spoken a word, glancing at his watch to mark every minute the speeches ran over their expected length.

In the end, Denise had insisted on a photo of Alice and her father together, urging them to pose in the shade of a tree while the sun blazed through the bleachers nearby. The picture had caught her just as she'd felt—shiny-faced, awkward, and relieved it was all over. Yet her father showed no signs of impatience or disinterest, and his smile wasn't the broad, automatic type he used when masking his feelings. Instead, he looked... proud of her.

Just then, she heard him finish the call and hang up. The office chair creaked as he turned in her direction. "Alice."

She swallowed back the sudden lump in her throat. "Hi, Dad. How are things?"

"Terrible." Despite the grim answer, he looked strangely gratified over the situation turning out just as expected. "We can't let people into the house. When I called in a handyman to install a ceiling fan, he took pictures of Fleur's bedroom and tried to sell them. Most of our neighbors are agreeing to interviews with the media, as are all of Fleur's friends. And this morning, a psychic showed up with her own film crew and claimed she could use Fleur's aura to locate the other riders. In short, it's an invasion of privacy from all angles."

All Alice could think to say was, "I'm sorry it's been so rough."

He waved it away. "I've kept most of it from Denise and Fleur. That's what matters."

"But what about you? That's enough stress for a heart attack."

"We went through worse with your mother."

Broaching that subject still felt raw and unexpected, and they both fell quiet. Alice picked at the hem of her sleeve. Her father got up and straightened one of the awards on the nearest wall. The hum from his computer sounded overloud.

Finally, he stiffly said, "How are you?"

She went with the shortest answer. "Nothing happened after that first day of reporters calling us. I think we live too far in the woods to be bothered."

He turned to look at her. "No, how are *you*? Are you worrying about any of this? Because you have the same hollows under your eyes as when your mother..."

Now it was her turn to be frank. "As when she left me and disappeared."

The words lodged like splinters. She didn't want to say anything else. But her father now wore a haunted expression that drove her to add, "I've been thinking about her. What happened at the resort brought up a lot of memories, but I still don't remember any new details. I wish I did."

He didn't look like he agreed that would be a good thing. "One of the child psychologists used to warn me that your stress-induced insomnia could become a problem well into adulthood. If you need help—"

"I'm fine, really. Colton makes sure I eat and sleep."

When her father grimaced at the mention of him, her tone changed. "Dad. He's good to me."

"I know," he said, voice falling quiet. "It's more and more obvious that he makes you happy, and you never had much chance of that."

The air between them had shifted into something raw and uncertain, vulnerable enough for honest questions and harsh answers. Alice suddenly felt terrified of the chance it provided, and of that same chance slipping away as soon as the world outside intruded on their private grief. Even as her heart clenched, she found herself saying, "Do you think she's really dead?"

He suddenly looked very, very tired. "She's been legally deceased for twelve years."

"But do you think that's what happened?"

"Alice..."

"She's nothing more than a few memories for me, but you knew her, Dad. You'd have the best chance at understanding why she left us. If she died, or if..." Then Alice stopped, feeling her eyes start to burn. "Or if she just never wanted to come back."

His sigh was interrupted by the sound of footsteps, and they both turned to look as Fleur leaned against the doorway, hair still damp from her shower. Aside from her sweatshirt being even baggier than before, as if she'd lost weight, she seemed the same, expression as bored as her tone. "Hey. I'm ready whenever."

Alice managed a smile. "I'll be right there."

When her sister disappeared back into the hallway, Alice started to follow. Then her father called her name. He had returned to his desk, a handful of papers already spread out and waiting, but his attention remained on her. The grey in his hair glinted as he said, "There's no way to know what happened to your mother. And in the end, no one needs the answer. We can still move on."

She only nodded, sensing the subject was as good as closed, and left him to his work.

Fleur waited in the dining room, notes spread all over the polished table while she flipped through a leather-bound tome of Shakespeare's works. In the next room over, Colton worked on a ladder. The prim furniture and delicate glass decor only magnified his ruggedness. The muscles in his arms bulged when he pulled off the old ceiling fan, holding its weight with ease while separating the wiring.

Before Alice could catch his attention, Fleur looked up and said, "Did you bring another copy?"

Alice brandished a worn paperback. "The same one I used in high school."

The clatter of pots drifted from the kitchen as she joined her sister. Fleur said nothing while Alice searched for the opening scene, seemingly focused on her notebook instead. Yet as soon as Denise turned on the blender, creating an effective noise barrier, Fleur dropped her pen and came alive. "You look horrible."

It was too true to take offense at. "It's been a rough week for everyone."

"Not really. Dad's in his element sending lawyers after people, and Mom's just happy we're all safe."

Alice studied her sister. "How about you?"

"I don't know. I hate having to talk to so many people. They want to hear things I can't tell them. I don't remember much about what happened, and what *is* clear seems too crazy to be real." Then she looked up at Alice. Her hair had fallen into her face, giving her a skittish, suspicious appearance, as if she expected yet another adult to reassure her that it was all over and didn't matter.

"It happened," said Alice, quietly. "And you're not crazy."

Fleur blew out a shaky breath. "So... you really changed into a wolf."

Alice nodded.

Her sister's focus switched to Colton. "And he's a maniac."

He didn't look away from his work. "When I feel like it."

"He's also very sweet when he feels like it," said Alice, smiling in response to his glance. Then she fell serious again. "But he's killed, if that's what you mean. We both have. And if you want to know anything about that night, I don't mind explaining what I can."

Fleur shrugged. "Not right now. I mean, we're safe, right?"

"Yes. I'm sure of it."

"Then that's good enough for me."

Alice simply nodded, so surprised by her sister's calm that she didn't know what to say.

Even as Fleur's gaze dropped to her notebook, she added, "Everyone acts like that night must be the worst experience of my life, but it just feels like a bad dream. You know, where you're scared shitless at the time, but once you wake up, it can't follow you. It stops being real. What happened with Hayley fucked me up so much more. Does that make me weird?"

Alice smiled a little. "Who's normal?"

Her sister nearly smiled back. Then the roar from the blender shut off, and her voice changed in an instant. "Anyway, thanks for coming over to help."

Alice took the cue and opened her copy of the play. "Don't thank me yet. Shakespeare was the only homework assignment I got a C on."

"That's still better than my first grade for this. Now that I'm trying to pass, I'm even more screwed."

"What are you stuck on?"

Fleur grabbed at some of her notes. "Every word. The assignment is pretty simple. We're supposed to write an essay describing what themes of family the play explores. I could do that on my own if I just understood what the characters are saying. But I don't. It's like trying to read a different language. Old English *is* a different language, right?"

"Um..." Alice hesitated, realizing she didn't know the answer.

"It's not in Old English," said Colton, already screwing the lightbulbs into the new fan. "It's in verse."

Fleur didn't look convinced. "What does that mean?"

"That it's hard to read," murmured Alice, flipping through a few pages. Then she shook her head. "All right, let's try the opening scene."

They struggled through until the simple lines of dialogue thickened into speeches too obtuse for Alice to puzzle out. She already had a throbbing headache when Fleur stopped taking notes and chewed on her pen instead. "None of this makes sense. Why does it matter that Horatio is a scholar?"

Alice glanced at Colton in a silent plea for help. He responded while testing the lights. "He's the most capable one in the group to face the spirit."

"Are you serious?" said Fleur.

"He reads a lot of classic lit," said Alice, thumbing ahead to find a dismaying amount of speeches. "And enjoys it. Shakespeare isn't even a stretch for him."

Colton didn't react, but Fleur still turned to him with a scoff. "You act like you're in pain whenever you have to talk. Reading doesn't seem like your thing at all."

At that, he finally glanced over. Alice could tell by his expression that he was ready to ignore her sister for the rest of the evening, and gave him a pleading look. The glint in his eyes softened just before he said, "Scholars knew Latin. Latin was used to exorcise evil spirits. Marcellus wanted to hide behind someone who could drive off the ghost if it turned out to be evil."

"Holy shit." Fleur stared at him. "And you can do that for the entire play? I mean, break it down so it makes sense?"

"Sure." Then he turned off the fan and began gathering up the tools he had used.

When Fleur realized he wasn't going to say anything else, she turned to Alice and hissed, "Make him help us. We're getting nowhere on our own."

Alice raised her eyebrows at the idea of anyone *making* Colton do something they wanted and he didn't. Yet at that moment, a dismayed "Oh, no!" came from the kitchen.

Fleur pounced on it. "Besides, Mom definitely needs help. She's making the pizza from scratch, and she's never tried this recipe before."

Alice hesitated, not wanting to drag Colton into another tedious task, but to her surprise, he jerked his head at the kitchen door and said, "Pizza's beyond me. *Hamlet* isn't."

The frustration melted from Fleur's face as he sat in one of the chairs across from them and added, "I won't go through the whole play. Just the best scenes for the theme."

"Sure. We're supposed to write about—"

"I heard."

As Alice handed over her copy, she mouthed *thank you* to him. A sudden smolder in his eyes told her how she could make it up to him. It left just as quickly when he turned his attention to the book. "Take notes because I'm not repeating myself. If something confuses you, say so."

Fleur nodded, pen ready.

Alice didn't wait any longer, catching the first hint of something burning in the kitchen. She hurried to it, unsure of what to expect.

It looked like a disaster. Sauce splattered the ceiling above the stove. A scorched pot had been shoved into a corner where it couldn't burn anything else. The blender had spilled over, its sides streaked with a grainy, sickly grey paste. In the middle of it all, Denise furiously chopped away at something on the cutting board while two round pizza pans waited nearby.

"Need any help?" said Alice, already grabbing the spare apron hanging by the fridge.

Denise sagged in relief. "Oh... would you?"

Alice scanned the recipe while twisting her hair into a quick bun. It didn't take long to realize the pizza was vegan and gluten-free, requiring a huge list of substitutions to mimic basic ingredients. "How far along are you?"

"I was almost ready to put it all together, but something went wrong with the cheese swap." Denise looked at the blender. "I'm not sure why it turned so sticky. Or grey."

Within a few minutes, Alice had cleaned out the previous attempt. As she started measuring the ingredients, Denise chattered away while chopping up sun-dried tomatoes and fresh herbs for the toppings. "Fleur's stayed home this past week. Her principal was very understanding. We're also lucky in how there are only a few more weeks of school before it's out for summer. We've been thinking about putting her in independent study in the fall. She seems to like the idea. I'm just glad she's talking to me at all."

There was a brightness in her voice that sounded artificial, and Alice suddenly realized how wildly she chopped at the basil. "Denise, you just did what you thought was best. What happened wasn't your fault."

Her stepmother sighed. "When I think of how lucky you and Fleur were, and how we might have been one more family hoping for a miracle, it makes my stomach turn. But I know I shouldn't feel so guilty. I realized that when Vanna tried blaming herself for it."

"Vanna?" said Alice, unable to keep the sharpness from her tone as she remembered Fleur's wild words from that chaotic night, her insistence that she had recognized a family friend as one of the witches. "Vanna Moore, your old college friend?"

"Yes. She was the one who recommended the resort. A few days ago, she called to make sure we were all fine. She couldn't believe what had happened."

Alice stared at the blender, feeling a muscle jump in her throat. A snarl bubbled there, thick as the paste forming in the wake of the blender's blades, and it took until the mock-cheese was the right consistency before she could sound calm. "Did she say anything else?"

"Oh, not much. She wanted to visit and offer her support, but her schedule just couldn't allow it. Her business has taken off in the last few years. She's a food blogger now, did I tell you that? Well, she started as that and then turned it into so much more. I'll get you a copy of her new cookbook. It's coming out next week."

Alice hoped the wordless noise she made sounded interested at the idea. She now remembered the woman from past social gatherings, distinguishable from the rest of Denise's friends only through the extra effort she put into the food when hosting a party. Alice wondered whether Vanna had even remembered she existed, much less expected her to be more than human. The thought somehow made her angrier. "Does she still live in the area?"

"No, she moved to Texas a few years ago. What was it called... Fort Worth. I think it's by Dallas, or maybe Houston. One of the bigger cities anyway." Then Denise saw that she was scraping the cheese from the blender. "That looks perfect! Now we just have to layer it all together. Here are the crusts."

They were flat, dark green, and slightly pulpy looking. Alice winced for Colton's sake.

As if sensing the turn of her thoughts, Denise brought him up while they began assembling the pizzas. "It's so nice of Colton to help with the fan. He's been a rock for our family since this all happened. Even your father is warming up to him. I don't think he'll have any objection at all to the wedding."

Alice blinked. "The wedding? What wedding?"

"Yours, whenever it happens. It's obvious that you're both very serious about each other." At Alice's silence, she looked over. "Aren't you?"

"Yes, but..." Alice struggled to explain how a ceremony seemed so inconsequential compared to what they had already fought through together. "It's just not on our minds right now."

"Maybe not, but it's a natural progression for many people. Your father and I have gone to so many in the past year, and most of them have been for couples about your age. People settle into the life they've made for themselves, find a loving partner, and feel ready to move on from there. There's nothing holding you back."

Alice could only stare while her stepmother spread the cheese over the sauce.

"Holding her back from what?" said her father, stepping into the kitchen. He looked tired but relaxed, and obviously hadn't caught the rest of their conversation.

Denise didn't enlighten him. "All done with work? Good, you can help me finish the pizzas so Alice isn't stuck in the kitchen."

"I don't mind," she started, but her parents waved her off.

"Go tell Fleur to gather up her homework," said Denise. "Dinner will be on the table in ten minutes."

As Alice approached the dining room, she saw that Colton and Fleur still sat at the table. Colton had leaned back in his chair, arms folded and book thrown aside, as if he hadn't needed more than a glance through it. Fleur was just the opposite, scribbling in her notebook with the same concentration that filled her words. "I think I'm good. The only thing I don't get is why Shakespeare put a play in the play. Is it a commentary about how all the characters are performing to each other to cover up their lies and schemes?"

Colton's gaze unerringly found Alice as she stopped in the doorway, but he answered without a pause. "More because the drunks in the audience couldn't remember what happened back at the beginning."

Fleur nodded, looking satisfied. "Thanks. I think I'll be able to pass now."

Just as Alice was about to mention dinner, her sister's face suddenly changed, and she started fidgeting with her pen.

Colton noticed it, too. "What?"

With her back to Alice, Fleur couldn't see that she was right there. "Is Alice all right? She looks really bad. I think she's taking it the hardest."

"She saw more."

Even as Alice felt herself flush, both embarrassed and touched by her sister's concern, Fleur said, "The rest are all dead, aren't they?"

"Yes." His tone was flat and pitiless.

Her sister fell quiet for a heartbeat. "I never saw a body before. Not until that night."

"You'll be fine." Then Colton cracked his neck and rose to his feet.

Fleur scoffed. "Thanks for the sympathy. But weirdly enough... yeah, I think I will be."

Alice stepped into the room, then, drawing her sister's attention. "Hey. Dinner is almost ready, so we need to set the table."

As Fleur gathered her notes, Colton handed Alice her copy of the play. His mere nearness worked like a balm on her spinning mind, and she smiled as he glanced toward the kitchen. "It doesn't smell like pizza."

"It's vegan," said Fleur, not missing a beat.

"What?"

"And gluten-free. The crust is just kale mashed together and baked until it's crisp. There's also some marinara sauce, and a bunch of vegetables." Then she grinned at him. "You'll be fine."

Alice bit her lip to keep her smile from growing. When her sister was out of earshot, she murmured, "Thanks for helping her."

He shrugged it off, stroking up her back with surprising gentleness. "They're all fine."

It was a sentiment reinforced by the sight of her family settling around the table with their pizza slices. Her father still looked tired, and every time Denise and Fleur spoke to each other, the words felt stiff and careful, but the first signs of recovery were there.

No lingering shadows haunting their thoughts. No savage questions that bit without relief. They had left the forest without taking anything except their memories, and even those were wrapped in the peace of knowing it was all over. Alice felt glad for them, very much so. And yet... she had never felt more isolated from her family. They were ready to move on. She wasn't.

Stars winked far above when they finally left for home. Alice sank back in her seat, relieved that the cab of Colton's truck had very little light. She already felt too exposed, too raw, and the shelter of night was a small relief. She couldn't bring herself to speak until they reached the highway. "Dinner wasn't that bad. As long as you didn't think of it as pizza."

A twitch of disgust was his only response, but she still sensed his attention and still remembered her promise to open up once they were alone. It made her entire body feel like a live wire, and she switched on the radio to distract herself.

"Hey, hey, hey, it's Johnny Kicks and the Rattler, coming to you live to shake up your Saturday night. And boy, have we got something to send shivers all over your body. Tell us about it, Rattles."

"You know those people missing somewhere in the Sierra National Forest? And how two were found really fast? The weird thing is, one of them has done this before. Alice Corrigan. Remember her? Maybe not if you're too young to buy a drink for your date, because it was twenty years ago when her mother dumped her in the forest and disappeared. She spent three days there and had to eat crickets to survive. Pretty creepy, right? Call in with your wildest theories about why this keeps happening to her, and we'll bless the one we like best with two—TWO—tickets to the Skyhorse concert happening next week at the—"

Alice snapped off the radio again, her breath coming quick and hard. Colton's hand found her thigh and squeezed it. Her fingers clung to his as she fought not to cry or scream.

"I am so sick of people thinking they have all the answers when they don't know a fucking thing," she said in a low voice.

In the darkness of the cab, she sensed Colton turning to her, but only dropped her face into her hands and muttered, "I just want to be home. Please."

That drew a low growl from him, but neither of them spoke for the rest of the drive.

Once they parked and got inside, Alice heard the metallic slam of the large deadbolt Colton had installed. Locking into place. Locking the rest of the world out. Before she could switch on the lights, he caught her shoulders from behind and steered her into the bedroom, the air between them now thick as tar.

Moonlight shone through the windows, too soft and diffuse to reveal his face as he gently but unmistakably pushed her to sit on the bed. Then he sat beside her and said, "Enough. Talk to me. Whatever it is, I'm not letting you do this to yourself another night."

Her next breath was a slow sigh—a week's worth of strain slipping out of her. "The reason why I haven't opened up at all is because there's no way to fix what's bothering me. There's no way to find answers to the questions I have about my mother. No one will ever know or find out."

Then she smiled a little despite the burning in her eyes, reaching out to stroke the side of his face. Her fingers rasped against the day's growth of stubble. "Not even you. It's impossible."

At that, he tilted his head. The moonlight caught the color in his eyes, brightened them into something piercing. "Even if there's no answer, I can make you feel better in other ways."

It drew a small laugh out of her. "I could definitely use some stress relief. You probably could, too."

This growl of his was much different from the last one she'd heard. It felt like velvet against her skin as he pulled her onto his lap, noses brushing, hearts pounding. Then he caught a handful of her hair and pulled her head back to expose her throat. At the first scrape of his teeth, a shudder ran throughout her body, as bone-deep and exquisite as when she changed into her fur.

"I'm sorry," she murmured. "For this past week, I mean."

"No more apologies." His tongue pressed against her pulse with each word. Then he tore open her shirt with a jerk of his free hand, and she started gasping instead as that dangerous mouth found her breasts.

It wasn't long before he pinned her to the bed, fully dressed even as her clothes lay in shreds around her body. She waited, open and eager. Sweat prickled at the backs of her knees and against her neck even as the slickness on her breasts cooled with each breath, leaving her nipples hard and aching. He watched her writhe beneath him, the feral light in his eyes now wry.

She recognized that look and managed to say, "You're going to tease me, aren't you?"

He almost smiled before leaning in to flick his tongue against her nipple. The brief hint of heat and softness left her arching for more against the firm pressure of his hands. He only licked the salt from the skin over her ribs, ignoring how she twisted and offered him her nearest breast instead.

Eventually, he kissed up along her throat again, working his hips against hers in a slow, hard rhythm. The roughness of his jeans against her exposed, swollen cunt left her panting against his mouth. Then he shifted enough to put some of the pressure directly against her aching clit. Sweet heat filled her full, pushed her to the edge as she began to shake.

A heartbeat before she climaxed, he pulled back again. She almost howled in frustration while pushing herself up on her elbows, watching him strip to his skin. He was always feral, inhuman, but now he looked completely wild, the muscles in his chest and stomach covered in a light sheen of sweat, and his hard cock thick and throbbing as he stretched over her again.

She was greedy, wanting more than the brush of his erection against her thigh, wanting more than the cool air playing with the wet heat of her cunt. He just continued to tease, easing his cock along the planes of her body to drive her further into a frenzy. She felt the tip of the head against her stomach, soft as velvet, and the weight of the shaft, pulsing and hot. A thrust of his hips left her jerking against the sensation of him skimming over her skin, stoking an agonizing anticipation of its full length inside her.

Just when she thought she would pass out from sheer need, he straightened up, pulling her with him. She felt the lips of her cunt part as she straddled his lap, felt his hand catch her jaw and draw her close. She moaned into his mouth, already shifting her hips for the best angle, but he teased her again by pushing a hand between them.

She whined as his fingers slid along her slick lips, feather-light despite his rough kiss. Her own hands curled against the hard planes of his chest, running past the dusting of hair to find his lean stomach, delighting in the strength of the muscles there.

The heat of his mouth found her throat just as his thumb pressed in, and her body felt like it was on fire as she panted raggedly at the ceiling. His teeth caught her when she would have floated away, hands moving to her hips and bringing her onto his cock with one hard thrust. Her voice rose into something raw and frantic. Skin slick, fingers digging into his shoulders, she worked her hips with his, following his rhythm. Letting him take her to a place where fear didn't exist and agony was nothing more than primal pleasure.

She was limp long before he finished, the delicious friction of his cock driving her breaths quick and fast, begging for things she couldn't even name. His climax was quiet, a growl against her neck that pushed her into another of her own. Afterward, she turned her face into the comforting warmth of his throat, not wanting that hollowness to slip back inside her. "Don't pull out," she whispered. "Not yet."

He didn't, instead kissing the salt from her breasts, the movements of his mouth now slow and soothing.

Once her breathing slowed, the words slipped out easy and free, as slack as her body. "I always just wanted to know why she left us. An answer of any kind, even if it wasn't one I liked. Because if I knew why, then..."

She trailed away as the rest of it throbbed within her. Painful, insistent, old as a scar. Even in the dark, she blushed to reveal this out loud, to expose it to the monster that had tasted every inch of her, to the wolf she trusted her heart to. "If I knew why, then maybe the fear of loss wouldn't hurt me anymore. Or control me. Maybe I would know what to do whenever I was threatened by it again."

A dangerous jaw nuzzling against her cheek. A rasp of a voice stirring her hair. "You're thinking about the coven."

"Yes, and I'm so angry. They almost took my family, and what happened? They just slipped away, leaving even more questions behind. I'm glad my family is taking it so well. I really am. But I don't understand how they can just let it go. My father told me it's easier to live with the questions instead of the answers, but I can't believe that. I want each one of those witches to explain themselves. I want to find out why they did this."

"What's stopping you?" Then he tasted at the skin of her neck.

When she felt the edges of his teeth, she arched into them. "It seems too dangerous."

"I've hunted worse things than a coven. I'd keep you safe."

"I meant for you."

There was a rumble of a laugh against her. "Nothing's dangerous to me."

"Colton." She shifted enough to run a hand down his chest, fingers still sure of where the wound had been. "We met because a bullet badly hurt you. And the scar tissue is gone because a fire burned you alive."

"I was different then." His voice held a certain flatness that appeared whenever he wasn't about to explain himself further. "Believe me, I remember how to tear through this other world."

As she licked her lips, searching for some other excuse to use, some other rational argument to quell the hurt, and horror, and bloodthirst simmering in her heart, he caught her by the chin and gave her a long, lingering kiss. "Alice. Don't leash yourself."

She nodded and released a shuddering sigh, fingers tracing whatever parts of him she could reach. Worshipping his power and steadiness.

"What do you want?" said the nightmare creature that now held her close, the shadow that had slipped into her life and shown her a world where she need not be meek, and frightened, and hopeless.

Her answer was soft yet sure. "I want to continue the hunt."

CHAPTER EIGHT

The Hunt Begins

Alice glanced up from her phone and scanned the surrounding lines of traffic. Even though they remained unmoving, the navigation app repeated directions to take an exit nowhere in sight, its artificial voice somehow sounding annoyed. In the distance loomed overpasses, miles of concrete crossing over each other at dizzying heights. Construction cranes could also be seen, ponderous and stark while lifting their loads through an overcast sky. The metallic echo of their efforts blended into the rumble of idling engines.

"It's weird," she said, looking down again. "The map doesn't show any roadwork ahead."

Colton seemed undisturbed, hand easy on the wheel as they inched along. "Some part of I-35 is always being repaired."

She scrolled further along the map's route. The blue lines marking the highway snarled into what looked like a plate of spaghetti. "I think the directions are screwed up as well. It says we should be able to turn off right here."

"35 never follows rules either. It'll get better when we reach 20."

She shook her head and closed the app. "I'm glad you know where to go, because this thing doesn't."

The comment drew an amused glance, but for the next few miles, they both fell quiet. His silence held the sureness of an experienced hunter, the calm of having done this many times before. Hers was electric, charging the air into something hot and sharp despite the country ballad playing softly on the radio.

She hadn't known what to expect on her first visit to Texas, but the sheer breadth of it surprised her as much as the humidity it breathed. The sky stretched low and wide. The land on either side of the highway sprawled flat and endless. Striking differences from the rugged ridges of forest back home, but she found herself relishing them all the same.

"Enjoying yourself?" said Colton, suddenly, his gaze remaining on the road.

Still rare, the act of him speaking unprovoked. Still startling. She laughed to cover up her surprise. "I guess I am. It's interesting to see new things. I've never been in a place where pickups outnumber cars on the road, or where the sun looks so small. It doesn't seem as bright as in California."

Then she tugged at her seat belt, feeling as if her entire rib cage vibrated against it, as if her heart would surge until she could shift into her fur and run through this odd land, trying to find its end. "It's strange, because I've traveled before. I was with Magdalene on her biggest publicity tours, and before my father married Denise, I sometimes went with him on business trips abroad. But it also feels like I haven't seen much of the world at all. That I only sat in hotel rooms or convention centers and tried being on my best behavior instead of exploring what was around."

"That won't happen this time." His hand lightly squeezed hers, as much of a promise as his words.

She smiled. "What about you? You haven't needed directions once, so you must be really familiar with the area. Is it nice being back?"

"Sure."

When he said nothing else, she knew he was teasing. She managed a heartbeat before giving in. "Come on. You haven't said anything besides Fort Worth being 'easy' to get to. How do you know Texas so well?"

"Surprised you lasted a week without asking that."

"I wanted to see if you'd bring it up first. I think you enjoy dangling your mysterious past in front of me."

He almost grinned, eyes flashing with a feral excitement that appeared only on hunts. "I came here during the energy crisis in the 1970s. Texas was one of the Oil Patch states that thrived. All the other scavengers went to areas where humans were struggling. I wanted to be alone."

"Why?"

"When you're around them a little more, it'll be obvious."

She had been watching the trees and businesses flash past, amazed at how small and squat they seemed beneath the sky and its enormous clouds, but the disgust in his tone snuffed out her excitement. "Are you... will it be hard for you to step back into the supernatural world?"

He must have sensed her worry, because his hand squeezed hers again. "Whatever you're imagining, it's not that. There was no tragedy or downfall. I got sick of the chucklefucks, that's all."

"It's just hard to believe you're a complete misanthrope. If you were, you wouldn't have cared about a lonely girl trapped in a cabin."

"I wouldn't say I was nice to you when we first met." Simple words, but his deep voice turned them into something dark and rich. Thrilling like teeth against the neck, freeing like moonlight on fur.

Her own voice fell very soft. "No. I wouldn't have trusted you if you had been."

His hot glance sparked the air between them, but just then, green signs warned of upcoming exits. Traffic shifted in response, vehicles crossing lanes in fits and starts as the highway began to split. Colton swerved with the rest, guiding their truck through pockets of space until they turned onto the I-20 exit and left the confusion behind. Ahead loomed Fort Worth and its suburbia.

They reached the hotel and checked in without incident. Their room looked sleek and clean, beige furniture and floral decor invoking a bland elegance. Murmurs from neighboring rooms drifted through the walls, but there was a nice view of the street below and the city beyond. When she tested the bed, the slightest push of her hand made the springs squeak.

She smiled and raised an eyebrow at Colton, who shrugged and said, "Think that'll stop me?"

"No, just that you might actually break this bed."

When he approached with that silent stride, the muscles in her stomach tightened deliciously. It always amazed her, how much he could say without a single word. He moved for her in the way of a hunter, yet one with a hunger that had nothing to do with killing.

She sat on the bed, fingers already reaching for the fly of his jeans. She was tired and grimy from traveling, but at the moment, nothing felt more alluring than losing herself in him.

The heat of his skin only magnified her eagerness, as did his brief growl when her mouth moved past his hardening shaft and found the heaviness of his balls. Her fingers dug into his hips while she sucked at one and then the other, already panting. They were heavy despite him fucking her senseless the night before, and she began to massage whichever one wasn't in her mouth, loving how he swore under his breath in response.

She could never feel too filthy or depraved, not with him, and when his hand caught the back of her neck, she only rubbed her face against his sack, begging to be covered in every inch of his scent. Worshipping him with her tongue, her kiss, her breath.

He broke his silence to growl again, a deep one joined by his hand tugging her up to his thick, erect cock. It jerked at the first brush of her mouth, pre-cum already on her tongue as she took him in as deeply as possible. She sucked hard and fast, aching for the frenzy that she knew waited in his tense abs and twitching hips.

Salt and musk filling her senses, driving her arousal. Her own hips moved in the same rhythm as her mouth, stopping only when he caught the back of her shirt with both hands. Fabric ripped apart, slid from her skin. She moaned when he snapped off her bra as well. Then he started moving against her, hard thrusts that jolted her entire body, hand back to her neck to keep her face pressed close.

Yes, yes, yes. Her mouth couldn't say it but her heart did, each beat matching her primal need.

When he suddenly pulled out, she knew what was coming. She panted, arching her back so that his seed shot all over her bared, heaving breasts. Then she closed her eyes, lost in the sound of his snarl, in the heat trailing over her skin.

He was already breathing easily when his cock prodded her throat and then her parted lips, still hard. She smiled against its head before sucking him clean, finishing with a sigh.

She rested her cheek against his nearest hip, closing her eyes once more. Words came out easily, unfettered in this quiet, intimate moment. "What time is it?"

"Almost three." His voice sounded rougher than usual, perhaps from the softness of her breath against him.

"That's plenty of time to get to Vanna's book signing. And if we somehow miss it, or if she canceled the event, we can still search for her. Denise swears she lives here in Fort Worth. Unless Vanna lied to her. But her site bio said the same thing, so..."

His hand traced the curve of her cheek. "It doesn't matter what she does. We already know her scent from the ritual site. Once we catch it, we can follow it anywhere."

"Do you think she'll run once we find her?"

"She might try other things first. Probably bribery. Witches love that."

"Or she could attack us."

"Always possible."

He sounded so relaxed that she couldn't help asking, "How many times have you done this?"

"Done what?"

"Hunted people."

His answer was somehow both teasing and grim. "Too many times to count."

She bit her lip, now looking up at him. "And you're sure you won't get hurt?"

"Why aren't you as worried about yourself?"

Finding the honest answer wasn't hard, not when she still felt so delicious from her nipples growing sticky from his seed.

"It's only natural if I'm hurt doing this. I'm the one who wants to hunt them. It feels like a fair price to pay."

She didn't realize how terrible it sounded until his expression changed. Then he repeated, "Natural?"

"Well, that's what I learned to expect out of life. If I try to do something, I'll get hurt. Either because I'm not good enough to get it, or because I revealed that I wanted it at all. Pursuing things for myself has always felt dangerous."

"Because you'll be punished for it." His voice had grown very flat.

"Yes."

At that moment, he looked so wolf-like and wild that nobody would have thought him human. "You wanted me. Sought me out in the forest all on your own. How do you think you were punished for that? Through losing the pelt?"

She nodded. "It's pretty obvious as a consequence, isn't it?"

"No. It's not a consequence at all. Some crazy cunt wanted to keep you trapped. That's why it happened. You had people controlling your life until it seemed like the world, or fate, or whatever you could fucking call it, wanted you helpless."

"I know, but..." Then she faltered, feeling the truth behind his words sink in slick and unfamiliar, ill-fitting with the emotional pathways cut deep from years of living in fear. The fear had seeped away, but those yawning holes left behind still wished to be filled with what they were used to. "This all feels so new and strange. And I'm not sure I really have it in me. My teeth come out when I'm desperate or fighting back. I've never used them on my *own* hunt. Just to stop someone else's."

When she fell silent again, the weight of his body eased hers all the way onto the bed. His cock prodded at her lower stomach, but his gaze remained serious. "You're not helpless. You're not meant to be someone's trained pet. And when you let yourself be wild, you're the most beautiful creature I've ever seen."

She swallowed hard, sinking into the strength of his heartbeat against her own hummingbird-quick pulse. Something snarled deep within, something eager to draw blood.

"I'm ready," she murmured. "I'm just terrified of screwing this up."

"You won't. We'll be the dangerous things."

The rasp in his voice made her shiver, and she nodded even as he resettled his weight, pushing apart her thighs. Her breath quickened at the hot gleam in his eyes.

"When's the book signing end?"

"At five," she managed, already digging fingers into his shoulders. "And there's no reason we have to go there right away."

His hard kiss told her he agreed.

It was a short drive to the book shop, and any doubts Alice had over whether Vanna would be there melted at the sight of the window display filled with copies of her new cookbook,

Sweet Tooth. They stepped inside, sweating from the afternoon heat, and were greeted by a sign for the event.

Alice studied the image of Vanna smiling with a tray of frosted cookies, curious to see if she remembered the woman from any of her parents' parties. She did, and the memory of her laughing with Denise over mimosas on Sunday brunch mornings now made her shudder. "Her hair used to be shorter. Other than that, she looks the same."

Colton scanned the layout of the store. "It's being held upstairs. Want me to go with you?"

Alice glanced around as well. The ground floor held only a handful of people and had the hush of a library. Faint, classical music drifted through the wide spaces between the shelves, adding to an atmosphere that felt both open and comfortable. Nothing raked at her senses. Nothing left her uneasy. "Will she know you're not human?"

"Probably."

"Then I'll just go. It's better if she underestimates me."

He nodded, yellow tinging the green of his eyes. "I'll be close by."

A long line had already formed—mostly women Alice's age or older. As they all stood there, chatting lightly or scrolling on their phones, Alice grew increasingly aware of how casual she looked in her t-shirt, jeans, and sneakers. Every other woman in sight looked fashionable or at least well put-together: dresses or tops in bright colors accentuated with playful glitter or ruffles, hair styled to be as big and bold as their jewelry, and makeup that must have taken a solid hour to look as professional and smooth as it did. She began feeling glad she had packed more formal clothes.

As the line shuffled along, she heard Vanna's voice, as airy and sweet as one of her confections, but still couldn't see her. Copies of the cookbook were displayed within reach every step of the way, and Alice soon grabbed a copy and thumbed through it out of boredom.

She realized none of this was necessary. If she wished to merely remove the threat to her family, Colton would show her the quickest way to kill the witch without being caught. Yet that was only half of her purpose. She also wanted to get a good look at Vanna, and to give Vanna a good look at her. She wanted the other witch to realize she'd fucked up. Most importantly, she wanted answers.

It took about twenty minutes to reach the front of the line. There sat Vanna behind a rustic wooden table, her pink and white dress as frothy as sea foam. The colors precisely matched the cupcakes on the cover of her book, sparking sudden insight for Alice. This was all very important to the witch, to the point where she had planned out every detail.

Vanna wasn't alone. A woman sat beside her, one with that particular professional appearance that Alice understood at a glance. It had to be Vanna's agent, or publicist, or other key figure needed to boost her career. There to make sure Vanna did well in her first big public outing. It was something Alice had seen many times thanks to Magdalene and her literary circles. She was glad the woman was present; it meant Vanna couldn't just run off.

When it was Alice's turn to have her copy signed, she stepped forward smoothly, for once thankful that her parents' parties had taught her how to put on a smile even while her heart slavered.

"What's your name?" Vanna had already looked down at the book in front of her, pen poised against the first page.

"It's for my stepmother," said Alice, amazed at how pleasant she sounded. "I wanted to do this as a surprise. She'll really treasure it."

"That's so sweet of you. Her name, then?"

"Denise."

At that, Vanna's head snapped up. For one moment, her smile changed into something more like a rictus grin. She recovered quickly, voice growing warm even as her eyes remained sharp. "Alice! I can't believe I didn't recognize you. Why didn't you tell me you were in town?"

"Like I said, it's a surprise for Denise. I wanted to keep it completely secret. She's really excited for you." Alice's gaze flickered over as the other woman looked up from her phone, suddenly interested.

"You're an old friend? Good. We don't have many of those. Come to the private release party tonight."

Vanna cleared her throat. "Heidi, don't rope her into something she knows nothing about. Then she'll have to go even if she isn't interested."

"The more people who can spread this, the better." Heidi's focus jumped back to Alice. "I'm her publicist. We're trying to get the widest reach possible. All you need to do is post about the party on your social media accounts. We'll tell you what hashtags to use."

Hot glee rose within Alice at such an opportunity, but she knew better than to seem overly eager. "It sounds great, but I don't want to crash something that's private."

"We call it that because 'exclusive' sounds too elitist, but we still want control over who gets in. So far, we have about 60 people, all with substantial followings, but we still need that human factor. That sense of genuine emotion from friends or family excited to see Vanna realize her dream."

"Heidi," murmured Vanna, her excited expression frozen in place. "Are you sure about this? I don't want to force her into anything."

"Forcing her? She's a friend. Friends want to help each other. Right?" Then the woman looked at Alice.

Alice put on her most practiced smile. "That's been my experience."

A muscle jumped in Vanna's throat. "Seven o'clock for cocktails and confections. Give me your phone number and I'll text the address."

Alice pulled a drive thru receipt out of her pocket and offered it. "You can just write it on the back of this."

As Vanna's pen dug into the paper with a violence she couldn't otherwise reveal, her publicist added, "Bring anyone else who might be interested."

"Thanks." Then Alice took back her copy of the cookbook. "I can't wait."

CHAPTER NINE

The Party

Vanna's house looked gorgeous from the outside, a sprawling single story built from brick and wood. Clusters of oak trees and swathes of lawn offered privacy from neighbors. Traffic cones indicated where guests could park on the street.

Alice studied the property carefully while getting out of the truck. When Colton joined her, hand sliding down her back, she smiled up at him. "Ready?"

In his understated suit, he looked sharp and hungry, blending into the thickness of night as easily as when he wore his fur. "Sure. What do you want to do while we're here?"

"Get her to talk. Unless you think it's better to first—"

He interrupted her with a shake of his head. "Do what feels right. I'll tell you when there's trouble."

A waiter let them in, balancing his tray of empty glasses on one hand while bubbly music washed over them. Alice's first impression was of constant laughter, polished people, and colors bright as confetti. Both the guests and rooms had the slick look of liquor bottles or neon signs—picture perfect, attractive, and bewildering in such large groups.

There was even a small film crew and a photographer busy at work, obvious among all the sparkling bodies in their plain t-shirts and worn shorts. At the first click in her direction, she almost froze, but Colton ushered her along.

"Don't worry about it," he murmured as they moved past the first groups of people.

"But their footage..."

"Won't make it out. We're in a witch's house. She won't want evidence of us being here. We'll be blurs on any film, nothing more."

Before she could respond to the dark implications behind those words, she saw Heidi, who spotted them at the same time and hurried over, already frowning. "Don't look straight into the cameras. You have to seem natural. And don't worry about what to say, because there's no audio equipment. This is all for what will be a voice-over segment. Why are you wearing black?"

"It has some gold at the neck."

"This is a release party, not a funeral. And your makeup is much too nude. We want all the girls to have eyeshadow that brings to mind sprinkles on a cupcake. Go down the hall and into the second room on the left to see the makeup artist. She'll give you some pop." Heidi next surveyed Colton. "Put a smile on, sweetie."

Then she was gone, vanishing into the crush of bodies that waited in every room beyond.

Alice exchanged a glance with Colton, her brief amusement fading as a fresh thought came to her. In the roar of so many conversations, they had more privacy than if they were alone, but she still drew closer, lips brushing against his ear to make sure her words were heard over the grinding bass. "Is there anyone else here who isn't human?"

"No. She didn't have time to give us a distraction."

A waiter walked up with a large tray of cocktails. The rims were crusted with gold sprinkles. "Miss? Sir?"

"What is it?" said Colton, sounding like he dreaded the answer.

"A cake batter martini with frosting-flavored vodka and white chocolate liqueur."

Alice took one out of politeness. Colton didn't. "Any plain liquor around?"

"There's a full bar to your right, sir. Toby Buck is the bartender." At their blank stares, he elaborated. "The fella who's been winning all the awards in the past two years. It's amazing Ms. Moore pulled him away from Dallas long enough to be at her party."

As they drifted in that direction, Alice murmured, "If Vanna's trying this hard, why isn't she living in Dallas? It seems like she's already rubbing shoulders with the right people."

"It's a place for millionaires, and she isn't. Despite how it looks, your family's much richer." He said it matter of factly, without a hint of judgment, but she still looked at him in surprise as he added, "It's probably why she picked your sister and stepmother to be butchered. Jealousy over Denise being able to buy bigger diamonds."

For a moment, she couldn't imagine anyone being that petty. Then she thought back to the pitiful remains at the ritual site and winced, falling quiet as they moved through the rooms.

Despite the odd fits and starts to conversations as people reacted to the passing cameras, Alice still recognized the preening. She had seen it many times while out with Magdalene, a strange mixture of people trying to learn who was worth listening to and who could be abandoned at the first chance.

Yet while the parties and events on Magdalene's book tours had remained very restrained, more about networking with the right critics, editors, and other industry figures, this party of Vanna's seemed all about whipping up a reality as frothy as a marshmallow and just as calculated for easy consumption.

The largest room held a huge display of cupcakes stacked in five tiers, handwritten tags noting the flavors of each as well as the page number of its recipe in the book. All around it, people chatted, posed, and ate, pulling together for selfies and then parting again, their movements as rhythmic and repetitive as waves against a shore.

After that, Alice caught glimpses of the kitchen through its saloon-style doors, a seething pit of waiters fighting for space with the catering staff as they all added finishing touches to fresh trays of sweets. A towering cake decorated with lavender fondant and gold polka dots waited in the middle of the chaos, obviously meant for some sort of grand finale.

When they reached the right room, Alice was surprised by how restrained it looked in comparison to what she'd just seen; the only extravagance was a three-level champagne fountain set in the center. The bar itself looked quiet and comfortable, burnished in chestnut and gold. Syrupy liqueurs and sweet-flavored vodka filled rows of glass shelves, their bottles shining from the yellow lights beneath. The bartender was a man in his early thirties, laughing with a handful of women his age and rattling a chrome cocktail shaker as polished as his smile.

Vanna was there as well, glittering brightest of all while she talked and sipped at a cake batter martini. Something about her seeming so normal and happy while she mimicked the kind of people she had torn apart left Alice swallowing back a snarl. It took everything she had to keep a pleasant expression in place when she and Colton moved nearer.

Vanna waved as if excited to see her and then pulled her into a hug. As soon as her face was angled away from the nearest camera, though, she hissed into Alice's ear, "You little bitch. What do you want?"

Alice pulled back, feeling the spit in her mouth thicken from the urge to bite. "An explanation."

"I'm not about to abandon the party to speak with you. What's there to say?"

"Plenty. I have a lot of questions, and I won't leave until I have the answers."

The other woman smiled lightly. "Unless you're willing to make a scene, that's not happening. I've been at this longer than you. I'm better at it. What can you threaten me with? You won't have your dog kill me in front of my wonderful guests."

Alice stiffened at the insult toward Colton, but Vanna was already brushing past, infuriatingly smug. The sting of defeat replaced the churning in her heart, and she felt as deflated as when she had tried bringing down her first buck and found her jaws snapping on thin air. "I fucked up."

"No. It's good she's refusing to talk. Means she's frightened." Colton eyed the bar and the man behind it.

"She's right, though. I can't keep bothering her in front of so many people. She'll turn it against me."

"I'll take care of that." He ran a hand along her arm in a brief caress and then stepped away. "Keep chasing her. It'll leave her focused on your movements."

"What are you going to do?"

He only winked, the hunting excitement back in his eyes.

Despite the party's glamor, it soon proved as dull as any of her parents' gatherings. Alice always made sure she remained within a few groups of Vanna, who always made sure to stay out of speaking reach. Meaningless conversations rose and fell as she gave compliments over dresses and listened to tales of luxury trips abroad. Celebrity names were sprinkled in like sugar pearls, meant to be noticed and appraised in the constant dance of inciting envy in others and burning with it at the same time.

She slipped through it all, refusing to be distracted. Vanna's smile grew tighter each time their eyes met, and that was enough to keep her steady and focused as the party bubbled on. Waiters passed by with trays of mini cheesecakes and lemon bars drizzled with white chocolate. Drinks were replenished until the buzz of conversations grew into a droning roar.

The film crew appeared in and out of sight, obviously trying to catch as much footage as possible. Alice avoided being directly caught by their cameras, but she did overhear Vanna's publicist snapping at them as much as the guests. One in particular, a girl who looked a few years younger than Alice, seemed outright flustered, her face red against her video camera each time Heidi barked out an order.

Colton never appeared, but Alice didn't expect him to; she had recognized that look. Not many would call him playful, but he could be... it was just that his idea of play involved teeth.

Whatever he planned, she stuck to her part of it, eventually pinning Vanna into a room the color of butter. Alice had just offered to help a sick-looking girl, who admitted to feeling nauseous from taking so many bites of marshmallow-stuffed brownies for the cameras, when a crash and a collective gasp cut through all conversation. Then the screams started. Alice watched Vanna's face tighten before everyone moved toward the noise.

The glittering cupcake display was now a splattered mess on the floor. As Alice heard people ask each other if they knew what happened, she looked over to the other side of the room and saw Colton at the edge of the gathering crowd. There was a bottle of whisky in his hand, already half-empty. When their eyes met, he merely winked again.

One of the guests shouted that frosting had gotten all over her favorite shoes. Another, that some of the blueberries flying through the air had hit her phone and now it wasn't working. All other phones were angled toward the pile of crumbs and frosting, and Vanna was soon rubbing at her temple even as Heidi ordered the nearest waiters to start cleaning it up.

The film crew knew enough to stop and take a break. Curious about how much time she had left, Alice approached the girl she had seen earlier, the one who had looked so nervous. "How much longer could this take?"

The girl lowered the equipment from her shoulder and sighed. "We probably won't be done until after midnight. And that's if nothing else happens."

As soon as the girl was called away by another member of the crew, Vanna took her place, looking ready to throttle Alice. "You little—"

Alice interrupted. "It'll stop if you talk to me."

The other woman scoffed, but Heidi appeared then, silencing whatever else she might have said. "Vanna, Hubert Ritter is here. Where the hell is the 25 Year Laphroaig? You know it's the only thing he drinks."

"Why would I know that? Ask the bartender."

"He's *gone*."

Alice and Vanna both looked across the room at Colton, who swallowed the last mouthful of whisky and let the bottle drop.

A vein visibly throbbed in Vanna's neck as she turned away with Heidi. "We'll give him whatever we have. Jim Beam, Jameson's, it all tastes the same."

"He's the biggest name we could pull in. You don't give someone like that cheap liquor."

"Where are those people going?" said Vanna, her voice sharpening for the first time as a notable cluster of girls moved for the front door, some of them indignantly flicking frosting from their dresses.

"They're leaving," said Heidi, her voice flat. "That's why I was trying to find you. The champagne fountain has a plug in it and stopped running. The refrigerator broke about ten minutes ago. There was also a minor problem with the film crew, but I already resolved that. In my professional opinion, everything's turning into a shitshow, so have your face freshened up while I do damage control. We'll have the toast early while the cameras can still capture a full room."

Vanna seemed ready to argue until she noticed Alice again. Then she forced a pained smile. "Not ideal, but we'll just have to work with it, won't we? Give me fifteen minutes."

Alice considered trailing after her, but decided it was safe enough to leave her trapped in the makeup chair. Colton had slipped back out of sight and didn't reappear even when Heidi began calling people together. Unwilling to listen to any more bullshit, Alice moved for the nearest door outside.

It wasn't until she reached fresh air—humid as it was— that she realized how it had smelled overwhelmingly sweet inside, like being suffocated by cotton candy. For a few heartbeats, she stood in the grass and merely watched the clouds cover the stars. Then someone sniffled.

The girl from the film crew sat on a narrow cement pathway that bordered the house, the stub of a cigarette in one hand. She looked even more upset than before, gaze vacant and blonde hair tumbling free of its clip. From her red nose and eyes, it was obvious she'd been crying.

"Are you all right?" said Alice, stepping closer.

The other girl tried a watery smile. "I'm not sure. I was fired about five minutes ago. She won't even let me finish out this night."

"Vanna?"

"Her publicist. That lady is..." Then she shook her head. "No. I shouldn't say it."

"Rant away if you want. It won't bother me."

"I'm just really mad right now. That's all."

The girl looked too miserable to walk away from. Alice found herself sinking down to the damp cement next to her, uncaring of her dress. "Whatever her reason was, you couldn't have done anything that bad."

That drew out a bitter laugh, and the girl looked up with a mixture of defiance and shame. "I worked in porn."

Alice just shrugged.

The lack of reaction seemed to shock her. "You're not from around here, are you?"

"No. The heathen state of California." Then she smiled a little. "I'm Alice."

"Caroline." The girl's voice still sounded thick with tears, but also a bit steadier. "I got out of it as soon as I could. I'd hang around with the crew and ask how all the equipment worked until I learned enough to get into film production. I can use a camera as well as any film student. I thought that'd be enough to get into a legitimate career."

Alice could read between the lines. "But Vanna's publicist somehow found out."

Caroline nodded, looking ready to cry again. "Just tonight, I guess. She told my boss that they'll go to a different company if I stay. Vanna's image can't be connected to something so sordid."

Alice couldn't help it. She laughed.

Caroline's eyes widened. "You know, don't you? You know she's not as perfect as she appears."

What way was there to imply the horrors she had seen? "Do you?"

"Sure. I'm a local gal. Born and raised here. Vanna Moore's cupcakes glitter, but her business practices don't. When she first opened her bakery, she bribed whoever she could on the city's zoning board to make sure no other restaurant or coffee shop made it onto her block. The one that already existed closed down within a year over zoning violations. Nothing can be proven, but... Vanna has stepped on a lot of people's dreams to get where she is. Maybe I was naive to think it wouldn't happen to me."

After that, silence fell. Crickets sang. Clouds floated past the moon, heavy and thick with rain. Alice swallowed back her anger. She had already hated Vanna, but the hypocrisy to her actions added a fresh layer of contempt.

When she felt sure she could sound calm, she asked, "Do you have a way to get home?"

"I called a ride. That's what I'm waiting for. In fact, that's it right there."

As headlights flashed at them, they both rose to their feet. Caroline offered a final, faint smile. "Thanks for talking to me."

Alice nodded, wishing there was more she could do for the other girl. "It says nothing about you. I mean, why they fired you. It says a lot more about them."

"Maybe. But that can't stop the past from following me." Then she was gone, swallowed up in the dark as the shadowy car waited by the driveway.

After it disappeared down the street, Alice smoothed the front of her dress, hating how helpless she felt. Some part of her sensed Colton was nearby, and she looked up to find him walking toward her, silent and relaxed. When he wrapped an arm around her, she leaned into him, feeling herself shake.

His voice brushed the top of her head. "You all right?"

"Just impatient." After another breath, she looked up at him. "Let's hit her hard."

"Already did." Then he offered her a plate with a slice of cake on it. It had the same lavender fondant and gold polka dots as the one hidden in the kitchen.

"You didn't..."

A shriek went up from somewhere in the house.

Alice bit back something between a laugh and a gasp. "How did you avoid getting caught? People were guarding that thing."

He just gave her a sly look.

The front door flung open, bathing the lawn in yellow light. Within moments, Vanna appeared, looking ready to kill. "You asshole. You just fucked yourself over, too. The party is ruined. Over. There's nothing else to sabotage."

"Never said I'd stop with the party." Then he took a bite from the cake.

"You..." Vanna's body suddenly hunched, as if she were about to attack them both.

"Try it," growled Alice, some part of her hoping she would.

As guests began trickling out, already on their phones to call a ride home, Vanna straightened up again, still glaring. "Fine. I'll speak to you tonight after everyone's left. But only with you and only for half an hour. And if I see you after this, I'm going to—"

"Any threats and I'll kill you right now." Colton sounded calm, but for the first time he was truly looking at Vanna.

The witch made a hissing sound alien to her sparkling appearance. "Half an hour. That's it. Now if you'll excuse me, I have to convince my publicist to stop crying."

When she disappeared back inside, Alice felt her skin break out into shivers. Of fear or excitement, she couldn't say.

The house looked much dimmer and greyer without the music, confections, and guests. A few of the catering staff had remained to clean up, too tired to spare Alice and Colton a single glance. The lingering smells of buttercream and liquor followed them into back rooms that had been off-limits during the party. A home office. A bedroom. Sterile glimpses of a facade.

All ease had left Colton's movements, and Alice could feel his tension spike when Vanna waved her into a room that seemed more like a small study, sleek and geometric and colorless.

"Well?" said the other woman, when she hesitated in the doorway. "This is what you wanted, isn't it?"

Alice nodded at Colton, firm in her decision. She knew it was the only reason he allowed the door to close behind her. Impossible to understand the emotions tangling behind her ribs. They seethed like a pit of snakes, leaving her breath shallow and fast. Only caution rose above the rest, and she remained stiff and standing while Vanna sat in one of the beige chairs near the window.

"Don't look so uptight. Do you think I'd try anything with that monster of yours waiting outside?" A certain calm had come over Vanna, her previous fury softened to a cynical gleam in her eyes. She had changed out of her dress and into the type of fluffy, shapeless robe that Denise loved to wear.

A wave of disorientation passed through Alice, a sense of facing a creature that mimicked many identities without ever revealing her own. It left her words blunt, perhaps too much so. "Why not? You hate me as much as I hate you."

"A perfect stalemate." The other woman reached for the glass and wine bottle waiting on a nearby table. "In truth, I expected to see you again. We all felt Portia die."

Alice finally sat in the chair closest to the door, muscles tight, ready to lunge. "You don't seem upset by it."

"We hated each other to the point where I feel like I owe you a favor." Then Vanna cocked her head at her. "Even though you're here to kill me."

"I saw what you did to the bodies," said Alice, voice low. "You were going to butcher my family."

"They aren't your family. They're human. And weak as you are, you're one of us. What happened to your mother? She should have taught you some of this."

When Alice only curled her fingers into the arms of the chair, the other woman leaned back in her seat. "You're vibrating with rage right now. Are you aware of that? But you're curious, too. It's all right. Both feelings are very natural to us."

"I'm not like you."

"Well, I will admit you're extremely weak. Barely perceptible as a witch. I'm not sure what you could do even with a coven's power behind your will. You do know what a coven is, don't you?"

"You can mock me all you like. I don't care."

At that, the smile faded from Vanna's face. A more speculative look replaced it. "You really are curious. What do you want to know?"

"What were you doing that night?"

"Our most treasured ritual. Summoning our king." Then Vanna took a large gulp of wine, the line of her mouth shrinking into something bitter.

"For what?"

"To see if he was ready to sow his seed. You don't look enlightened. Do I need to explain further? Fine. Portia offered her daughter in the hopes he would find her acceptable. He didn't. Portia looked even more crushed than when he refused *her*." Vanna laughed, the most genuine emotion she'd yet shown.

"But... if you're all part of his coven..."

"There's a difference between belonging to him and bearing his heir. Our king is very particular. Strangely..." Vanna paused and then laughed again. "No, you'll need to hear this first. It's hard for us to have children. We're so used to consuming things that the little body growing within our own often doesn't stand a chance. Most pregnant witches have to feed constantly to bring their baby to term."

"You mean, on people?" whispered Alice.

"Obviously." Then she smiled again, a hot, vicious one that dared Alice to deny the implications.

Alice swallowed hard. "Always?"

"Always. It takes a very doting mother."

It felt like her heart stopped beating and shriveled up instead. Like one more breath would fracture her.

"What's wrong? Don't you want to know anything more?"

Alice just closed her eyes, unsure if she was going to scream or throw up.

There was a long pause before Vanna spoke again, her tone sliding into something free of mockery. "You know, a better way to learn answers is to find out for yourself. If you want to know what it means to be a witch, join our coven."

"Excuse me?" said Alice, looking up to make sure the words weren't further sarcasm.

Yet Vanna appeared serious. "You have a good chance. It's not like we hold any hard feelings over Portia. After all, our king didn't care about her."

For a moment, Alice could only stare. Was she serious? Could the attempt to stop her hunt be this clumsy? This oblivious to what her heart wanted? "You've spent all of this conversation mocking me for being weak, ignorant, and pathetic, but now I'm supposed to believe your coven would actually want me?"

Vanna's smile looked small and strange. "It's the very weakness to your nature that makes you a good prospect for our king. Ironically, witches whelped from normal men don't have any problems with carrying their children. It's as easy for them as with human women. You could have a real chance at gaining the most prestigious position in our coven as soon as you're introduced to it."

Alice started shaking, fingernails digging into the arms of her chair and peeling away ribbons of wood.

Vanna noticed, and her voice quickly rose. "Hear me out."

Alice just bared her teeth.

"Fine. Then leave. There are still people here. Are you willing to kill witnesses that heard you attack me? Do you have that ruthlessness?" Vanna matched gazes, unblinking.

Alice rose from her seat, trembling as she took a step back. "No. I'm not like you."

"Not like me?" Vanna stood as well. "Then what do you think you are? It's time to face reality, little girl. You're *exactly* like the rest of us. We took from the flesh our mothers fed on. The sooner you accept that, the sooner you'll realize it's simply natural for us to take whatever else we want."

Her heart hammered in her chest. Her bones ached to change. Only the awareness of the door slamming open and Colton lunging through it kept her still. Vanna recoiled at the sight of his bared teeth, her voice growing hoarse. "Witnesses. You'll have to kill them, too."

Colton just snarled, a thundering noise that filled the room. Yet even as the witch cowered, Alice managed to catch his arm. "Please. I got what I wanted. Let's get out of here."

His response was a terse nod, but his gaze remained on Vanna for a moment longer.

Vanna watched them warily as they turned to leave, but couldn't resist some parting words. "Then it's settled. The next time we see each other, one of us won't walk away."

Alice refused to answer, knowing gut-deep that as soon as she opened her mouth, the urge to sink her teeth into Vanna's throat would overwhelm her. She didn't speak until they were out of the house and alone in their truck, safely driving away. "Well. I wanted answers."

When Colton offered his hand, she clutched at it, feeling like it was the only thing keeping her from being swept away.

After miles of silence, she finally said, "How much did you overhear?"

"Enough." His fingers flexed against hers. "Witches know how to twist things. She knew it was hurting you."

"But it *is* true, isn't it?"

"I didn't know your mother. Neither did she. There's no way to know what she fed on. Whatever she did, it says nothing about you."

A bitter laugh escaped her. "I said that to someone earlier tonight. Almost those exact words. Now I'm not sure I believe that."

There was a soft growl from him before she wiped at her eyes and looked ahead, taking in the angry clouds. At the first flash of lightning, Alice leaned closer to the window, some part of her wanting to get lost in something, anything. Then thunder cracked loud and low. "The weather looks pretty bad, but... do you mind if we drive around some more? I don't feel like going back to the hotel and being surrounded by people."

"It smells like nothing more than rain. You want a better view? There are plenty of back roads that will show you more."

She nodded, fingers tight against his, gaze fixed on a storm that matched the one in her heart.

Under those same roiling clouds, a naked figure squatted in an open stretch of grassland as if daring lightning to strike her. Vanna Moore looked very different from her party hostess role, hair now disheveled and clotted with drying blood, fingers curling against the worn granite of a gravestone. Whenever lightning flashed, the cross from a nearby historic church cast its shadow over her face.

She waited. She had called and knew the power behind her coven would respond. Not her king, no. She had lost her chance at his favor. But there were other things attached to the coven, other things that might be pulled close out of curiosity.

When she saw him, she remained still, giving away her tension through quickened breathing. The figure approached with the silence of a shadow, long and lean, panting hard enough to reveal sharp, white teeth. Even in the churning darkness of the storm, his eyes glowed.

A black wolf entered the graveyard, but a man rose before Vanna.

She smiled up at him to hide her fear. "I thought your kind couldn't stand holy ground."

"Don't believe everything you hear."

She stood as well, fingers digging along the hard planes of his chest in a gesture that might have been threatening, might have been teasing. "You better be as good as the hag mother promised."

"I am." Then he licked the blood trailing between her breasts.

She swallowed hard as he pulled her close but let his teeth replace his tongue. In between the stinging flashes of lightning, she whispered one final thing. "I need the girl alive and unbroken. She might be precious."

CHAPTER TEN

A Challenger

The thunderstorm above had spent itself, nothing more than a film of clouds and the smell of ozone. The one in Alice's heart, however, continued to rage. She trembled despite her exhaustion, limbs tightening each time her mind circled back to what Vanna had said.

In the darkness, Colton was hardly more than eyes intent on her face and a hand warm against her own. Silent. At ease in his ability to wait in the shadows without having to fear whatever else might hide there. Patient as only a hunter can be.

She didn't want to talk—no words could crystallize how she felt at that moment—but sitting there in silence somehow felt worse. "I didn't expect easy answers, but I thought they'd bring some form of closure. Or that I'd understand more about myself. Instead, it feels like I know less than ever. This is all starting to feel like a bad decision. *My* bad decision. I'm sorry."

"Never apologize. Not to me."

"I know. I'm just so angry, and confused, and scared."

She felt him move, sharp and sudden despite the small space of the truck's cab, as if ready to chase away whatever tried to terrify her. Before he could ask who or what it was, she added, "It's not just what Vanna said, but what she did. The way she threw a party less than two weeks after trying to sacrifice an old friend. As if it all meant nothing to her. And she expected me to do the same, acting like I was naive to be mad about her trying to cut out and eat Denise and Fleur's hearts. Naive... and weak."

Then she felt herself slump, a movement that stirred scents of buttercream and brandy from the folds of her dress. It was a sickeningly sweet reminder of Vanna's party, and for a moment, she had to resist ripping off everything until there was only her skin. "Maybe she's right."

"No." Colton's fingers brushed her face, his touch as charged as the storm-churned air. "You're neither of those things."

"It felt like it tonight." The truck's cab suddenly seemed too small and too familiar in the way it trapped her and held her still, and her confusion threatened to boil over into panic. "I need some fresh air."

Her high heels sank into the sodden grass as she climbed out and took a few steps, but she didn't care, closing her eyes against the sharp breeze. When she opened them again, Colton was approaching, movements smooth and sure despite the uneven ground. "You did well tonight."

If the words had come from anyone else, she would have taken them as sarcasm. As it was, her disbelief must have bled into her expression, because he added, "You got her frightened. Didn't lose her. Cornered her and made her talk."

She nodded but still glanced away. "I should have killed her, too, instead of waiting for a better chance."

When he only shrugged, she insisted, "You would have."

"I don't like people. It makes things easier." Then he stepped close, leaning in until she looked at him. As the stars emerged from the clouds, somehow bigger and brighter while the world dripped around them, his eyes glowed like the monster from the woods that he truly was. "What is this? Your scent is thick with shame."

Silence was still her first instinct, still her first attempt to shove away the ugly feelings squirming within her heart like parasites. Breaking it was its own agony, and she tensed against the reveal of her many vulnerabilities. "I don't know if I can explain it very well, but if you really want to know..."

"I want to know whatever hurts you."

Tears that had been held back now threatened to spill out. Not from anger or grief—not anymore. From the sheer relief of that brusque voice brushing her like a kiss. Promising she was no longer alone. "I don't think about Magdalene like before. Each day, it feels like I leave her further behind. But sometimes, I try to work out what first drew me in, maybe to avoid being fooled by a mask again. And what I remember is being so amazed that she didn't care about anyone except herself. It's easy to look back and beat myself up for not recognizing what that meant, but I really didn't. I admired how nothing fazed her. That she couldn't be hurt by other people or even her own feelings because she was so self-absorbed."

The words had streamed out faster and faster, spurred on by her embarrassment of her younger self's stupidity. In a sick voice, she added, "Well, it's still there. That horrible envy toward people who can use others and not feel anything. I had it while sitting across from Vanna tonight, even while wanting to tear out her throat. I sat there, and seethed, and envied because some part of me wants to be like that instead of always feeling so much, and being so damn sensitive, and... and weak!"

Her next breath hitched, and she had to stop. The burning in her eyes spilled over as she pressed her cheek against Colton's chest, her fingers curling into claws against the crisp lines of his suit.

"Alice." He stroked up the bare skin of her back, trying to soothe her shivering. "You're not weak."

Her reply came out as a child's wail. "Then why did my mother leave me?"

Then her body collapsed against his, shuddering as if bone and sinew were coming apart. Her cries were high and breathless, as lost as when she'd screamed for a figure who had disappeared into the forest and had never come back out.

The heart of a beast runs on simple mechanisms. To fight, to fuck, to feed. Throbbing urges, base needs. Even in the midst of her grief, the girl clings to such purity, burying her face against her beloved with the same reverence as kneeling in prayer. Perhaps the same desperation as well.

Her jaws can lengthen into a wolf's, can crack bone and tear flesh, and yet her heart will still flinch like a human's, will still question its inner workings in confusion over what is her will and what isn't. Sometimes, she feels like scar tissue has left her too feeble to act on anything. Sometimes, she hates herself so much that she can't breathe.

The monster that is her lover now pulls her closer. He's watched her without wavering, calm only because it's what she needs. His blood seethes, shaking off the weight of his years. His senses sharpen, ready to hunt something down and savage it. At times, she marvels over how he acts so calm and dispassionate, as if his ruthless nature is that of an executioner's —quick, cold, efficient.

It isn't. He's fast because he's hunted so much and for so long. He's indifferent because his kills are now small hungers compared to the urge to keep her safe. He's been tired for far too long and yet the mere press of her hands stirs his appetites, awakens his viciousness. Reminds him that he's still alive.

For her, he's willing to give anything, even the words he's so reluctant to use...

Alice's crying dwindled to uneven breathing before his voice grew clear to her, low and steady as he kept holding her. "There's nothing wrong with you. It wasn't your fault she left."

She wanted to believe that. With him saying it, she nearly could. "I just don't understand."

"Understand what?"

"Anything." Then she managed a bitter laugh. "Not even myself."

"You do. Enough to change into a wolf. Enough to know what you really want. That's more than any other witch I've met."

Slowly, she nodded, turning her face enough to look out at the dark grassland stretching in all directions. The sky once more seemed vast, endless with stars. The desire to change into her fur started as an ache that quickly grew into a heavy throbbing.

"And you," she whispered, and felt him tense in response. "I always want you. Even when everything else is too bewildering, I know that."

She took in a breath, ready to spend the rest of the night running by his side as a wolf, when his arms tightened against her. Then he said, very flatly, "The stupid bitch."

"Vanna?" The thick dullness behind her eyes from so much crying now evaporated in a flash. "Is she already coming after us?"

"Not her. She's sent someone else." He stared in the direction of the city. "Another vargr."

Shock shivered through her. Of all the things she'd imagined Vanna doing in revenge, drawing in another vargr hadn't been among them. It seemed unfathomable that anyone with the same wildness and hunger as Colton would take orders. "Do you recognize him?"

"No."

"We better leave." She twisted toward the truck.

Colton only looked at her. Even in the dark, his eyes gleamed. "We're not running from the fucker."

"But we don't know anything about him."

"I know what he wants." Then he did move for the truck, his hand gentle against her back even as a growl deepened his voice. "Whatever the witch promised him, there's only one reason he'd agree to come after us."

"Which is?"

His answer was a hot, meaningful stare. It left her quiet while they got in, but her pulse picked up at the start of the engine. "What's the plan?"

"Our scents are strongest at the hotel. He'll look there first." He drove calmly, at a safe speed, but his knuckles were tight against the wheel.

They reached city limits in half an hour, the truck's wheels throwing up water from the flooded streets. Everything glittered from lights reflecting off puddles and wet cars. At the sight of the hotel, Alice felt herself start to pant, bones aching to change into a form that she could trust, a form that she knew was dangerous.

Even though it was past midnight, the building shone from the many lights outlining its bulk. The site across the street, however, looked dark and isolated, a blot of shadows among bright nightlife. A chain link fence protected construction equipment and the rubble of a demolished structure. The sidewalk was blocked by signs, deterring foot traffic.

Colton parked there, eyeing the hotel in the distance. "He's already in there. Probably in our fucking room."

Alice didn't bother asking how he'd managed it. Colton could slip past any boundary he wished; she imagined other vargr had a similar gift.

Without any change in his expression, Colton leaned over to open the glovebox. He pulled out a lighter and said, "Get into the driver's seat and wait. I'll be back in five minutes."

She tried to sound calm. "What are you going to do?"

"Flush him out."

"What if he's friendly?"

"He won't be."

"Well, what if he's dangerous?"

"He will be."

"Colton." The sound of his name and the brush of her hand drove some of the hunter's edge from his movements, and he paused to look at her. "Don't leave me in the dark about things. Let me help. He can't be stronger than both of us together."

For a moment, the lethal chill left his eyes, but all he said was, "We're not the ones who have to worry. Trust me?"

It was the one thing she never had to think about, and she nodded, hands clammy with nerves.

Despite the late hour, there were plenty of people out and about. He slipped among them unnoticed, quickly disappearing into the hotel. For a few minutes, she watched and waited, fingers clutching the steering wheel. It was impossible not to think of the other times she'd seen him hurt, or of how vicious this other vargr might be. The construction site gave off a sour, metallic odor, stoking the sick feeling in her stomach.

Then a fire alarm pierced the air, shrill and insistent. Alice leaned closer to the windshield as people streamed out from the hotel's exits. First a few, and then many, milling around in confusion at the edges of the parking lot. Even from across the street, she recognized Colton's silhouette and felt her shoulders hunch, body ready to change at the first sign of trouble.

Yet he returned to her as calmly as he'd left, motioning at her to roll down the window rather than open the door. "Once he's out, he'll catch my scent and follow it."

A distant siren could already be heard. Alice scanned a fresh wave of people hurrying outside. "Do you think he'll try to talk at all?"

"Only to throw his weight around. He'll misread my scent and think I'm hardly more than a pup."

Before she could ask what he meant by that, the air thickened with a new presence. Hot as spite, aggressive and curious. Even Alice, who didn't have heightened senses in her human form, smelled it as a distinctive musk. Bloodlust and vigor ready to explode into violence.

Colton stepped away from the truck as the first fire engine pulled into the parking lot, its lights highlighting one figure crossing the stream of others.

He looked like a typical young businessman, well-groomed and well-dressed as if ready to sink into the city's nightlife, but Alice still felt her skin crawl. He moved too much like Colton —not with the heavy steps of humans oblivious to their instincts, but with the caution of something wild. The shadows around the street lamps seemed to leap toward him, flickering at his feet like flames, and the tilt of his head suggested he was using scent as much as sight to find his way. He had to be the other vargr.

When he turned in their direction, Colton let out a low, long growl but otherwise said nothing as the other vargr began to approach, movements smooth and casual. Unnoticed by others.

Alice realized she was frightened, terrified in fact, but reached for the door handle anyway, prepared to face him.

"No," said Colton, quietly. Then he glanced at her, and for the first time, she saw how thin his composure truly was, saw the killing frenzy in the darkness of his eyes. "If he so much as touches you, I'll go fucking nuts."

As the vargr closed in, Alice caught a better view of him. Lean and handsome, with an arrogant set to his mouth. Dark hair cut short and teeth bright and sharp as he grinned. "Nice little trick. She told me you had no sense of humor."

When Colton said nothing, just watched him fixedly, the other vargr stopped a few feet away and glanced at Alice instead. She hated the feeling of his gaze and bared her teeth in response.

"And she said *you* were polite." His smile changed. "The name's Giove. Remember it, because it's what you'll be—"

The rest of his words were cut off by Colton's quick uppercut to his jaw. The other vargr's head snapped back sickeningly. His legs wobbled. Colton grabbed him by the collar and punched him again, this time flush in the face.

It wiped away his smile and left blood running down that crisp, white shirt. "Are you fucking crazy? You don't even know who I'm with."

"Doesn't matter." Colton's voice had deepened into something completely inhuman. "You're not controlling this conversation."

The other vargr—Giove—wrenched against Colton's grip as he laughed, still incredulous. "Doesn't matter? They're the oldest coven in Europe. They survived the witch hunts."

Colton just slammed him against the construction fence, the squeal of metal highlighting Giove's yelp as he was pinned by the throat, barbed wire scraping at his neck and shoulders. "I'm only interested in the witch that called you here. Where does she want you to take—"

"Alice?" said Giove, the bloodiness of his grin both obscene and gleeful as he emphasized her name, turning his knowledge of it into a taunt.

Colton's next punch was a liver shot that echoed throughout the lot. The other vargr crumpled. "How the fuck are you this strong?"

"What did she do to get you to come after us?"

"What do you think? Anyway, it sounded like fun." When Giove's gaze flickered over to her, Colton snarled, a sound that shattered the air. The other vargr quickly looked away and spat out more blood. "Stealing someone else's cumdump always is."

This time, Colton's knuckles cracked bone. The other vargr howled, a ragged sound cut off by the unexpected approach of footsteps. Alice's head snapped toward the noise. Even in the darkness, her eyes picked out the slow, shrunken silhouette of an old woman rounding the corner of the blocked sidewalk, the squat heels of her shoes clicking against the asphalt.

"Colton," she hissed, recognizing the danger.

Giove saw the woman, too. "Help!" His voice cracked with fear. "Help, I'm being mugged!"

His face had lost its sneer, and his bloody, disheveled appearance looked truly desperate as he fought against Colton, who didn't even glance over while punching him again. The old woman stopped, shock clear on her face. Her fingers tightened against her fringed purse.

"No—" started Alice, aware of how sharp and broken the word already sounded.

Just as she threw open the door, a gunshot shattered the air. In the deafening silence that followed, Colton staggered and swore, somehow remaining upright even as blood welled from the front of his suit.

As the old woman fired again, Alice shrieked and lunged at the same time as Giove. She went to Colton, who had collapsed. Giove, to the woman, wrenching at the gun and going for her throat. Alice flinched at the third shot, her hands already bloody against Colton's chest as she realized both bullets had gone through the heart. In the uneven darkness, she couldn't see his face, but he didn't respond to her voice— didn't move at all.

The scrape of shoes. The smell of blood intensifying. She looked over to see Giove pulling himself upright and away from the old woman's limp body. The gun was by his feet, but he ignored it, instead turning in Alice's direction.

The thought of that smirk returning to his face sent her running to the truck, snarling as if she were in her fur. It felt like the bullets had shattered her and all her panic, leaving nothing except a raging, heedless creature that started the truck and stomped on the gas pedal. Colton's blood left her fingers slick on the steering wheel as she hurtled toward the other vargr. Tears trailed down her raw face.

Headlights caught Giove's stunned expression an instant before she slammed into him, crashing through the fence in a screech of metal. Her foot felt glued to the pedal as blood splattered on the windshield.

Then a wall of concrete flashed before her. The entire world seemed to shatter from the impact, the force throwing her forward and crushing her still with bone-cracking pressure. Pain lanced through her, searing and shapeless as the truck's engine hissed weakly and died.

She heard nothing. Saw nothing. Just sat there, panting and wondering how much of her was left. Before she could do more than blink at how the side of her head felt hot and sticky, a groan came from somewhere in the crumpled metal of the truck's grille. As chips of concrete settled on the ruined hood, the other vargr tried pulling himself free, pain and irritation mingling on a face cut from broken glass.

"That... wasn't nice." The truck creaked as he wedged himself free and fell back to the ground, crouching on hands and knees like a beast. Bone cracked as he shuddered, and Alice realized he was already healing. "You'll have to do a lot to make it up to me."

Her fingers clawed for the door handle, still numb from the shock of the crash. Instinctively, she knew being stuck in the truck was as good as being caught in a trap, and her mind turned frantic even as her movements remained slow and dazed.

"What did she promise you?" she growled, trying to hide her weakness. The door refused to budge.

"Not you, if that's what you're thinking. Though I'm definitely having you anyway." Then the other vargr pulled himself upright on the remains of the truck's hood, eyes already gleaming at her. Just as he reached through the broken glass of the window, an arm wrapped around his throat and wrenched him back, cutting off his snarl.

"Colton!" gasped Alice.

His eyes looked nearly black as he choked Giove, dragging him away despite the other vargr's struggles. There was a broken concrete pillar nearby, twisted spires of rebar sticking out into the air. Giove seemed to sense the danger, because he fought even harder.

Fresh blood ran down Colton's front as he shook off the attempt, twisting enough to throw the other vargr backwards against the pillar. Giove screamed as the rebar skewered him from neck to belly, trapping him like an insect pinned in a display box. Then he spat something in a language Alice didn't understand, a language that sounded old and forgotten in the humid night air.

Colton bared his teeth while twisting some of the longer pieces of rebar up, preventing the other vargr from easily sliding himself off the steel. He answered back in the same tongue, and Giove's face paled.

At that, Alice renewed her efforts to escape the truck. Within a heartbeat, Colton was there, ripping the door open.

"Easy." His voice seethed as he reached for her, strong and sure despite the dark stains on his shirt.

Alice could only stare, still panting as he pulled her out of the truck. When she tried to walk, her body refused to cooperate, feeling boneless and heavy. Something scraped and moved whenever she breathed.

"What hurts?" he said, easing her hands away from his shirt to examine them.

She insisted, pulling at his collar until the ugly wounds on his chest were visible. "Oh, God..."

"They're already healing." He sounded terse while running careful fingers along her arms. "Alice?"

"My ribs," she admitted. "It hurts to breathe."

Just then, police lights flashed somewhere down the street. So did flashlights.

Giove snarled, thick and bubbling. "Ah, fuck it."

Then came the wet sound of tearing flesh. By the time Alice looked, the other vargr had shifted into his fur, eyes glowing balefully before he disappeared into the night with his tail between his legs.

Alice's fingers tightened against Colton's shirt just as he said, "He's running. Given up already."

"Bastard." She barely recognized her own voice.

"We'll find him. He's not getting away without answers." Colton scented the air a final time, amazingly calm despite his bloodied appearance, but when he turned to her, she saw clear concern in his eyes. "Can you walk?"

With this kind of pain, she wasn't sure for how long. "Where are we going?"

"Back to the hotel."

"They might not allow anyone inside yet."

"We'll still get in."

Her heels sounded overloud next to his silent stride. Her panic at being caught by people who would ask questions that couldn't be answered soon congealed into exhaustion. By the time they used the chaos of staff, guests, and firefighters to slip through one of the back doors and then up the fire escape to reach their floor, the left side of her ribs throbbed with each step.

Once they reached their room, it was easy to see that Giove had gone over every inch, leaving their luggage in shreds.

"He was thorough," murmured Alice, wondering if there were any of her clothes left to change into.

When Colton didn't answer, she looked over and found him staring at one of her dresses, a black one that made the white splatter on it all the more obvious. A muscle jumped in his jaw.

"He jacked off on it," she said, stepping back. "Some kind of message?"

"Making his claim."

She nodded, taking one breath and then another to make sure her next words came out calmly. "I don't want to let him get away tonight. I want to keep chasing him."

They were at opposite ends of the room, Colton by another white stain left on the bed sheets, and she by the opened dresser drawer spilling her shirts. When their gazes met, he said, "How bad is your pain?"

"It's manageable. My ribs aren't scraping so much as cramping right now."

"You're probably already healing."

She thought so, too, but had to admit, "I'm not sure I could run or change into my fur. But I can drive. Or could, if I hadn't crashed the truck."

"I'll get another one." His voice gave away nothing of what he thought, and neither did his expression.

It left her unsure, and she quickly glanced away, realizing there was no time to sink into an emotional tar-pit with Giove still out there. "I need to change."

Colton nodded. "Pack up whatever you want. We won't be coming back."

After he left to find a new truck, she pulled out a pair of jeans that looked untouched. Her sneakers also seemed all right, but she had to settle for one of Colton's t-shirts. Her ribs burned as she raised her arms to pull it on, and once she was finished, she sank down onto the bed and shivered against the feeling—more painful than any injury—that she was very bad at all of this.

It was no trouble to leave the hotel again. She didn't ask where Colton had found the new truck, and he didn't offer. It navigated the still-wet back roads with ease, yet sharp focus filled his slightest movement while he searched for that invisible track the other vargr had left behind, somehow sensed by him as a fellow creature of gravedirt and shadow. The stars drifted through the sky.

Just as the truck's clock clicked to 3:00 AM, he tensed and said, "He's nearby."

Alice scanned the flat swathes of grass and mesquite, trying to pick out where a wolf might hide and lick its wounds. Then she saw a squat, single-story house in the distance, unlit and all on its own. Her stomach tightened.

Colton saw it, too, growling briefly while guiding the truck off the road, weaving through the smoothest areas of the land to bring them closer.

"Where is he?" whispered Alice, trying to pick out which of the many shadows would be the dangerous one.

"Inside. Feeding to heal himself."

The very simplicity of the words added to their brutality, and she swallowed hard, all other questions withering in her throat.

They parked several yards from the front of the house. Before Alice could get out, Colton stopped her with a brush of his hand. Wildness had returned to his eyes. "Let me handle him. He'll be reckless with bloodlust. Aggressive."

"I want to at least check and see if anyone's alive."

His glance suggested it was a faint chance at best, but he nodded. He left the truck as a wolf; she, as a girl with ribs that still ached. She pressed a hand against her side, wanting to change into her fur. Wondering if she could. Then the first hint of blood drifted to her, heavy in the air, and her concentration shrank to what waited inside the house. The front door was in splinters, and she wished she didn't feel so afraid of what they would find.

The black wolf went first, silent and bristling. Despite the dimness of the rooms, it was easy to hear the wet, ripping sounds of the other vargr feeding. To smell the metallic sharpness of blood and sour stink of terror. The living room revealed nothing, and neither did the kitchen beside it. That left the hallway.

Halfway down, the black wolf doubled back long enough to press against her, warning her into stillness. Her fingers buried into the thick fur between his shoulders even as the gluttonous noise continued. There was a body lying there in the dark, abandoned in its pool of blood.

A man, she thought, unable to see much more than the white of his undershirt. The black wolf slipped ahead again, and as she followed, carefully avoiding the body, she noticed one of the arms had frenzied bites all over it. The hand was entirely gone.

Light splashed out from a doorway at the end of the hall— Alice guessed it was a bedroom. The noises were coming from in there. This door had also been broken into, hanging feebly from one hinge. At the edge of the shadows, the black wolf's careful stride exploded into a lunge, and he disappeared inside.

Alice quickly followed, hissing in a breath at the carnage. It *was* a bedroom, with the limp body of a woman on the bed. Alice glanced over the slack face and exposed, glistening ribcage, and then at the vargr crouched between the spread legs, teeth red as he snarled at them both.

The black wolf didn't give him a chance to do anything else, bowling into him with enough force to send them both crashing through the nearest window. In the aftermath of broken glass, Alice shivered, unable to keep from staring at the body. When she finally did look away, her gaze found family photographs on the bedside table. In her mind's eye, Giove's smirk surfaced, stretching into a bloody leer.

Then the fury she'd held back all night came crashing down, obliterating her last thread of caution. Despite the weakness in her bones, she willed herself to change. She wanted her teeth, wanted to use them on the other vargr until he screamed.

Yet as soon as her claws appeared, something in her ribcage snapped. Agony flooded her full, and her yelp sounded thick, even bubbly. Her body lurched back into its frail skin, shaking and sweating. Despite the sharp jabbing that came with each breath, she slammed her fist against the door, wanting to howl over being so useless.

She fought through enough of the pain to walk back outside, unafraid despite the fresh silence. A glance around proved Colton and Giove both gone, the hunt now a distant chase between two swift wolves. The air felt colder than before. The stars looked as hard and bright as diamonds.

Then she heard a yelp. Not from where they had been fighting, but from around the back.

Alice followed the noise and paused at the sight of a doghouse. A chain rattled weakly, and then she saw the dog, slumped on its side near a cluster of bushes. It whined when she approached but didn't move. One step closer cleared her view. Revealed what the vargr had done.

She dropped to her knees beside the dog, hands moving on instinct from her years as a vet student. Trying to stop the bleeding, trying to stop the inevitable. When it looked at her, eyes wide with panic, her face crumpled. "Oh, honey. I'm so sorry."

Then she petted its short, thick fur while it whimpered, legs twitching in its final throes.

Deeper into the wild land, unseen in the shadows, two wolves fought. Both dark as pitch, both aggressive and going for blood, but one held the sharpness of panic in each movement, tongue already lolling from exhaustion. The second moved without fear, frenzied in his attack.

They were both bloody, but the black wolf seemed only sharper for it, ripping at legs, belly, throat. Bleeding his opponent, terrorizing him with each snap of the jaws. The other vargr panted harder.

A dodge in the wrong direction gave the black wolf just what he wanted, and his next bite caught a shoulder and pierced it. The other vargr snarled and snapped back, but the black wolf was faster, teeth meeting teeth.

A sickening crack, and the other vargr wrenched away with a scream, lower jaw gaping oddly. It was broken. The black wolf pressed in and bit again, intent on ripping it off. Unrelenting, savage, driven by the idea of the other vargr wanting to put those teeth to his precious Alice.

His opponent screamed again, breaking free long enough to flee. The black wolf followed, tearing at the other wolf whenever he slowed. When the dim shape of an abandoned well appeared, squat as a frog and still smelling of water, his teeth caught and dragged down the exhausted vargr, nearly hamstringing him.

Beaten, bleeding, his opponent somehow changed form, pleading through a shattered jaw. "Enough. I'm warned off, all right? I'll leave you alone."

The black wolf circled in silence, breathing lightly, utterly intent. There was nothing to suggest that this fight had even been hard for him. For the first time in centuries, Giove felt true fear. "Who the fuck are you?"

The black wolf's muzzle wrinkled in a silent snarl, the meaning behind it perfectly clear. *Talk or else.*

Giove panted against the damp grass for a few moments and then gave in. "Round Rock. I'm supposed to take the girl to Round Rock in three days. Drop her off in the back room at the witch's bakery after it's closed. That's all I know."

There was a thundering growl from the black wolf. Teeth were inches from Giove's face, red with his own blood.

"That's it, I swear. There's nothing else to get out of me." He knew better than to meet that fearsome gaze while adding, "Look, I'll just disappear. I won't say anything to the witch."

At that, the black wolf changed over as well. Nothing of the rage in his attacks showed through in his next words. "I know you won't."

Then he grabbed Giove by the neck in a choke even tighter than before and dragged him toward the well. The other vargr struggled, his panic filling the air and overwhelming his scent as he realized what was about to happen. "What the fuck are you —I just *helped* you."

The black wolf tightened his grip, choking the sniveling voice down to nothing. His own broke into a snarl. "I know what you would have done to her during those three days. Yet you think I'll let you go?"

There was a final, froth-filled insult from the other vargr before the black wolf pulled him to the stone rim and threw him in without ceremony. It was an old well, a deep well, and it took several seconds before he heard the splash from the body.

Despite his own wounds, he changed back into his fur without hesitation, running lightly, easily, intent on returning to Alice.

He found her behind the house, sitting very still while mechanically petting the body of a dog. Silent as he was, she didn't look up until he nuzzled at the tears on her cheeks. When he changed over into his skin, she just stared, fingers now trembling against the dog's fur. The scent of her agony matched the expression on her face.

"Alice," he said, very gently, drawing her hand away. "It's gone."

"And we need to leave." Her voice sounded thin.

When he nodded, she looked down at the dog again. "He didn't have a chance. I couldn't do anything for him."

The black wolf hesitated, never sure of what to say to this exquisite creature always so ready to love something wholly and unconditionally. "Because of you, he wasn't scared and alone at the end."

Her mouth trembled, but she didn't say anything else while he eased her upright. As they walked to the truck, she leaned against him despite her pain, finding comfort in his touch even as the rest of the world slipped away.

CHAPTER ELEVEN

Grandma's House

It was a picturesque inn they'd found, a historic country house with the interior transformed into modern-day suites, and their room was very nice. Big windows filled the air with buttery light. Fresh flowers added color and sweetness. Outside, trucks rumbled on the highway. The smells of hash browns and coffee drifted over from the diner next door. In the face of such a simple morning, the events of last night bewildered like a bad dream. Alice wished she could set them aside as such.

She knew her battered body needed rest; although her ribs had stopped shifting with each breath, they still ached, and some of the bruises on her skin were as big as her palm. Yet every time she closed her eyes, images rose up savage as teeth, ripping through her exhaustion.

The sound of the lock turning in the door broke into her grey thoughts, and she glanced up as Colton stepped inside. He seemed miles away from the vicious creature of the night before, instead just one man among many in his simple shirt, jeans, and boots. In the bright sunlight, his eyes looked very sharp and the fresh stubble on his jaw very dark.

Then she realized he had a white bakery bag, the bottom already stained with grease. "Donuts?" she said, surprised to feel herself smile.

He nodded. "Thought you might be hungry."

Lingering tension filled his movements while he sat beside her on the bed, but his attention felt easy and comfortable. He really didn't seem to think she'd done anything stupid last night.

When she made no move to open the bag, he said, "How are you?"

"My ribs feel better." Her fingers drifted to his t-shirt, all too aware of the new scars hidden beneath. "What about you? Are you sure you're okay?"

"I'm fine." Terse words, but they held an expectant undertone, a readiness to answer anything else she asked. When she merely nodded, surprise flickered in his eyes. "No more questions?"

She shook her head, quiet until his hand caught hers, gentle against the bruises on her knuckles. "I thought you hated explaining things."

"I do. But I like your curiosity."

The words drew another dim smile from her. "I'm just really tired. Maybe I'll try to sleep."

He studied her intently, then nodded. "Rest as long as you want. We're safe here. I took care of everything from last night."

In bed, the heaviness of her eyelids spread to the rest of her body. This time, a thick numbness protected her from the torment of memory, pulling her into darkness until it felt like her limbs were trapped in tar.

The oak trees appeared first. Ancient specimens, bleached as exposed bone, the bark on their trunks so withered that it seemed like wrinkled faces peered at her. Such attention felt suffocating, and she soon turned away, looking up at a sky as black as pitch. No sun. No moon. Nothing that could guide her out of this grim forest. She had to be in the shadow world.

Despite the eerie stillness, familiarity gnawed at her heart. The red, uneven earth erupting in rock and root, the gasps of space between the shrubs and sticks tangling together... this wasn't a forest she had ever raced through as a wolf. Instead, it lived in her nightmares, preserved itself in her memories.

This was where her mother had left her.

Light winked. Then she realized she was looking at the side mirror of a car, fractured but held in place by plants that had grown over the roof. The car itself was hardly more than a shell —paint worn away and windows punctured through with vines—and yet she still knew it. Of course she did; she had screamed in it for days, had bitten at the fabric seats like an animal.

A sick pit formed in her stomach as she approached her mother's car. In the mundane world, it had been towed away soon after Alice had been discovered. Examined for evidence and found lacking, it had then been returned to her father and quickly sold. Yet here it looked untouched, left to decay among the weeds and poison oak. When Alice ran a hand along the roof, it stirred up flakes of rust. The backseat still had the stain from where she'd once spilled apple juice.

She looked up again, unerringly finding two distant oaks that leaned into each other, branches twining together like fingers. She had stared at those trees for hours after her mother had disappeared between them, searching for the slightest hint of movement, for the smallest sign that she was coming back. She had waited, cried, and then finally kicked and writhed her way out of the car seat. Yet she had also stayed put, because that was what her mother had said to do, and she had been too scared to disobey.

Stay there. I'll be right back.

Standing there in the shadow world, a place she hated for exposing her deepest vulnerabilities to those who only wanted to feed on her fear or humiliation, she knew that whatever waited inside the dark mouth of that forest would hurt her. There would be nothing tender. Nothing loving. Just a terrible truth that would reveal and mutilate at the same time, used like a razor blade against flesh.

But what if she's there? Can I really turn away when I've always wanted to go back to this part of my past and learn what I couldn't the first time?

In the utter silence, her first step sounded overloud against the dead leaves. Her next was quieter, as was her third. By the time she reached the two oaks, her heartbeat overwhelmed everything else, hard and fast as she crossed the invisible line into forestland she had never been able to see.

No squirrels or birds. No insects. Just straw-colored grass scratching against her legs and branches catching at her hair and shoulders. It was then she realized her clothes were gone, and that dirt streaked her bare skin as if she'd already walked for hours. The sky gleamed like black ink as the ground grew uneven, angling upwards.

Just as the first wisps of mist drifted between the trees, something stirred at the edge of her senses. A murmur that matched her pulse. It urged her closer while she pushed past shrubs, avoided poison oak, and broke branches that blocked her way. She felt herself sweating.

Then she reached a point where the ground plunged down to a dried river bed, the worn rocks leaving each step treacherous. Even as she stopped, the voice cleared into one word repeated over and over.

Alice. Alice! AlicealicealicealiceALICE.

She looked across to the other bank and caught a hint of movement among a cluster of trees growing on a massive, rotting log, their roots weaving over its surface like a net. In the shadows of their overhanging branches, a figure shifted, the curve of a back becoming apparent along with bony shoulders.

Alice felt her breath constrict into something tight and fast, felt a question burn in her throat. *Mother?*

She scrambled down the steep earth and over the rocks, heedless and shaking. At the edge of the other bank, she paused, uncertainty sharpening her desperation.

The figure turned as if to peer at her, still hidden in the gloom. Silent until Alice took the final step needed to bring her to the edge of the shadows. "You found me at last."

Disappointment seared her heart like a brand. There was nothing familiar about that voice. "You're not the person I was looking for."

A chuckle. "That's life for you."

"Are you with the coven?" said Alice, but she suspected the answer even as she spoke the words. She sensed age and an odd, petty glee in the figure, not the dismissal and malice she was coming to expect.

"Them? They're nothing. Just some empty rituals and a grubby king. Although, I'm very glad you squabbled with them and made your presence known. I'd given up all hope."

Alice frowned, only half-understanding what that meant. "Who are you?"

"At this point, hardly anything." Then the figure leaned forward and revealed itself.

Empty eye sockets. Thin, grey hair barely attached to the scalp. A horrible grin made by exposed teeth. Alice found herself looking at a creature that was little more than a skeleton and some skin.

She swallowed hard, refusing to lose her composure. "I heard you calling me. You knew my name."

"Of course. Doesn't every grandmother wish to see her granddaughter?" Then the figure spread its arms in a grotesque mimicry of a hug.

Alice flinched back. "My grandmother died years ago. They found her remains near her cabin."

"So skeptical! I didn't say I was alive. But it's possible to linger beyond the body. To wait and hope for some way back. Or do you dismiss the idea of ghosts as well?"

A shiver ran down her spine as she thought of Magdalene. It flared into a strange panic at the idea that this really could be her grandmother. As her gaze dropped to the damp earth around the figure, searching for some hint that it was at all true, the smoothness of bone among rotting leaves grew apparent. Only a few pieces were left, stained with age and covered in teeth marks. They'd been gnawed on.

"I believe in ghosts," she said in a low voice. "And it's obvious you're a witch."

The figure nodded. "Year after year, I've wasted away while waiting here. Starving down to petrified bone. You can't imagine what it feels like to shrivel as the hunger digs in."

Alice jerked her chin at the scattered remains. "You caught something."

There was a moment of silence. The witch's jawbone quivered slightly before she said, "It was long ago, and not nearly enough. I'll always be like this unless you help me."

"I don't know if you're even really my grandmother. We never met. I wouldn't be able to recognize her, and I don't see how she could recognize me."

"You look like your mother. Especially the shape of your nose and mouth."

Something must have changed in Alice's expression, because the witch gave a laugh that sounded like a wheeze. "I see that's a sore spot. So, it's only her that you care about. Why not your old granny as well?"

"She *ate* people," said Alice, still shocked that every witch she met expected her to accept that, and easily as well.

"And your mother helped. At least until she ran away and became some human's housewife." The witch's voice grew sour. "I suppose you've turned out much the same. Who's ruling your life? A nice lawyer? A bank branch manager? I'm sure it's someone who doesn't understand the sweet taste of blood. Who just wants to breed enough well-heeled children to fill his house."

Alice stared at the witch, fresh horror surging. Anyone from the coven would have known about Colton and what he meant to her. This wasn't a trick. This *was* her grandmother.

"You sound like the others," she murmured. "Throwing all the insults you can and then expecting me to just take it."

The words seemed to infuriate the witch, for she lurched from the shadows, jumbled from the ribs down in the way of bones unearthed from a grave. "Are you scolding me? You, the little wretch living warm and well-fed while I'm suffering out here? You're as selfish as your mother. I called her for so long, trying to reach through to her little haven."

Alice met her grandmother's anger with a streak of her own, words tumbling out high and hot. "Did she ever respond? Is that why she left me that day?"

"Is that what you want? Answers?"

"Yes. I want to know if she's still alive. If she's been dead for years. I want to know what happened. I want to understand so I can finally move on." Her heart felt like it was being split in half, in agony from the possibility of finding out as much as the terror of remaining ignorant.

Her grandmother, however, had fallen very calm. The shadows in her eye sockets flickered as she said, "Help me, and I'll help you."

A strange sound came out of Alice. A laugh, she realized, brief and breathless. "Is that all it is? Just a trade in need?"

"Don't sneer at the chance like a spoiled brat. It's a good start to becoming precious to each other. You'll get your answers, and I'll build back my power."

Despite the stark differences, Alice was reminded of the preening witches she had already faced. As she watched the pitiful figure before her, trying to find some answer that revealed the roaring in her heart, she suddenly said, "I found the wolf pelt in your cabin."

"Oh? And what happened?"

"It worked."

For a moment, the raspy breathing stilled. "How?"

She didn't have a better answer than, *I wanted to escape.*

Her lack of response drew out an annoyed huff. "Do you still have it with you?"

"No. And I don't need it now." Simple words, but she suddenly realized the truth behind them, realized how her hunger didn't match the witches she had met. She wasn't greedy for the power of controlling the world around her, for making dead skins twitch with life or hearts throb with envy. She already knew how false words could be and wanted no comfort in ones that worshipped her. The brilliance of a crown faded to nothing compared to the freedom of running beneath a full moon. Her lust was her own, good and bad.

She found herself stepping back, stepping away, raw but sure.

Her grandmother hissed, "Don't be a fool. That coven can't give you anything more than I could."

"I'm not joining the coven. I'm hunting them."

"Then that's it? You'll just turn your back on your old granny and leave?"

"I'm not like you. I don't *want* to be like you." Then Alice shook her head. "Don't call for me again. I won't answer."

The witch's voice rose. "Do you think I'll let you go that easy? After what happened with your mother, do you think I'll suffer through the same thing twice?"

Something charged the air between them. Alice bared her teeth, skin breaking out into shivers. "You don't want me. You just want meat. I'm no one's prey."

Just as she turned around, ready to climb down the bank, she heard the witch chuckle. Her body tensed, but it was too late. The ground crumbled beneath her, tumbling her down toward the dried river bed. She flailed, squeezing her eyes shut against the expected pain of flesh breaking against rock.

She landed hard, breathless and confused at the softness against her shoulder blades, at the pressure of a strap against her chest and stomach. Then she realized it was a seatbelt holding her stiff and still, and her eyelids snapped open. She was sitting in a car's backseat, held in place while branches raked against the filthy windshield.

"No," she whispered, realizing she was in her mother's car. Her arms were caught fast by vines that had grown through the windows. She felt frozen from head to toe. Then she screamed. "No!"

Her grandmother's voice filled her ears, a disembodied presence that remained calm even as she started thrashing. "Blood returns to blood."

Alice just shrieked again, fighting against the restraints. "Let me out!"

"So much fussing. I chose my camp well. You're not in a place where anyone can find you, much less hear you."

She turned into a wild, heedless thing, snarling while clawing free of the seatbelt and tearing into the vines with her teeth. They bled like something alive, but she only bit harder, frothing. "Not again! Never again."

Her grandmother cried out as if in pain as Alice ripped her hands from the bleeding plants and wrenched at the door. When it wouldn't open, she attacked the nearest window with the same frenzy. The sting of sliced fists meant nothing compared to the brittle crack of glass. It shattered, flooding her with blistering light.

She crawled through without flinching, ignoring the hot agony of glass biting into her palms and scraping her sides, forcing herself forward until she half-fell, half-slithered to the ground. Panting, aware of the heavy smell of blood, she felt either sweat or tears run down her face while her hair fell into her eyes, blinding her.

Then her grandmother's voice cut through the air, sharp and shocked. "No. Not you. Not *you*."

Alice just shuddered, trying to crawl away from the car and the prickle of glass against her skin. When a scream rang out, thin and ragged, she only redoubled her efforts.

Then hands caught her, and now *she* was screaming, expecting the hardness of bony limbs, the pressure of rotting skin shoving her back into her worst nightmare.

"Alice. *Alice.*" A voice rough as a growl, a voice that her heart recognized through its animal panic.

She collapsed, now understanding what had happened, his name already on her lips. "Colton."

The world spun as he brushed hair back from her face, and then she realized he was leaning over her, that the softness of blankets and sheets pressed against her back. That she wore the fluffy robe she'd fallen asleep in, and that the ceiling above glowed with warm morning light.

A simple nightmare?

Yet the idea faded from her mind even before she took in his bloodied state, and how his pupils were constricted to pinpoints. Then the throbbing of sliced skin and the grit of dirt between her toes sank into her senses, and she hissed out her next breath while gingerly sitting up.

"Alice," he repeated, now stroking the curve of her cheek, and she saw everything in his eyes that he never put into words. Fury and concern mingling with a tenderness that made her ache.

"Was that really her?" she asked, knowing he could answer the question. Knowing that he would no matter how painful the answer might be. "Was that my grandmother?"

"Yes."

She stared at the clotting trails on his jaw and throat. "Is that her blood?"

His voice darkened. "I will never be gentle with anyone who hurts you."

It wasn't an apology, and she didn't want one. Instead, she started to reach for him, pausing only when she saw the fresh cuts on her arm. He noticed them, too, growling at their sluggish bleeding.

"It's okay," she said, and was surprised by how true that felt. "I'm okay."

He looked up from her wounds, his expression clear despite his silence. The killing rage lingered in his eyes, but she also saw a particular scrutiny that appeared whenever she tried to hide her pain and put on a pleasant mask.

"No," she said, catching his hand with hers. "I don't mean it like that. My body is hurt, but I'm not... not broken up over it. I'm too angry to be. No, I'm not even angry. I'm *furious*. She only saw me as something to use, just like the rest of them. I'm never going to get the answers I want. Not when they think they can use that to keep me meek and confused."

Then she did touch his face, running fingers along that dangerous jaw without a hint of repulsion, even when they came away sticky with her grandmother's blood. "I'm sick of asking questions, and I'm sick of being laughed at."

New intensity warmed his gaze. "Ready to use your teeth?"

She nodded. "They're going to learn to leave me the hell alone."

CHAPTER TWELVE

Recovery

Within minutes of returning from the shadow world, Alice realized her arm wasn't healing. Blood streamed from the cuts alarmingly fast, clotting the grime left on her skin from crawling through a rusted car and then damp leaf litter.

"It hurts more, too," she gritted between her teeth, trying to keep still while Colton studied the wounds. The towel he held beneath her arm had already soaked through. "Did she do something to me?"

"No. There's glass lodged under the skin. Your body's trying to get rid of it and finish healing." His thumb ran over an uninjured area of her wrist, warm and comforting. Then his voice turned grim. "I need to pick it all out."

Soon, she found herself staring at the gentle yellow of the bathroom walls, the floor tiles cold against her muddied feet. She had to sit on the closed toilet to stretch her arm over the sink while leaving enough light and space for him to work.

Two of the fluffy white hand towels set by the soap were already stained red and left crumpled on the floor.

"We might get kicked out for this," she murmured, while he took tweezers from her makeup bag. "Me making such a mess, I mean."

The lighter in his other hand snapped to life before he replied. "It'll be fine. I'll handle things."

As she watched him sterilize the tweezer's tips in the flame, she had no trouble believing that. Aware that he was almost ready, she turned on the faucet and adjusted it to a gentle warmth, not looking forward to the next step.

The water shocked her pain into something searing, and when he growled, she knew it had flooded her scent. Her fingers found his and squeezed tightly while blood and dirt swirled down the drain. Once the water ran clean, she sucked in a breath to steady herself and then looked down at her mangled flesh.

It appeared about as bad as it felt, fresh blood welling up to replace what had washed away. Yet she had seen worse as a vet intern, and watched unflinchingly when Colton leaned in with the tweezers.

Chips of glass landed against the porcelain, red and glittering. The smell of blood filled the air. Strangely, she grew calmer by the moment, the throbbing agony somehow easing the turmoil that had filled her full from the night she and Colton had found the remains of the coven's ritual. It was as if removing the glass embedded in her flesh also removed the fear and confusion piercing her heart.

Perhaps she wasn't ready to heal, but she was bleeding clean.

And the tongue that always felt so tender against her wounds? The teeth that tore at her nightmares? The wolf with his unrelenting hunts, his quick brutality, his shameless hunger? He was there with her, his fury filling the room while blood dried on his jaw.

A dangerous sight, horrifying to some, but she only relaxed, watching the last pieces of the shadow world swirl down the drain.

"It's all right," she said, softly, aware of his tight shoulders and simmering silence. "It feels better than when the glass was still in there."

He growled without looking up from the task. Among the old-fashioned decor of framed, cross-stitched quotes from the Bible, he looked like the wild beast that he truly was, rugged and seething and ready to kill.

She reached out with her good hand and brushed his face, unflinching against the dark blood. "I really mean it. I don't think I can be hurt anymore, at least not by witches. After facing my grandmother and realizing I was nothing more than fat and bone and opportunity to her... Well, I don't see how Vanna or anyone else from the coven could cut as deeply."

At that, he looked up with the full force of his attention. It reminded her of the first morning they had spent together at the cabin, watery light spilling through the windows as his eyes pierced her through. The shock of such scrutiny when she was used to the sting of dismissal. The thrill of facing a beast honest about his nature. The realization that he could devour her without destroying her as well.

Now the thrill felt deeper, sweeter, and she grew breathless when he moved his head enough to lick her fingers clean. "They'll still die screaming."

She shuddered but not from revulsion, wanting to feel that velvet tongue against much more than just her hand. The longing sharpened as he eased her arm beneath the running water again, this time without an answering spike of pain. The cleaned cuts were already healing.

"Looks like it's all out," he said, still curt. Then his hand eased over to her ribs. "Does anything else hurt?"

Yet she was already tired of being careful with her injuries and simply shrugged off her robe, the sudden heat in his gaze stoking her own. "Let's find out."

She was the urgent one, kissing the rough stubble on his chin and sucking at the red trails on his throat while he stroked the length of her spine. They were both filthy, the shower mere feet away, but she didn't want to stop touching him for even a second, pressing closer as he teased the dimples in her lower back. When his fingers ran over the curve of her ass and then pushed in, she gasped and arched.

Too much, too fast. Her ribs spasmed in the wrong way, and her yelp sounded more like a wolf than a girl's as she went limp against him, frustrated and throbbing.

"They were all right until I broke out of the car," she panted, while he eyed the angry swelling on her side. "It must have reinjured them. And the worst part is that it's my fault for hurting them in the first place. God, I can't believe this. I'm so stupid."

At that, he gave a growl that sounded more like a sigh. Then his hand rubbed her hip, slow and soothing. "One day, you'll stop believing all the people who told you that."

When she looked at him, startled, he added, "No hunt is perfect."

"But... I crashed the truck."

He shrugged. "I didn't break that fucker's jaw before he could call out for help."

The blunt words drew her gaze to his shirt, and when she tugged at it in a silent request, he pulled it off. So close to each other, the heat of his skin was palpable, but it wasn't lust that ran through her as she hesitantly touched the new scars on his chest. They looked much like the one that had brought them together.

"Perfect heart shot," he said, voice rumbling against her fingers. "It's always the little old ladies."

A certain dark amusement filled his words, as if he'd been shot too many times to feel anything else. Yet when she leaned forward and kissed the marks, he tensed, as if softness stunned him more than any form of brutality.

"I was so scared when that happened," she whispered.

"I know. I could smell it while getting you out of the truck."

"No, it wasn't from facing Giove."

His eyes grew lethal at the sound of the other vargr's name, but he said nothing as she continued. "You were shot. The last time that happened, you bled out. You couldn't even move."

"I was different then." The terse answer was softened by the brush of his lips against hers. "There wasn't much to me. There was even less when we met."

An obvious evasion. A familiar reluctance to reveal why his invincibility had grown over time. It didn't scare her, his secrecy, but sometimes she wondered at how little she knew about his past. "I think you like teasing me with non-answers."

His laugh was brief, hardly more than a huff of breath. Then he leaned in to erase the last inch of space between them. His kiss was hungry and hot, raw in the best way possible. When they broke off, the scrape of his teeth lingered on her lips, as delicious as the new roughness in his voice. "No need to worry about me."

Then he brushed her ribs. "Or these. I got the fucker to talk a little. We have three days before the witch knows something went wrong with her plans. With food and sleep, it'll be enough to heal."

In the shower, the hot water felt as luxurious as his attention while they washed the blood and dirt off each other, and her frustration with her ribs flared once more. At the first brush of his cock against her hip, her lust surged into something as insistent as the pain, and she found herself bracing against the slick, marble walls in an unmistakable signal, hair in her face and breath quick and harsh.

He only nipped at her neck. "Not yet. The thrusting would break them again."

She groaned, amazed at his self-control. "I know. It's a bad idea beyond belief. It's just... I need to feel you against me. In me."

"You will." His tongue somehow felt hotter than the steam reducing her view of him to a shadow.

"No, not in a few days. I need it now."

"Alice. Do you think you're the only one desperate to fuck?" Then he shifted enough to push his erect cock against her. When she stroked it, it jerked against her grip, thick and throbbing. "As soon as we're finished cleaning up, I'll be all over you."

By the time they were out of the shower, her need had worked itself into a slow burn that sparked at his every touch. Even with the bed bloody and dirty from her return from the shadow world, she was more than ready to use it.

He stopped her with a jerk of his head toward the vintage, backless couch set near the fireplace. Made of dark oak and upholstered in red velvet, it looked sturdy yet was as narrow as a bench, one end gently sloping up to mimic the support of a pillow behind the head.

She glanced at it, her hand already sliding down to stroke his balls. "We can't both lie on that."

"No. Just you." Then he gave her a rare smile, even rarer because it was playful, his tongue licking at one of his upper canines.

Fresh lust filled her when she understood the implication. Her skin felt flushed as she settled against the soft fabric, ribs quiet. The chill of water droplets lingering on her breasts and stomach faded beneath the heat of his gaze. Even in the gentle lamplight, he looked feral, inhuman, and she licked her lips in unfeigned excitement.

His eyes darkened as he spread her legs, thumbs stroking along her inner thighs. Then he eased between them, crouching over her like a beast. The sight of him looming above quickened her breath, fired her anticipation into something scorching. She traced his arms and shoulders, then his chest and stomach, worshipping the strength in those hard muscles. Before she could reach his cock, he caught her hands and pinned them over her head.

"Later," he said, and then sucked at the tender part of her throat where her pulse beat hard and fast.

The sweet frustration of not being able to touch him was magnified by kisses trailing past her collar bones, and her nipples felt tender even before he caught one between his teeth and tugged. She cried out, voice thick with need as he sucked at the other.

Then she heard a muffled noise behind the nearest wall— the sound of a door creaking open.

"Oh, shit. Neighbors," she managed, suddenly aware of how living alone in the forest had erased all self-restraint.

"Do you care?" He licked just below her belly button, the rough stubble on his jaw inches from her swollen cunt. She suddenly felt very wet.

One breath, two, and then something howled deep within her heart, scorning all embarrassment and doubt. "No," she said, and spread her legs wider.

She felt him smile against her inner thigh. Then he licked her outer folds, the heat of his tongue shocking. When she jerked in response, his hands caught her hips, holding them in place. Keeping her from reinjuring her ribs. Driving her wild.

He was relentless, sucking and nipping until her breaths turned into gasps and her legs shook. The hint of his teeth pushed her somewhere exquisite. The tenderness of his kisses kept her there. Dimly, she was aware of begging him with his name, of her nails digging into the cushion and her nipples hardening into points, but with each heartbeat, her senses dwindled to the heat of his attention.

He didn't stop when the first climax ripped through her, instead squeezing her slick flesh to drive her into another. A sheen of sweat covered her skin as he licked at the fluids of her excitement, tongue slipping in deep to drive her voice high.

Then his teeth grazed against her clit, and she gave up trying to pace her reactions, letting his hunger and control drive her into the delicious freedom of being mindless as a beast. One release blurred into the next, until her insatiable need eased into complete exhaustion, until she could only murmur his name and feel him growl against her in response.

Her haze cleared when he pulled away, his absence shocking until she saw him rubbing his cock with fast, hard strokes. She pushed herself upright enough to lap at the precum trailing from its head.

"Greedy," he said, but sounded amused. His free hand brushed her cheek before his voice roughened into something closer to a growl. "Lie back."

She did, smiling at what he was about to do. And when his breathing changed, she found herself panting along even before his seed striped her breasts and stomach, depraved and thrilling.

Afterward, she felt light enough to float, a warm glow filling her full. Even her ribs seemed stronger, taking the pressure of each breath easily, without strain. He didn't even seem spent while tracing the curves of her body, relaxed yet intent. Absorbing her every movement as if he'd never grow tired of seeing her.

"Thank you," she murmured.

"Always so sweet." His thumb ran over her mouth.

She shifted enough to look at him and grew aware of the lingering stickiness on her skin. "Does this have anything to do with what Giove did to my clothes?"

His easy expression didn't change. "We're not subtle."

She smiled, amazed at how she never felt shame in his presence. Yet the presence of the rest of the world tugged at the edge of her mind, just enough for her to ask, "Will he be a problem when we hunt down Vanna?"

"No."

The utter confidence of the answer widened her grin. "Everything's always so terrified of you. Even other monsters waiting in the dark."

"Most go for the easy prey and start feeling invincible. Live like that for a few centuries, and you get stupid and lazy." His fingers continued to stroke along her body, lulling her.

For a while, she dozed, unaware of her afterglow fading to the chill of dried sweat until she heard him move to light the logs in the hearth. She shifted enough to watch, thinking back to the first fire they'd shared together in those long, dark hours of blood and whispered stories, of gunshot wounds and yellow eyes intent on her face.

What a strange night. Her first glimpse of the world beyond her own. Her first taste of keeping company with a beast. She had never been one to wonder about the flexibility of fate— whether her path had been decided at birth by the cold glitter of the stars, or whether chance and chaos shaped it day by day, erratic and indifferent. All she knew was that he had transformed her life into something so much more than a dull march of enduring each day because she feared anything else. That she now knew how delicious it felt to have sharp teeth of her own.

"You weren't either of those when we met," she said, drawing his attention just as he finished. The first hint of flames rimmed him in gold as she added, "Stupid or lazy, I mean. You were so... free. And you made me feel like I could be the same."

He returned to her, eyes gleaming as brightly as when he was a wolf. A moment of rare hesitation, as if he considered replying with words, but then his mouth caught hers, slow and tender while their bodies pressed together, coaxing her to relax back against the couch.

Safe, her heart quiet and her body exhausted, she felt the darkness of sleep—*true* sleep—descend even as his voice rumbled in her ear. "I'll keep you from slipping away this time."

When he pulled back, she couldn't keep from reaching after him, eyes already closed. A heartbeat passed before a cold nose nuzzled back. Then a velvet tongue licked her hand. The black wolf circled around her once, claws clicking against the hardwood floor, before pacing the boundaries of the room as if to satisfy himself that everything was well and calm.

After he finished and settled beside her, she turned enough to stroke between his shoulder blades, silent because no words were needed. Then she let herself drift off, her last perception that of fur beneath her fingers.

She slept for a full day, waking up to fading bruises and a ravenous appetite.

"Everything's fine," said Colton, when she looked at the nearest clock and then the freshly made bed. He sat on its edge, his posture suggesting he'd been watching her for some time.

When he offered no further explanation, she tested her ribs by carefully arching her back, not missing how his eyes followed the rise of her breasts. Her skin was still marked by his dried seed, but she felt no shame while sitting up, her side merely tender rather than agonizing.

As she studied her arm, finding scabs that were already flaking off, she said, "I don't know I want to do more, eat or go after Vanna."

"Save the bitch for tomorrow and enjoy tonight."

"Are you sure?"

"I'm sure. She's expecting to find you in Round Rock, which is only 150 miles away. We can drive there in the morning and spend the day finding her hiding places. Until then..." He shrugged. "Best way to recover from a hunt is to rest and eat well."

She nodded and stretched again. "I'm definitely rested up, so where can we eat?"

This time, their shower together was brief yet playful. He washed her hair while she sucked his cock, and she shaved that dangerous jaw while he tweaked her nipples. She laughed when her stomach wouldn't stop growling, spurred on by his promise of the amount of food any Texan steakhouse would offer.

In the bright light of day, she studied their surroundings as he drove to one, rolling her window down despite the humidity. Some of the buildings looked similar to the historic gold mining towns that were back home, the original architecture preserved. Others looked modern, brick and plaster sandwiched together in neat rows along the streets. "Where are we?"

"About forty miles from Fort Worth." He looked almost excited while navigating the wide streets with clear familiarity, a specific steakhouse obviously in mind.

"You know this area, don't you?" When he nodded, she added, "What about Round Rock?"

That drew a glance from him. "Are you worrying about tomorrow?"

"It's more that I was thinking..." Then she stopped, the words feeling foolish there on the tip of her tongue.

"Go on." His hand slid along her thigh, easy and soothing.

"It's just an idea I had about what to do with Vanna. But maybe it's not a good one."

"Let's hear it."

"Once she's dead, the media will probably find out her connection to Denise. I don't want more scrutiny on my family. But I remembered something Caroline—she was part of the film crew at Vanna's party—told me. She said Vanna is known for bribing local zoning boards and making other shady business deals. If we can make sure enough evidence is found, then most people will focus on that for their conspiracy theories. Believe me, it won't take much. You should see what people have made up with the little information known about my mother's disappearance."

"You're talking about looking through her finances."

"Yes. I don't think they'll be hard to find. Most people are careless about hiding discrepancies in their own records." Then she realized he was looking at her with his full attention while they waited at a red light. "What?"

"You know how to do that?" He didn't sound skeptical. He sounded... impressed.

She blushed, somehow more flustered that he was taking her seriously than if he'd dismissed the idea. "Well, that's what my father does. He's a forensic accountant. Even before I was out of high school, I knew the basics of examining finances. He's never mentioned any of this?"

At that, he raised an eyebrow. "Do you ever see us talking to each other when we don't have to?"

"Fair enough. Anyway, I was pretty good at it, and I still know what to look for. All I'd need are Vanna's personal records."

"Should be doable." Then, unexpectedly, he added, "Did you like it? Accounting?"

"Yes," she said, a little surprised by the answer. "Looking back, it was really satisfying to track down things. In a way, it was like hunting. But I've seen enough through my father to know it's a very cold, clinical career, and that I wouldn't like the people involved in it. I always wanted to be a veterinarian instead. Spend my time being around animals and helping them."

Then her voice trailed off, and she shifted in her seat with the same discomfort that needled her heart whenever she admitted to being a trust fund baby. The near pain of revealing a part of herself ripe for others' contempt.

Yet she could never feel shame in his presence, or fear from his attention, and after a moment, she admitted, "I think a lot of people would look at me and see wasted potential. And I'm definitely the fuck-up among the children from my parents' social circles. Everyone else my age is already years into their career. A few are married. But I don't want that life. I never did, even when I had a chance to be good at it."

His hand moved to hers, folding their fingers together. "You're not a fuck-up. You just know yourself."

"Not back then. Even now, I barely understand who I am. All I had was some kind of blind instinct." Then she laughed a little and looked over at him. "You're the real reason why I'm sure I could never be an accountant living in her office, or a lawyer's wife bored in his mansion. Not without regretting every day of it. Nothing could make me as happy as running beside you through the forest."

The green in his eyes warmed, as feral and tender as the scrape of his teeth against her skin, but all he said was, "That's it on the right."

When she realized he meant the steakhouse, she looked over at the squat, wide building, her fingers squeezing his in fresh excitement. The hunger gnawing at her stomach flared into a roar at the first hints of sweet mesquite and meat drippings.

Inside, it was busy but not overly so, and the hostess quickly seated them at a table off to the side. The lighting was warm and dim, burnishing the wood paneling of the walls. TV monitors flickered from all corners of the room, playing football highlight reels. Most of the other people there were in groups of three or more, casual in their t-shirts and baseball caps, so lost in conversations punctuated by laughter that she felt as private as if they were alone.

She glanced over the list of specials. "Any suggestions?"

"It's all good." He pulled over the basket of fresh rolls that had been given with their menus and offered one to her.

Pillowy softness melted on her tongue as she bit into it. "Oh, my God. These taste homemade."

She shoved the rest in her mouth and reached for another, this time adding a pat of butter. "Denise would be horrified by this. Saturated fat on top of refined carbs. Fried everything on the menu. Platefuls of meat."

Colton had already eaten two himself, menu set aside as if he knew what he wanted. "What do you think about it?"

"It all sounds mouthwatering. There's a lot I've heard about but never tried. It's going to be hard to decide."

"Get as much as you want. If you don't finish it, I will."

When she hesitated, his voice turned serious. "You need this. Not just to replace what your body lost, but to let yourself enjoy something. Fucking aside, you've barely smiled since the day your sister was taken."

After a moment, she nodded, scanning the menu with fresh eyes.

When the server stopped by, they ordered drinks and appetizers. Alice wasn't surprised Colton went with a double whiskey, something he always enjoyed with steak. She declined to get any alcohol but decided to try the fried green tomatoes and stuffed jalapenos, rubbing her thumb along the edge of her menu once they were alone again.

"Still worried?" he said, resting his forearms on the table to lean closer. He looked relaxed in his seat, but never took his eyes off her. The heat of his attention felt magnified by the dim lighting.

"Not really. I was just thinking that this almost feels like a date. I've never been out to dinner with anyone besides friends or my parents."

When he said nothing, just gave her a slight tilt of his head that meant he heard more beneath those words, she added, "In high school, dating meant going out to the movies or ending up in someone's car. And later on, Magdalene always preferred poetry readings or coffee shops. Even when we ate out as a regular occasion, it was never pleasant. But this... this feels special. And nice. That's all."

The appetizers arrived then, still sizzling from the fryer, but she had the feeling his attention was on her more than anything else, even when the server took their entree orders.

A comfortable silence followed the man's departure until she reached for a stuffed jalapeno. "You told him you wanted the 1 ¼ inch steak. How does a steak come in inches?"

"It's the thickness of the cut."

His offhand familiarity drew out her curiosity, and all the questions that had turned in her mind from the moment they arrived in Texas now spilled out. "You haven't talked much about living out here, but you seem to know every area we end up in. Where else have you been? Why did you keep traveling around? What kind of work did you do?"

"There's all your questions," he said, eyes dark with amusement. Then he drank half his whiskey without answering.

She didn't protest only because she had a mouthful of stuffed jalapeno, lost in the rich cream cheese and zing of heat. When she finished it, she added, "And why did you leave? This is *amazing*."

He tortured her with another heartbeat of silence before giving in. "I moved all over the state until I found a job that fit. Worked in oil fields, on oil rigs, did some welding, and finally ended up on a ranch not too far from where we're going tomorrow."

"You worked with livestock?" She couldn't imagine it. Horses were terrified of him. She doubted cows were any different.

"No. The man did raise cattle, but that's not what I was there for. He hired me to keep his land from being overrun by mesquite. You know anything about mesquite?" When she shook her head, he grudgingly elaborated. "It's a tree that grows like a weed. Takes over everything if you don't cut it down. If you own a lot of land, it's a nightmare, and he had around 100,000 acres. He gave me a trailer and a chainsaw so I could live out there on the property, driving around and cutting down what I could each day, every day."

"What else did you do?"

"That's it."

"That's it?" She stared at him, a suspicion forming in her mind. "Did you ever leave the place?"

"Never had to. Fuel and food were left by the gate every week." Then he started eating the tomato slices, not even bothering with a fork.

She took one, too, but absently, still fixated on what his words didn't reveal as much as what they did. "So, you never saw anyone else? Never had anyone to talk to?"

"Closest thing was the radio in the trailer, but it broke after a few years."

"But..." She groped for words, her fork frozen. "That must have been so lonely."

He shrugged.

"Well, what happened? What made you leave?"

"A flash flood caught the trailer one night and swept it away. When I managed to crawl out, I kept going west. They probably thought I drowned."

"Colton, that's horrible."

"No, it worked out all right. I'd been there for fifteen years. People would have started wondering why I never aged."

"Fifteen—" Horror choked her throat. The tomato slice had been pulverized by her fork. He had spoken about it so dispassionately, as if years of isolation were normal for him, and that somehow made it all the worse.

Then he caught her hand. "Alice. It's all right. It's what I wanted at the time."

Slowly, she nodded. "I know you don't like people, but... that's such a long time."

"Not for me. I've spent far longer than that living alone in the woods." His thumb brushed over her knuckles, coaxing her to relax again. "What else do you want to hear about? More about my other jobs?"

It was an obvious attempt to change the subject, but she took it, mood slowly brightening as she learned more about him. The arrival of their entrees, huge and crackling with melted fat, was further distraction, and she found herself staring at Colton's plate. "I have never seen a steak that big in my life."

Then she looked down at the pile of meat on hers, sausage and brisket fighting for space with the huge scoops of potato salad and coleslaw. Her stomach growled again, hardly satisfied by the appetizers.

Whether it was from their hunt, her body healing from multiple injuries, or simply how delicious everything tasted, she soon found herself with an empty plate. Colton had finished before her, now working through the rest of his whiskey at a slower pace.

"Wow," she said, tempted to lick the traces off her plate.

"Want dessert?" he asked, eyes glinting as if he already knew the answer.

"Please."

He ordered the cobbler, but she was caught by the list of coffee cocktails, and ordered one with tequila.

"Believe it or not, I've never tried tequila," she said, as a massive confection of coffee topped with real whipped cream was placed before her. "When people smuggled liquor into my college dorm, it was always vodka."

"It's strong," he said, pushing the cobbler between them to make sharing easier.

"I'll just sip until I feel it."

The first taste hit her like a hammer, and she almost coughed. By the third, she pushed it away, feeling her senses spin. "All yours. You weren't kidding."

He finished it off without even wincing. She watched, the warmth of the alcohol stealing over her until the lighting turned into a haze and she felt flushed. She wasn't used to anything besides wine, or even drinking when she felt good, and bit her lip to keep words from spilling out. Silly words, honest words. Words about how she loved the color of his hair, and how he never hurt her, and the way he said so much with his eyes.

Something about her expression must have given her away, because he raised his eyebrows and said, "Feeling it?"

"Very. But not in a bad way. Everything just feels... blurred. Slurred. What a great dinner."

When they left the restaurant, her steps were unsteady enough that he guided her to the truck. She got in without trouble yet felt like her awareness had been suspended on a string, trailing after them a second too slow while they drove back to the inn.

She stared at the moon, so small in the vast sky, and now the words came out on their own, soft but clear. "I used to be so scared of everything. It shaped my day. It filled my nights. I grew so used to it that I forgot I could feel anything else. And then I met you, and I wasn't afraid at all. Even though I should have been. So, I think I'm easy enough to figure out. But you..."

Then she turned to him, finding his shape there in the dark. "I don't know what you saw in me. At that point, I was barely even a person."

There was a soft growl from him. Then his hand found hers. "Has this been biting at you for awhile?"

"For-*ever*. Probably since the night of the mudslide, when you stayed with me." Sad words, but she didn't feel sad at all, just weightless and warm. "And lately, with the way you handled Giove and my grandmother... every time I see how powerful you are, I wonder why you're not ruling an empire somewhere. Every other witch and wolf I've met would do it in a heartbeat."

"Fuck that. Ruling an empire means dealing with people."

"And having a crown." Then she giggled, trying to imagine him wearing one. If he said anything else, she didn't hear it.

They reached their room without incident. She was dimly aware of the bed waiting with fresh sheets, and the whisper of her body sliding beneath them. The ceiling swam until it disappeared entirely.

Eventually, the neon glow of the tableside clock glared at her, revealing how much time had passed. Her mouth and throat felt very dry, the flavor of tequila still sharp and repulsive. Before she could do more than shift, Colton was there, still dressed and holding a glass of water. "Slept it off?"

"I think so." She sipped at the water gratefully. "I really didn't mean to do that. I'm sorry."

"Why? You were asleep for a few hours, that's all."

"I know, but..." Then she groaned and sank back against the bed. "God, I'm such a mess. I can't even recover without screwing it up. This entire hunt must be so frustrating for you."

"No." There wasn't an ounce of hesitation in the reply.

She looked at him, unable to understand it. "Why? Why are you even with me? You could be anywhere, hunting anything. Even other vargr are terrified of you, and yet you're here, watching me underestimate tequila."

At that, he settled next to her. "So many questions."

She pushed herself upright, intent on a firm answer, feeling both desperate and terribly vulnerable. "Because I can never figure out what made you stay that night. What makes you want to wake up each morning beside me. Beside *me*."

He sighed against her neck, breath hot against the pulse in her throat, before pulling her closer, effortlessly easing her onto his lap. As she settled against him, running fingers up the back of his neck and into his thick, dark hair, his gaze remained intent on her face. "What did you notice about me when we first met?"

She swallowed hard, trying to keep her voice from trembling. "You were very primal. Very mysterious."

"I was a mess," he said, flatly. "Starving, and tired, and barely able to speak."

Ribs visible beneath his skin. Eyes feral and suspicious. Words rusted over. And... badly injured from a bullet to the chest.

When her fingers hesitantly traced over his current scars, he nodded, sensing her silent comparison. "And weak."

"But why?"

He shrugged. "I stopped caring about anything. Had for a long time. We can't die, Alice, but it's easy to waste away and let the years slip by until you forget how to live. Then you start forgetting things about yourself. Who you are, what you've done. Hell, even where you are."

What happens to a wild beast that loses the will to fight? It becomes a body left in the woods. Scavenger-gnawed bones scattered among the leaves. Yet what about a creature that cannot be killed? That *must* endure because its own grave has spat it back out? What is it reduced to?

Tears burned in Alice's eyes as she considered the horror behind the answer. *Something that knows there's no escape.*

Without looking up, she said, "You told me that being turned into a vargr was punishment, but I never really understood that. I didn't think you'd have to be afraid of anything if you can't die. That if you can change into something so vicious, then nothing can ever hurt you. But loneliness can, can't it?"

He growled softly, coaxing her into meeting his eyes. Their green had shifted into something warm and heavy as he said, "Not anymore."

When her mouth started trembling, he licked it. "Do you think I liked cutting mesquite for fifteen years? I didn't. But I also didn't fucking care. It was as good as anything else because it was as meaningless as everything else. I'd lost myself. Not that there was much leftover from the grave, but what there was went away with my will to live. Strength. Memory. Hunger. By the time we met, I'd been rotting in the forest like a fucking log. I looked like a man, but I was hardly even that. I was pitiful."

"No." She might have called herself a thousand insults and on a bad day believed them, but she wouldn't let him do such a thing to himself, not when everything he'd given her throbbed in her heart. "You weren't pitiful. You *saved* me."

"Alice." His nose brushed hers. "What do you think you did for me?"

Tears seared down her cheeks, but she was smiling while he pulled her closer. The moon wheeled overhead as his kiss sank into the scars on her heart, and as her fingers traced the scars over his.

CHAPTER THIRTEEN

The Coven

The hag king hunched beneath a colorless sunrise. His skin steamed in the air while he shook scraps of flesh from his antlers. His slashed sides heaved. The fight had been a hard one.

His rival twitched a final time, power and ambition reduced to mangled flesh against churned earth. A warlock that had wanted more land. A warlock that had wished to be a conqueror as well as a king. Now, a mere body drowned in its own blood.

The howls of the rival's coven could still be heard, invisible among the pines and mist as they fled. The witches belonging to the hag king spurred them on with taunts and branches broken into switches, scratching and spitting at one whenever she stumbled.

Only the hag mother stayed by her king's side, already tending to his wounds. Against his bristling filth, her immaculate skin glowed like the moon, and her expression matched the tenderness in her fingers while she wiped the blood away with her own hair. He appeared unaware of it all, those massive antlers cutting at nothing as he shook his head and seethed. Sweat and aggression filled his every movement.

Soon, his other witches returned, exhilarated from the chase. Their switches were bloody, and a few still laughed breathlessly. They all surrounded their king with shining eyes, new eagerness filling their movements as they took in his impatience and thick, erect cock. Which of them would have the honor of being his first? Gain the biggest taste of his power?

The hag mother remained intent on his injuries, but one of the others approached without being told—Faustine, the youngest of the coven and also the boldest. In silence, she crouched in front of their king and stroked his matted beard. His eyes remained hidden in shadow, but she thought he looked back at her.

When he let her fingers trail down his neck, her mouth curved into a small, triumphant smile. Then she shifted closer, ignoring the soft laugh from the hag mother.

Just as her bare breasts brushed against his arm, he moved. A casual twitch, effortless on his part, and yet she was still flung away from him. Her shriek echoed through the trees. Then he vanished, leaving the hag mother with mud on her fingers and blood clotting her long, dark hair.

Their smiles disappeared with him. The excitement that had filled the air now soured into something metallic, something closer to fear. Faustine rose to her feet, cheeks burning, and rejoined the others as they all stared at the lifeless body of the rival warlock.

"It's time to finish things," said the hag mother. She alone seemed unshaken while kneeling beside the remains, a knife already in hand. "Start a fire."

"It won't collect nearly as much power as when *he* burns enemies."

It could have come from any of them, that whisper, for their faces were all etched with the same frustration.

Then one stepped away from the rest—Vanna, far removed from her usual stylish appearance. "Maybe, but he's obviously not coming back. I'll find some kindling."

The others watched suspiciously as she disappeared into the trees. A witch only moved against the mood of her coven if she had a scheme that could give her some safety, an assurance that standing out would result in a sweet reward instead of a painful tumble down the pecking order. When she only returned with thin branches, they all began working together with the grim harmony of pallbearers carrying a casket.

The flames devoured the severed body parts with the same hunger the witches felt deep inside. The sting of their king's absence could at least be soothed by the flush of power from his burning rival. A rare meal, much more potent than any human or stray witch. The most satisfying flesh always came from enemies. More than one imagined that the only thing sweeter would be that of their own coven-sisters.

By the time the hag mother cut out the heart, they had lost all restraint. Glutted, frenzied, they left in different ways. One used the wind, turning as swift and insubstantial as the air, traveling unnoticed by any of the towns she passed above except for a strange chill felt by people still asleep in their beds.

Another conjured a mare out of sticks and rode it, the sweat and blood on her skin drying into grime from the speed of the beast. A third hunted until she found a hiker and turned *him* into a horse, laughing as she spurred him on until white foam lathered his coat. She abandoned him panting and shaking at the edge of a gorge, water far beyond his reach.

Only the hag mother simply disappeared like their king, and only she wore a smile when they all met in a mansion protected by the forest. The building was centuries old, a fortress against prying eyes and modern convention. It was his, just like they were, and they expected him to be there.

He wasn't.

Left to themselves, each witch found another until they were all in the grand parlor that held furniture and mementos from their time spent ravaging high society in England throughout the 19th century. There among portraits of themselves, they settled into red velvet chairs and picked at their freshly washed hair. All held the same dire thoughts yet dared not reveal them for fear of criticism.

Together, without smoke and shadow and mud blurring their features, they grew distinct from each other.

There was Vanna, reclining in her seat as if posing for photos, wearing a skintight dress and high heels. She easily looked the oldest among them, having kept the same face and letting it age slightly. Her gold earrings glittered as she swiveled her head to watch Cleo pace the length of the massive hearth.

Cleo had recently changed her appearance and still seemed uncomfortable with it, pushing thick-framed glasses up her nose in between tracing the spines of books stacked along the mantelpiece. Her blonde hair looked as unkempt as her baggy sweater and ripped leggings, but the effect lent her a careless grace as enchanting as polished beauty to the right eye. Whenever she passed in front of the flames, dimming the entire room, Faustine glared in her direction.

Ah, yes, Faustine, still sulking from her failed offer to their king. She now sat on the floor, painfully aware of how his open disinterest had erased any chance of her influencing the coven's decisions. Her hands shook with rage while she braided Marie's hair, who was absorbed in playing a game of knucklebones. The two witches looked like sisters, one brunette and one blonde, with the same pointed face and wide eyes. They often shared clothes and mimicked each other's makeup. Truly, the only notable difference was that Faustine always spoke up with her own thoughts, and Marie merely echoed them.

The last figure in the room was the hag mother herself. She sat in a chair close to the fire, her posture as regal as the opulent dress she wore, a relic from 1870s France. While the rest sulked, or worried, or schemed, she watched the flames and smiled.

None of the others knew her true name. She had never revealed it or anything else intimate about herself. Her expression remained as constant and tranquil as a death mask's, but something about her eyes looked ancient.

There were whispers that she had survived the witch hunts of Europe; indeed, that she had been at their king's side the entire time. Whether it was true or not, the rest of the coven remained wary, unsure of her true strength and what she might do if they ever displeased her too much. Under the weight of her silence, no one dared point out the obvious.

No one... except Vanna. "He's getting worse."

Her composure nearly rivaled the hag mother's, but spite gleamed in her eyes while she lit a cigarette and waited for a response. "Oh, don't be such cowards. It's the simple truth. He's weakening. I know I wasn't the only one who felt him struggle throughout the fight."

Cleo paced beside the hearth again. "No, you're right. He used to fuck us for hours afterward. Perhaps he misses Portia."

Faustine scoffed. "No one misses that bitch."

"Or her daughter," added Marie.

"Then why isn't he here?" said Cleo, eyes flashing behind her glasses. When her question was met with sullen glances, she insisted, "Something's wrong."

At that, the hag mother rose from her chair, hushing the rest of the room. "The answer is very simple. It's just not the one you hope for. He left because there's nothing here that will satisfy him."

Then she left in a rustle of silk, as if she, too, had grown tired of being disappointed by them.

Once she was out of earshot, Vanna smiled. "She wouldn't complain even if he pissed on her."

That drew a laugh from Faustine and then Marie.

Cleo merely scowled and returned her attention to the books. "We do everything he asks and everything he could want. Everything!"

"You're just mad because you were the first to lose his interest," said Faustine. "Brilliant little Cleo with her knowledge of rare rituals and her collection of precious artifacts. You were so sure of passing even the hag mother in his favor."

"Shut up," said Cleo, her cheeks flaming red.

"It's true," said Marie, looking up from the teeth rattling in her hand. "No one cares how smart you are if you're totally boring."

"You—"

Before Cleo could choke out anything more, Vanna straightened up in her seat. "Let's avoid getting into a fight until we decide what to do."

"Don't act so above it all. He doesn't like you any better."

When Marie opened her mouth to chime in, Vanna flicked cigarette ash onto her head, and the smell of burning hair filled the room. The other witch screamed.

"Bitch," hissed Faustine, quickly brushing it off.

Cleo watched in silence, looking sick of them all.

Vanna waited until Marie stopped whimpering. Then she said, "We need to think clearly about this. If he's weak from wanting nothing to do with us, then new blood needs to be brought in. Someone to catch his interest and make him care again."

Faustine rose to her feet, Marie close behind. "Do what you want. Or at least, what you *can* on your own. We wasted a lot on Portia's schemes, and look how that turned out. Neither of us will help you with anything."

Vanna showed no disappointment as they left the room, or when Cleo slunk out soon afterward. In truth, this was exactly what she'd hoped for: a show of sharing her idea with the rest without the headache of actually arguing with them.

Her skin tingled from the blood of the defeated warlock while she prowled around the parlor, stopping before the portrait of their king. She stared at it for some time, all satisfaction draining away as she faced what he had been.

It was a stuffy painting—all the ones from that time were— and yet the intensity of their king shone through. He had called himself Edric back then, and had ravaged the glittering cities of Europe in every way possible. Vanna couldn't remember ever loving anyone, not in the way others had described it, but her heart had always burned for bigger and bigger tastes of his power, and she supposed that was much the same. She certainly grieved over the loss of it.

She sensed more than heard the hag mother join her. For a moment, they only stared at the portrait. Then the older witch said, "The others have gone. There's no reason to stay."

"I wanted to talk with you."

"A new member of the coven. I overheard." The other witch sighed. "I suppose what happened to Portia wasn't enough to dissuade your own ideas."

"Perhaps he wants an heir. Perhaps just a new fuck. Either way, it's obvious that Portia was on the right track. He needs fresh blood. True youth, not stolen faces."

"You're much kinder to Portia now that she's dead." The hag mother almost sounded amused. "Who do you have in mind?"

"Her killer."

Shock was an emotion long lost to the older witch. So was any sense of disgust. Instead, she only raised an eyebrow. "What does she hope for in return?"

"Absolutely nothing. The very idea repulsed her."

"She's unwilling?" The hag mother looked a little more interested. "He might enjoy that. It could be refreshing."

Vanna nodded. "She's different from us in every way. Raised by her human father. Guileless. Weak. The only reason she managed to kill Portia was because she—"

"Ah, let me guess. She keeps company with a black wolf that can change into a man. Is this why you asked to use my connections to the vargr? To solve any complications surrounding her?"

"Yes. On her own, she'll be easy to deal with."

"What do you propose?" said the hag mother, her voice soft. In the warm glow of the firelight, her eyes had gone very dark. She was truly considering this.

"By the time I fly back, everything will be ready to introduce her to our king. All I need is for you to invoke him. He doesn't respond to me anymore." A trace of bitterness imbued Vanna's last words.

When the other witch only studied her, she added, "If he wants her, he wants her. If he doesn't... we can have fun with Portia's killer."

"And you'd be happy with either result. Always the ruthless planner, Vanna. I've heard you still torment the descendants of that one girl who crossed you. Some silly little human that should have been nothing to you, and yet here you are today, five generations into your revenge with no end in sight. How many bodies in her family cemetery are you to blame for?"

"I've never counted," said Vanna, the words so smooth they were obviously a lie.

"We'll see if this scheme works just as well."

"Then you do think he wants someone new."

"I never assume I know his will. I simply serve it. That's why I've lasted this long."

The two witches turned toward the portrait again. When the hag mother spoke, all traces of humor had vanished from her voice. "He's changed because he's felt disappointment for too long. If he doesn't remember his hunger, we'll soon become the ones chased away in shame while others cut out his heart and eat it. So. Present your little witch and I'll call him. What spot have you chosen?"

"The cemetery you just mentioned."

The hag mother's mouth twitched toward a smile. "Of course. I'll meet you there."

Vanna left the mansion feeling completely pleased with herself, all earlier frustration replaced with hot anticipation. The sensation lasted through a long transatlantic flight and a late arrival in Austin. Sunlight slanted through the airport's windows as she turned her phone back on while waiting for her luggage.

Messages beeped to life, several of them, but she only turned her phone off again, not wanting to be distracted. Whatever they were, it didn't matter. Olive knew how to handle things. She had been Vanna's acolyte for years and had never made a mistake. Whatever she couldn't do, Aaron did. Some poppets could be sullen or disobedient, but Aaron was steady, loyal, and best of all, had no moral qualms... about anything. He followed instructions to the letter, and Vanna had given him very clear ones.

The traffic in Austin proved as terrible as always. It took her over an hour to reach Round Rock, the air hot and humid and tinged red while the sun sank behind the horizon. She smoked with the windows down, focusing on nothing in particular as she entered the downtown area.

Suddenly, her skin prickled, and the thin burn of nicotine disappeared under the caustic stench of true, devouring fire. Smoke thickened the air. Red lights flashed as she rounded a corner. Then she jerked in her seat. Countless police cars and fire engines crowded around her bakery. The roof looked charred, burned through.

"What the fuck?" she muttered, slowing down as police waved her away, warning her the street was closed.

A pit opened up in her stomach as she parked and got out, joining a small crowd watching from the sidewalk.

"Was there a fire?" she said to the nearest person, an older woman who craned her neck in hopes of a better view.

"They already put it out, but everyone's saying there's much more inside." The woman's voice lowered to a whisper. "A murder. Can you believe it?"

She took Vanna's sudden silence as a sign of shock and nodded. "Neither could I. They're not saying how it happened, just that the poor man was already dead when they found him. And there's a young woman, too, but she survived. That's her on the stretcher there."

Then the woman pointed toward an ambulance just visible among the police cars.

Vanna felt the blood drain from her face as she recognized Olive being loaded into the back, trails of red splattered on her neck and the front of her white jacket. Her acolyte's eyes looked glassy with shock, and Vanna had no doubt that the dead man was Aaron.

"Has to be related to drugs," said a man in front of them. "Whoever did it dragged the body onto piles of papers. I saw the trail of blood. Who does that? There's something bigger here than how it looks."

"Papers?" murmured Vanna, still feeling like the ground had dropped out from under her. Then she saw Olive shift against the stretcher, as if already sensing the other witch's presence.

Aware that the stupid girl was dazed enough to scream her name if she saw her, Vanna slipped back to her car. She retreated down a different street and quickly found herself locked in slow traffic. Her hand shook as she turned on her phone again, painfully sure those messages were no longer trivial. Then she began checking them.

The first was a male voice she barely recognized, snarling like the wolf he was. "What the *fuck* did you send me into? Never call me again, you fucking bitch."

The next was from Olive. "Giove isn't answering his phone. You told him to come at sundown, didn't you? It's just that... I'm at the back door, and it's unlocked, and there's no one here. Aaron is checking things out right now."

Her second message had arrived ten minutes after that. Olive now sounded hysterical. "Something happened. *Something happened.* She still has the wolf with her, and they've just killed Aaron. I'm hiding down here in the secret room. I can't tell what they're doing now. Oh, God, Vanna, the wolf tore him apart. *I don't want to be next.*"

"Shit," hissed Vanna, even as her voicemail loaded up the final message.

She recognized this voice immediately and felt her mouth move in a silent snarl as Denise's stepdaughter said, "It's over, Vanna. We made sure they'll find everything you tried to hide."

Even as she slowed to a stop at a red light, her mind raced frantically, recalculating everything. The horizon ahead glimmered red from the sunset, and cars began turning on their headlights. Shadows spread everywhere, and the air no longer seemed humid but instead very cool. A chill ran down her spine—the chill of being watched. The muscles in her neck felt stiff as she looked to the left, finding a hedge between buildings.

Two pairs of eyes glowed at her. Even as she sucked in a breath, sharp muzzles and rangy limbs grew apparent. Wolves, one black as coal and the other grey as smoke.

"You little bitch," murmured Vanna, fingers strangling the steering wheel.

When the lighter one licked its chops, she stomped on the gas pedal, ignoring the screeching brakes and honking horns as she ran the red light. It felt like the night chased after her.

Her car flew down streets and then country roads, flashing through the rugged wildland as shadows thickened into true night. There were no signs for where she wanted to go, no hint at all that what she sought even existed. Yet she drove without hesitation, having long memorized every inch of the journey there.

Her heart pounded in a way it hadn't for years, and she realized she sweated from fear as much as rage. All thoughts of trapping the girl had shifted into saving herself. One witch alone had no chance, but if she could meet the hag mother and call their king... that required fresh blood though. Something she didn't yet have.

When she grew close, she pulled off the road and turned on her emergency lights. Then she got out and waited for a sympathetic driver to stop and help, all the while wondering just how fast wolves could travel...

Wolf-Alice ran swift and sure beside her lover, vicious exhilaration beating within her like a second heart. In this form, she could smell as well as he, and needed no guidance on following the witch's scent into what she'd heard the locals call *hill country*.

Deer fled their presence. The moon gleamed like a sickle. It felt as if her paws barely touched the ground, as if her body would never fall exhausted. Their hunt had reached a fever pitch.

When the oil and tar of the nearby road exploded into engine grease and spilled blood, the black wolf slowed, his patience steadying her excitement. She followed his lead, panting lightly as they approached the source.

A car and a truck were pulled off to the side, both with their headlights and engines shut off. The car reeked of Vanna and her fear; the truck held a stranger's scent.

Wolf-Alice wrinkled her muzzle in a silent growl, already guessing what had happened even before they circled around to a pool of blood where the man's scent grew sharp with shock and pain. Another body to be used for a ritual.

They followed the trail, silent as only wild beasts can be. The glint of a fire appeared in the distance. Wolf-Alice paused at that and then at the new smells of worn stone and faint decay, unsure until she saw gravestones sticking up from the ground, as stubby and uneven as rotting teeth. Vanna had fled to a cemetery, an old one from the look of it.

She and the black wolf slunk among the headstones, invisible in the shadows as two figures in the middle of the cemetery grew apparent, naked and hunched close to the ground. Graves yawned around them, dug up to reach the pitiful bones inside.

Wolf-Alice watched as a dirt-smeared Vanna positioned skulls in a large circle around the limp body of a man. She looked nothing like the sleek, smug woman that had thrown a party for her book release. Instead, she panted like a trapped animal, scratching at the dirt with frantic sweeps of her arms as the first stinging hints of magic filled the air. She smelled terrified.

"I'm ready," she said, turning to the second woman, who Wolf-Alice dimly recognized as one of the witches at the ritual that now seemed so long ago. "Let's finish it."

This other witch was calmer, less disheveled, and moved with a stately grace as she crouched close. When she brandished a knife over the body, Wolf-Alice snarled and lunged.

Vanna's head snapped up, and for a moment their eyes met. Her voice rose into a shriek. "They're here. Hurry!"

The other witch started like a deer. Then the two wolves reached the edge of the firelight and she darted away, disappearing into the darkness beyond.

"No, you bitch!" Vanna grabbed the knife and plunged it into the body, ripping the abdomen open. The reek of magic grew overwhelming as she dropped the knife and shoved her hand inside. Her face had turned into a mask of hatred.

Then they were on her, teeth against unprotected flesh. The witch screamed, shrill and furious, before the black wolf found her throat and crushed it. The cemetery fell eerily silent, the smell of hot blood joining the harsh smoke from the fire.

Wolf-Alice tore until she knew the damage was too much to recover from and then circled away to the other body, changing back into her skin.

"Too late again," she murmured. Yet this time, she shivered with rage. Despite the man's stillness, she inched closer. She had to make sure there was no chance of saving him. She couldn't live with herself if she didn't at least try.

After seeing what had been done to him, she was glad he was clearly dead. Some part of her sensed the second witch lingering nearby, and she looked up without thinking about where to turn, finding the other woman crouched up in a tree.

She watched Alice intently, silently. Alice stared back while pulling the knife out of the body and throwing it aside.

Before the other witch could react, the smell of magic grew unbearable. Mist slid among the gravestones, glowing strangely, and the black wolf growled. Then he was there against Alice, pushing her away with his weight.

She let him, stumbling in shock as the body began twitching. The skulls around it chattered like living things.

Antlers pierced through the ruined flesh of the abdomen. Alice heard a soft exclamation from the witch above but couldn't look away as bone and meat ripped open and fell aside.

"My king," managed Vanna, voice broken. "Please!"

A final bite from the black wolf silenced her entirely. The figure that emerged from the ruined body didn't even react, instead shaking the blood from his skin.

The hag king. A chill ran through Alice's entire being as his head turned in her direction. She couldn't see his face; he was hardly more than a silhouette in the strange mist. Yet she knew bone-deep that he saw her standing there, naked and bloodied and furious. The feeling of his attention was repulsive.

Those huge antlers lowered slightly, as if he studied her more closely. The air fell very still and quiet. Then he beckoned her to come to him.

Did he think it would be that easy? Did he think she would go back to a life of meek worship? Her growl was as loud as the black wolf's, and when the hag king tilted his head as if puzzled or amused, her body shifted into its fur without hesitation, every fiber of her being focused on attacking this creature that looked at her and only saw prey.

Yet as soon as they lunged, the hag king was gone, and the second witch with him. Only the bodies remained.

The bodies... and the two wolves prowling among the fading magic, both aware that the nature of the hunt had just changed.

CHAPTER FOURTEEN

The Hole

The nightclub didn't have a name, but everyone knew about it and called it The Hole. Its entrance wasn't particularly secret or difficult to find—a rusted door in a back alley that opened to a rough stone tunnel. No bouncer, no lights... no sign that anything waited beyond.

The descent was long enough and dark enough to sting the most audacious spirit, yet just as animal instinct threatened to overwhelm curiosity, neon stripes appeared, shifting from blue to pink as they scaled massive walls. Their harsh glow revealed the broken columns and stone arches of Roman ruins.

Music next. Modern, throbbing, and electric, its presence reassuring visitors that this experience would be the same as every other club. By the time the dancefloor appeared, the soundstage glittering among the ancient remains like a neon crystal, even the gimmick of being far underground vanished against the crush of bodies. Fear lost to excitement, and most

danced and drank and fucked without discovering what hid
further beyond.

The coven had funded The Hole from its beginning, but
the hag mother never enjoyed visiting it. The convenience of
endless tourists that could be taken without a trace didn't
outweigh the irritation of deafening music and bewildering
lighting. She also hated the owner. Yet on this day, she needed
to see him, and moved through the crowd with grim resolve.

She was recognized by the bartender as soon as she stepped
up to his counter. "Where is he?"

The man was hardly more than a silhouette against the
purple glow of the shelves behind him. The bottles of liquor
glimmered like jewels. "In the back. He doesn't want to be
disturbed."

Despite the warning, no one stopped her from entering the
hallway of private rooms that could be rented out to the right
people for the right reasons. The music faded to muffled beats
and then to nothing at all. The walls changed into carved
stone. Tallow candles replaced the neon, the one hint to
humans who had wandered too far that this area wasn't for
them. The air felt hot and greasy from their acrid smoke.

Then doors appeared, neat rows of red on either side.
Muffled chanting could be heard in one of the rooms she
passed. In another, scratching and snuffling. The hag mother
smiled, already feeling back in her element.

Each door looked identical and could be locked from the
inside, but she knew which one to go to and had the key for it.

As she stepped inside, chains rattled. A muffled moan rose above a growl.

Candles flickered in their stands, illuminating a massive bed and the two figures on it—a woman on her back, naked except for a blindfold and the cuffs restraining her hands and keeping her legs apart, and a man hunched over her like a beast, his tongue lapping at the sweat on her breasts as she panted.

"Not now," he said, without so much as a glance over.

The hag mother found the light switch and flicked it on. "Let's not play coy. I'm more important than any whore you found for the night."

At the sound of her voice, the woman gasped against her gag, limbs jerking against the chains in an attempt to cover herself. The man only thrust harder, his teeth now on her neck.

Then the hag mother spoke in a German dialect that had died out four centuries before. "It's about the wolf you recommended to one of our witches. He failed, and now she's dead."

At that, the man paused and looked up. In the modern lighting, his features were clear. Sharp and dangerous and all the more handsome for it, like a knife blade honed to perfection. When the hag mother noticed the bright yellow of his eyes, she kept her expression cold, well aware she faced a wolf on the edge of bloodlust.

The girl beneath him whimpered, cheeks flushing as if embarrassed by the presence of another. A small noise, but it drained all threat from the vargr. He shook his head while stroking the girl's hair. "You're such a pain in the ass. Wait in the other room."

Then he bit the girl's throat and finished as she shrieked.

The hag mother lingered long enough to watch him release the girl from the bindings with surprising gentleness, and to catch her smile when he murmured to her. Satisfied that he truly was done, the witch walked into the small lounge off to the side and made herself a gin and tonic at the bar.

Some part of her felt tempted to kill the girl just to gauge his reaction. From her brief experiences with him and the other vargr, she'd sensed a strange allure between the black wolves and human girls. The focus of a predator finding its ideal prey, or something more? Even as she mused over the answer, he appeared, cleaned up and fully dressed.

His navy suit stood out against the warm lighting and cream furniture, yet like any vargr, he moved with a hunter's natural silence. His eyes had softened into a human blue and now held a mocking glint as he sat beside her. "All right. What do you want to bitch about?"

"Always so crude, Adair," murmured the witch, and finished her drink. "And disappointing. Despite your many reassurances, Giove botched everything he was asked to do."

Adair laughed. "I thought he could handle it. It's not my fault he grew careless enough to get fucked up by a brat like Shane."

"It wasn't Shane."

"Had to be. He's the only one in California."

The witch reached out and straightened his tie. "You were wrong. When I found Giove, he told me next to nothing before disappearing again, but it was still enough. This strange wolf understood Giove's native speech and replied in it. It's a dialect that's been dead in Italy for over 300 years. You said Shane isn't even 150."

"He isn't." The derision left Adair's voice. "What did the mystery man say?"

"Nothing helpful. From what I understand, Giove swore at him and said he couldn't be killed. The other vargr said he'd soon wish he could be." The witch paused. "You've gone very pale. Do you know who it is?"

"Did he say anything else?"

"No. Apparently, he's quite the silent type."

Adair shoved himself up from the chair. "Shit. It sounds like... but that doesn't make any sense."

"In what way? You're being very unclear," said the hag mother, watching him pace the length of the room. He looked openly agitated.

"If it's who I'm thinking of, then you should already be dead. He doesn't fuck around. He never fucks around. How did you cross paths with him? Why is he killing members of your coven?"

She stirred the ice in her glass while debating how much to tell him. "One of our rituals angered a witch who would have lost family to it. She's young, raised by humans, and charmingly determined to hunt us down. He's helping her. I believe they're lovers."

"Fuck. *Fuck*." Adair now rubbed at his face with both hands. "It's him. He must be holding back on the slaughter for her. Going at a teaching pace. I can't believe that asshole actually found someone who could stand him."

The hag mother smiled slightly, enjoying his panic. "My turn to ask questions. Who is he?"

"He's been called different things over the years, but no one knows his real name. He's old, the oldest wolf known."

"What do *you* call him?"

Adair straightened up again, his expression bleak. "A killer."

"So dramatic!"

He stared at the witch. "If you weren't so young, you wouldn't have that smug fucking grin on your face. You've never lived through what he does. He doesn't go after humans like you or me. *We're* his prey, and he was a terror until he grew sick of it all. He disappeared 500 years ago, just long enough for you fucking baby witches to build kingdoms and believe they could last."

"This is all fascinating, but what, exactly, is your point?"

"That your delusions of grandeur are about to be torn apart."

"We've faced persistent enemies before," said the hag mother, voice bland. Then she rose from her chair to fully face him. "But I do believe we'll need your help. And this time, I won't accept a substitute in your place."

He laughed, but it was a brief, disbelieving sound. "As far as I'm concerned, I'm talking to a dead woman."

"Adair, I have no patience for negotiations. Not tonight."

When she left the room, he followed after her, his words sliding into a growl. "Give the girl what she wants and hope you're not included. If you survive, call it a life lesson and move on. That's your best chance out of this. And whatever you do, don't hurt or kill her. Don't even threaten it."

By now they were out in the hallway, the hag mother's heels striking sharply against the stone floor. "I don't think you quite understand the situation. We don't want to harm the girl at all. Quite the opposite."

"What?"

"Our king has seen her and made his wishes clear. She's to become part of the coven."

"You can't be serious."

"I never question his will. Now, come see me tomorrow night so we can finalize your part in the plans and what you'll want in return." After she checked her watch, she added, "No more arguing. I have a few things scheduled tonight that I really can't miss."

Then she was gone, disappearing as silently as a candle's flame, leaving Adair to snarl at empty air.

Hours later, he found her enraptured in a ballet performance of *Romeo and Juliet*.

"This is a private box," she murmured, as he sat beside her.

He lit a cigarette despite the no-smoking policy, glancing over their surroundings with obvious disinterest. "Our conversation wasn't over."

To any outsider, they looked like a glamorous couple, he in his stark tuxedo and she in a glittering ombre gown. If the shadows appeared a bit darker around them, well, it was easily dismissed as a trick of the eyes.

The witch in particular seemed much changed. Her reserved manner had thawed into something softer, and her smile seemed of actual delight as she watched the performance. After a brief silence, words slipped out of her as if by their own will. "This was the first place he took me to after I became his. This opera house, in this very box. I'd never seen such luxury before. Such beauty. I couldn't believe the dancers were mere humans, and that I could experience such joy watching them. They were performing for him. For *me*. It was then I realized just how many doors he could open. How the smallest taste of his power was more precious than anything else I could hope to know."

She looked at Adair with shining eyes.

He sighed. "You're all so fucked in the head."

Her gaze dimmed again. Then her smile faded into its usual hardness. "You're wrong once more, Adair. I looked into this mysterious wolf after our earlier conversation. He's been glimpsed here and there for the last century, always shunning contact as soon as it's made. A quiet hermit in the forest hardly sounds like your vicious killer."

"It's him. He went into isolation to waste away and forget everything. It's the closest we can get to killing ourselves."

"He missed quite a lot. The world isn't the same as it was back then."

Despite her dismissive words, Adair didn't snap. Instead, he slumped back in his seat, his gaze growing distant. "2,000 years ago, I was just like you—convinced I could take what I wanted without anyone stopping me. Then I crossed paths with him. He killed me. When I came back into myself, he killed me again. And again. And *again*. Every time I woke up, he was there, waiting for me to see him and realize it wasn't over. He didn't stop until I forgot how to scream."

The hag mother raised an eyebrow. "You nearly made me feel pity. I'm telling you, it will be different this time. Our coven survived centuries of witch hunts. If entire populations of humans can't destroy us—"

"Who told you that whopper of a lie? Your king?" A certain malicious amusement slid into his next words. "Humans burned each other in ignorance, or greed, or fear. If they caught a real witch, it was a matter of chance. Want to know who really killed the major covens in Europe? *He* did. Your precious Edric was too insignificant to be noticed at the time. Maybe he's got a gold crown now, but it's taken from the remains left by the real killer."

"Enough," hissed the hag mother, the first cracks showing in her composure.

"If you don't face the truth now, it'll bite you in the ass later. The Cathars' Crusade, the witches of Athens, Theodosius' final years... do you think any genuine witches who died in those events did so at the hands of blind, stupid humans? It was his favorite trick to slip in wherever they butchered each other and find the nasty things like us that were feeding on the chaos."

"I suppose he killed all the Druids as well?"

Adair's voice grew hot. "No, you sarcastic cunt. That was a different vargr, one who went nuts after his lover was taken from him. Seeing a pattern yet?"

The hag mother drew in a deep breath. "You're severely underestimating my king."

"No. Just your state of denial. It's fucking baffling. How many from your coven are dead from believing they could use this girl?" When her mouth only tightened in reply, he added, "And yet here we are. What makes you think a plan that failed for others will succeed for *you*?"

"You never criticized our plans when it meant financing your club. If it wasn't for our money, our influence, and our power, you wouldn't be where you are today."

Adair shrugged. "I'm lazy and a coward. It was easier to work with you than build up something on my own."

For several heartbeats, silence fell between them. Tension sharpened the air into something jagged. Finally, the witch said, "And will you now work against us?"

"Fuck no. I'm not interfering with his hunt. The only reason I'm doing *this* is because I hoped to somehow convince you to drop your plan and save us all from a goddamn extinction event. We're flourishing in the shadows of the humans because he left. Don't bring him back. Your fucking scavenger king isn't worth—"

The hag mother stabbed him, her eyes bright and furious. For a moment, he only stared as the pristine white of his tuxedo shirt bloomed red.

"You went too far," she murmured, gripping the knife's handle so hard the skin over her knuckles looked ready to split. "He is worth *anything*."

Then Adair laughed. His teeth flashed.

The witch's expression changed as his hand wrenched hers —not away, but closer, pushing the blade in to the hilt. It left their faces inches apart. His eyes glinted gold. "Your only hope is that he's forgotten more than he remembers from centuries of wasting away. Otherwise, you're completely fucked."

In one quick movement, he shoved her away again and then pulled the knife out. He didn't seem affected at all, even when fresh blood ran down his chest. In the silence that followed, he took a long drag from his cigarette and sighed. "The only thing I'm not sure of is the girl herself. Why kill thousands of witches and then shack up with one?"

The hag mother returned her attention to the dancers below, her face smoothing out as she sank into the performance once more. "I'll be sure to ask him that."

"Ask? No one *asks* him anything."

CHAPTER FIFTEEN

The Hermit

"When were you last in England?" said Alice, watching the countryside unfold before them. They were on the open level of a tour bus as sedate as their surroundings. A guide pointed out spots and provided local history while the other passengers listened and took photos.

It leant a sense of privacy as strong as if they were alone in the woods, but Colton still leaned in until his mouth brushed her ear. "The Second World War."

The gentle hills looked greener than she believed grass and trees could ever be, but there was a brooding quality to the overcast sky that she couldn't quite place. They had left Texas in the middle of a thunderstorm, sweating from the suffocating humidity, but the dampness to this air somehow felt heavier, like the chill of a gravestone.

Despite the goose down jacket she wore against the cold, she shuddered convulsively. "Did you see any fighting?"

"No. I'd long grown tired of killing." The flatness behind the words left them more sinister than the fiercest growl.

Sinister, and yet she only turned to him with a smile. If she was overdressed for the cold weather with her gloves and fur-lined boots, then he was beyond casual in comparison, wearing nothing more than a flannel over his t-shirt. His eyes looked sharp yet relaxed, revealing little of what he thought. "Are you familiar with this area?"

"Only with traveling through it. It's been another's territory since the Romans invaded, and I never felt like taking it away."

As with most of his answers, it left her with more questions. Just then, the bus crested a hill, revealing a patchwork of fields and trees below. Buildings clustered together in the very center, bright white and brick red and dark brown. Even from that distance, their shapes and colors marked them as centuries-old relics. It was a striking view, as if this little town had somehow hidden itself from time, protected and unchanged, while the rest of the world moved on.

Colton nodded, sensing her next question. "That's it. He won't be there but should catch our scents."

She bit her lip, unsure of how she felt about meeting another vargr. "And you really think he'll be friendlier than Giove?"

"No reason for him not to be."

The tour guide announced the name of the town as they entered it, but Alice immediately forgot it, overcome by what she saw. Every street and building looked like history captured and preserved from different periods, and the man's cheerful narration couldn't hide the sense of something ancient gutted into a shell of itself, all nastiness cleaned out and covered up with quaint charm. She had always hated the glassy eyes of taxidermied animals and now felt the same aversion as the bus took them into the main square.

They got off with a handful of other tourists at a 16th-century pub, admittedly beautiful with its thatched roof and whitewashed walls. Its interior was much more modern, offering both tables and bar seats. She didn't miss how Colton guided them to the far corner of the bar, or how he made sure his stool blocked hers from the rest of the room.

Her eerie feeling only grew as they settled in, and she still couldn't say why. The lighting was warm and cozy, and the air smelled like beer and roasting meat. The bartender was a grandmotherly woman in a cable-knit sweater who never stopped smiling, and the conversations from the other customers rarely rose above a murmur. All in all, it should have been a comforting atmosphere to anyone exhausted from sightseeing.

Yet if she closed her eyes, she thought she heard something else beneath the hiss of beer taps and the bartender's cheerful teasing toward another group of tourists. A whisper of a noise, a faint scream that echoed as if she were in a vast land and not a crowded little pub...

Colton's hand squeezed her knee, bringing her back just as the bartender turned her attention to them. Even as her skin crawled, Alice smiled politely while he ordered a pair of stouts and a ploughman's lunch for them to share.

When they were alone again, she murmured, "Something feels... strange. Not dangerous, exactly, but nasty and lingering."

"The whole area is soaked through with magic." He must have caught the sudden alarm in her expression, because he stroked along her leg and added, "Nothing new or even active. It's as dead as the people who cast it. You're sensing what's been left behind. Think of it as bloodstains."

That was a mild way of putting it. Some part of her knew that any concentration on the traces of scent and sound would reveal their terrible origins. Whatever this magic was, it hadn't belonged to witches but could be sensed by them. She shook her head, not wanting to sink to those depths. Since the night the hag king had shown interest in her, she hadn't wanted to think about her heritage as a witch at all, or what it might mean. "What happened here?"

Colton didn't respond immediately, at first because their beers arrived and then because he seemed to choose his words with care. "The people who lived here would offer sacrifices to their gods, usually at the nearby peat bog. At first it was only for formal rituals, but the Roman invasions left them desperate. It became a constant begging."

Her love of mythology sometimes pulled her interest into the history surrounding favorite legends and lore. She knew enough to fill in the details. Some of the victims would have been human.

She thought about how casual Colton seemed in another vargr's territory compared to his feral aggression toward Giove's mere scent on the wind. He must have felt sure this vargr wouldn't pose any threat toward her, and it didn't take much to think through the implications behind that.

A woman at a nearby table shifted in her seat while laughing, and for one sickening moment, the glint of her earrings sharpened into the flash of a bloodied sickle. Alice blinked the phantom away and looked at Colton again. "Something horrible happened to him, didn't it?"

He didn't ask who she meant. There was no need to. Instead, he studied her intently, something there and gone again in his eyes before she could understand it. "He fell in love with a girl. Before he could take her away, she was sacrificed to the bog."

"And he's stayed here all this time?"

Colton shrugged. "It's where she is."

She quickly drank from her glass to stop her mouth from trembling. Colton shifted in his seat, leaning closer as he recognized how near she was to crying. "Alice..."

"I'm fine," she said, quickly. "It's just... sad." She couldn't bring herself to add why those words had stabbed so deep, but it hung there heavy in her mind. *Is that what you would do if I ever...?*

Then the ploughman's lunch arrived. She eyed the piles of meat and cheese and bread, trying to regain her composure. "I always feel so up and down, like I react more than I should. Not like you. You're always so steady."

He raised his eyebrows. "I've been thinking up ways to gut that fucker from the moment he beckoned at you. Trust me, I'm not feeling any calmer about what's happened."

"You don't show it."

"My way of showing things usually involves murder." When she only smiled, he shook his head and added, "Still not scared of me?"

"Never." Her smile widened, kindling a sudden smolder in his eyes. For the first time since that night, she felt herself relax enough to ask the question that had lived in her heart like a parasite. "How much trouble are we in now that the hag king wants me?"

"We'll find out." The indifference in his voice didn't match the heat in his gaze. "Worried about anything in particular?"

She sipped at her beer again. It was thick and bitter and good, and she hoped it would numb the edges of these next words. "I'm worried they'll somehow compel me to join them. They seem so confident about getting what they want, as if they know something I don't."

"Confidence looks the same as delusion."

She laughed a little but quickly fell serious. "I'm also scared of the dreams I had about my mother before all this started. Were they just nightmares, or did they mean something? I've always obsessed over why she left me. Maybe I should've thought harder on why she left at all. And after meeting my grandmother and all the other witches, I keep asking myself whether I'm the delusional one."

Then she looked away, hearing her voice catch with fear. "What if I can't keep this life because of what I am? What if it's my fate as a witch to lose myself and end up like them? How can I resist whatever they accepted?"

"Alice." He leaned in close and cupped her chin, coaxing her to look up at him. His eyes had darkened into something feral. "You're nothing like them. And I'd find you no matter what."

Just as she nodded, they both felt it—a subtle shift in the air. A presence that overwhelmed the ancient traces of death, smoke, and fear with its own agonies and bloody deeds. The skin on the back of her neck prickled as the shadows in the room flickered and then darkened. The other vargr had arrived.

Colton said nothing but shifted in his seat to further block her as the pub's front door opened, revealing a flash of the street traffic before someone stepped inside. Alice dropped her gaze to her beer, aware that her manner was much too stiff to come off as oblivious to the true nature of the man taking the stool nearest to Colton's.

The bartender came over immediately, all former cheer gone. She set a beer before the man without a word between them. Then she retreated to the other end of the bar and began drying glasses with a rag, giving herself a reason to keep her attention away from their corner.

The man took a long drink from his beer. Without looking up, he said, "Bringing any trouble with you?"

His accent was as thick as the other locals', but Alice couldn't glean much else about him. Even pushed back, the hood of his thick winter coat obscured his features, and she was suddenly reminded of how Colton had worn similar clothing when they'd met. A beast hiding what he was. A beast perhaps forgetting what he was.

"No." Colton sounded casual. "Stamping it out."

"Might be harder than you expect. Most who'd recognize your nature are too young to know what you've done. Or they think it's exaggerated. The black wolves aren't looked at with any caution these days. We either keep to ourselves or hide what we are."

"Some of these humans know."

Despite their terse words, Alice didn't need clarification. It was obvious many of the locals in the room understood what had joined them. She read it in their twitching shoulders and nervous glances. The fact surprised her, and she wondered what the other vargr did to be known and accepted, if just barely.

"Not enough of them," replied the other vargr, sounding tired. "I'm in the middle of convincing the local kingpin to leave me the fuck alone. Can't say I'm happy to find you here either."

Alice brushed Colton's arm to signal she was about to speak. "All we want is information. We're trying to learn more about the coven we're hunting. If you don't want to help, we'll move on."

The other vargr still didn't look at her, but she sensed the gesture was meant to be polite. "I don't see how local gossip is needed. You're with a butcher who's the best at doing this. Just kill whoever you find and eventually they'll be the right ones."

"I don't want that. I want the witches who tried to torture and eat my family."

At that, the other vargr finally turned to them, his gaze flickering from Colton to her. He was good-looking in his own blunt way, rugged features magnified by a beard, but it was his eyes that truly struck her. They were the saddest she'd ever seen, pain crystallized into the color of slate. She was surprised by how utterly neutral his attention felt, without interest or calculation.

When his study of her lasted a few seconds too long, Colton growled, a brief yet clear warning.

The other vargr raised an eyebrow but returned his focus to his beer. He didn't seem nervous or suspicious so much as very, very tired. "I'm called Ambrose now. Ambris was too odd for modern tongues."

When Colton gave his name, he nodded and not-quite-looked at Alice again. "Can I speak hers, or will you throw me down a well, too?"

"So, you do hear things."

"Never said I didn't. But I don't go anywhere beyond this village. My life's very quiet. I run a rescue shelter for dogs and I like it very much. I don't want anyone fucking it up." Then he sighed and finished the rest of his beer. "But I'll talk if you want. Not here, though. At the shelter. I hate this village. I keep thinking about burning it down."

Alice remained silent, unsure of how to respond. Colton, however, looked almost amused. "Rumor has it you're their local guardian."

The other vargr grimaced while putting change on the counter. "Their presence helps protect the peatland. That's the only reason they're alive."

"I've been listening when they think I can't understand. They like you much more than you like them. They're even afraid this kingpin might kill you if you keep resisting him."

At that, Ambrose scoffed. "No one can do that. The point of our curse is to survive while anything we love rots to time. That's why I don't understand you coming here. It's not like it'll matter in the end."

Then his gaze found Alice's face, piercing through her as if he sensed her own doubts about their hunt. She forced herself calm and stared back at him, refusing to crumple. "We'd still like your help."

The other vargr nodded and rose from his seat. "I'll wait outside."

After he left, she murmured, "I wouldn't call him friendly."

She didn't miss how the bartender's shoulders sagged in relief when the door shut behind him. Then Colton's hand returned to her thigh, warm and reassuring, and he kissed her until she relaxed again. "He is compared to the rest of us. But if you're uncomfortable around him—"

"No," she whispered against his mouth. It wasn't a lie, not completely. The vargr himself didn't repulse her, not like Giove, but the bare glimpse of him, grief-riddled and worn down, sharpened the fears that had only grown from admitting their existence. She once thought nothing could terrify her more than being alone, but now she also dreaded what would happen to those *she* left behind.

Yet there was no time to dwell on it, not when the mere thoughts threatened to freeze her in place, and so she made herself smile. "Besides, he likes dogs, so he can't be that bad. I say we find out what we can."

CHAPTER SIXTEEN

A Future Seen in the Past

Ambrose seemed much happier out in the elements, even sounding friendly as he said, "It's not too long a walk. Maybe an hour or so. I don't drive."

When Colton remained silent, Alice nodded politely, appreciating the chance to stretch her legs and take in the view. Once they left the town and its lush border of fields and trees, the grass turned tough and weedy-looking. The land wasn't truly flat, with mild rises and falls, yet she saw nowhere to hide and nowhere to rest, just scrubby, soft ground marked by occasional paths created from generations of feet.

Ambrose and Colton ignored both these and the crumbling walls that emerged from the ground and sank back in just as quickly, but Alice found herself studying the moss-covered stone. It was easy to imagine the land swallowing anything else that tried to exist. There weren't even any trees or bushes. She felt very small and intrusive in the middle of such harsh beauty.

Out in the wild, both vargr slipped into their nature even as they remained in human form. Silent, focused. Unrelenting. Neither of them spoke and kept yards apart, always aware of each other. Shoulders tight with caution. Steps careful as if ready to spring into a lunge. They had come to an agreement, but that didn't mean they were at ease with each other.

If they were hyper-cautious, then she was growing ever more distracted. The ghostly sensations she'd experienced back in the town were magnified out here, as abrasive as the wind cutting at her face. Voices hissed among the bristling deergrass. A scream once came from a distant ridge of forest. Whenever she stepped onto damp ground, she glanced down, half-expecting blood to well up around her shoes.

Impossible to guess how much time had passed before their path reached the crest of a slope and revealed the dark, dense earth on the other side. Pools of water, black and sluggish, reflected the grey sky. The smell of decaying plants thickened the air.

A hump rose in the very middle, and after a moment she recognized it as the remains of a tree. It must have been ancient, all branches snapped off and the bark too weathered to tell its original color. It looked less like a stump than a growth on the earth, misshapen and unnerving.

Ambrose must have sensed the subject of her attention, because without looking back, he said, "That's the bog. No one goes there but me."

The chill she had felt back at the pub now felt like ice-cold terror—but not her own. She squeezed her eyes shut, trying to calm down. Yet when she looked up again, the stump had turned into a mammoth white tree, gnarled and leafless. Blood trailed down its bark. Scraps of skin dangled from its branches.

Her breath caught in her throat. Dimly, she heard the sound of her name, there and gone against the growing whispers. Indistinct words rose to the rhythm of her pulse as fresh trails of red ran down the trunk, urging her closer for all that her feet didn't move.

A great, throbbing heart remained in there somewhere, as if the tree itself had absorbed all flesh fed to the bog and all blood spilled into its water. It was dead but somehow still hungered, aware of her in the way of a normal plant following the sunlight.

Closer, it hissed. The whispers echoed the word. *Closer so you can sink down and sleep. You won't even feel it when your bones begin to melt...*

A hand grabbed her chin, forcing her to look away from the tree. Her mind cleared in a flash, and she realized she was gasping for breath, bile sour in her throat as she stared into Colton's feral eyes.

"It—" she started to say, gaze instinctively darting back toward the tree.

"No." His voice came out as a snarl, and he stepped closer to fill her view. "Don't look anywhere else. Just at me."

"I'm sorry," she murmured, pressing the back of her hand against her mouth. Her heart jumped in her chest. Her thoughts felt sluggish. She wasn't sure if she was about to cry or throw up. "I just looked at the tree, and then it... it's where they performed the sacrifices, isn't it? They fed people to that thing."

"They thought it was god-touched," murmured Ambrose. He stared at her, surprise sharpening his eyes, but his next words were toward Colton, who remained intent on her. "She's sensitive. Most don't know it's more than a stump."

"It's a tree of death," she managed, and thought she heard a ghostly cackle.

"And power. You'd be amazed at the number of witches who thought they could run me off and use the tree for their own purposes."

"How can you stand being near it? Can't you hear the whispers?"

"All the time. It sings to itself like a madman at night. But she's in that same mud somewhere, deep down, and she's the one I visit. Not it."

Alice shuddered, but in the next moment, Colton's thumb brushed over her mouth, keeping her grounded. As the sick feeling slowly receded against the heat of his touch, she murmured, "I really don't want to get any closer to that tree."

"You think I'd let you?" When she tried to push hair out of her face with trembling fingers, he did it for her.

It was a small act, yet from the corner of her eye, she saw Ambrose abruptly circle away. From his expression, he was remembering times when he had been able to touch someone with such care. He stared at the distant stump and said, "The shelter's off to the left, far enough that you won't hear the tree. Just the dogs."

After a final breath to collect herself, she nodded. "That's fine. I love dogs."

The shelter looked well-constructed, with thought and care put into its design. A gate allowed one entry into the property, and from there, the gravel path split to different buildings, all of them modern and in good condition. The exercise fields had their own fences, and there were separate sheds for what she guessed was storage. Barking could already be heard.

As they approached, she started feeling better. Ambrose certainly cheered up, even appearing eager as he said, "I've run the shelter for 20 years now. It started as a way to save retired racing greyhounds, but I've worked up to enough steady donations and funding to accept any dog that's brought in. That's the office there, but I need to see them first. They know I'm back."

Inside, she was pleased to see that the cages were large and clean, with heated beds and a few toys for each dog. No one could doubt that they were happy to see him, yelping and jumping to get his attention. Their coats looked glossy and their eyes bright. Ambrose greeted each one through the bars of its cage, grinning for the first time.

"Meet your approval?" murmured Colton, picking up on her scrutiny of their surroundings.

She smiled a little. "It looks clean and well-run. And they're not afraid of him at all."

She had spoken quietly, but Ambrose still looked up from petting a yellow retriever mix. The dog snuffled at his face as he said, "I like dogs. They're the reason I get up in the morning. They can sense that along with what I am. And these ones need me as much as I need them. Rabbits, deer... even beasts of burden still have their prey fear. But a dog's been bred out of being a predator. All they know is trust and loyalty. What chance does a creature like that have against a human who decides to be cruel?"

As he looked down at the dog again, rubbing its ears while it panted happily, understanding cut through Alice. She knew the pain of feeling trapped by life as well as anyone, and the starkness of this insight about him left her quiet even as a middle-aged woman stepped out from one of the back rooms, already pulling on her coat.

She gave Alice and Colton a polite smile, obviously thinking they were there to adopt. "Mr. Oakes? I've just finished up, but Sean's never showed to take the dogs out."

"I'll take care of it."

It was a clear dismissal, but the woman hesitated. Her expression suggested she wanted to say far more than she could in front of company. "Mr. Gibbs messaged twice today."

Ambrose didn't even look up. "I'll take care of that, too. See you Monday."

After the woman left, the room fell silent. The dogs had all calmed down, settling in their beds or turning their attention elsewhere. Colton had already taken in the state of the shelter and now watched Ambrose without giving away a hint of what he thought. Ambrose didn't seem inclined to start up a conversation either, now scratching the dog's back.

"I can help walk the dogs," Alice found herself saying. "If it'll make things easier."

"I've done it alone before," came the even reply.

She hesitated and then decided to test her suspicions. "I meant if it'll be easier to have me out of the way. You haven't said a word to each other since the pub, and neither of you are comfortable right now. He doesn't like it when you look at me, and I don't think you like looking at me either. It's too painful."

Ambrose didn't look her way, but she still caught the surprise in his expression. After a moment, he nodded. "You can try Gracie here. She likes people but not other dogs, so we exercise her alone."

When she offered a hand, the dog sniffed her and resumed panting, dark eyes shining with excitement as Ambrose handed over a harness and leash.

Gracie behaved well as they walked out to one of the fields, whining and twitching from the urge to run while Alice shut the gate behind them. A rack of balls waited nearby, and when

Alice grabbed one, she briefly felt like she'd fallen back into time. A vet intern with vague dreams of owning her own clinic one day. A girl with fears that seeped away whenever she was around animals. Whenever she could *help* them.

She unhooked Gracie's leash and watched the dog race across the entire length of the field. Her heart felt lighter with each second. By the time Gracie returned for the ball raised in her hand, panting and jumping in the air, she was smiling, voice rising into a silly pitch she hadn't used for years.

Back near the gate, the two vargr watched.

Then Ambrose said, "You're an idiot."

"Fuck you."

The other vargr turned away. "You gave yourself a weakness. You would've stayed lonely before. Now you'll be a hopeless fuck like me."

"I forgot how much you blather on."

"I've barely said anything. Anyway, it's why you're here, isn't it? To hear what I know."

At that, Colton looked over at the other vargr. His voice remained flat. "What do you want in return?"

Ambrose lit a cigarette. The pain on his face was palpable. His silence lasted until his first breath of smoke. "Do you remember the language of her people? It's been dead for a thousand years. Maybe more. I'm starting to lose the words. I can only recall the sound of her voice."

When Colton replied, it wasn't in English. "I'll speak as much of it as I can."

"That's all I ask." Ambrose took another drag from his cigarette before adding, "She's very sensitive to body language. Very cautious. Was she living with someone abusive before you found her?"

"Why do you want to know?"

"Merely curious. Half the dogs I rescue are abused. You recognize the behavior after a while."

"Then why fucking ask?"

Ambrose laughed. "If I talk just as much, then you're just as hostile. I've told you, I want to remember as much of this language as possible. That means a lot of words."

Colton grimaced. "At least make them useful. What do you know about the Golden Stag coven?"

"They're a strong coven despite falling apart for the past century. Their king, Edric, isn't the most brutal warlock out there, but his hunger made up for it. They had a dominant reach across Europe. Probably the most influential and certainly the wealthiest."

"What changed?"

"He grew obsessed with a particular witch and tried to breed an heir to his crown. She died pregnant with his child." Then Ambrose's voice darkened with disgust. "It'd be a very tragic story, except that he was the one who killed her. No one knows why, only that he did it in a blind rage. Apparently, he's been very sorry ever since."

Colton growled softly. "Is that so?"

"I'd call it sulking. You know how these kings are when they don't get what they want. Well, it seems he wanted her after all, or perhaps just the child. Since her death, he's withdrawn from everything. No more parties. No more conquests. His coven's desperate to raise his spirits again. Rumor suggests they're looking for a replacement to the girl he killed."

Colton's expression remained inscrutable. "Who's likely to help him?"

"There are two covens old enough to remember you. Flavius up in Scotland, and Matera over in Italy. They won't. All the rest are too young. They might, they might not. There are about 20 major covens across Europe and countless smaller ones feeding on their scraps. Without you, there's been nothing to keep them in check."

"What about Michel?"

Ambrose stared at him. "Michel? He's dead. He's been dead for eight hundred years. You were the one who killed him."

"Hm. That's right."

"...you were nearly there, weren't you? Wasted to nothing. Even your scent has worn away."

When the words drew a mere shrug in response, the other vargr added, "This Edric is no different from any other warlock. He won't back down. And they're all arrogant these days. Overconfident. If he wants her..."

"I never said he did."

"I'm not a fucking idiot. You smell like buried rage."

They both fell silent. Happy barking drew their attention back to the field. Alice now looked as muddy as Gracie, laughing as the dog bounded around her with the ball in her mouth.

With a shake of his head, Ambrose circled away. The cigarette had burned to a nub between his fingers. "We're fated to remain alone. You can't protect her forever. She'll die. Everything does except for us."

Colton didn't acknowledge the words, but when he faced the other vargr, his eyes gleamed with sudden viciousness. "One more thing. Any recent visitors asking these same questions about me?"

Ambrose met his stare, unflinching. "Do you really think you can intimidate me?"

The older vargr tilted his head in the direction of the distant tree. "I think anyone could if they knew how to go about it."

Ambrose looked away first, somehow appearing even more tired. "So, that's why you're here. I wondered. It's not about information at all. You just want to know if the coven was clever enough to seek me out. They've already got a vargr in their pocket. Adair."

"He wouldn't help with this. Just piss himself and run."

The other vargr raised an eyebrow but didn't argue.

Just then, a car appeared in the distance. Dark in color yet otherwise nondescript, it took the side road that would lead to the shelter. Both vargr watched with sudden tension.

"Your kingpin?" said Colton, briefly scenting the wind. There were four men, two of them with guns.

Ambrose nodded. "Better be quick about any further questions. I shook off his first warning, so he won't be friendly this time."

Yet Colton was already walking toward the field, drawing the attention of Alice, who also watched the car with sudden caution. At the jerk of his head, she quickly leashed the dog and hurried over.

"What is it?" she said, absently soothing Gracie as she whined.

A storage shed and tall hedges blocked most of their view from the property entrance, but Colton didn't answer until he seemed sure they hadn't been noticed. "Time to go. Looks like Mr. Gibbs is tired of leaving messages."

"You mean, the man threatening him?" She glanced over at Ambrose, who had walked over to meet the visitors at the property gate. The men who got out looked as nondescript as the car. Only the one in the nicest coat smiled while they all went into the office. "Will he be okay?"

"It's not like they can kill him."

"But what about the dogs?" When he shrugged, she insisted, "Colton, what if they try to hurt the dogs?"

The disinterest in his eyes faded when he saw her distress, but in the next moment, they both heard footsteps. Then Gracie barked, lunging against her leash. Her fur bristled along her back.

A shared glance, and then Alice eased back with the dog, trying to quiet her while Colton stepped behind the nearest hedge. She kept herself out in the open, trying to look surprised and nervous when the man appeared in view and saw her.

He was short and as muscular as a bodybuilder, with a neck thicker than his head. He flashed her a big grin and barked back at the agitated dog, who was now throwing up pebbles with her lunges. Alice pulled her back further, eyeing the fresh blood on his too-tight shirt.

"Unfriendly, is he? You work for Oakes?"

She remained silent, realizing her American accent would give things away. He was almost close enough to the hedge. Her teeth ached as she edged away again. Her arm hurt from holding onto Gracie.

"Better answer my questions. It'd be a shame to ruin such a pretty face." Then he took another step.

Colton lunged out. The dog's barking grew frenzied as the man managed to pull out a gun, but in one vicious movement, Colton caught the hand holding it and forced the nozzle under the man's chin. The man managed a scream before the gun went off. His face disappeared in a spray of blood.

Gracie flinched back against Alice, subdued into whining. Alice crouched down to pet her, trying to soothe her trembling while Colton shoved the body away. As she tied the leash to the nearest pole, he looked at her. There was nothing human in his gaze. "Ready?"

She nodded, feeling her own bloodlust rise.

They approached the office as wolves, silent and unnoticed. In her fur, it was easy to catch the smell of Ambrose's blood. The men's sweat smelled like menace and uncertainty, and she bared her teeth while they circled around the building, taking in the nuances of the three they were about to kill—trying to find which of them had the remaining gun.

A voice drifted out as they prowled. "I don't think we're getting anywhere, Mr. Oakes."

Ambrose's reply sounded strained yet calm. "That's because intimidation won't work on me. You know what I am."

"I've heard the barmy old stories, but I'm a very practical man."

Just then, the black wolf twitched his ears at her. She understood the signal and followed as he ran toward the nearest window. His power shattered the glass; her speed caught the arm aiming the gun at Ambrose's face.

She bit until bone cracked and then lunged for the throat to stop the screams. Her jaws locked in tight despite the fingers flailing at her head. Blood soaked into her fur while she waited through the choking, trusting the black wolf to finish the others.

Once, she glanced up and caught sight of Ambrose pulling at a letter opener that had been driven through his hand to pin it against his desk. He bled from the nose but looked irritated more than anything, grimacing when the yelling rose into shrieks as the black wolf ripped into a man's belly. By the time he freed himself, it was all over. As the terror in the air faded, she could smell Ambrose's surprise that they'd helped him.

Only Mr. Gibbs was still alive, bleeding from a crippling bite to the leg. He had squeezed himself back into a corner, sweating and speechless at the sight of his dead men and the black wolf pacing nearby.

With a sigh, Ambrose rose from his chair and glanced at her. "There are towels in the back room and extra clothes if you need them."

Realizing the fighting was finished, she went into the back and changed form. The black wolf followed yet remained in his fur, circling around her while she washed up at the sink. As she wrapped a worn towel around herself, she heard Ambrose speak.

"They're not like me. They're active against threats. I told you not to send a man after them."

She approached the doorway in time to watch Ambrose crouch before Mr. Gibbs. Despite the fact that the man had made him bleed, had wanted to break him, there was no malice or glee on the vargr's face, just a grim weariness of having done this many times before. "I'm more diplomatic. I pay taxes. I keep presentable. And I listen to people when they claim they want a nice chat."

Then he showed the man his hand as it healed, leaving only dried blood behind. "I realize this is hard to hear for someone like yourself, but there's nothing to be done. I won't give you what you want. There's no way to make me."

"Christ," muttered the man, grabbing at his leg. "Something's got to kill you. You can't survive everything, you bastard."

Ambrose's hand tightened into a fist. Alice tensed instinctively, and beside her, the black wolf growled. The air suddenly charged.

"Do you think I like this?" For the first time, Ambrose's voice lost its calm. In one swift move, he grabbed the man by his shirt collar, eyes darkening. "Do you think I like being like this? That nothing affects me?"

The man stuttered as Ambrose's grip moved to his neck, squeezing with each word. "Every night, I close my eyes and hope I won't wake up in the morning. That this world and its scum won't be there. There's no end for me. No escape."

As Mr. Gibb's fingers scratched at his hands, Ambrose rose to his feet, dragging the man up with him. "The one bit of hope I found was taken before I could even understand what she was to me. Yet you think I *want* this. That this is all a big fucking laugh."

Then he slammed the man against the wall, voice thickening into a snarl. "I want to die. I've wanted to die for two thousand fucking years. Let me die!"

With those last words, he wrenched the man's head. Blood splattered.

Alice kept very still as the twitching body slid back to the ground. Ambrose remained standing, panting as he stared off into the distance. He didn't seem to realize there was only a head left in his grip.

She must have made a noise. A hiss of breath, perhaps, or her nails digging into the doorway. Whatever it was, the other vargr suddenly looked at her. There was no rational thought left in his eyes. When his shoulders hunched, she knew he was about to lunge.

Then Colton was there with bared teeth, slamming into the other vargr. Howls rose up from the shelter as he shook off Ambrose's attacks and pinned him back against the door, easily holding the other vargr despite his rabid struggling.

Alice's pulse hammered in her ears as Colton growled, "What was her name?"

The other vargr's eyes looked black with rage, yet a gleam of confusion appeared in them even as he snarled. The barking outside grew frenzied.

Colton tightened his grip. "Her *name*. I know you'll never lose it, even when the rest of your mind is fucked."

"Brea." The word was choked with froth.

Colton nodded. "And what was the first thing she ever told you?"

Ambrose panted for a few moments. "She said, "You don't scare me.""

Then his legs gave out, and he collapsed to the ground. Despite his bloodied face and hands, he suddenly looked pitiful.

When Colton circled away in silence, he didn't stir. The barking grew louder, nearer, and Alice looked over in time to see Gracie jump through the broken window. The dog ran over to Ambrose, tail wagging madly while she whimpered. As she licked at the blood on his face, he slowly started petting her.

Alice found herself glancing away, feeling as though her attention had suddenly grown intrusive.

"Ready to go?" murmured Colton in her ear. He sounded as steady as always, but the hunter's gleam hadn't yet left his eyes.

Even as she nodded, Ambrose looked up at them. He still sounded unsteady as he said, "Wait. You helped my dogs. I appreciate that. A witch from the Golden Stag coven did come to me. The one who lives up in Scotland and specializes in finding rare and lost magic. I didn't help her, but what she offered would interest you."

"We're listening," said Colton.

As Gracie sat beside him, tail still wagging, he said, "She claims she found a way to control life and death. A ritual that can raise Brea from the dead... or send me back."

When Alice stiffened, his gaze flickered to her. The weariness had returned to his face while he added, "I didn't believe what she offered. There's no reason to. How can they raise the dead when they can't even raise their king's cock? As for myself, I know there's no escape from this. We're not affected by magic once we come back from the grave. We survive everything. That's our fate."

Much later, when night had fallen and they had finished traveling for the day, Alice looked up from the flames crackling in the fireplace and said, "I feel so bad for him."

She had already showered and wrapped herself up in a thick robe against the cold drafts of the Scottish countryside. Colton had remained fully dressed, shoes silent while he paced around the room. They were in a medieval castle renovated into a modern hotel, but she didn't sense anything unpleasant in the ancient stone and intricate tapestries. Colton, though, was definitely on edge, responding to her comment with a brief growl.

"What is it?" she said, softly.

He shrugged, and in the next moment crouched beside her to feed another log to the fire. She read the tension in his broad shoulders and simmering silence, and then fell quiet as well, understanding that he struggled for the words he usually scorned.

Before he could find them, her phone rang with a Facetime request. She checked it and sighed. "It's Denise. She must not realize what time it is here. She mentioned wanting to call and check in on us."

As he prowled out of view, she put on a pleasant smile and accepted the request.

Denise beamed at her from thousands of miles away. "Honey! How are you? It's not too late over there, is it?"

"No, it's fine. We were going to stay up for a few more hours."

"Are you sure? You look tired."

"It's just jet-lag."

"Oh, that's perfectly understandable. If you want to get some rest, I can call later."

"No," said Alice, quickly. "I'd love to see everyone now."

With a start, she realized it was true. They were close to the next witch, but all hunting excitement had long left her heart. She felt raw, and angry, and grief-stricken for reasons she couldn't name.

Denise smiled again. "I'm so excited to hear how England went. I'm trying to convince Tom that we should all go on a family trip abroad next summer. I don't think he'll let us vacation anywhere near a forest ever again."

"How are things going?"

Her stepmother fell serious. "I feel so lucky. They still haven't found any of the other horseback riders. When I think of what I'd be doing right now if Fleur was still missing... I don't think I could do anything at all. I think I'd stop functioning. The experts warned us that she could have nightmares or show other signs of trauma, but she insists she feels fine. Oh, and she got 100% on her essay and wants to thank you and Colton. Let me just..."

The screen lurched and spun while Denise walked with her phone. When it fell still again, Fleur was in view, turning from the kitchen sink long enough to pop one of her earbuds out and wave. There was sauce all over her sweatshirt, but she didn't seem to care. "Hey. Thanks."

When she turned away again, Denise swiveled the phone back to herself. "We're making dinner right now. Vegan macaroni and cheese. Did you know you can use cauliflower in place of pasta? You wouldn't think it'd work, but..."

As her stepmother barreled on, Alice swallowed a lump in her throat. Suddenly, she realized how badly she wanted all this to be over. She *missed* them. Not the faint regret that had chilled her at times while living with Magdalene, but something raw and frustrated. Something that proved she'd built up enough of a life for herself that leaving it made her homesick. She'd always grieved for lost things, but the pain of those waiting for her to come back felt new and awkward.

They talked about little nothings for several minutes before Denise said, "You really do look tired, sweetheart. Your father will be off work in another hour, but I think we should let you go for tonight. We can't wait until you're back home."

Her heart squeezed painfully. "I can't either. Bye."

There was a final chirp of, "Love you!"

Then she was left staring at a blank screen.

"Your scent's full of grief." Colton's voice sounded unexpectedly gentle.

She looked up as he approached, still feeling hollow. "I miss them." Even as tears burned in her eyes, she laughed and added, "I never thought I'd grow so close to them. But I have, and I miss them."

In the following silence, she ran fingers through her hair, drying it with the heat from the fire. Within a few breaths, his hand replaced hers, and she had to close her eyes against the sensation. Some part of her still wondered how someone so casual about carnage could also lick at the scars of her heart with such care. A nightmare had found her, and yet she felt safe in his presence even while the rest of the world tried to steal what it wished.

"Alice."

At the sound of his voice, she looked at him again. In the firelight, his eyes were as yellow as when he was a wolf. "Do you want to go back to them?"

She blinked, confused. "The hunt isn't over."

When he sighed, she sensed he was about to reveal the words he'd fought with in silence. "You could go home. I could stay here and finish it."

"No." She didn't even have to think about it. When he continued to study her, she added, "Is that what you want? To hunt the rest of the coven alone? But... I'm a good hunter. I know I can do this. I've made some mistakes, but I can—"

"Alice. That's not it. You've done nothing wrong on this hunt. As for what I want..." Then he broke off with a grimace.

She stroked the side of his face, fingers rasping against his stubble as she sensed his frustration. "Whatever it is, I want to hear it. I won't mind."

"It's nothing like that. It's just finding the fucking words." Their noses brushed before he added, "All I want is to be with you. You're the reason each day means something, and I'm miserable whenever you're out of sight. But it'd be the safer way."

The words, grudging as they were, left her pressing her face against his neck to hide her tears. "You could be in just as much danger. You heard what that witch told Ambrose."

"He's skeptical for a good reason. There's no way to get rid of us. Many have tried. Never works."

For a while, she only listened to his heartbeat while he continued to dry her hair. When she felt sure she could speak steadily, she said, "I want to do this. I went into this hunt meaning to finish it. I don't think I could live with myself if I just—just went home and had you do the rest. I know you wouldn't hold it against me, but I'd hold it against myself."

His voice rumbled against her. "Even though you're afraid?"

"Yes. I need to know that I'm *not* my mother. That I won't run away when the world feels too threatening." Then she straightened up enough to look at him, and her next words came out as fiercely as a growl. "I want to stay. Nothing's going to keep me from this, and nothing's going to keep me from *you*. Not even my fear."

He never showed much emotion, this wolf hiding as a man, yet a savage light filled his eyes as he nodded. Then he caught her chin just how she liked, angling her head so that his mouth could devour hers.

She lost herself in the slide of his tongue and the scrape of his teeth, feeling all the emotions that had bludgeoned her mind throughout the day now melt into simple heat. When they broke off, she whispered against his mouth, "Make me forget everything for tonight. Just for a little while."

His growl went straight down her spine. A final, tender kiss, and then he turned ferocious, ripping her robe open. She barely had time to feel the cold air before he was on her.

A thick rug was placed close to the hearth, and that was where she found herself on hands and knees, begging him with each twitch of her hips to go harder, rougher. Drops of his sweat fell on her back and shoulders. The floor creaked from his thrusts jolting her. In the dim firelight, the rest of the world faded to his relentless rhythm and possessive hands.

She arched, feeling his power turn the desperation of the day into something clean and blinding, and was panting even before fingers slid over her hip and between her legs. As they pressed against her clit, she howled instead, lost in her climax.

When thought returned to her, she was on her back with his cock still deep inside, hard and unrelenting as he licked at her breasts.

"More?" she managed.

She felt him smile before he bit her nipple, leaving her gasping. "Haven't even started."

Long afterward, her skin burning from his teeth, she whispered, "I love you, and I know you love me. But I don't want you to end up like him if something ever happens. I don't want you to give up."

When he tensed against her, she insisted, "Please. Promise me."

"I can't." His voice sounded very flat even as his touch remained tender. "Not without lying to you."

CHAPTER SEVENTEEN

Tricked

The witch who called herself Cleo stood among the lonely ruins, moving only to adjust her spectacles against the harsh winds. She looked far out of place among the crumbling walls of the castle, more like a young tourist in her thick coat, ripped jeans, and sturdy hiking boots.

A deceptive sight—she knew this place better than anyone and yet glanced at the stones scattered in the green pastures without a hint of affection. She had been born in this area and had stared at the castle quite often as a child. Always hating how pitiful it looked, like the carcass of a mighty beast. Always hating how the moldering arches were the grandest things she could ever hope to see.

It was sheer familiarity that brought her here, and all her attention remained fixed on the heavy book in her arms. It was an old, ugly-looking thing—its leather binding had cracked with age, and blood and grime spattered every page. Yet its presence gave her the confidence to pull off her scarf and let the wind whip her scent for miles. Eventually, the beast that had killed two from her coven would find it and track it.

Portia and Vanna had both been fools; they had believed the power of their king would protect them. She knew better. He was the keystone to their rituals, the raw strength that granted their wishes true... and his force worked through *their* words and *their* plans. In the end, their flaws had failed them. She intended to do better.

She knew nothing about the black wolves, and apparently her coven-sisters hadn't known enough. Yet within the tattered pages of this grimoire, ancient witches shared rituals and abilities otherwise lost to time. Her research had revealed no insight into what sort of magic put a man in his grave and pulled him back out as a wolf, but she had found something even better: a way to end immortality.

From the satchel beside her, she withdrew a long dagger. The dark, triangular blade gleamed like an oil slick. Sigils appeared on its surface as she placed it on the book.

"Not yet," she said, softly, and the sigils brightened as if the dagger sensed her words. "Not until the end."

Then she put both objects back in the satchel and found a broken wall to sit on, ignoring how her brief movement ignited a rattle of metal. Ah, yes, her first line of defense, even now fanning out around her new position. Silent, obedient, standing at attention as if the decrepit stones were still a worthy castle: fully armored knights with their weapons at ready. The bones inside them had belonged to medieval warriors, but now they were unthinking, unliving things, nothing more than puppets to her commands.

There were twelve of them of course—twelve to represent her king's crown of antlers. Cleo couldn't remember the last time she had thought of him with anything close to affection, but it never hurt to ingratiate herself to his ego. She doubted *any* of the coven truly adored him. Merely his power.

They all waited, alert to the first sign of intruders...

Clouds had slipped between the nearby mountains when she caught sight of them. From that distance, they were mere blots against the rugged landscape, easy to mistake as lost backpackers or tourists. Yet they moved with purpose, and her skin prickled at the exact moment their path turned in her direction.

When they were near enough to make out their faces, she wondered how Portia and Vanna had ever underestimated the vargr. Even in human form, he looked feral, the glint in his eyes suggesting he had already decided how to kill her. If she hadn't met Adair and learned what the famed black wolves were really like, she would have been terrified.

She studied the witch beside him with far less caution. Jealousy was something she hated to feel, but there it was, worming its way into her heart at the sight of the girl who had captured their king's attention with her mere appearance.

It was easy to see why. Even as this Alice studied her with open hatred, she possessed a vulnerable air that they had all lost centuries ago. To think that his tastes could be so simple... so blind to other options. It was infuriating.

She struggled to keep her reaction hidden while they slowed to study the motionless knights. When they remained silent, she called out, "They're here for my protection and won't attack unless I tell them. You've killed two members of my coven. I didn't think you'd be any friendlier with me, even though I've done nothing to harm you."

"Yet," said the girl. If the vargr beside her had an air of impassive brutality, then she was unrestrained emotion, her voice shaking with anger.

Cleo remained sitting, remained still and composed. She had prepared for a fight, but that didn't mean she was averse to taking an easier way out. The vargr wasn't about to listen; he eyed the knights without a hint of doubt, ready to attack. The girl, though, might be open to persuasion. "It's possible to avoid any further killing. To find a peaceful way out of this."

"If this is some trick..."

"I swear I'm being sincere. I'm sure your companion can smell as much. There's plenty of magic I could use to get the first blow in, but I'm trying to negotiate, not attack." Cleo watched the vargr from the corner of her eye. Strange, how he made her nervous in a way that Adair didn't. He seemed much closer to the savage side of his nature, and she fervently hoped the girl would take the smart way out.

The girl nodded. "Go on."

Cleo sighed and glanced around at the harsh rock puncturing through the green grass. "There used to be a village here before a plague wiped it out. I grew up in it. I had a miserable childhood, believing I'd be nothing more than an ignorant hedge witch using charms to give her goats more milk than her neighbors'. That I would marry some brute and breed for him like I was a farm animal myself until I was discovered and burned for what I could do. I hated every part of my life, including its future.

"When a warlock came for me, I didn't like him any more than the village boys. But I understood that becoming his was far better than any other option. He could give me the power to find my true joy in life. Books. Knowledge. New experiences." Her fingers stroked the satchel until she realized the vargr was now watching her.

She quickly folded her hands and added, "That warlock wasn't Edric. I've been in several covens and served several hag kings. Just because they want you now doesn't mean they want you forever."

The girl shook her head. "Why are you telling me this?"

"I'm saying Edric will lose interest in you. He certainly has with the rest of us. Why not take the best way out for both parties? Join the coven while he wants you and leave it again when he's finished."

The girl laughed, a high, disbelieving sound.

Cleo stiffened. She hated being sneered at. "Don't dismiss it that quickly. It's a lot more rational than your current campaign of death. You'd have to leave the child behind, but that—"

"You're a few words away from a ruined throat," said the vargr. His voice sounded rough as a growl and unnervingly flat.

Cleo resisted the urge to reach for the knife. As her gaze darted back to the girl, she said, "I'm just pointing out that you don't have to like the hag king—or the rest of us—to be part of the coven. Pretend enough to get by and then use the power he gives you for what you truly want. Why turn away this opportunity when you can exploit it?"

"Let him use me so I can use him. Does that sum it up?" The girl had fallen serious again, and the bitterness in her voice suggested she was anything but convinced. The vargr eyed the knights once more.

Cleo tried a final time, refusing to fail that quickly. "What would you really lose? Even as his, you can keep your own sense of self. It merely has to stay hidden. It's a shame that my coven-sisters have repulsed you with their behavior, but it doesn't have to be yours. You can remain better than them."

"Is that what you think *you* are? Do you think you're better?"

"Completely. They really believe they can win his eternal favor and always be his special one. I've never had such delusions."

"But you still want him. You still sacrifice people in his name. And right now, you're aching to win me over peacefully because you're sure he'll notice you for it." The girl's voice dipped into a growl as she added, "You would've eaten my stepmother and sister along with the others. You do what they do. You say what they say. How can you call yourself better when you act exactly like them?"

With a hiss, Cleo rose from her seat, finally fed up. "You're thinking like a child. Become his, get more from it than you ever could on your own, and then go back to the life you want, including your wolf. Believe me, this is the only peaceful way."

"We're way past the point of that," said the girl. Her eyes changed color as she and the vargr both circled away.

Cleo resisted the urge to spit. "So be it. You're both such fools."

Then the knights jumped past her, axes and swords raised high.

The vargr snarled something at the girl and lunged at the nearest one. Cleo watched from the corner of her eye while grabbing at the satchel, interested in how the girl struggled with changing into a wolf. It looked painful, as if she did it out of sheer willpower rather than any formal knowledge or spell, but she also seemed used to it, shaking her fur in place and growling as Cleo straightened up with the grimoire and dagger.

Cleo kept her expression blank—not an easy task as the vargr disarmed the first knight and beheaded it with its own axe. He obviously knew what he was doing, and the bastard was *strong*. Even as the armor crumpled, revealing the cracked bone inside, she pressed her palm against the grimoire, flooding the rest of the knights with extra speed.

The she-wolf tried pulling a knight down with her weight, but her teeth glanced off the armor. She avoided the stab of its sword without fear and circled around to try again.

Cleo bit back a curse; she had commanded the knights not to injure the girl. The vargr yelled at the she-wolf again, words blurred by the rattle of armor as the knights attempted to swarm him. Cleo guessed that he was telling her to flee and felt her breath fall shallow at the idea.

It further constricted when yellow eyes met hers and revealed what flashed through the she-wolf's mind: if Cleo commanded them, then stopping her might stop them all. Her fingers began to sweat against the book.

Two more knights crumpled to the ground, but another caught the vargr's side with its sword, staggering him. At that, the she-wolf snarled and lunged for Cleo, who ran further back into the ruins. The vargr roared something, his words muffled by the frantic beat of her heart as she stopped beneath an archway that stood alone. The grimoire also sweated in her hands, the human skin it had been bound with now heating up from the force of this next spell.

Just as she turned with the book tight to her chest, teeth latched onto her arm and pulled her to the ground. Goose down from her coat exploded into the air. Her arm felt like it was being ripped out of its socket. Everything was fur and muscle and snarling.

Then the book twisted beneath her stiff fingers, and she knew the she-wolf had swallowed enough blood.

"Get back!" she screamed, panic driving her voice high, and then the power was there, invisible but as forceful as slashing antlers.

Another knight fell while the she-wolf was flung away, yet the rest continued blocking the vargr from reaching her. Cleo panted as the she-wolf struggled upright as a girl again, confusion clear on her blood-smeared face. Only a few feet separated them, but all fear drained from Cleo while she shrugged off her ruined coat and pulled up the sleeves of her shirt.

"Your black wolf isn't the only invincible thing," she said, sneaking a glance as another knight fell. She would have to be quick. "But he's strong enough that we didn't think we could keep him from protecting you. Instead, we found a way to make sure you couldn't stand being near him. All it takes is a taste of blood."

Even as the girl grabbed at a nearby sword, the will to fight still on her face, Cleo used the dagger on her own arm, spilling more blood onto the opened grimoire. The girl screamed, contorting with the pages. Somewhere beyond the mass of metal, the vargr snarled again.

Cleo called the remaining knights to separate them and then ignored everything except her work, gritting her teeth while carving sigils into the ground and using her wounded arm to drip blood onto them. Then she bowed her head, feeling the hag king's will respond. The grimoire pulsed like a heart from the sudden flush of power. It coursed through her as well, exhilarating and hot as it followed her blood to the girl. The screaming abruptly stopped.

It had been so long since she'd felt her king's strength fill her full. For several breaths, Cleo forgot where she was and what was happening. The rush felt as explosive as a climax, as searing as a knife wound. She felt like she could crack the entire world from pounding her fist against the ground. She felt like she could crush every person she hated by sheer force of will. There was nothing sweeter than a warlock's power and her will to guide it.

When her eyes cleared again, she was shaking and panting, kneeling on the grass with the book clutched to her like a child. The vargr was through all but two of the knights, his hunter's instinct severing the plates of armor into heaps of over-decorated metal. The blood on his face magnified the wild rage in his eyes.

The remaining knights blocked his view but not hers, and she smiled at what she saw, voice rising even as he crippled them into useless bones. "Too late! She won't recognize you now. She can't."

Then her gaze darted back to what stumbled up from where the girl had been. A doe, panicked yet unsteady on her delicate legs. Wide eyes glanced over the vargr with mindless terror.

"Alice," he murmured. Despite the blood staining his clothes, it was the first time he sounded desperate.

At the sound of his voice, the doe shied away. The flash of the surrounding metal further frightened her, and she fled, out of sight in a second.

Cleo let her go; the rest of the coven had their own parts to play, and she wasn't yet finished with hers. "Follow her if you like. She'll never stop running from you. She's not yours anymore."

When the black wolf looked at her again, the glint in his eyes had turned murderous.

Despite the pain throbbing in her arm, she flattened her hand against the grimoire once more. "And now to take care of you."

As he stepped over a pile of armor, sword in hand, the ground groaned. The grass lurched and bubbled from sudden pressure beneath it.

"An entire village was lost to plague and buried here," she said, remaining calm even as the earth around her roiled and shook. "My village. Old skeletons aren't very strong, but there are a lot of them."

The black wolf just growled as the first of the bodies struggled up from the earth, stained bones held together by rags and roots. As they staggered upright, surrounding him, Cleo shook her head, readying the dagger. "How long can even you last? The hunt is over."

CHAPTER EIGHTEEN

The King

Her head hurt. Her limbs refused to move. Darkness overwhelmed, and she felt indistinct in a familiar way. Remembering more felt like raking fingers through fog. At last, she recalled past experiences of a night filled with sex and drugs fading into a morning of discomfort and bile. When she tried moving her hands and found them restrained above her head, she blearily wondered whose place she'd been left at, and if Magdalene had already gone home.

Then she grew aware of a copper taste in her mouth— blood. The fight at the castle flashed into her mind, and her next breath came out as a gasp. Her hands wrenched against their restraints as she tried remembering what had happened after that horrible convulsion of muscle and bone, worse than any shift into her fur. There had been the knights, and the smell of Colton's blood, and the witch's triumphant smile...

Fingers brushed her cheek. She jerked away as the rustle of silk and the sweetness of perfume filled her senses. Her skin prickled even before candlelight flickered into being, revealing only the bed she was on and the woman sitting in the chair beside it.

She looked like a figure from a classical painting, remote and regal in an opulent dress of red and gold. Jewels glittered against pale skin and dark hair. Her smile didn't reach her eyes, which held a knowing glint that belied her smooth, youthful face. Despite the finery, Alice recognized her.

"It's you," she said, voice hoarse. "The witch who was with Vanna."

"Yes. I'm the hag mother of the coven. You may call me Ermentrude. Not many know my name, but then again you are... very special."

Alice just fought harder against the rope, closing her eyes and willing herself to change. The effort felt as useless as nails scratching at glass. "What did you do to me? What did you do to him?"

"I'm sure Cleo had no time to explain. She's terrible at hiding her resentment toward the rest of us, but she can be very clever. It was her idea to turn you into a deer whenever your black wolf is too close." The hag mother sounded very gentle, which somehow made her words hurt all the worse. "A chase without end. Even if he could catch you, you'd be nothing more than a terrified animal in his presence."

"No!" She writhed against the bed, trying to bite at the rope keeping her in place. "I don't believe you. I don't believe you!"

She flinched when the hag mother pressed a hand on her brow, as concerned as a mother tending to her feverish child. "Hush. It'll do no good to fight. Your time with him is over. Hush, now."

And then it felt like she was bleeding out, all frenzy fading to a grey numbness. Her thoughts slipped and slid, unable to hold on to anything except the hag mother's words. She couldn't even speak. Dimly, she grew aware of the witch somehow smothering her will, and just as quickly smothering her panic over the realization.

"That's better. There's nothing to be afraid of. Once you've been inducted into the coven, you won't grieve for your old life. Everything will feel right and natural. This is all any of us were ever meant for." The witch stroked her hair before adding, "I'm sorry you knew so little about it before. Your mother shouldn't have isolated you."

When Alice managed to twitch away, the witch let her. "Yes, I've heard you're very sensitive about her. It's understandable and very unfortunate. Leaving you behind was just her misguided attempt at keeping you away from other witches. Every mother wants her child to be safe. What she didn't realize was that belonging to a coven is safety itself."

Fury tore a hole through the haze keeping her quiet. "You don't know anything about my mother."

Surprise flickered in the witch's gaze, but she answered smoothly enough. "I've never met her, if that's what you mean. Yet it's easy enough to understand her actions. A witch only hides among humans when she tries to turn her back on her nature. It's a pointless gesture. We can never change what we are."

Then she rose from her seat. "Ah, but we must return to this subject later. Your coven-sisters have arrived to help prepare for your induction. This is Faustine on the left and Marie on the right."

The pressure keeping her still lifted enough for her to shift and catch sight of two witches approaching the bed. They could have been sisters, except for one having brown hair and the other being a blonde. Their expressions wavered between brittle obedience, uncertain hope, and open suspicion as they studied her.

"Did you bring everything?" said the hag mother, her tone much less tender with them.

"Yes," said the brunette—Faustine.

"Good. Then let's start."

Alice couldn't see what they held but still cringed away as they all moved closer. She thought she caught a sliver of something that looked like bone in Faustine's hand as the witch said, "This will keep you from hurting yourself when we untie you."

"It'll just feel like a pinch," added Marie.

Then her neck itched and burned, and only the hag mother's control kept her still and silent. Within a breath, the pain chilled into that same numbness she'd felt when Portia and her acolytes had trapped her. The thought that she was as helpless now as she had been then drove her to weakly scratch at the ropes holding her still.

The hag mother approached with a knife and cut through the restraints, taking Alice's hands and placing them at her sides. "Bear with us. There will be time for explanations later. At this moment, there's simply too much to do. He'll be here very soon."

The magic dampening her will intensified into something suffocating, and the things that happened next were as fitful and bewildering as waking from a nightmare and falling back into it.

They moved her limbs like a puppet's, washing every inch of her body with water filled with fresh rose petals. The younger witches dried her skin with their own long hair. The feeling of their fingers wasn't as neutral as the hag mother's, and one even gave her a vicious pinch when the elder witch wasn't looking, knowing she couldn't react.

Once Faustine and Marie were finished, they left her sitting upright. As they stepped out of her line of sight, the hag mother began untangling her hair with an antique silver comb. The faint clink of porcelain warned her that the younger witches weren't finished with their tasks, and her muscles tensed as they returned with pots of cosmetics.

Brushes powdered her cheeks and painted her lips. Foundation hid the redness from the bone splinter lodged beneath her skin. She had never felt more like a doll. When they began rouging her nipples, she managed a strangled growl.

Just then, the hag mother spoke, and the magic binding her now narrowed her focus to each word. "I can sense you're still confused by this opportunity. Let me reassure you, he can bring any wish true, even those that seem impossible. Do you want to find your mother? Or perhaps replace the parts of yourself that you've always despised? You can even forget what it means to fear. To feel alone. Why turn away this chance merely because you thought you were happy before? Haven't you ever felt the same conviction in the past, the same sense that everything was fine before a change showed you how inferior your life had been?"

Her head suddenly ached, a throbbing, intrusive pain, as if the elder witch wormed her way inside. When the hag mother spoke again, she sounded pleased. "Magdalene. He can take away all the memories of her and the pain they cause. The price to pay can hardly even be called that."

The witch rested a hand on Alice's lower stomach. The rings on her fingers felt cold enough to burn. "An heir. You're very lucky. It's an exquisite honor. Poor Portia was right all along. She just couldn't admit both she and her daughter were inferior choices."

Then all three witches carefully placed her back on the bed, now sprinkled with flower petals. The hag mother's hand pressed between her hips once more, igniting deep cramps. It hurt worse than the bone sliver had, but the magic constricted her reaction to a mere shudder.

"Just pushing your body to a more receptive state," murmured the witch, pulling away again as the spasms eased into a heavy soreness. "Making sure you're ready for our king's seed. There will be more time for languor and privacy later."

For a moment, the pain cleared the haze keeping her body still and her words lost. She bared her teeth at the hag mother. "You're afraid. That's why you're rushing into this. You're still terrified of Colton finding me."

Her defiance drew a sidelong glance from Faustine. The hag mother remained serene. "Kings hunt wolves. Not the other way around. Cleo is making sure he won't be a problem. Now, *hush.* He approaches."

The thickness smothered her thoughts once more, this time taking away even her surroundings. Visions overwhelmed her senses, vivid and immediate.

Heavy jewels against her throat and wrists. A gorgeous dress tight against her skin. An etched glass goblet waited before her, filled with chocolate mousse and strawberries dipped in gold leaf. Everything seemed bright and glittery, and she realized she was in an elegant restaurant.

Beautiful people surrounded her, all lost in their own conversations. Waiters slipped among the white-clothed tables, efficient yet unobtrusive. The only one who paid attention to her was the figure on the other side of her table, his face in shadow. He wore a tuxedo like the rest of the men and had a quick aside in French to a passing waiter, but massive antlers rose from his head, shocking in their size and brutality. He could only be the hag king.

They loomed above her as he tipped his head in greeting. "You know who I am, but do you know my name? It's Edric."

When she merely stared at his antlers, he said, "Do they disturb you?"

His voice didn't match the rest of his appearance; it was reedy, even high-pitched compared to... to...

She frowned, unsure of who she had been thinking about. She just remembered another voice being darker, rougher, always ready to dip into a growl. The champagne glass before her sparkled, catching her attention and coaxing it away from her confusion. Realizing the hag king waited for an answer, she said, "All of this is disturbing."

"My apologies. Perhaps more privacy?" He inclined his head once more, and suddenly they were in a gondola, water lapping gently at its sides. Despite the night sky, everything looked clear and bright from the waxing moon, and she could see that the gondolier guiding their boat wore a white Venetian mask without eye holes.

Her thoughts seemed to lurch with the water. "What do you want from me?"

"A second chance." Shadows still covered his face, but his movements were fluid and suggestive, making up for his hidden expression. "I had an attempt at happiness long ago and lost it."

"You already have witches who adore you."

"They adore my power. It's been too long since I've had the pleasure of anyone pure in their motives. From the moment you looked at me, I knew you were different. Special."

The words gave her the wrong kind of shiver, and she glanced away, looking out at the moon as the gondola continued along a placid river. The buildings on either side were quiet, unlit, but she thought she heard an echo of a noise she should know, thought that there must be fear in her heart for a reason. "You want a child from me."

When he nodded, she added, "Is that what you wanted from your first chance at happiness, too?"

He tightened up. It was a small movement, but even the gondolier turned slightly in response. "I thought she was perfect. She wasn't. You'll be different."

"What was her flaw?"

The gondolier quickly renewed his concentration on his rowing. The air thickened before Edric said, "She lost the child."

"A miscarriage? You can't blame that on her."

It was as if she hadn't even spoken, for his hands curled into fists, and his antlers slashed at the air as he continued. "She turned out to be the same as all the rest. Selfish, greedy. Pretending to cherish my presence to get what she truly wanted. If she'd cared, she would never have betrayed me."

"But that's not something she could have—"

Then he pointed at her. "You'll be different."

Her surroundings slipped and slid again, and now she found herself dancing with him in a grand ballroom. She moved mechanically, aware of his breath hot against her cheek. Her heart hammered in her chest as if she'd been terrified, but she couldn't remember why. She couldn't even remember what his last words had been.

They danced quickly, deftly, circling with other couples until she felt dizzy. The sound of his voice was the only steady thing to cling to as the orchestra pushed them on. "You'll be perfect as my queen."

"Perfect?" she murmured, not sure why the praise made her want to shudder.

"With Ermentrude looking after the rest of the coven, there's nothing you'll have to worry about. No one else will have their wishes granted faster or know such wealth and power." When she started to speak, his finger brushed her mouth to silence her. "What more could you ask for?"

What more could there be?

Even as her mind struggled to answer, that strange call reached the very edge of her hearing. It was so alien to the glamour of their surroundings, piercing her heart until she gasped, remembering. A howl from far away, trying to reach her. It couldn't move closer, not yet, but it was calling to her, waiting for her to answer.

She hissed in another breath, tears filling her eyes even as she started to say a name—*his* name—but darkness suddenly enveloped her. She sank, her voice lost with the rest of her being until she found herself limp on the bed once more.

As she shuddered, mind still thick and confused, the three witches all stared at her, stripped down to their skin. When they turned toward the hag king emerging from the shadows, she began shaking her head, realizing gut-deep what was happening. The introduction was finished, and now he was ready to claim her.

She caught only hints of detail as he approached. Unkempt hair past his shoulders, mud and blood streaking his arms and torso. One corner of his mouth quirked up, as if he was amused by her resistance.

When he stretched over her, darkness seemed to fill her view. Not the welcome gloom of the woods but instead a yawning emptiness. Even the air seemed to squeeze itself from her lungs. There would be nothing of her left once he was done.

"Let him take you," breathed the hag mother, her eyes shining.

Then he leaned in, his mouth angling for hers. She thought of the moon, of being able to run far away and hide in the safety of shadows. Then she bit as hard as she could, catching skin and ripping it with her teeth.

As the hag king roared in pain, she spat his blood back at him. "Never. *Never.*"

He recoiled for a moment, just long enough for her fury to twist at her bones, twist at the magic that had caged her. Even as her body convulsed, her will wrenched even harder, taking in the surrounding power and working frantically.

Too late. A bellow of rage shattered her. Those wicked horns slashed down. Pain exploded in her chest, and then she couldn't breathe. Her howl of defiance choked on the blood bubbling in her mouth.

As the hag king's darkness melted into an endless abyss, she heard a voice hiss, "Stupid girl. It's all lost now."

The words were in her grandmother's dry voice, in the hoarse shriek of her mother, and finally in her own broken whisper. Then there was only the hag mother with her knife, leaning in while the other two witches watched with shining smiles.

CHAPTER NINETEEN

Gruesome Discovery

The city didn't smell right as Adair drove through its streets. It made him nervous. He had lived too long to ignore his instincts, and his weekend off from The Hole had been spent preparing to turn tail and run at the first hint of the other vargr.

He could be out of Amsterdam and settled into a new life in under a day; that wasn't the problem. The problem was that he couldn't figure out where the motherfucker was. The Golden Stag coven had gone quiet, refusing to talk since he'd insulted their king. His other sources hadn't found any trails of bodies to follow. And no one could get that miserable bastard rotting in his peat bog to say anything. It all left him feeling as paranoid as a rabbit.

Humans were everywhere, overwhelming shining windows and hot electricity with their insatiable lust and fear. So was the thin hunger of a few younger witches who hadn't attached themselves to a coven, searching for easy prey that could disappear without drawing attention.

All in all, a normal night. Yet he had lived in this city for decades and knew its throbbing underbelly well. Something was off. He decided to stop by the club to check on it, and was halfway there when powerful magic seeped into his senses, thick and indistinguishable like smoke. His paranoia hardened into dread.

The Hole was empty—not part of his orders. Near the unlit soundstage, he scented the air carefully and then broke off with a grimace. The Golden Stag warlock and his bitches were holding a ritual. Ignoring his warnings about attracting the wrong type of attention, as fucking usual. They smelled glutted, satisfied. Finished.

Unlike the other black wolves, he'd never developed a hatred for magic, but so much and at such close range left him with a burning nose and a sour taste at the back of his mouth. To hell with it; he would just leave and take the club's loss of revenue out of the coven's cut for the month.

Even as he turned to go, it hit him: a scent that still made him cringe and whine. A mere trace, so faint it must have been on someone else's skin, but still unmistakable in its age and violence. The oldest of the black wolves and the most feared until he had let himself be forgotten. The only one to wear his scent that closely would have to be...

"You're fucking kidding me," he muttered to himself, lengthening his stride as he reached the hallway of secret rooms. The smell of blood was overwhelming even before he unlocked the door.

For a moment, he could only stare, even when one of the figures inside looked up and hissed. The warlock hunched near the hearth, sulking while the two younger witches cooed and patted a cloth against the vicious bite mark on his chin.

Ermentrude gave him the same smile as when they'd last argued, but said nothing while feeding something to the fire. There was almost as much blood on her as there was on the bed.

"What did you do?" he said, well-aware of what burning flesh smelled like.

"We made a mistake." There wasn't a hint of regret in her voice as she wiped her mouth clean with a lace handkerchief. "Did you ever think you'd hear me admit as much? I'm sure you're thoroughly enjoying the fact you were correct."

Adair said nothing when she passed by, instead staring into the hearth. At the sight of blackened bone smoking among the embers, he turned away and lit a cigarette with unsteady fingers. It took a few drags before he could speak again. "I smell his blood," he said, jerking his head in the warlock's direction. "She attacked him?"

"Does that make a difference?"

"No. No, we're all fucked now."

"I don't see why. We'll keep looking for someone who can pique his interest *and* cherish it. Eventually—"

Adair moved so quickly that the witch never saw him coming. His fist caught her jaw with a crack that filled the room. The hag king didn't look up, but the other two witches watched wide-eyed as she dropped to the ground.

The hag mother had only a moment to spit out blood before Adair pinned her to the ground with one shoe to her neck. "There's no more 'eventually,' you fucking idiot. You ate her. You *burned* her. And you did it in *my fucking club.*"

When she tried to respond, he kicked her in the face, breaking more bones. Then the warlock rose to his full height, lowering his antlers in threat. Their points were still bloody.

Adair turned toward him, flicking his cigarette to the side. "What? You think you can fight me? You look like you haven't so much as wiped your nose in centuries. Sniveling like a baby over one fucking bite. What do you think *he'll* do after finding out you killed her?"

The hag king was the first to look away, shaking his antlers again in irritation. As the two younger witches crawled close to clutch at his legs, he said, "She was false."

Then he pulled away from their hands and was gone. In the silence that filled the room, the younger witches scowled at the empty air between them but knew enough to flinch back from Adair as he approached. "I have no idea what that's supposed to mean. Why didn't you just let her go?"

"That's not nearly... punishment enough for refusing our king," managed the hag mother, her voice muffled as she clutched at her jaw.

"Oh, I get it. You still think you have the upper hand. Why give up on your delusions when you can double down instead?"

One of the younger witches glanced over at the hag mother and then tried to sound confident. "What's there to fear? Cleo already took care of the vargr."

"He's dead, too," added the other, and then shrank away as Adair crouched before them.

A question hissed out between his clenched teeth, strangled by its obvious answer. "If he's dead, then where *is* dear Cleo?"

CHAPTER TWENTY

No More Words

The witch wiped at the blood trailing from her nose, no longer smiling. Her hand shook while she drew sigils on the opened book in her arms. The grimoire had withered into a pitiful thing, its pages crumbling like dead leaves each time her grip tightened. Her appearance hadn't fared any better, hair gone thin and white and spectacles sinking into pallid, wrinkled skin.

More undead bodies pushed their way up from the dirt, oblivious as they crawled over piles of savaged remains. The moon faded against a brightening sky, but the black wolf showed no signs of slowing.

When he cut through two at once with a sword taken from one of the crumpled knights, the witch's composure finally shattered. "This can't be possible. It's been hours. Hours!"

"Think this is my first fucking mob?" The black wolf ripped a skull off its neck and shoved the twitching body aside.

Unlike the witch, he had grown faster, angrier, and brutally efficient. "Think there's anything I haven't fought by now?"

The witch dropped the grimoire and grabbed for the dagger. Pages fluttered all around as she said, "This. It's the Mortal Maker of legend. No one believed it could be real, but I found it."

The black wolf just growled, breaking through a new round of rotting skeletons. Blood and grime streaked his face like war paint, but his teeth flashed white as he snarled at the witch.

She flinched back, licking chapped lips. "It ends even immortal lives. I found it in a tomb hidden deep in a cave in—"

"France." He hacked through rib cages, toppling the last of the undead between them. He let the crumpled bodies take the sword with them. "Held in the right hand of a skeleton. Who do you think crushed its skull?"

The witch raised the dagger high. It trembled in her hands. "Everything can die. You just have to find the right method."

Then she ran at him. He let her, dodging her wild strikes. The green of his eyes was still bright with rage, but he moved deliberately, drawing her out to the sluggish moat that ran along part of the ruins. Just as she realized the danger, he caught her hands and wrenched them, plunging the blade into her stomach. Her scream was cut off when he twisted them further. "I die all the time, you stupid bitch. Then I come back."

Her panting turned shallow as he changed the pressure of his grip, angling the dagger up toward her ribs in a wordless threat. "Where is she?"

"It's too late. Killing me won't stop anything. By now, she's his and—"

The blade went up an inch. "Where?"

The witch's voice grew hoarse. "The Hole. It's a club we own in Amsterdam."

When she tried to say more, he ripped the dagger up and out, slashing all the way to the throat. He threw the twitching body into the water and waited to make sure. His sweat steamed in the cold dawn air. His clothes stuck to his skin, wet with his own blood. Yet all he could think about was Alice and the sound of her screams.

By the time true sunlight rimmed the ruins in gold, the black wolf was gone.

The city had much changed since he'd last visited it, now a thriving spider web of canals and buildings. It was also cleaner, and he quickly found her scent, slender as a thread among the writhing human masses.

He found a door, and then an underground tunnel. Even in the darkness, he sensed the utter stillness that waited beyond. No one was there. Only scent remained, lingering like ghosts. He ignored the hundreds of humans that had come and gone, ignored the dormant electricity of the soundstage and the clean chill of Roman marble.

It was the hallway that held his attention, the hallway and what it revealed before he even stepped into it. The warlock's musk. The frenzy from the witches. And blood, all of it Alice's.

The black wolf had long forgotten how to be frightened, but he still knew pain. It felt like he'd been shot as he found the right room, hearing nothing.

Inside, he circled the rich furniture with his usual hunter's care, memorizing each scent and where he found it. He bared his teeth at the bed soaked with her blood and the warlock's sweat, but his growl ended in a whine when he found hair in the fireplace.

Parts had been crisped by the flames, but the ends had escaped damage, glimmering in the same way as when he couldn't resist tangling fingers in the strands by her face. He slowly reached out until he saw what else was in the hearth.

Impossible to accept. If he did, it would crush him. Instead, he slipped into the shadow world, now in his fur and racing through its utter stillness in search of some hint of her scent, some sign that she hadn't passed through this final, thin barrier between her death and what waited beyond the grave.

His desperation choked him until he began to howl among the lifeless trees and empty clearings. It was a piercing sound, recognizable to any. A wolf calling for another. A wolf that paused for an answer and heard only an echo.

When he came back into himself in that room far underground, he remained crouched there by the hearth, one hand clenched beside the strands of hair. Unmoving even when he sensed someone approaching. The man's scent was unknown to him and overwhelmed by that particular sourness a witch's magical servant always had. He could also smell that fucking dagger, and knew the witch's body must have been found.

"They thought you might find your way here. I'm sure you know what they want." The man paused, as if waiting for a response. When there wasn't any, he shrugged and pulled out the dagger. "Thanks for making it easy on me. Any final words?"

Beasts accept whatever they find. Their hearts beat steady through injury, thirst, and starvation. Their paths remain sure in their will to survive. But what of the heart of a beast that still remembers being a man? What will it turn to when it realizes *what* it has been damned to survive?

In one movement, the black wolf turned and lunged. The man's eyes bulged as he was grabbed by the throat, and then bulged again when those vicious fingers dug further in. The black wolf's eyes had darkened, pupils expanding until the color of his irises disappeared. Blood sprayed them both as he ripped out the man's throat with one jerk of his hand. He remained expressionless while letting him drop to the floor, gurgling and twitching.

The man was beyond hearing, but the black wolf still answered in a language too old to be remembered by anyone else, voice thick as a snarl while he shoved the dagger's blade into a crack in the hearth and snapped it off at the hilt. "No. No more words."

CHAPTER TWENTY-ONE

Endless Slaughter

Adair let the empty bottle drop next to his chair and reached for a new one without looking at the label. Beyond glittered the Tyrrhenian Sea, blue as a jewel. A few yachts cut through the waves, blindingly white beneath the afternoon sun. It was a dream of a day, tranquil and lush, and he was doing his best to get shit-faced.

At the sound of footsteps, his hand darted for the pugio he always kept sheathed beneath his suit jacket, but even as his fingers found the hilt, they relaxed again. He turned and glared at his human assistant, a business grad with great credentials and a sad misunderstanding of what it meant to join the murky world of things that went bump in the night. "You're still here? I told all the staff to leave."

The man shrugged. "I must have more loyalty than the rest."

"I don't even know your fucking name."

"It's Trevor."

"I didn't say I cared either." He drank from the new bottle and grimaced. It was brandy. He hated brandy. "Did that tech geek finish the map before he left?"

"Yes, sir."

"And you've been adding entries to it? Good. Show me."

Within minutes, he studied an image of Europe on a laptop. A pinprick in red—his club in Amsterdam—expanded in four stages. It looked like a red stripe slicing southeast down to Italy. The image replayed twice before he said, "What time was the last entry?"

"Two hours ago."

"He's already in Rome," muttered Adair. Then he resumed drinking.

His assistant fidgeted while waiting for him to speak again. When he didn't, the man said, "How could even a vargr kill so many witches in four days? The data has to be wrong."

"You're the one who added it in. Did you contact the covens in these areas?"

"Well, yes."

"Reach any of them?"

"No, but—"

"Of course not, because he's on a goddamn rampage. Is this your idea of loyalty, Travis? Giving me shit over what's obvious?"

"It's Trevor, sir."

"Whatever." Adair sighed and slid further down in his chair. The grapevines twining around the columns of the deck fluttered from a gentle breeze, and singing could be heard in the distance. Yet he was too old and too careful to be lulled by such calm, and the alcohol was barely working. "What about our sources in the human media? Have they noticed anything?"

"Only a few reports of strange howling at night. The timing of the complaints match his path. Sir, if you're that worried, why not reach out to him and see if he's willing to make a deal? Perhaps your safety in return for passing on information, or—"

"All he wants is blood. And right now, he's getting it from witches who can't believe this is happening."

Trevor cleared his throat. "Some do. That's what I came to talk to you about. There's a meeting of six covens being held in underground Rome. The Golden Stag coven is leading it to discuss what to do."

Just hearing about those bitches made his eye twitch. As he reached for a pack of cigarettes, he growled, "And they want me there."

"Their hag mother seemed to know you wouldn't go. She's suggesting you join via video."

"Like I can set that shit up on my own."

"I did it for you, sir." When Adair looked at him again, he added, "She was very insistent."

"So, that's why you stuck around. You're secretly in her pocket." He thought about killing the man to wipe that look off his face and then realized the other vargr would do a far better job than he ever could. "Fine. We're all fucked anyway."

He'd gone through half the bottle and two more cigarettes by the time his assistant had everything working, but his eyesight was clear enough to recognize the carvings on the marble columns lit by candlelight, and then the witches and warlocks seated at the ancient table.

They were in Roman ruins that had been taken over like moss growing on a fallen tree, modified with velvet chairs and frescoes of wild stags. There was even a rack of antlers sprouting from one of the walls, gleaming gold and carefully situated above the central chair.

"Jesus Christ," muttered Adair, unsurprised that Edric wasn't sitting in it. He wasn't there at all.

The sound of his voice drew all attention to him. Each figure had dressed in their finest despite the dust and grime, but appeared annoyed more than anything at being there. It amazed him how they all looked the same despite being fiercely competitive with each other for land, blood, and money. The same expressions, the same hairstyles and board meeting-sterile clothes... hell, they probably even fucked the same way.

Then Ermentrude sat in the central chair, giving him her usual infuriating smile. Close to her were the two younger witches he had seen before. "Adair. Thank you for joining us. You don't look so well. Have you been drinking?"

"Like a fish. If I'm drunk enough by the time he finds me, I might not even care. Where's Edric? Still nursing his wounds?"

She ignored the question to murmur something to the warlock on her right, and Adair used the moment to glance over the line of faces again. "Looks like Matera ducked out as well."

"He decided not to come. He feels safe from having—"

"An immortality spell." Adair laughed. "I'm sure that'll work out real well for him."

None of them liked being laughed at. They all stiffened in their seats, and he heard more than one who thought he didn't know Catalan mutter about barking dogs.

Ermentrude hated it most of all. Her eyes glittered poison at him as she said, "We caught him."

"You caught him," he repeated, unsure if he heard correctly. When he saw smugness infect the expressions around the table, he grinned. "Let me guess. One of your men, dressed in the uniform of the local cops, arrested him and took him to an undisclosed location of your choice."

When their smiles faded again, he added, "Do you really think he hasn't done any of this before? Hell, *I've* done it. It's the easiest way to find a good source of information when the scent goes cold. And you can always sniff out a witch's servant. Did you see the arrest?"

Ermentrude's voice turned glacial. "The man has a bodycam."

"Is it still active?"

"We're working on it. There was a connection failure. We've sent a second man out to investigate. He'll patch through to the conference when he arrives."

"Sure." Adair lit a fresh cigarette and then rubbed at his eyes. He hadn't slept since finding the girl's remains. As they waited, he studied Ermentrude's appearance. "You look different. Your hair is a different color."

"Yes. Hers was admittedly beautiful, and I didn't see any reason to waste it. If you hadn't been in such hysterics the last time we spoke, you would have noticed it then."

"You took her fucking hair." He finished what was left in the bottle. "He's going to spend centuries killing us."

"I've told you, we've—" The rest of her words were interrupted by a new connection.

Adair watched another window flicker onto his screen. From the shakiness of the footage, he guessed it was the live bodycam of the second man. His accent was thick, a dialect he wasn't used to, but words weren't necessary. The visuals, jittery as they were, revealed everything.

Shattered windshield glass glittered on the pavement. A torn-off car door grew visible within a few steps. The man's breath quickened at the first pool of blood. At the sight of teeth scattered like pebbles, the camera twisted violently, and vomiting could be heard. The camera shook and shuddered, barely catching a severed arm, and then the car left in a ditch.

In the silence that followed, Adair raised his eyebrows. "You tell me. Think your man kept his mouth shut about your whereabouts?"

The expressions around the table had radically changed. The other witches and warlocks began turning toward

Ermentrude, voices rising as they demanded an explanation. The younger witches from her coven looked openly shocked.

Adair glanced at his assistant, who had also paled. "You know the funny thing about using underground ruins as a hiding place? It doesn't work if the fucker hunting you down remembers walking through it as a thriving city. They're in what used to be an enormous garden. The owner was a rich, influential man who liked to keep parrots in parts of it. I hated the little bastards. He'd laugh whenever one tried biting your nose off."

"Sir, I don't really know what you're talking about. Maybe you need some water."

"What I'm saying is, if I were doing all this, I'd drop a match from the nearest sewer above and be done with it. They could be fireballed to death in a second."

"Fireballed?" repeated his assistant, watching the figures rise from their seats in growing agitation, now arguing with each other. Ermentrude seemed unruffled but rose with the rest, her voice smothered beneath theirs.

Adair was nearly enjoying himself now. "Lost ruins are forgotten but not untouched. Plenty of things leak down from modern cities. Electrical wiring, chemicals, and gas from corroded pipes. All you need to know is where they are."

"Shouldn't we warn them?"

"Why? Anyway, that's not what he's going to do. Not right away." Then he looked at his assistant, not missing how the man's collar had gone damp with nervous sweat. "I like you,

Tyler, but you're as stupid as these witches if you thought everything was going to be all right."

Before his assistant could respond, Ermentrude suddenly hunched over, her face contorting into a mask of agony. Behind her, the witch with the blonde hair screamed and clapped hands over her eyes. Blood trailed between her fingers, dark and thick.

"What the fuck?" muttered Adair, leaning closer to the screen.

Ermentrude's hair fell out in large hunks, slithering down her shoulders and crumbling into ash as she tried to clutch at it. All the others watched in horror, arguments forgotten.

"Is it him?" said Trevor, somehow even paler. The blonde witch pulled her hands away from her face while she choked and gagged. Her fingers were now smeared in cinders, but her sockets remained empty, rotting. The third girl was already throwing up black bile.

"No. He doesn't use magic. And if they'd lost all the spells keeping them young, they'd look like withered husks. This is... their bodies are losing what they took from the girl. Could I be that fucking lucky?" Then he rose from his chair and leaned over the balcony edge to catch sight of the rising moon. It looked heavy, white, and perfectly full.

Bottles rolled in all directions as he lunged for the stairs winding up to the helipad on the roof, leaving his assistant looking after him in confusion. "Sir? What are you...?"

"I need the helicopter."

"The pilot left with everyone else."

The words already sounded faint. "I can fly the fucking thing myself."

At the sound of screams coming from the laptop's speakers, Trevor turned to the screen again. Then he jerked back instinctively. Blood blotted out half of the conference window. Chairs were upturned, and two crumpled bodies bled on the floor. The rest of the witches and warlocks were nowhere to be seen.

Only the hag mother of the Golden Stag remained, struggling against a bloodsoaked man. Her head was caught between his hands, and he didn't flinch when she scratched at his grip.

"Oh, shit," murmured Trevor, realizing the figure must have been the vargr.

Then the vargr pushed his thumbs into her eyes, gouging them out. The witch's scream was cut off when he threw her back onto the golden rack of antlers, impaling her through.

"Oh, *shit*." Then he heard the helicopter roar to life and ran for the stairs. "Mr. Richardson, don't leave yet! Wait for me."

But the helicopter was already slicing through the sky, rising at a sharp angle before straightening out and cutting northwest. By the time Trevor fled the house, the screen only showed the ruins going up in flames.

CHAPTER TWENTY-TWO

From the Ashes

The throb of a pulse came to her first, shrinking the overwhelming darkness. Giving it shape, giving it a sense of time. Her pulse, she realized. Her heartbeat. Then her lungs convulsed, choking on gritty ash.

She fought for air, lashing out until her claws scraped against brick and then a plush carpet. With a convulsive lurch, she pulled herself away from the cold cinders and panted in deep breaths. Her fur bristled as smells pressed in, sharp and revealing.

The chill of underground stone layered with traces of countless visitors—most faint with age, but a few raw and fresh. The rot of a body that had never made it out of the room. Old sweat souring on bedsheets. And most strongly, dried blood revealing the agony of its owner—herself. Alice.

That's who I am. Alice.

The thought cut through her confusion, and she began moving with purpose, sniffing through the darkness until she picked out used candle wax, each hardened trail brimming with the different scents of the original beehives. The nearby matches were easy to find, caustic with sulphur. She changed form without thinking, needing several tries to light the candles. Her fingers continued to shake as their warm glow illuminated the room.

She saw the body first. Bloated, savaged, unknown to her beyond the lingering sting of magic. A biting smell, much worse than that of rotting flesh because of what it made her remember: the witches circling her while the hag king loomed above. The blade of a knife gleaming close to her face. And then...

Her scream shattered the air as the rest all rushed back into her mind. Then she screamed again. Not out of helplessness or panic—no, her heart burned so hotly that the rest of her body felt ready to ignite. Her rage consumed the sullen traces of the hag king and the glee from his witches as she turned away from the corpse, baring her teeth at the stained bed.

The movement brought her close enough to the empty hearth to catch a scent she could never forget. Colton. Her next breath came out as a gasp. She clutched the mantelpiece, fingers matching the traces of scent left behind by his. Then the nuances grew clear; a fury hotter than any fire, a savage mindlessness that smelled unbreakable.

She didn't realize she was crying until wetness stung her cheeks. As she slowly sank to her knees by the fireplace, she looked at the scattered cinders and then at the ash smearing her skin. She could smell her own death and knew he would have as well. Worst of all, she could smell his wracking guilt that he hadn't found her in time.

"You did," she said, even though she was alone in the room. "I heard you calling."

Just then, she heard a whisper of noise. The lightest of footsteps. Yet it was the new scent that sent her upright, a scent more like a presence with its vast age and sharp teeth. A vargr, one she didn't know.

Slipping back into the nearest corner and its shadows, she willed herself to change. In her rush to reach the protection of fang and fur, she didn't even notice the smoothness of her shift. The stranger reached the doorway, in human form and already cautious.

When he stepped through, she lunged, jaws finding an arm thrown out to protect his throat. She bit until she tasted blood and then ducked away, circling to face him as he swore. Her snarl warned him that she was ready to rip him apart.

In response, he flicked on the lights and examined his savaged arm with a grimace. He looked lean and sharp in his suit, but he was also unshaven and missing his tie, and watched her with more wariness than she would have expected as he said, "You bite hard for a female. No wonder Edric sniveled."

Her growl deepened at the sound of the name.

He quickly added, "Look, I'm here to help. I partner with the coven on other things, but I was against this fucking idea from the start. Do you know what happened to you?"

After a hesitation, she returned to the shadows, keeping the bed between them. Then she shifted back into her skin. "I died. I refused him and they killed me. I didn't see you in this room, but I can smell your presence everywhere."

He nodded, flexing his arm and wiping off the blood with a nearby drape. "This is my club. I didn't find out what happened until it was too late."

She eyed him, taking in his disheveled state. He looked like he'd spent hours traveling. "And once you did, you fled."

"Well, you were fucking charcoal. I didn't think there was any way of fixing their stupidity."

"You're not very nice," she said, and then pulled the nearest sheet free and wrapped it around herself. Some part of her hated that it brought the hag king's scent close to her skin, but she was also shivering and feeling more miserable by the minute as memories of what had happened pressed in.

The vargr laughed. "You'd rip into me again if I tried to be. I can smell it. You don't trust 'nice,' but that's obvious, considering who you picked for a lover."

Urgency swept aside all caution. "Do you know Colton? Do you know where he is?"

Each question sent him back a step. "No offense, but don't get too close. I don't want him ripping my head off because our scents mingled. I can give you everything you need to get to him."

"Why should I believe that? You could be tricking me. You could still be working with the coven."

"You tell me. You can smell lies."

She'd already sensed his age, but now the frustration that stemmed from it reached her. He fully understood how history repeated itself, locked to human behavior and the hunting patterns of those who preyed on it. "You're terrified. You saw all this coming and no one listened."

"Gold star for you," he muttered, already on his phone.

She brushed aside his sarcasm, too intent on what was important. "Colton. Is he all right? Did they hurt him?"

He laughed without looking up. "He's butchered all the covens from Amsterdam down into fucking Rome. They can't do shit to him."

"I need to find him."

"Five minutes and I can have everything set up."

"No." She moved for the door, not wanting to waste any more time.

He slid away, keeping a wide berth between them, but followed her out in the hall. "No?"

"Just because I think you're being sincere doesn't mean I'm going to take whatever you offer." The hallway stretched ahead into the darkness, but hints of fresh air already reached her.

"What do you want?" he said, sounding resigned. A grim note had joined his scent—the expectation of her turning out like all the other witches he'd known, demanding more. Just because of what she meant to Colton, she had him by the balls. He knew it and expected her to know it *and* use it.

She stopped to look at him. "I don't care about any of that," she said, knowing he'd understand what she referred to. "If I did, I would have accepted the hag king's offer."

For the first time, the sardonic glint left his eyes. "You really are different. Maybe that's why you were able to change."

When she only stared, he added, "What do you think you are? You said it yourself: you died. What's the only thing that comes back from its grave?"

It made it real, saying the words out loud. "A vargr."

Then she shuddered, only now beginning to understand how her life had changed. "They didn't do this to me. The coven. They wouldn't know how. I just remember... spitting his blood into his face and feeling like I was doing *more*. That whatever they did to me wouldn't stick. I don't know. I never learned anything about being a witch."

"They take. But you've figured that out already."

The sourness to his voice made her glance up again. She had his scent but still didn't quite understand him. "Why do you want to help me?"

"I was being slightly... glib before. He's unstoppable right now. No one's going to hurt him. But he's gone mad. Probably can't even speak at this point."

Her heart clenched as she remembered the distinctive void in Colton's scent by the fireplace. "How are you so sure?"

"I've seen it before. Not with him. It was another vargr, maybe one you know. The miserable bastard in the peat bog."

"Ambrose," she murmured.

The other vargr nodded. "I met him after he lost his girl and went on a rampage, killing all the Druids he could find. He didn't recognize anyone or anything. Completely mindless. And he hasn't been right in the head since."

Her voice cracked. "Where's Colton?"

"He's butchering the Serrano coven in Naples. Their den looks like an abandoned church in the slums. Just follow your nose. Or the screams." Then he carefully moved past her and unlocked one of the many red doors stretching down the hallway. It revealed what looked like a billiards room, but she could smell the grimy paper of money.

She remained in the doorway while he circled the pool table, opening secret compartments in it and withdrawing a stack of Euro banknotes. A passport and credit card quickly followed. Without looking up, he said, "He knows you died in my club, and you're the only one who can possibly snap him out of his blood rage. Believe me, helping you is entirely selfish on my part."

"All right. I still don't trust you enough to let you book any flights or trains for me, but I'll take those and some clothes."

"I have extra uniforms for the staff. Take your pick." Then he took a pool cue and pushed the pile over to the end of the table closest to her. "Tell him I helped you and had *nothing* to do with taking and killing you. The name is Adair."

She nodded.

"Adair," he insisted. "It's A-D-A—"

"I'll remember it." She felt almost calm now, all focus on finding Colton as soon as possible.

The inner quiet lasted longer than expected, disappearing into the rawness of her heart only when she began searching for Colton's scent. Fearless despite the unfamiliar streets. Intent despite the crowds of people muddying her senses.

Adair's description proved true. The old church looked in absolute disrepair. She found her way inside through a broken window. The reek of blood overwhelmed the rotten wood of the pews and the mold and droppings from bird nests in the rafters. Screaming could be heard somewhere below.

It didn't take long to find a door in the ground that opened to stone stairs set in a dank tunnel. She smelled the warlock and his witches, their desperation as withered as their magic. Then she caught Colton's scent, searing and blood-filled, and hurried down.

The stairs opened to a massive stone room decorated with marble statues and tapestries. There were also empty pedestals and crumpled suits of armor that tugged at her memory. Her attention then jumped to a long wooden table offering a terrible feast. Opened skulls and gnawed rib bones waited among grapes and cheese. Crystal glasses held both blood and wine. Several chairs were knocked over, their ivory upholstery splattered red.

Then she looked down to the far end of the room and felt her heart jump in her chest. A gaping maw of a hearth breathed flames, reducing the black wolf to a silhouette while he ripped at the twitching hands of a body. He was so covered in blood that it dripped from his fur.

At her gasp, he looked over and fell still.

Her breath turned shallow, but not because she was frightened. "Colton."

When she started to approach, he growled—a violent, mindless sound. His emptiness smelled absolute.

"It's me," she said, stopping again. "It's not some trick of theirs."

He just snarled, teeth flashing.

"Colton..." She swallowed hard, wondering how much of him had been lost with her. From his scent, he had willed himself into complete hollowness, driven by rage alone.

When she spoke again, her voice shook. "I'm not scared of you. I never was. The first time I saw you, it was through the window of a rundown cabin. It was night, and I was scared of lying awake while the hours crawled by. Wishing I could be someone else. Then you appeared. I thought you were just a wolf coming out of the woods, but when you looked at me, I forgot what it felt like to be afraid."

The black wolf had fallen silent, moving closer with the slow, stiff movements of a predator uncertain what to do.

She didn't flinch back, even with all the savaged bodies surrounding her. "You didn't scare me when you killed Magdalene either. Do you remember the first time we went somewhere together after her death? It was to the grocery store. We were out of food. You told me to pick my favorite type of coffee because you liked anything, and I stood there for ten minutes, not knowing what to do. I'd never had the chance to find out what I liked, much less drink it.

"And I remember being so scared, because it made me realize I didn't know how to have my own life. I'd spent too many years under someone else's control. How could I be a functioning person if I cried while trying to choose coffee? You came back ten minutes later and found me panicking because I still hadn't picked one. Do you remember what you said? You were so calm about it. Everything about living suddenly seemed so terrifying. Everything except you."

Something flickered in those feral eyes, but before she could recognize it, one of the bodies off to her left suddenly cracked some of its bones back into place, its armor gleaming as it reached for a nearby knife.

The black wolf was on it before the blade could do more than point at her. She kept very still as he changed form to wrench the head off. Then he took the dagger from the body's quivering hand and stabbed it into a crack between the armor, snapping it off at the hilt.

In the dim, erratic lighting, she couldn't see his face as he approached, empty-handed but still with that careful hunter's step. Blood dripped down his jaw and chest as she looked at him, feeling her eyes burn. "Colton. Please, come back to me."

He still showed no reaction to his name as he leaned in close, taking in her scent, but she kept facing him, kept her throat exposed to those dangerous teeth. "I heard you howling for me. The coven tried everything they could to make me forget you, but I still heard your call. Do you think I could have resisted the hag king if you hadn't shown me how to use my teeth? Do you think you don't save me every day just by being in my life?"

At last, the tears came, and she roughly wiped at her face before looking up again, leaving her mouth inches from his. "I used to be so afraid of disappearing like my mother, of being called away to somewhere where I'd never be found. But then I realized *nothing* could keep me from finding my way back to you. Now I'm here, and I don't know how this happened or what it's done to me, and I'm terrified. But you don't scare me. I will never be scared of you."

Then her eyes blurred over too much to see. Her heart was in worse agony than when the hag king's antlers had pierced it through, and her next breath came out as an ugly cry, all words spent.

Thumbs brushed the tears from her raw cheeks. Then his deep voice pressed against her lips, hoarse yet steady. "Alice."

She clung to him, crying into his bloodied neck while he held her tightly, as if she were a phantom that might yet fade. He was covered in gore; she, in the lingering ashes of her grave. It didn't matter. He touched her with exquisite tenderness, as if memorizing every inch of her body. As if he would never be complete again without feeling her against him.

She touched him with equal care, finding his new scars and unshaven jaw. When it left her fingers bloody, he licked them clean, gaze still on her face. She shivered, ready to replace the ache of tears with the sting of his teeth. Her yelp of protest filled the room when he pulled back with a shake of his head. "Not here. We'll go somewhere safe."

"To rest?" she said, realizing he probably hadn't stopped his rampage from the moment she was taken.

At that, he pulled her close again, fingers brushing the hair by her cheek. "No. So I can fuck you for hours."

Some of the usual flatness had returned to his voice, but the look in his eyes was still raw, as if he wouldn't quite believe she was there until he had tasted every part of her.

She nodded, feeling exhausted, and grimy, and beautifully alive.

CHAPTER TWENTY-THREE

The First One Known

Sunlight streamed through the window, outlining her reflection in gold while she stared into the mirror, dimly aware of Colton turning on the shower to warm the water. She looked exhausted, puffy-eyed. Her hair had fallen out of its sloppy bun, and stains dappled the sleek red dress she'd gotten from Adair. There was even a lingering smudge of ash on her jaw—her ash. Her remains.

At the sound of footsteps, she looked over and managed to smile at Colton, fresh tears running down her raw cheeks just from seeing him. Even as he moved with a predator's silence, his scent seethed with concern for her. The lingering hints of violence—a feral gleam in his eyes, blood drying beneath his clothes—were the only signs he'd been berserk for days. That horrible emptiness she'd sensed had gone.

She hadn't asked where he'd found the clothes or the apartment they were now in. For once, questions and their answers didn't matter. All that mattered was him, and the savage attention of his gaze, and the power and heat of his hands as he pulled her close.

"I heard you howling," she murmured, turning her head until her cheek pressed against his heartbeat. "I thought I was trapped and alone against the coven, but then I heard you."

His rage sharpened the air around them, but his touch remained soothing. "Tell me as much as you want. Or as little."

She understood the implications behind those terse words. The room where she'd died had remained a tableau of smells and stains. He knew terrible things had happened there but wouldn't pressure her to reveal them. She also understood why —despite his hunger intensifying each moment from feeling her against him—he kept himself from ripping off her clothes and covering her in his scent.

"The hag king didn't do anything to me," she murmured, and watched a muscle jump in his jaw. "I bit him as soon as he tried."

"They killed you for it," said Colton, his voice very flat. His eyes looked as wild as when he was a wolf.

"Yes, but I don't remember too much of what the witches did to me afterward. I don't think I want to. It all feels very raw, like it hasn't yet sunk in. All I really want to know is whether we're safe."

"It's safe. Not all of the coven is dead, but I've done enough to keep everyone away. You can take as long as you want to rest and recover."

She nodded. The part of her that howled with fury whenever she thought of what the witches had done to her now panted in glee over the chance to hunt the ones who remained. Later, though. When she better understood what she'd become. When she could think of anything besides Colton.

"Rest is the last thing on my mind," she said, and then licked at the callused thumb still against her lips.

His eyes darkened. "I can't be gentle. Not after four days of believing you were dead."

She smiled while reaching for the sleeves of her dress. "Good."

Too slow for his need. He grabbed the low neckline of her dress and tore it off with one jerk of his hand. She gasped at the rush of cold air on her skin, and then at the teeth at her throat, hips already working against the rough denim of his jeans.

By the time they reached the shower, her neck throbbed on both sides, as intense as pain but so much sweeter. The hot water felt almost as good as his hands running over her body, rough and insatiable. Digging into her hips, squeezing her ass. Following the line of her back up to her shoulders and pulling her ever closer. Even with water spraying over them, she could feel the slipperiness of precum against her lower stomach.

Then he caught her chin, raising her mouth to his. His other hand snarled deep in her hair, keeping her still through their jaw-cracking kiss. Her heart felt like it was on fire.

This was the kind of hunger she loved, a hunger that devoured without demanding anything in return. A hunger that freed instead of smothered. A hunger that left her wild and unafraid.

Just as she grew dizzy from lack of air, he broke off and licked her earlobe, distracting her from how his hand had released her chin and now skimmed past the sensitive skin of her stomach. Then his fingers slid between her legs, igniting hot pressure against her clit.

She gasped, and when his fingers flexed again, bit his shoulder in a frenzy. At the smell of his blood, she grew breathless for a different reason. "I'm so sorry. I didn't mean to. I—"

He laughed against her ear. "Fuck apologies. I like your teeth."

Then his fingers pushed deep into her cunt, and the rest of her words washed away with the last of the ash on her skin.

Her climax left her jerking against his hand, ready to collapse then and there. Instead, she found herself bracing against the tiled wall, arching her back as he grabbed her hips from behind. She was panting even before his cock pressed into her slick folds, turning the afterburn of his touch into fresh heat.

He moved hard and fast, shaking water droplets from her skin, but his thumbs stroked the dimples in her lower back with surprising gentleness, intensifying the power in his thrusts. She felt like she was about to come undone in the most glorious way possible.

She came before he did, voice rising above the steam and water, sweat trickling down her neck and breasts. Only his grip kept her standing. Then he growled against her and pushed in so deep she nearly climaxed again, shuddering as he bit her neck and finished.

They stayed in the shower long enough to wash off their sweat. Her previous exhaustion had sweetened into something cleaner, softer, but her hands still shook as she settled on the bed and started drying her hair. When he noticed, he pulled her onto his lap and did it for her, combing fingers through the long strands to check for snarls.

She sighed against him, ready to pass out. "You're very sweet."

"Not many would agree."

The words drew a grin out of her. Memories of the bloody chamber and its terrible feast far beneath a crumbling church already seemed so far away, and so did Adair's obvious dread. But she did remember those stiff, strange knights surrounding him, and the sound of his snarl as he fought back. "You know how to use a sword."

He seemed unsurprised by the jump in subject. "For a while, you had to."

"What other weapons can you use?"

"Anything that doesn't need a horse. Even trained ones were too scared to stay near me."

Her smile faded as she thought about riding with Fleur on that fateful day, and how much had changed since then. "I guess that'll now be my problem, too. God, I haven't even thought about what all this means. What type of attention will I bring to us?"

"Alice." His voice brushed against her temple. "It's all right."

"Are you sure? It doesn't seem like new vargr appear very often."

He shrugged. "Not very. The last one turned up during the First World War."

"So, I might be the newest one for awhile."

She chewed on her lip until he stopped her with a kiss, his tongue soothing the teeth marks left behind. Then he said, "You'll handle it better than most. You're already used to changing into a wolf, and you have me."

She thought of Adair's open panic and then of Giove's shock and fear. She also thought of the freedom of running effortlessly through the night, each stride filling her with joy. She never felt so comfortable in her body as when she was in her fur and he was there beside her, chasing the moon together.

When she nodded, he added, "It's true that some vargr like to fuck with the younger ones, especially when they're still confused about what they are. Others are fine with a few fights to decide territory and dominance. And then there's the older fuckers like me who don't care at all."

"Is that how they are with female vargr, too?" Her worry had faded to the edge of her thoughts, chased away by the sensation of his hand stroking along her back. He always made her feel so safe.

"Don't know. You're the first one known."

When she spoke again, she couldn't keep the shyness from her voice. "Is my scent really different? Now that I'm a vargr?"

At that, the brush of his fingers coaxed her to look up again. Then the nightmare creature that was her lover kissed her slowly, fiercely, thrilling her with his teeth as much as his tongue. "You're still my Alice."

The words left her eyes burning, and she closed them as his mouth remained hot against hers, the weight of his body pressing her back against the bed.

She felt inflamed even before he eased her legs apart. Her senses narrowed to him and him alone, taking in everything. The hard muscles in his arms as he braced hands on either side of her. The clean musk of his skin. The scrape of his unshaven jaw as he licked at the suck marks he'd left earlier. Her breath quickened at the heaviness of his cock against her thigh.

"Again?" she murmured, stroking along his shaft and then finding his thick sack. His balls constricted at her touch, feeling heavy, overfull.

His growl sounded amused, but he held back until he caught the rising lust in her scent, until her legs wrapped around him. He pushed in slowly, making sure she felt every inch. Teasing her. She sighed at the delicious burn and teased back. Arching until her nipples brushed him. Running fingers along his broad shoulders and back.

In response, he began thrusting hard, deep, and slow, never looking away from her face. The green in his eyes had darkened with a tenderness he never trusted to words.

After her first climax, his rhythm grew relentless, jolting her until the bed creaked. When she arched again, past words, he nearly smiled before shifting position enough to hook her legs over his shoulders, changing the angle of his thrusts. Her nails ripped at the sheets in fresh bliss as he snarled through his own climax.

For several breaths, she remained desperate and shaking, calming only when he stroked her feverish skin, his touch now feather-light and soothing. After he eased her down to a warm afterglow, he shifted his weight enough to settle beside her. She curled against him, feeling delicious.

He was already breathing easily, already back in control while tracing aimless patterns along her back. Eyes clear and intent as he watched her. She felt ready to pass out but managed to say, "You still outlast me."

All his tension had bled away, and the rasp in his voice sounded almost teasing as his hand slid over her hip and between her legs, drawing another shiver out of her. "You're exhausted. Settling back into yourself. It's normal when your body has to rebuild itself."

She made a humming noise, his warmth lulling her close to sleep. She wasn't sure she had another orgasm in her, but she was greedy enough to hope so. "I'm going to have so many questions when I wake back up. I don't even know where we are."

"One of the cliffside villages of Agerola. About an hour from Naples." His thumb pushed in, and the sweet pressure against her clit made her gasp. He licked her open mouth before adding, "I know the area well. You're safe here."

Then those rough fingers coaxed her into a final release, a frantic twitch of her hips that took the last of her energy. As she let herself sink toward sleep, she murmured, "Do you remember the first night we slept in the same bed? I don't even feel like that girl anymore."

His response sank deep into her heart, soothing scars old and new. "You are. You've just found your teeth."

CHAPTER TWENTY-FOUR

A Painful Answer

The tantalizing smells of fresh coffee and buttery pastry woke Alice from a dreamless sleep. She shifted, growing aware of warm sunlight and clean cotton sheets against her bare skin. Traffic could be heard outside, and birds, too.

Then Colton's hand brushed her cheek, and she opened her eyes to find him fully dressed and alert. A sweet ache filled her heart as she smiled.

He gave her one of his rare smiles back. "How are you?"

"Sore, but in the best way." She sat up and stretched, reminded of that similar morning in Texas. Her body felt much better now compared to then, not in true pain so much as uncertain and tender. New. She was reminded of when she'd tried taking a martial arts class—the next day, every muscle and tendon in her body had felt raw, even the ones she hadn't known existed.

When her gaze fell on the steaming cups of coffee and sugar-dusted pastries waiting on the bedside table, he said, "Thought you might be hungry."

Ravenous, but as he settled beside her on the bed, the first thing she did was move closer to him, sinking into his scent and all that it held. His vast age and experience, heavy as stone. Blood that had long been washed off his skin but still marked what he was: a killer with the purity of a beast, never tormented by the bodies he left behind. Enigmatic even to sensitive noses, revealing little and offering less.

Terrifying glimpses, but she rested her head against his shoulder without fear, sensing new threads weaving into his scent as he nuzzled her in return. His love and protectiveness, one tender as a tongue and the other savage as teeth.

"This hardly feels real," she murmured. "I don't know how I came back."

"You're here. That's all that matters."

She smiled, knowing it really was that simple for him. "Maybe, but I like learning answers."

"I've noticed." Then he shifted enough to look at her. "There aren't many vargr because few people know the ritual. And when it's performed, most of the time nothing happens."

"But it *is* considered a punishment."

He shrugged. "For most of us. It can be used for other reasons. The vargr pining after your friend—he was brought back by his granny. He'd been murdered, and she wanted him to have a second chance. The only thing we all have in common is dying angry."

She nodded, remembering her rage at feeling so helpless. "It wasn't the coven who did it. I'm sure of that. In their eyes, as soon as he stopped wanting me, I stopped being worth their attention, even for punishment. They just wanted to—"

Then she stopped, bile rising in her throat. When she spoke again, the words were as vicious as the bite she'd given the hag king. "To *feed*. I wanted to tear them apart so badly. I still do."

"Who says you can't?" he said, voice lowering into a growl. "He's still alive. So are two of his witches."

Her anger felt clean and savage, matching his until it seemed her skin would spark wherever he touched her. "And the hag mother?"

"Dead. Always kill the true believers first. It turns the rest into cowards."

Dark exhilaration rose through her, but she sobered just as quickly. "I want to do this right. Throughout this hunt, I've done everything wrong. Screwed up."

He traced the curve of her cheek. "First hunts are like that. With more experience, you'll make less mistakes."

"I know, but... when we find the hag king, I want to be able to rip into him as well as you can. I want him to know it's *me* bleeding him dry."

His eyes never looked absent while he thought. Instead, they turned piercing. "All right. We'll stay here for a week or two and practice hunting. It'll also give you time to recover. Get used to yourself. Feeling wobbly?"

"A little," she admitted. "Is this normal?"

He nodded and offered one of the pastries. "Eating helps."

She reached for it, already smelling the butter and lemon zest. It looked like a croissant but was sweeter, softer, and stuffed with cream. She ate two before even thinking about her coffee. It was rich and strong, chasing away the last of her haze. "I'm glad you're here to help me through all of this. I was so confused when I woke up in that room. I couldn't imagine what I would have felt like if I knew nothing about vargr."

When guilt and anger spiked through his scent, she looked up at him. "Colton. Don't feel bad about not being there. You were still protecting me. The owner of the club helped out only because he was terrified of you."

At that, he grimaced. "I smelled the fucker."

"He said his name was Adair, and that he had nothing to do with what happened. I don't think he did. He wasn't there with the coven anyway." She was surprised by how calm she felt while discussing it. "Maybe it was his club, but... I'm not interested in going after him. He's nothing to me."

It felt like her first shaky step in returning to their hunt, if only in deciding what to do. She glanced up at Colton with a half-smile. "It still feels uncomfortable to make decisions. I guess death didn't take that away."

"No." Then he licked the traces of foam from her lips. "You weren't meant to be leashed. You'll remember how to live without it."

It was exactly what he had told her in the grocery store while she'd tried not to cry over coffee, now so long ago. It was what she'd asked him to remember in that underground chamber filled with death. Her breath hitched. "I wasn't sure you heard me."

"Every word." His voice sounded casual, but his eyes said so much more, and when her fingers brushed his unshaven jaw, he moved in, catching her chin to give her a devouring kiss.

A car horn startled her into breaking it off. Her teeth suddenly felt very sharp against her lips. She'd grown out her fangs without effort or thought, merely reacting to a noise and the possible threat hiding behind it. Colton seemed amused, glancing at the mirror in a silent signal for her to look, too. Her irises had shifted into a wild gold.

"It's that easy?" she said, trying to figure out how to change them back.

"You'll learn to control it." Then he kissed her again, now slow and soothing, licking her teeth until they were blunt and human. When she checked her reflection, her eyes were back to normal. "Just need to get used to sharper senses."

She understood what he meant when they left the apartment to explore the village. She wore sunglasses just in case, but scent overwhelmed her much more than sound. Smells pressed in from all around, as strong as when she was a wolf. It felt disorienting to understand strangers with one breath.

She knew who was angry, or worried, or sick, or pregnant. She knew who had bled that morning from shaving too hastily and who had drunk too much the night before. The cafes all breathed their own special blend of coffee and milk, of butter and yeast and candied orange. Cars and scooters radiated hot plastic and gasoline. When they passed by a man with cologne reeking of cedar and vetiver, she sneezed.

Disorienting, but not distressing. Her fascination grew with each street. She didn't miss how the roads sloped in one direction or another, or how turning a corner often revealed untamed earth rising sharply above apartment buildings and businesses, making it clear they were in a village that existed in pockets along the mountainside, as hardy and surprising as flowers growing from cracks in a rock.

She didn't know how much time had passed before she caught the first hint of saltwater. She looked over at Colton, confident that he'd also smelled it. "Are we near the ocean?"

"Far above it. There are some trails that give you a good view."

The idea of seeing it turned her curiosity into sheer excitement. "Are any of them nearby? I feel strong enough to try it."

He seemed to know exactly where to go, leading them into a side alley and through an iron gate rusted with age and left open. Trees and shrubs swallowed civilization from sight as effectively as the forests back home. Their path turned into dusty earth and chipped rock, narrow and twisting as it led them up. They walked in silence for some time, meeting no one else.

Considering how exhausted she'd been the day before, she was surprised by how long she lasted before feeling winded. When weariness slipped into her scent, Colton stopped beside a slab of rock that had pierced through the earth, its surface worn smooth by the elements.

As they sat together, comfortable and wordless, she studied the village below, red roofs bright against the surrounding greenery. The ocean glittered beyond, deep blue and gentle. A few speedboats cut white lines through it, too far away to be heard. After the hectic smells of the village, this peace felt like sweet relief, and she found her attention drifting between the lulling rhythm of those distant waves and Colton's quiet presence, his face giving away nothing of what he thought.

He'd told her that he knew the area, but she couldn't guess whether he was glad to be back. Throughout their hunt, he'd never seemed to care about the places they visited, showing familiarity only in how to travel through them and which language to use to be understood.

Just then, he said, "You're studying me more than the view."

A wry glance followed the words. Under the bright sun, his pupils had constricted to pinpoints and there was a bead of sweat running down his neck, but he otherwise seemed unaffected by the hike.

Any casual observer would have considered him a normal man, but she well understood why even the other vargr were unnerved in his presence. Sometimes, he seemed so remote from the pettiness of thought and the weakness of flesh, his motives primal and pure. The other black wolves knew how to use their teeth and disdained humans as blind and feeble, yet only he seemed truly comfortable with being a beast.

"Where's your birthplace?" she said, voice soft.

He seemed unsurprised by the question. "Don't know. I don't remember much about being human."

"What about childhood memories? Or family?" At the shake of his head, she added, "Isn't there any place you can call home?"

"Sure. Wherever you are."

When she blushed, overcome by the words as much as the tender gleam in his eyes, he wrapped an arm around her shoulders, coaxing her to lean into him. "Lands change and so do the people living there. Sharing a bed with you means more than wherever I was born."

Birds wheeled lazily on the wind currents far below as he added, "Worried about forgetting the same things?"

"No. I think my past is too much a part of me to ever fade." The words left a lingering bitterness in her mouth. She had entered the world of witches and escaped again without receiving the answers about her mother that she'd hoped for.

"Nothing about coming back as a vargr feels like a curse. If anything, I feel... free. I'm not afraid anymore."

Her lack of fear only grew in the days that followed. They would hike in the morning, finding ruins that Colton remembered. She would sit and study the worn bricks while he told her how old they were and what life had been like when they were new. She asked about the eruption of Vesuvius, and whether wolves really had been revered by ancient Italians, and countless other questions, always receiving answers.

His patience extended into their night hunts, tracking elusive boar and skittish rabbits. They never killed; there was no need to. Chasing prey over the steep mountainsides strengthened her stamina and perfected her timing.

They fucked whenever they had the privacy. It was then that he turned teasing, pinning her hands behind her back while she straddled his lap, his thumbs stroking her wrists with surprising tenderness even as his teeth left her in a frenzy. The bed threatened to break from the power of his thrusts, so she often found herself face down on the flat couch in the living room, panting against the cushion while her fingers dug at the fabric in ecstasy. Afterwards, her sleep would always be quiet and mindless... at least, at first.

He had warned her about vargr losing the ability to dream, and, in its place, gaining the chance to relive experiences. Within a week, memories appeared to her while she slept. Much like dreams, some cut and some confused, bringing back to life moments she had long forgotten.

The terror of her mother screaming at her for getting crayon marks on a white table. The awkwardness of her first kiss with a boy named Stefan Fisher, both of them so nervous that his braces ended up gouging her lower lip. The bubbling excitement of receiving an acceptance letter from UC Davis, her first choice for college.

And then one night, she sank into a memory of being woken by the creak of her bedroom door. At the sight of her mother's silhouette, she squeezed her eyes shut again. She might get yelled at if she was found awake, so she remained very still, even when footsteps approached. Her heart pounded hard enough to make her ribs ache.

A hand brushed her face. Pulled the sheets up to cover her against the cold. Then her mother started to whisper, sounding so different from the loud, frustrated voice that filled the day. Her words were small and trembling. "It's too late. It's too late for me. All I can do is make sure it's never too late for you."

She tried not to twitch as her mother stroked her cheek again. They never touched. It was her father who hugged her, and held her hand while walking, and showed her how to hold crayons and draw with them.

"You'll never know your grandmother, not while I can help it. Not her, not any of us. But that's not enough. It's never enough, running away. I learned that early on and began collecting everything I could find, much more than Mom ever knew. Rituals long forgotten and spells thought to be lost. The rarest magic. The most forbidden curses. I'll tell you them all, my poor daughter. I'll plant their power in your heart like seeds. It's the best I can do. Please, be better than me. You can't just run whenever they find you. You have to *escape*."

Then she woke up with wet cheeks, tears trailing down in a ghostly imitation of her mother's fingers. At the first hitch of her breath, Colton shifted against her, his voice rough with sleep yet already alert. "Alice?"

"I know how I became a vargr." Even as she spoke, it was as if she could taste the hag king's blood in her mouth, her fury transforming her death with all the potent magic of the ritual she unleashed by refusing him. Heart bright even as she bled out. "My mother knew about the curse, and she told it to me. She…"

Then her voice cracked, and she had to swallow hard before explaining it all to him. Once she finished, she let out a shaky sigh. "Just last night, I relived a memory of her yelling at my father that I was the biggest mistake of her life. Nothing's simple, is it?"

The black wolf never spoke the answer when it was obvious. Instead, he kissed the tears from her face, his mouth gentle even as his voice remained harsh as a growl. "You're not a mistake."

"I know. And I know why she left me in the forest that day, too. She was scared." Then she closed her eyes, remembering white knuckles against the steering wheel and a simmering tension in the air. Signs that now seemed so clear to her. "I think… I think she *was* supposed to take me along with her.

Whoever called her away, whether it was my grandmother or another witch, they wanted me, too. And that's what she was so scared of—me ending up just like her. So she left me behind at the very last minute, because she couldn't escape but thought I could."

Then her heart clenched in grief and agony and terrible, terrible relief. The question that had always haunted her finally had its answer.

Her next breath came out as a sob, and for several minutes, she simply shuddered, clutching at the shoulders of a nightmare creature that scared all other monsters lurking in the dark. He held her tightly, chasing away her trembling with the warmth of his hands and the steady beat of his heart.

When the anguish choking her scent finally faded, he nuzzled at her. "Want to stay up for awhile?"

"Please," she said, grateful that he understood.

Within minutes, she was curled up on the couch, clutching both the fistful of tissues and the cup of coffee he'd given her. When he sat beside her, she leaned into his reassuring heat, all out of words. It felt like her heart had been cut open and drained. Finally able to heal. Would this erase all the ways her mother had hurt her? No, but it was the final piece of her past that could be left behind.

She stared at the mild yellow wallpaper of the room until his nose brushed her temple. Then she weakly smiled at him. "I'm all right. Just... not ready to sleep. My mind is filled with so much noise."

He studied her. In the warm lamplight, his eyes were dark and intent. "I could tell you a story."

When she looked at him in open surprise, he added, "What about the one with the two wolves that live in the sky?"

It was the same myth she had told him on their first night together, when it had been his heart struggling to heal. Her eyes burned for a new reason. "I'd love that."

Then she shifted closer until she could rest her head against his chest, closing her eyes as he began to talk. He remembered it without trouble, the words reverberating all the way to her bones while he ran fingers through her hair.

Alice didn't realize she'd fallen back asleep until she opened her eyes to a room softly lit by the sunrise. Colton was still awake, still holding her close, and she had the feeling he'd watched her the entire time. She rubbed at her raw face and said, "I missed the ending again."

He traced the curve of her ear. "There is none. Their hunt continues to this day."

She nodded, aware of how sore but whole her heart felt. "I don't want ours to do the same. I'm ready to move on. I'm ready to finish the hunt."

CHAPTER TWENTY-FIVE

A Final Fight

Faustine stuck her tongue out at a portrait of the hag mother while stuffing yet another dress into the garbage bag, trying to get the yards of brown silk brocade all inside. She had gone through half of the dead witch's closet without finding anything worth keeping. "Can you believe these clothes? She had no taste at all."

"Some of her jewelry is nice," said Marie, seated at the nearby dressing table. Gold bracelets marched up her arms. Ruby, sapphire, and emerald rings flashed on her fingers. She posed with her chin in her hands and studied the effect in the mirror. "I guess these eyes aren't too bad. Why did we lose everything we took from that little bitch? Hers were nice."

Faustine pulled out a pair of Georgian-era shoes of silk and leather dyed blue and embroidered with silver flowers. She grimaced at their pointed toes and threw them in with the dress. The bag was starting to bulge. "Who cares? At least her pet wolf gave up looking for us."

"Are you sure?"

There was skepticism in Marie's voice, not fear, and Faustine immediately looked up. She couldn't remember the last time the other witch had questioned her. "We're alive, aren't we? No one can find this mansion unless our king wills it."

"Edric doesn't do anything except sulk in the mud. If the hag mother's death couldn't stir him up, what chance do we have? Let's just leave him and find a new coven." Then Marie held a pair of diamond earrings to her ears. They glittered against her fair hair, and she smiled.

Faustine tied off the bag and shoved it toward a heap of others. "The other covens are shattered by that bastard wolf. Edric is our best option. Now take these out. They're starting to pile up."

"In a minute. I'm busy."

"With what? You don't expect to wear those, do you? They're old-fashioned and ugly."

"I like them." Marie's fingers curled protectively against their rings. "Anyway, you're the one who wanted to move into these rooms. Why don't *you* take out their garbage?"

Faustine scoffed, rising to her feet. "You're letting those jewels go to your head. You aren't the new hag mother of the coven, and you definitely aren't its queen."

"Neither are you."

For a moment, Faustine only stared at her. Then she smiled, wide and fixed, and approached the other witch from behind.

As she tucked Marie's hair behind her ears to better reveal the earrings, she said, "Playing dress up doesn't make you an adult. I was the smart one in this coven, no matter how many books Cleo read. The rest were always jealous. Now they're just dead. So, let me do the thinking, all right? You got this far by being a follower, not a leader. It's your natural role."

Then she straightened up again, missing the hatred that flickered in the other witch's expression. "Take out the trash. I need to check the other closets and see how bad they are."

As soon as she was out of the room, Marie scowled and muttered, "You're not a leader either. Just a basic bitch."

The sourness in her face faded as she opened another drawer in the jewelry box, revealing a three-strand pearl necklace waiting in a bed of red velvet. After so many years of living on the unsatisfying scraps of magic and luxury available to lower members of the coven, resisting the hag mother's jewelry proved impossible.

Her gaze dropped from the mirror while she put it on. The gold clasp was fiddly, but the strands already felt as luxurious as silk against her neck. She was smiling even before she looked into the mirror again.

Then she jerked, the necklace rattling like loose teeth. A second reflection had joined her own.

"You?" she gasped, recognizing the witch they had killed. But it couldn't be. She had been burned to ash. She couldn't be back as real flesh and blood.

"Me," growled the other girl. The word revealed a mouth full of fangs.

Then she caught Marie's head and smashed it into the mirror. Glass shattered, slicing into her skin. Before Marie could scream, the girl did it again. This time, something in her face cracked. The world exploded into hot blood and searing pain.

The hands holding her disappeared, but in the next moment, terrible pressure squeezed her neck, unrelenting as she began to choke. Teeth. That's what it was. Teeth and fur and bone-chipping force.

The last thing she heard was the sound of pearls scattering on the floor.

Faustine returned in a worse mood than before. The rest of the rooms were even fuller, and there were no poppets left to clean them out. When she saw the pile of garbage bags still waiting by the door, her thoughts further soured. "Marie, what the fuck? We're stuck here together until we can figure out what to do, so you might as well..."

The rest of her words faded as she stepped past the silk folding screens that blocked her view of the inner rooms. Blood splattered the gold-striped wallpaper and plush carpet. The chair had been knocked back from the dressing table, its pale blue upholstery stained red.

And there by the mirror waited Marie's head, studded with broken glass and staring at her. Her body slumped on the ground, surrounded by precious gems from the upturned jewelry box. The hands were still twitching.

Then a black wolf slunk out from the nearby shadows, yellow eyes fixed on Faustine's horrified face.

A strangled noise escaped her as she whirled, already reaching for one of the ornate daggers mounted on the walls, but a second black wolf blocked her way. Bigger, burlier, stalking toward her with deliberation.

"Two?" she managed, finding her voice at last.

The one near Marie flashed bloodied teeth in response.

Faustine turned and fled back through the door. The only thought that broke through her panic was that she would be all right if she made it to the trophy room...

The she-wolf felt like laughing. Her heart beat as fast as that of the frantic witch running from them, but for a much different reason. She was finally able to fight, to turn the sneers of those who had used her and then burned her like trash into screams instead.

The black wolf picked up on her bloodthirst, his steadiness sharpening into swift brutality while they tracked the witch to a room that reeked of metal both precious and practical— weapons.

The witch's scent was faint; she hadn't stayed. They slipped through the doorway and found walls bristling with daggers, swords, halberds, and dueling pistols. Deadly tools that had been refined into works of art over generations of humanity. One was clearly missing, its outline visible from years of dust and grime dulling the wood behind it: a dueling pistol inlaid with silver, the other of the pair left behind in panic. A chest of drawers had been touched as well, the witch's sweat lingering with the heaviness of the lead balls she'd taken to load the pistol.

Terror marked stairs and hallways, finally bringing them to an indoor atrium thick with tall, broad-leafed plants. A shallow pond marked the center of the room, lapping against a massive marble water fountain depicting a woman twining against a stag. The witch sat on the stag's back, trying to load the dueling pistol with shaking hands.

The she-wolf ached to attack, aware that she could cross the distance between them in seconds. A quiet growl from the black wolf reminded her to remain cautious, and they both melted into the shadows of nearby rubber plants while the witch was distracted.

The witch looked up just as the leaves fell still. The panic in her scent increased, and then she called out to them, her voice high and cracked. "It wasn't my fault. Edric chose to kill her, not me. And if you want to know where he is, then I can't help you. He didn't tell me."

The black wolf let himself be seen long enough for the pistol to swing in his direction. Long enough for the she-wolf to slink closer toward the pond. When the witch aimed wildly, trying to find him, the she-wolf fell still, anticipation rising as the witch spoke again, fingers clenched around one of the marble antlers. "It's not a lie. No one has seen him since the ritual. He likes hiding in the forest whenever he's upset. Go after him! I didn't want anything to do with this."

The she-wolf's muzzle wrinkled in a silent snarl as she remembered this witch's gleeful smile when the hag mother had started cutting her open. Sensing her frustration, the black wolf flashed his eyes at the witch as an obvious distraction.

Obvious, but the witch went for it, shooting while he disappeared again. With the pistol empty, the she-wolf attacked, crossing the distance within a breath. The witch fumbled for the lead balls in her pocket, but the she-wolf was already there, lunging up the massive statue with a swiftness honed from chasing prey over uneven mountainsides.

Her teeth raked the witch's arm with such force that the pistol was flung out of her hand. Then they were falling into the pond together, rock and cement scraping against the she-wolf's fur while her frenzied attack churned the water into froth. Dimly, she was aware of the black wolf tearing at the screaming witch as well, his jaws efficient yet just as brutal as her raw wrath.

The pond was red by the time they climbed out, shaking their fur dry while waiting to be sure the witch was truly dead. Her ears were already pricked toward the forest that bordered the mansion. One figure left to hunt, his scent already clear to her. It felt like agony to wait and make sure the mansion caught on fire and burned everything inside.

Wild excitement filled her when they ran past the first of the trees, seeking the deeper gloom. Despite the nearing dawn, the moon looked bright and big, its light reducing the forest to a harsh land of bone and charcoal. They crossed streams and ducked gnarled branches, paws sure against the moss and ferns as the hag king's odor grew ever stronger.

Breathing it drove the she-wolf's rage to a fever pitch. She caught a similar change in the black wolf's scent. He was steadier than she and had been throughout this hunt, but that didn't mean he was *calmer*. The same fury that had slaughtered covens and terrified all the other monsters now focused fully on the warlock. Her delight felt as savage as her teeth as they ran together in perfect harmony, his power complementing her speed.

And then there was the hag king, the moonlight picking out the curve of his spine and the tines of his antlers as he hunched beneath a massive oak. Unmoving, unaware. Lost in the same sullen malice that had choked her as much as her blood.

This time, they attacked with pure aggression, his jaws cracking the warlock's nearest arm and hers ripping into his side. The taste of his blood was as sweet as his roar of pain. Her teeth glanced off ribs, unable to keep him down, and she ducked away as his antlers swung toward her in a wicked slash.

The black wolf still had a grip on his arm and now wrenched it, twisting the warlock away from her. The snap of bone cut through the clearing. The hag king bellowed again, and then the stink of magic filled the air.

They broke off their attack, circling from a safe distance as the warlock's form convulsed. Shadows hid most of his writhing, but within a breath, a stag rose from the bloodied ground, stamping and shaking his antlers. Then he pivoted to aim those dangerous tines at the black wolf.

The stag's lack of concern toward the she-wolf only further infuriated her. She lunged, ripping into the meat of his back legs to hamstring him. Blood steamed in the air. By the time the stag turned, she was gone.

Just out of reach, she snarled, putting all her hatred and rage into it. The black wolf used the chance to rip into the stag's other flank. These weren't killing bites, but they would hurt and exhaust him.

The hag king shook his head at them again, snorting. Then he fled further into the forest, perhaps believing he could outrun them. Her tongue lolled out in a laugh at the idea.

They followed. Exhilaration filled her full whenever the shape in front of them stumbled. Weariness soon entered the stag's scent, but she remained tireless. As the black wolf ran beside her, it felt like their hearts beat as one.

When at last the hag king slowed, she was the first upon him, her swiftness joined by the black wolf's power. Her teeth caught the stag's hind leg, stumbling him. The black wolf's jaws caught his neck, bringing him down. Then she began ripping at the belly while the stag foamed and thrashed against the grip on his throat, unable to escape.

The black wolf watched his Alice as blood soaked her pitch-dark fur. She had never looked more beautiful, vicious with rage and confidence. Sometimes, she watched him with unknowing wistfulness, certain that she would never be as wild or unafraid. Yet in this moment, there was nothing tame about her. She took her revenge on the warlock that had used her like prey with the ferocity of a born wolf. She anticipated his struggles with the ruthlessness of a human.

She was stunning.

Blood ran over the moss in thin rivers by the time the stag gave a final, convulsive lurch and changed form. Terror filled the hag king's scent as he struggled to breathe. His throat and belly were a ruined mess.

The she-wolf backed away from the limp body and shifted back into her own skin. She breathed lightly, easily, crouching to make sure the warlock could see her face. See who had killed him.

The sunrise lit her in gold, revealing her in full. His eyes widened. She couldn't tell whether the twitch of his face was a grimace or a sneer, but she recognized the disbelief filling his scent. It was the same as when she had ripped at his mouth instead of kissing him back.

Filled with the calm of a finished hunt, she only stared while his fingers twitched, trying to bring her under his control. A useless effort; her will was hers and hers alone. When it didn't work, he tried to hurt her instead, managing to swing his antlers in threat.

The black wolf changed form and caught them before they even came close. The muscles in his arms bulged as he wrenched them the other way, snapping the hag king's neck.

The warlock went limp, but the black wolf still snarled, all his power thrown into pulling the antlers in opposite directions until they gave with a great *crack*, leaving only broken stumps behind.

Alice watched in silence, rising to her feet only when Colton approached. In the glow of the new day, he somehow looked more inhuman than when he had been a wolf, eyes hot and piercing against the blood covering his face.

She smiled at him, feeling lighter with each word. "I'm ready to go home."

Forever

"It sounds like a wonderful trip." Denise's voice filled the kitchen, slightly tinny from being on speakerphone. "We can't wait to see you tomorrow and hear all about it."

"Is there anything we can bring over? Maybe dessert or wine?" said Alice, half of her attention on splitting the row of shortcakes that had been cooling on the counter since morning. The strawberries were already ready.

"Just yourselves." Then her stepmother's voice lowered to a more confidential tone. "You know, your father and I both thought you two left on a secret honeymoon and would come back unveiling wedding rings. You're not about to, are you?"

"No," said Alice, trying not to laugh at her stepmother's excitement. After all they had been through, proving their commitment to each other was the furthest thing from her mind. "I needed to get away and clear my head about some things, and I did."

"Honey, I'm so glad. I'll just say one final thing on the subject: your father would never admit it, but he's fine with the idea of you two marrying. He's working from home today. Do you want to say hi?"

"Sure." They hadn't spoken since she and Colton had started the hunt. The usual anxiety wormed into her heart as she waited, yet less so than before. She wasn't sure she'd ever be comfortable with her father, but in a strange way, the things she had learned about her mother helped steady her view of him as well.

When his voice came through, it still held the flatness of his professional tone. "Alice."

She took the speakerphone off. Even though she was alone in the house, it somehow felt more private. "Hi, Dad. How are you?"

"Well enough. What about you? You sound tired. Six weeks is a long time away."

"I know, but I needed it. I feel much better about some things and ready to move on from others."

"That's good." There was a brief silence before he said, "We're looking forward to seeing you tomorrow, although I told Denise you should have a few more days to recover."

"I'm fine, really. In fact, Colton's coming home after lunch so we can take a long drive. There's just one more thing I want to see before we're done traveling."

"Is it about your mother?" Her surprised silence must have been answer enough, because he then added, "The anniversary of her disappearance was yesterday. It's not hard to make the connection."

Alice hesitated, unsure of whether to tell her father what she had remembered. Unsure of how much *could* be understood by someone who had never seen that dark, furtive world hiding in the shadows of his own. "What made you move forward, Dad? After Mom disappeared, I mean."

Her father sighed. "I knew I had to keep life as normal as possible for you. I'm not saying I succeeded. Just that I tried."

She bit her lip, hearing the same pain in his voice that she had heard in the memory of her mother at her bedside. It rubbed her heart raw to realize the cold behavior that had once made her fear him stemmed in part from his own fears. She didn't know what to think, much less what to say. "I'm fine now. Really. I realized that... that she didn't leave because she hated me."

There was a long pause, long enough that she thought she'd made a mistake in opening up. Then her father cleared his throat. "I'm glad. There was never any reason to blame yourself. She loved you, but she was also sick."

Alice closed her eyes, aware that it was as close to the truth as he would get, or would possibly even want. "Thanks, Dad."

For a moment, he almost sounded reassuring. "Get some rest. We'll see you tomorrow."

"Okay. Can't wait," she said, and felt surprised by how much she meant it.

She had just finished whipping the cream when the rumble of Colton's truck reached her. She looked out the window in time to catch him walking up the driveway. The smells of sawdust and tree sap mingled with his own clean musk, already brimming with impatience and lust. Excitement filled her own scent as she waved.

She filled one of the shortcakes while he unlocked the front door, and had it ready on a plate by the time he appeared in the kitchen doorway. Even now, she grew breathless beneath the weight of his gaze. "Hungry?"

"Starving," he said, pushing the plate out of the way before she could offer it to him. Then his mouth was on hers, tongue flicking at the roof of her mouth as his hips pinned hers against the counter. Playful and savage, teasing and perverse. She managed a laugh as he ripped her sweater open, and then all thought disappeared under the delicious heat of his attention.

She found herself bent over while he took her from behind, each thrust hard enough to raise her on tiptoe. She panted, breasts hanging out from her ruined sweater and hair falling into her face. Already desperate, she pushed a hand between her legs and found her clit, her fingers as unrelenting as his cock.

"I love you," she whispered, feeling herself shiver from the truth of it.

His rhythm didn't falter, but in the next moment, his hand joined hers, twining their fingers together until the pressure against her clit made her feel ready to melt.

"Words," he murmured into her ear. The rasp in his voice sounded almost tender.

Then his teeth caught her neck, right where her pulse pounded hard and fast. His next thrust went in so deep she cried out, shuddering against their clasped hands.

Afterwards, she curled against him while they shared one of the shortcakes. She had only a few bites, nerves stealing away her usual just-fucked appetite.

He noticed. "Sure you want to do this?"

Despite her uncertainty, she smiled. "I'm sure. It's just... I haven't been to that place since she left me there. I don't know what to expect, or see, or even feel."

She absently glanced down at the empty plate before adding, "I want to move on, but it feels strange, too. I spent so much of my life obsessed with my mother. I'm scared of seeing how much space is left behind."

His nose brushed hers, coaxing her to look up again. His eyes were still dark and relaxed from their hard fuck, their color reminding her of the forest outside. "What's your favorite coffee?"

"Any light roast with chocolate notes." Then she laughed a little, understanding the implications behind his question. Any empty space could be filled. Sometimes slowly and painfully, but it would happen.

She didn't talk much on the drive to the Eldorado National Forest, not at first. When she turned on the radio, she was greeted by the oily voices of the local shock jocks.

"Come on, Rattles. You're screwing with me. I never heard of that."

"It's true. If you had extra nipples, you'd be burned for witchcraft."

"Who has extra nipples? No one has more than two except for the three-boobed lady from Total Recall."

"That's because we burned everybody who did."

"So, you're saying witches have three boobs?"

"I'm saying we killed off a genetic mutation, man, and it was one of the good ones."

With a sigh, Alice turned the radio off again. "I think I already understand why vargr stop paying attention to people."

Still, it had been weirdly reassuring to glimpse the rest of the world and its oblivious spinning, and she began talking about the memories she had remembered from the night before. Little ones, meaningless ones, yet he listened intently, his hand occasionally squeezing her thigh. The landscape around them shifted into oak trees and scrubby wild grass.

Amazing, how easy it was to direct him off the highway and to the right area of the park. Picking apart her feelings proved impossible, especially when she realized how much had remained unchanged. Gravel-covered ground served as an informal parking lot for those who wished to weave through the oaks and manzanita on their own rather than use one of the hiking trails. It wasn't an official entrance but popular enough that other cars were there.

There still weren't any fences blocking the way. Her mother had driven further in, much further. The small car had struggled against the uneven ground; Colton's truck wouldn't. Yet Alice found herself wanting to walk those last 100 or so yards. Wanting the chance to absorb what she had missed as an unknowing child.

Her hand clutched his while they walked, but her mind felt surprisingly clear. Some of the wild grass had already turned yellow, dry as straw and just as pleasant-smelling. She also caught traces of deer, raccoons, and even a cougar. The hot asphalt and acrid gasoline of the highway faded to nothing while they traveled further into the wilderness. The powdery, red earth clung to their feet.

And then...

"We're here," she murmured, looking at the two trees that leaned into each other in a natural arch.

For awhile, she simply sat on a nearby rock and stared at the surrounding forest. It had changed with time. The trees were taller, bearing scars from bad weather. The rock she had looked at as a child whenever the endless leaves had started to overwhelm her sense of up and down was now surrounded by poison oak. There was no hint of the tire marks from her mother's car. The land, too, had moved on.

A certain calm came over her as she got to her feet again. Then she looked at Colton, who waited nearby. Tears filled her eyes for reasons she couldn't name. "There's nothing waiting for me here. It's just a forest."

As they began the drive home, she held his hand with both of hers, feeling as raw and relieved as the night she had left Magdalene's body in the morgue. She remembered every word of the conversation she'd had with him afterward, their bodies steaming the cramped confines of her car. How her hope had outweighed any fear of damning herself by continuing to want him.

Her life felt as changed now as it had then, as enormous with possibilities and as unnerving with having to rebuild herself.

When she kissed the rough calluses on his hand, he glanced over. "Thinking of that night?"

She laughed. "Were you?"

He nodded. "You were scared, but not of me. I couldn't believe it."

"Well, I couldn't believe you wanted to stay. I thought you'd leave since I was only human again."

"Never. But you weren't ready to hear that."

It was true. Her heart had still been constricted by Magdalene's grip, had still hardly believed it had escaped. Any promise would have terrified her. She softly repeated what he had told her instead. "'Until we tire of each other.' What would you say today?"

At that, he looked at her. Most would have called him expressionless, but his intent gaze promised things that only a beast could give: savage passion, and moonlit hunts, and a tongue tender against any wounds life might deliver. "Forever."

As the forest behind them disappeared from view, she found herself smiling. Her heart was her own... and still so full.

About the Author

I've always loved writing about monsters and the girls who love them, which means I write a lot of werewolf romance. In my spare time I like to do things where I don't have to take myself seriously, like bike riding with my husband, baking anything that sounds good, and painting monsters and horses.

I like scotch, wine, and cats.

Enough about me; if you want to know more about my work, my personal website is juliemidnight.com, and my Instagram handle is @juliemidnighter